I0561970

Christine
&
Alexandra

One Love, One Lifetime

Book One

Published by New Generation Publishing in 2012

Copyright © C. A. Barrington 2012

First Edition

The author asserts the moral right under the Copyright, Designs and Patents Act 1988 to be identified as the author of this work.

Some characters names (only a few) in this book have been changed to protect identity. All places are the actual places and correct. The storyline is as factual as can be remembered, any mistakes are purely the fault of the author.

All Rights reserved. No part of this publication may be reproduced, stored in a retrieval system or transmitted, in any form or by any means without the prior consent of the author, nor be otherwise circulated in any form of binding or cover other than that which it is published and without a similar condition being imposed on the subsequent purchaser.

www.newgeneration-publishing.com

 **New Generation Publishing**

For Alexandra
Mon cœur est à toi pour toujours

And in Memory of my mother Alice

ACKNOWLEDGMENTS

Thanks to Juliet Haw, for encouragement, your blinding belief in the book and editing of first drafts – your life was taken far too young my friend.

To Alice Walker, your unflinching support, ideas, editing and friendship were second to none.

Thanks to my dear friend Flo in Devon for giving up your bedroom and providing good food, fine wine, much fun and laughter, and for allowing me to be part of your lovely family.

To Richard (Tricky), for the use of your farm in France and my nephews – Brendan, for your house in Radcliffe, and Jonathan for your house in Cape Town – All delicious places in which to write – thank you, thank you.

Also a special thanks to Darin Jewell at the Inspira Group for your faith, confidence, huge guidance and unstinting help every step of the way.

And to beloved Hogwarts, thank you.

Prologue

Déjà vu in Kenya

I arrived at Jomo Kenyatta airport in the dark African night amid a spectacular storm, with thunder rumbling and lightning flashing. As the plane came in to land it did not dampen the excitement of at last being in the country I had so achingly longed to visit for nigh on fifty years: Kenya.

A young Kenyan medical student and part-time taxi driver had been sent to meet me at the airport; his driving was incredible as all traffic in central Nairobi was at a standstill due to the storm which had wreaked havoc with massive metal hoardings, electricity pylons and trees. All matter of debris strewn across the roads did nothing to dull my ardour and I honestly found it exciting whilst holding on for dear life to every handhold in the taxi I could find as the car swerved or swam through flooded roads. The journey to our destination in one of Nairobi's outer suburbs, Karen, took two hours longer than the usual half hour it requires in normal conditions.

I found it hard to believe that I would be

spending the next three years in Kenya at such a ripe old age in my life. Even more incredulous was that I would be living in an old fieldstone gatehouse on an estate that was once part of Mbogani Farm, the farm as depicted and immortalised by Karen Blixen in her book 'Out Of Africa', which was her home and coffee plantation where she lived, grieved and loved during all the seventeen years she spent in Kenya. Her book was published in 1937 six years before I was born. I had read it as a young teenager and it had a profound effect upon me as it ignited a lifelong passion to explore Africa and, I believed at the time, if only for me, it was the greatest love story.

So, I felt in good company with a strange karma surrounding me as I stepped out of that dark African night into the fieldstone cottage where a warm fire burned in the grate, set out was an abundance of food, wine and beautiful white roses, but most of all, my own love's bright smile was there waiting. The long road I had travelled getting to Kenya started with a telephone call from Germany to our home in South Africa twelve months earlier to the day, so there was much to celebrate and we did so in style.

The storm did not abate through the night, with the sounds of falling branches from the ancient trees around the house crashing onto our corrugated tin roof, together with bush babies clambering over it and the haunting sound of tree hyrax screeching at one another, and a strange bed to boot. Sleep, for once in my life, did not come easily. Excitement, a new life, the sounds and smell of Africa surrounded me and I could not wait to explore the new day.

Bright sunshine greeted me as I walked out the next morning to see for the first time the surroundings of what was to be my home for the next three years. The twenty-eight hectare estate was the first piece of Mbogani Farm that was sold to the farm manager at the time after Karen Blixen finally left Kenya for good to return to her home in Denmark, and it was beautiful. The grass was lush and green, tall trees surrounded us, vegetable gardens were full and flourishing. There were magnificent polo ponies to watch and a lovely old manor house where the owners lived. This would do well - very well in indeed. The contrast of the journey from down-town Nairobi the previous evening and the area of Karen was like being in two different countries. I was soon to discover both had equal merits, both had disadvantages – they had the best of both worlds, in fact.

Having acclimatised myself to the immediate surroundings on the estate and getting to know the people, the animals and, most importantly, the owners, I decided it was time to visit the Karen Blixen museum established now in the original Mbogani Farmhouse, a five minute walk from Hogwarts – the name I affectionately gave our new home.

There was calmness about me and I knew I had chosen the day well to visit the museum. No cars or matatus were in the parking area, for which I was duly thankful. It was peaceful and quiet with an unusual serenity as I stepped into a piece of history that had been a source of fascination since I was sixteen years old. And it was all as I had imagined from the description in the book and later the film – very atmospheric with the rooms left exactly as they were those many, many years ago. Today there was a fire burning in the grate of the dining room, giving off a gentle scented aroma of wood smoke. Photographs of Denys Finch Hatton adorned the walls and appeared in frames on the furniture – how wonderfully handsome he was.

Outside, behind the farmhouse, I sat at the millstone table where Karen Blixen sat quietly each evening to enjoy her final cigarette of the day, looking across at the far distant Ngong Hills, thinking of Denys a long way away on one of his hunting safaris, and praying for his safe return to Mbogani. I sat in wonderment of the moment looking across at the Ngong Hills as she once did, thinking how romantic it all must have been, though I knew in my heart of hearts it was not always the case.

A shiver ran down my spine and a strong feeling of déjà vu embraced me as I sat at the humble millstone table. My own love story was on my mind, because it's the reason I was in Kenya. Living so close to Mbogani Farm was merely a coincidence.

The time was right, the situation was perfect. Looking out across the Ngong Hills I decide to write our story, our beautiful and unusual love story.

Chapter One

Her Bright Smile

25th December, the year 2002, was a Christmas Day no more unusual than any other, yet unbeknown to me it was going to be one that would change my life forever.

Since leaving England, my country of birth, to go and live in South Africa, it had become the custom to spend Christmas with the family at my niece's farm in Elgin, the beautiful apple growing region of the Western Cape. We would all gather together on the 24th to celebrate both my birthday and Christmas on the eve of Christmas Day. It was always a splendid affair with the largest tree imaginable, surrounded by what felt like a million presents – dinner itself a truly magnificent feast with excellent wine to compliment it. Towards midnight the local village farm workers' choir (sic) gathered together on the lawn in front of the house and sung Christmas carols, albeit a trifle out of tune, as by midnight they would be three sheets to the wind! Still, we loved it and their rendition-ing of a slurred "We wish you a Merry Christmas" stays happily in my memory.

The great day dawned to early rustling of feet up and down the passage outside my bedroom door – the sound of young teenagers anxious for the grown-ups to get up and have breakfast before the grand opening of presents. I personally think this is unfair to expect the younger generation to wait until nearly lunchtime on Christmas day to open the long-awaited presents – but hey! That is the family custom... or is it me, part of the older generation, who cannot bear to wait for the opening of those beautifully gift wrapped presents lying temptingly under that good tree?

Present opening being over, drools, thanks, and wonderment duly proffered, we settled down to a glass of champagne followed by a scrumptious help-yourself lunch. Hadn't I heard everyone say last evening after supper that they would not be able to eat again for a week? At least I thought I did, including myself - yet there we were again not thirteen hours later, tucking into another feast. Once lunch was over, I decided to brave the pool for a quick swim before heading off back to Cape Town where I was expected by guests from England, who were staying at my house in Chelsea, where another Christmas dinner and my dogs, Hettie, Harry and Josh, awaited me.

By the end of the day it was all too much. The fabulous food and company at the farm, the one and a half hour drive back to Cape Town (speeding fine too hefty to mention) followed by another good dinner eventually took its toll – I needed to get away from everyone. There was an overwhelming and compelling desire to escape to my small Mediterranean-style flat overlooking the sea in the naval port of Simon's Town. Drawing me like a magnet, this is where I longed to be, alone and at peace; so I made my apologies and drove away, offering an invitation to my guests, James and Elspeth, to join me in Simon's Town the following day where we would lunch at the yacht club and perhaps take James sailing. Fortunately they were good friends and preferred to have the house to themselves anyway – though of course they would never admit that to me – but I knew!

The flat is in a mountainside security complex called Sea View Heights, which forms part of the Table Mountain Nature Reserve. There is nothing fancy about the complex other than the lovely drive up to it, but the view from my top floor flat is, to say the least, spectacular – spanning False Bay and the Atlantic Ocean from the front and a view of the mountain reserve from the rest of the windows. A piece of paradise this little place of mine.

Arriving back at the flat that evening felt good. There was a positive feeling about the need to be there – more than I have ever felt before since buying the flat. I unloaded my bag and presents from the car and took them inside, then remembered my next door neighbour, a Scots lady called Lynn. She was probably on her own and I felt I should at least wish her a happy Christmas before going to bed, so I gingerly walked the few yards to her front door. Before I knocked it suddenly dawned on me that Lynn had mentioned having a visitor from Malawi over for Christmas. I had forgotten, so she wasn't alone and would be happily ensconced chatting merrily to her buddy.

I unpacked my clothes and presents, poured myself a glass of wine, had a luxurious bath soaking in one of my birthday gifts, avocado oil and milk, then spread out on the sofa with an exciting novel by Ian Rankin.

Waking up the next morning to a cacophony of dawn chorus, the outer bedroom door was open onto the balcony and I could feel a gentle breeze on my face. Magic mornings, I call them. In a few moments I would look through the bedroom window – or, braver, go out onto the balcony and look across the bay, where the sun would be rising up from behind the mountains, sending a burst of cadmium orange the entire length of the range and filling the sky like a brilliant red flame. Moments like these are what life is all about, being surrounded by the splendours of the world that we live in.

My early morning indulgence of coffee was brewing in the bodum with the delicious aroma of Arabica permeating the flat, when I remembered I had left the milk, bought on the way back the evening before, in the car. Wrapping a brightly coloured kikoi around my waist and donning a white t-shirt, I surreptitiously sneaked out to the car to retrieve it.

Clutching the rescued milk, I walked back along the communal passageway Lynn and I share to our flats. Her front door was open and I could hear the sound of Mozart's Horn Concerto faintly in the background – Lynn is an early riser.

'Good morning,' I said, knocking lightly on the open door and popping my head inside.

'And a good morning to you,' replied Lynn in her lilting Scottish accent. She was busying herself as usual in the kitchen, her petite figure and black cropped hair belying her age. Her friend was there, cutting up sweet melon, and she turned around. 'Hello,' she said. Gob-smacked would be the best description of my surprise at seeing a thirty-something young lady, very attractive – with a smile to light up the darkest of Africa, standing there in Lynn's kitchen. 'This is Alex, my friend from Malawi, and this is Chris, my next door neighbour,' Lynn nonchalantly said, making the introductions while she still had her marigold gloved hands in the sink.

'Hi! I've heard such a lot about you,' said the radiant smile.

'Nice to meet you,' was all I could summon up to say. I had clearly assumed that her friend would be Lynn's age, sixtyish. They had both worked together for the Voluntary Services Organisation in Malawi until, and I remembered now Lynn telling me, Alex had been offered a high-powered job funded by USAid in Malawi, which she had already started. Therefore her friend would only be entitled to a few days leave over Christmas, and South Africa was the closest destination.

Once I was back in the flat and at last enjoying my lovely fresh mug of coffee topped with frothy milk, I sat gazing out over False Bay and debated whether there would be enough wind to sail before lunch or after. Better still – if the weather was clement enough, we could take a picnic lunch and have it on board Tradewind out in the bay. What could be better? But Elspeth would not like it one little bit; it would therefore make sense to decide when we met up at the yacht club. Neptune's, the club restaurant, could make us a picnic lunch quickly if we should decide to go sailing. With that settled in my mind I took a quick shower and got ready to prepare myself for the day.

There was a knock on the door, and I shouted out to whoever it was to come in. It was Lynn.

'Hi Chris, Alex and I were just wondering what was happening at the yacht club on New Year's Eve?'

'As far as I know there will be the usual New Year's Eve party with a live band, dancing, plenty of food and drink. At midnight the Navy let off out-of-date flares which we donate to them from our various boats when they are no longer acceptable within the required safety regulations – it's quite a display. Also there will be the lone piper in full Scottish regalia,' I added, as I knew this would appeal to Lynn.

'That sounds great. What does it cost, and do we have to book?'

'I'm not really sure, but I can ask when I go to the yacht club this morning and let you know.'

At that moment Alex appeared in the doorway and came over to join us. 'I've just been asking Chris about New Year's Eve,' Lynn explained to her.

'It's usually quite a bash at the yacht club,' I explained, 'but there is also a huge party being held in Jubilee Square – they cordon it off from all traffic – it reverberates with live music, food stalls, restaurants and plenty of people. Not my scene I'm afraid – too cold and noisy.'

Lynn looked thoughtful, 'Why don't we come to the yacht club with you this morning and find out if we can get tickets, see what time it all starts?'

'Great idea,' agreed Alex enthusiastically.

'That's fine by me. I can be ready in five minutes; I'll give you a shout when I'm leaving.'

They left the flat and I gathered my things together in the hope that James and I would be sailing later. It was still looking too calm, but the wind might hopefully pick up in the afternoon.

Lynn and Alex followed me down to the yacht club in Lynn's car because they knew I would be out to lunch or sailing and besides, they both had things that they wanted to do. We met up at the yacht club where the receptionist informed us that you could buy tickets for the New Year's Eve bash either on the night or there and then from her. Alex asked me what I was doing for New Year, and for the life of me I had no idea. 'I'll have to liaise with my visitors and friends before I decide,' I told them.

'It would be really nice if we could all get together and make up a party, have dinner in a restaurant and then go onto the yacht club,' Alex suggested, with Lynn nodding in agreement.

'Sounds good to me, but we would definitely have to book at a restaurant – Simon's Town has become very popular as a New Year's Eve venue,' I told them.

As we were saying our goodbyes and making arrangements to discuss our plans further in the week, Alex suddenly asked, 'Is there any chance we could look at your yacht whilst we're here?' Obviously Lynn must have told her I had a boat.

'With pleasure,' I said, surreptitiously looking

15

at my watch, as I did not want to be late for James, Elspeth (Sarah's father and step-mother) and my great friend Sarah, who I had also invited, when they arrived - but I was a sucker for any chance to show off Tradewind. 'It's probably a good time now while the sea is calm.' So we wandered off down to the marina.

There was something enlightening and enthusiastic about Alex's company. Her high spirits were immediately contagious, and I felt my own spirits rise. We had only met a couple of hours previously but her charm and broken German accent were captivating and such a pleasure. I was a natural optimist and of late it was becoming unhealthily clear that a great many people surrounding me appeared to be radiating negative vibes – which I was finding harder and harder to tolerate – so being with Alex was like a breath of fresh air.

After showing them Tradewind, Lynn and Alex left to go and get on with their day. I met James, Elspeth and Sarah and we decided not to go sailing but opted instead to lunch at a local fish restaurant on the town jetty. It was a lovely sunny day, and as we sat eating scrumptious fresh fish and drinking chilled, dry white wine, everything was perfect. I was thinking about New Year's Eve.

'Penny for your thoughts,' Sarah asked.

'Sorry! I was just thinking about what we could do on New Year's Eve.'

'Well, you can count us out. Elspeth and I are going to take Nola out for dinner somewhere quiet and without too much razzamatazz – we cannot bear all that noise and things at our age,'

James said without too much ado. Nola was James's first wife, Sarah's mother, and my dear friend. After the usual period of bitterness that seems to follow a divorce, James and Nola remained friends, and even Elspeth was accepted now. They were all in their late seventies and I doubted the bash at the yacht club was "quite up their street".

Sarah looked surprised; she obviously had not been included in their arrangements. 'What are you thinking of doing?' She was looking at me so I told her what was happening at the yacht club and Lynn's suggestion. 'Mind if I join you? It sounds a good idea – dinner and then on to the yacht club for the build-up to midnight. We wouldn't want to spend the entire evening at the club with all that noise going on, would we?'

A brainwave suddenly hit me. 'I think we should celebrate and ring in the New Year with champagne on board Tradewind. Now, what do you think of that?'

'Jolly good idea,' agreed Sarah, chinking her wineglass against mine in a cheer of agreement.

'Which one is your boat?' Elspeth asked as we were finishing lunch.

'Over there on the first walk-on marina, the one with the white hull and black sail cover,' I said pointing over as best I could into the direction of where Tradewind was moored. Lucky it was on the first walk-on and near the clubhouse, otherwise it would have been impossible to point it out amongst all the many different boats moored there.

James's eyes lit up. 'Can we go on board and

have a look at her after lunch?'

'Of course we can,' I enthused. We finished our lunch in companionable chit-chat, downed the rest of the vino and headed off to Tradewind. Sarah declined to join us as she wanted to visit the local toy museum.

'She's lovely,' James said stepping gingerly from the jetty over the guard rail of the boat. Elspeth, tight-lipped and stiff chose to stay safely on terra firma. We looked around the cockpit before descending into the cabin area. I was showing an enthusiastic, knowledgeable gentleman, a once experienced fighter pilot now an eminent QC in London, around my prized yacht and I could not have been happier. With his intelligent knowledge, he quizzed and questioned me about every detail.

'Tell me Chris, how did a Lancashire lass like you get into sailing?'

'Well James, after finishing work one Friday afternoon, Sarah and I decided to take the dogs for a walk and swim on Long beach here in Simon's Town followed by a fish and chips supper at the Salty Sea Dog restaurant down by the Simon's Town jetty. After finishing the walk it was a little too early for us to eat so I suggested that it might be nice to go to the yacht club and have a walk around the marina and look at the lovely boats – we would then be ready for supper by about seven.

'It was a particularly beautiful afternoon and the marina with its neatly set out rows of yachts and powerboats shone in glimmering water, magnificent in the idyllic and most perfect setting imaginable. Moored alongside the working jetty was the prettiest of boats with a "For Sale" sign giving a contact telephone number. 'I wonder how much a small yacht like that would cost.' I remarked to Sarah. 'Phone and ask,' she nonchalantly replied. With some disappointment there was no response to the number supplied, so we strolled around the rest of the marina before leaving to have a delightful meal where we discussed, in great excitement, the prospect of a boat in my life.

'I eventually managed to get through to the number the following morning, which turned out to be the chandlery at False Bay Yacht Club. I was told the price of the yacht and given a brief inventory – we made arrangements to have a sail in her the following week, which I did, and that was it, I was hooked! The marina berth where my little twenty-one-foot yacht called Moksa is moored was also for sale. I negotiated to purchase that as well and was promptly told that I would have to become a member of the Yacht Club to own a boat and keep it there, the same applied if I bought the marina berth. I did not want to belong to a Yacht Club – any Yacht Club. So there I was, in a dilemma: get rid of my newly acquired and precious boat plus the marina berth, or belong to the Yacht Club. In the end there was no contest. And just to round it off – I had not a clue what to do with Moksa, as I had no idea how to sail. 'Learn to sail,' suggested Sarah when discussing this dilemma.

'What?' I replied. 'Are you mad? I'm in my mid-fifties. I can't learn to sail at this time of life.'

'Then why on earth did you buy the boat if you

don't intend to use it?'

'So learn to sail I did. I completed a course offered by an Olympic sailor called Ian Ainslie. I learnt the rudiments of sailing and gained confidence to be out in the bay, to move around on the deck of a boat in different weather conditions. It was exhilarating. I read and gained knowledge from books, seafaring friends, sailors, boat builders and yarn spinners – anywhere I could! I spent as many hours as possible on the water. We even entered a few races and I became quite competitive!

'So racing became a passion, and my thoughts of cruising fell away into oblivion. I eventually graduated to a larger yacht with which, beyond all my expectations, we won many races. I am very proud of Tradewind and what we have achieved together. This would not have happened without the fantastic support of all my fellow sailors and racers at False Bay Yacht Club, who have been immeasurably helpful and unbelievably great.

'Yes – owning a yacht is a financial bottomless pit but I have not regretted one cent that I have spent on my wonderful hobby. I feel eternally grateful that I fell into the world of yachting before it was too late; to have learned how to sail and won races at my age is the greatest feeling imaginable. And to think that it all came about by going for a fish and chip supper – well, all I can say is that it was the most expensive fish-and-chips in the world.'

'What an amazing story,' James said shaking his head in disbelief.

'I'd take you for a sail, James, but I think there

is zero wind. It looks like a millpond out there – not much point going along on the engine. Maybe we could try again tomorrow?'

'I would like that very much,' he enthused.

We closed up Tradewind and set forth back to the clubhouse where Elspeth was waiting for us, sitting supremely under a large palm tree on the lawn. 'You both look like a couple of naughty children,' she remarked as we sat down beside her.

Chapter Two

A Powerful Attraction

The following evening, Sarah and I had been invited to dinner by Bernard, a neighbour, who owned the flat below mine in Sea View Heights. Bernard was a good friend of Sarah's and it was through her that we had originally met, although we both lived in the same village of Chelsea. Once a very successful ballet dancer and choreographer with Cape Town Ballet, he was now retired and since then Bernard had studied Pilates. He went on to convert a barn on his property into a Pilates studio which today is one of the most advanced and successful Pilates studios in South Africa. I liked Bernard a lot. Bright and intelligent with a wicked sense of humour, dinner with him was always a treat where copious amounts of wine would be consumed and lots of laughter would be the best ingredient. I was looking forward to the evening.

We left the flat to make our way to Bernard's only to bump into Lynn and Alex on their way out as well. 'Hope you're going somewhere nice,' I asked them as we all went in single file along our communal walkway towards the steps. 'We're going to the same place as you,' Alex told us mischievously.

'Are you going to Bernard's as well?'

'Yes,' said Lynn. 'He told us you and Sarah were going for dinner and he thought we might like to join you, so here we are.'

'Good! The more the merrier,' I told them.

It was a balmy evening once again, and although Bernard's flat does not have the elevation that my flat has, his view is still superb and we all sat out on the balcony sipping our drinks and enjoying the moment. The talk was mostly centred on the work Lynn and Alex had done as volunteers in Malawi and of Alex's new consultancy position in the country. I must say that they made Malawi sound fascinating. Bernard told us all about his Pilates studio and how well it was going; doctors were now referring their patients to him from the nearby private hospital, so with that and their regular clients, it kept Bernard and his team very busy.

'How come you both own a flat in Sea View Heights?' Alex asked curiously.

Bernard shot me a knowing look and shook his head meaning he did not want to relay the story... it was mine to tell.

'Okay, here goes. A few months after purchasing Moksa I bumped into Bernard, who invited me to tea at his flat in Simon's Town. 'What a stunning view,' I remarked, entering Bernard's flat for the first time.

'Yes, that's exactly why I bought it, Chelsea - quaint as it might be does not harbour many views,' he offered, before I had chance to ask him his reasons for buying the flat.

'Just as we were finishing tea the architect of the complex, Matthew Gray, called in to see Bernard about something to do with the aesthetics committee. He introduced us and I commented on the complex and its design – then I asked him if he were, by any chance, to hear that the flat above Bernard's was for sale I would be interested - and specified clearly only the flat above, and no other. Matthew looked perturbed, so I explained. 'Top floor corner flat with even better views than Bernard's, commanding a one hundred and eighty degree vista of sea and mountain and overlooked by no-one.'

'Not much chance of that happening,' he responded. 'The present owners have had it since the complex was built; I doubt they would ever sell, though I have to say I haven't seen them here for some time. He's a busy anaesthetist at a private hospital so they don't get much chance to visit the flat,' Matthew threw back at me in a matter-of-fact manner.

'Three months later on New Year's Eve I got a telephone call from Matthew informing me that he had bumped into the owners of the flat above Bernard's in the local supermarket that morning. They had chatted amiably, and as each were saying their goodbyes the good doctor turned and mentioned to Matthew that he and his wife were thinking of selling the flat due to the pressure of his work. 'I might well have a buyer,' Matthew shouted after them. 'Phone me when you get home with your asking price.'

'This came like a bolt out of the blue. I confess here that I never gave the flat another thought after my tea with Bernard. We agreed to meet the following morning, New Year's Day, for Matthew to show me the flat. "Strike while the iron is hot," is my motto. I was not disappointed. The flat, once we had ploughed through the dark heavy furniture and rubbed through the salt-grimed windows, was beautiful. The views were second to none. Large glass sliding doors led out onto a small balcony which stretched the views even further, a huge expanse of Atlantic Ocean set out before me in False Bay. It was perfect.

'Suffice to say an offer was negotiated, a purchase price accepted, and by the end of New Year's Day I knew I was about to be the proud owner of a flat in Simon's Town. This was a fortuitous decision in hindsight to purchase the flat, as six months later I was voted onto the General Committee of False Bay Yacht Club, which began taking up an inordinate amount of my time.'

It was a really nice evening and I was enjoying listening to everyone chattering and hearing such a cheerful camaraderie going on. We discussed New Year's Eve once again and I told them my bright idea of celebrating at midnight aboard Tradewind.

'How wonderful,' was Alex's immediate response.

'Won't it be too cold to sit on a boat in the water at that time of night?'

'Yes Lynn, it might be cold but we can take sweaters or jackets and if it's really, really cold we can go into the cabin.' I told her. There was no way we would all fit into the cabin – although, bodies huddled together in the cockpit with champagne to cheer us along, we would be fine – but I was not going to inform Lynn of that.

'Well, it's a novel idea I suppose, being on a yacht for Hogmananny.'

Hogmanay is New Year's Eve in Scotland. I could feel Lynn was relenting because it didn't matter where you were in the world for New Year, nothing would ever compare to Hogmananny – Lynn's favourite name for Hogmanay – on Scotland's hallowed soil.

'Right,' I said. 'I must be going now, I have to play tennis tomorrow and do a whole lot of shopping for a lunch party on Sunday that I'm giving for a few sailing friends. Everyone here is welcome to join us, bearing in mind it might well be a squash.'

'Have another glass of wine – one for the road,' Bernard suggested, uncorking another bottle.

'Not tonight Bernard, no road to travel, no need for more vino!'

'Where do you play tennis?' Alex asked just as Sarah and I were getting up to leave.

'At Springfield Convent, a girl's school near where I live in Chelsea. A group of ex-parents run it and we play on Saturday afternoons. There are some really good players, both male and female. I enjoy playing with the men as you get a nice powerful game with plenty of exercise. Why? Do you play tennis?'

'Yes, well at least I used to play in Germany, but I haven't played at all since being in Malawi. I love playing, would there be any chance I could join you on Saturday?'

Alex looked very athletic and definitely in her early-thirties. Our club members were mostly people in their fifties, although a couple of younger people appeared occasionally. I was sure she would get some good games and not feel too out-of-place. 'Yes, I am certain the club would love to have you along – they enjoy new blood. If you can play you're okay! Be ready to leave here at two o'clock tomorrow afternoon. Is that okay?'

'Sure thing,' she answered with a beaming smile.

Sarah and I said our farewells and left. It had been a fun evening, in fact, a good day altogether. Back in the flat and safely in bed reading, my mind kept drifting back to Alex. During the evening I had once or twice noticed her looking at me, or was my imagination running riot? Whichever, it had unnerved me… perhaps I looked strange? Wore weird clothes? Finally I decided it was indeed my imagination and left it at that, before drifting off into a deep and peaceful sleep.

The following day I went to do some shopping for the forthcoming lunch the next day. I left Sarah in the flat working on her school schedule for the coming year. Sarah was a workaholic and a much-loved school principal who put everything into the better education of children, a person admired and loved by her staff, colleagues and friends alike – quite an accolade and much deserved. I arrived back at the flat carrying a ton of shopping, which Sarah volunteered to unpack and put away for me whilst I hurriedly changed into my tennis gear. When I went outside again I saw Alex was waiting by my car as I approached it. 'Wow, you look fit for the part,' I told her, noticing what looked like new kit, tennis shoes, shorts and a nice top.

'Thank you. Do you think I will be alright?'

I wasn't quite sure what she meant by that and thought perhaps I was missing something in the German accent. 'You'll be fine, the men will be suitably distracted having such a young and attractive player on the court – anyway they are a great bunch all of them, it will be a refreshing change.' And with that we left. It was a beautiful drive over the mountain to Chelsea. At one point you can see the ocean on both sides of the peninsula; it's a breathtaking view and it never ceases to give me immense pleasure to show this off to visitors. This day was no exception.

The tennis club crowd were pleased to see us and were delighted to have a visiting player – the club is a small group of past parents whose children went to Springfield school. There is a strong bond amongst them and it does not possess the egos and arrogance that a lot of other tennis clubs and its players seem to have, so Alex was welcomed with open arms. To top it off, she turned out to be an excellent player.

When we left the club some three hours later feeling pretty exhausted after a last set of mixed doubles, I told Alex that I needed to do some last minute shopping for lunch the following day in Constantia Village. There was a good delicatessen which I favoured a lot and they stocked a good selection of cheeses and other goodies – they stayed open until nine in the evening. Alex pushed the trolley around as I filled it – what a pleasure. 'Every home should have one,' I told her.

'You can have one if you want,' came the swift reply.

We both started laughing as we left the shop to make our way back to Simon's Town.

Chapter Three

Cut to the Chase

Sunday dawned to perfect weather. There was very little wind, balmily warm, which meant that we could spread out onto the balcony. When it comes to a party, the yacht club crowd excel and space for jollification is required. It was a small gathering, about twenty, as the flat is small. Lynn and Alex joined us for which I was grateful, as they mixed well with my friends and brought a different aspect to the usual banter of yacht talk.

'This is Alec and Lindsay,' I said introducing Alex to a couple who had just sailed around the world. Alec, with one leg, was fifty-odd; Lindsay, his girlfriend, was, hazarding a guess, Alex's age, a nice intelligent and bright girl full of character with her short, blonde hair, slender figure and a lovely personality. Lindsay, like Lynn, was also from Scotland. The two girls immediately got chatting and I left them to it.

Introducing Lynn was more difficult; she always put on a show of pique, drawing her lips tight as if she disapproved of everyone. 'This is Graham Heard,' I found myself saying to her as

Graham was squeezing passed us. The look of disgust on Lynn's face said it all, as Graham – in a somewhat scruffy-looking vest – put his beer bottle into his other hand and proffered Lynn his free one. Once again I made a hasty retreat and went to talk to Keith – my present sailing partner, laborious, large and strong Keith. Twenty-four years old going on forty who, unlike me, was a natural sailor, but old before his time.

Alex helped me throughout the entire afternoon – roasting two legs of lamb for such an occasion was probably a tad ambitious on my part, but with Alex's constant assistance, and the men attending to the drinks, all went smoothly. It was a good party.

The following few days were spent sailing and joining in the fun "racing round the cans" in the bay. They were casual, sun-filled days with a holiday atmosphere. One of the strangest things about being in South Africa at Christmas time is, of course, the weather. To hear "Jingle Bells" and "In the Bleak Midwinter" constantly being played in the shopping malls in heat sometimes soaring around 30 degrees Celsius is amusingly strange to say the least. This is something I have never quite come to terms with, as the Christmas season never really feels like it does in good old Blighty.

Lynn and Alex were conspicuous in their absence. Over the last few months Lynn had been patiently waiting for Alex to arrive in South Africa so that she could advise her on buying and setting up a computer system, and to this endeavour they were apparently encumbered – making constant trips back and forth to Cavendish Square, where there was an excellent computer store providing the largest and most competitive stock. Unfortunately, I was later to learn, something was missing or not working each time they arrived back home – a seventy kilometre round trip each time, and I believe they made four trips in all. Neither ladies were best pleased when we did eventually touch sides – Alex was due to return to Malawi in the early morning of 2nd January – so it had to be done in those few days.

Sarah had returned to the house in Chelsea to spend time with her father and Elspeth and her mother Nola, before returning to Simon's Town for the New Year festivities.

During the two days build up to New Year's Eve there were several changes to our plans. A few more people wanted to join us and Lynn suggested that we all meet up for drinks in her flat before heading off into Simon's Town to have dinner. I saw Alex pondering these arrangements. 'I think we should put the glasses, ice and champagne on board Tradewind during the afternoon so that we have nothing to carry and its all set-up ready for midnight,' she suggested.

'Good idea, nothing worse than trying to carry cool boxes and glasses with us tonight, and it will give the champagne time to settle,' I agreed.

The last day of the year heralded with beautiful sunshine and a nice gentle breeze. I had made an arrangement with Keith to go for a sail in the morning. This was a traditional thing to do on the last day of the year – but this particular year we were rounding off what we considered a successful racing season for us, having won a couple of twilight series and a medium distance – of which I was immensely proud. Tradewind is a cruising yacht and not at all built for racing, so our wins were pretty exceptional mainly thanks to Keith, the young yacht-racing enthusiast that he is, who managed to coax Tradewind around the marker buoys and across the finishing line with great alacrity.

After a fabulous sail, just following the wind along the coast towards Cape Point and back, we docked in our mooring to find Alex standing on the jetty waiting for our return. 'What a nice surprise,' I said, throwing her a line. 'Hold the boat steady would you – until we cleat the other lines and make her secure.'

'We watched you sailing out there – it looked great. When I saw you coming round the harbour wall and lowering the sail I thought I'd come down and meet you. Hope you don't mind.'

'No, not at all - we can always use an extra hand when we dock the boat, three hands are always better than two. By the way, the end of the harbour wall is called the 'bullnose', rounding the bullnose; the sail we were lowering is the mainsail.'

'And, just to add for your info on nautical terms,' blurted out Keith, 'the multi-coloured sail at the front is called a Genoa and it's attached to a roller-furler.'

'Heavens, Keith! I don't think Alex wants to know the in-depth rudiments of sailing.'

'Sure she does, she's a natural! Look how she's holding onto that line. Have you ever sailed, Alex? And by the way, my name's Keith, remem-

ber, we met at the party on Sunday,' he shouted -
then threw her a broad, burly grin.

'No, I have never sailed on a yacht but I've
been on boats before.'

'Come aboard.'

'Well I've come to put all this on Tradewind for
tonight,' she said pointing to a cardboard container and a cool-box standing at the end of the
jetty mooring.

'Aha, pre-empting me. I thought we were going to meet up later this afternoon to collect all the
goodies we need on board for midnight?'

'Already done - champagne, glasses, ice and a
few goodies that Lynn has thrown together for us
to nibble on. Can I pass them over, please?'

So there and then we packed Tradewind's
fridge with bags of ice and stood the bottles of
champagne into it ready for the evening – we left
the food in the cool-box Lynn had kindly sent. It
all looked good enough to eat and I wondered
then why on earth we were having dinner in a
restaurant, but by this time our numbers had crept
up to twelve so I suppose the finger food Lynn
had provided wouldn't go very far. Indeed, I was
wondering how on earth we were all going to fit
on the boat as it was anyway.

We left Tradewind looking all tickety-boo and
made our way back to the clubhouse. 'I must owe
you something for getting the champagne?' I
asked Alex when Keith had left us to go to the
cloakroom.

'You owe me nothing. It's my contribution.'

'Wow! That's a large contribution; we cannot
let you pay for all that.'

'I would like to. You've all been very hospitable to me, in fact, you've all been fantastic, especially you.'

An antenna went up. 'Oh, I don't see it that way, that's just how we are here in Cape Town – a cheerful, friendly crowd making visitors feel at home.'

This didn't sound very convincing even to my ears. I found myself being vaguely nervous suddenly, alone in Alex's' company. One of the brief encounters when we touched sides a couple of days ago when I was getting into my car to go for a walk on the beach. Alex came out from Lynn's flat and asked me where I was going, so I told her.

'Would you mind if I joined you?' she asked delightfully.

'No, not at all, we're heading off to Noordhoek beach.'

I had Harry, my Staffordshire Bull terrier, staying in the flat with me for a couple of days – Hettie and Josh were staying at the house in Chelsea with James and Elspeth – and his great love was walking on the beach and going for a swim in the cold Atlantic surf. I loved taking him to the beach, but it would also be nice to have some company, I felt oddly pleased. As we were about to leave, Lynn, who had apparently been out playing bowls, suddenly sped round the corner in her little silver car – she was a mean driver, and parked in her bay next to mine. 'We're just off to the beach to take Harry for a walk,' we told her in unison, as she stepped out of her car, 'would you like to join us?'

'No thank you, I've a few odds and ends to see

to – that damn computer has taken up so much of our time other things have got left behind.'

My heart rose and I felt somewhat relieved Lynn had declined and something inside me instinctively knew that Alex had not really wanted Lynn to join us either, but I had absolutely no idea why. So we left Lynn to her chores and drove the ten kilometres to the village of Noordhoek with its white sandy beach and wild Atlantic rollers, where surfers wait patiently for the big curl – such a beautiful sight which always reminded me of my early years in St Ives, Cornwall, and Porthmeor beach, when hunky flower power Australians adorned it and surfed the waves, whilst we girls paraded nonchalantly to and fro in the skimpiest of bikinis trying to look as cool and chilled-out as they did – those were the days my friend, we thought would never end. Reminiscing this to Alex made her laugh. The walk was refreshing and Harry just loved it.

The nervousness did not subside so that every little mark of attention or suggestion was magnified out of proportion – I was beginning to think that I was imagining signs that were truly not there. Was I going bonkers? This person was attached to me in an indefinite way… that I knew. What on earth was going on? I had to keep asking myself.

Little did I know that the stuff of madness was wavering there on the edge – a tidal wave more powerful than anything I was ever to know or experience again – would come thundering down and carry me away on its crest, rendering me helpless and paralysed in its wake.

Sarah returned from Fleur, the house in Chelsea, leaving James and Elspeth to have their evening dinner with her mother, Nola, as planned, quiet and dignified.

Dearest Lynn, clearly excited as any Scot on Hogmanay, had invited a few of us to her flat for a glass of champagne before we left for the Salty Sea Dog... the restaurant unanimously chosen by everyone in our party to have dinner that evening, which, surprisingly, still had room for us when making our booking. A friend of Lynn's, Bill, was there in the flat – rudderless without his wife – semi-separated, and I could soon see why, British, boring and at least eighty years old. My heart dropped – could we put up with his mindless banter all evening, and how on earth were we going to haul him on board Tradewind? I was being uncharitable I know, but a negative bore is a bore is a bore – no getting away from it. Even the car journey from the flat to Simon's Town did not bode well when he started on my beloved English football. God help me, I prayed, to get through this night!

The Salty Sea Dog was packed with people and full of good cheer. I engineered a seat as far away from Bill as possible making it clear to Lynn that he was her responsibility; we'd never met the guy before. To say we were a tad overcrowded at the dinner table would have been an understatement; a sardine tin would have had more room. However, we squeezed in and because of the festive occasion, it did not matter a jot. Alex wedged herself in next to me, when actually, she could have sat anywhere.

A good dinner over, it was time to move on. 'Let's go and meet up with Allan and Kathy over at Bertha's restaurant then we can all go to the yacht club together.' I suggested. Allan and Kathy were my very good friends; Allan's rather elderly father was staying with them for the holidays. He would not be deterred from being on Tradewind at midnight he'd adamantly told Allan in no uncertain terms. So now there were two octogenarians in tow.

Our party, now all together made it to the yacht club by 11pm. Lynn suddenly flew up the stairs as we reached the entrance to the club house, and quite literally seemed to disappear. I followed the music belting out from upstairs in the Crow's Nest bar, and lo and behold, there was Lynn in the middle of the floor dancing and gyrating away with an unknown gentleman. I could not believe my eyes. Quiet, timid Lynn had suddenly come alive. I saw no sign of Bill; we left him behind at the security gate still fumbling in his pockets for the entrance fee. The yacht club was humming with people dancing or out on the balcony drinking and just enjoying the music, some members were partying outside on the lawn and barbecuing. It was a laid-back atmosphere with a good vibe.

Wow! I could dance when I wanted to and this evening was no exception... what a time I was having. Lynn had definitely set the tone, and I was in the mood. Was that a tap on the shoulder I felt? Turning round I found Alex standing there looking a bit cross.

'I think we should be making our way to the

boat. I've rounded everyone up and they're making their way down, we have about ten minutes until midnight,' Alex suggested rather curtly.

If I didn't know better, I had the distinct feeling this interruption by Alex was to get me off the dance floor, not necessarily to get me down to the boat. She had stayed very close to me throughout the evening; this brief respite on the dance floor was a huge separation after the intimacy we had shared during the last few days. I realised that now.

'Right, I'll be with you in just a moment.'

'No, I'll wait for you. We need to get going straight away; otherwise it will be too late.'

I got the message loud and clear. 'Let's get going then.'

There was action everywhere. It was indeed only a few minutes to midnight and suddenly as if everyone realised just in time, people scattered to where and to whom they wanted to be with to spend those last few seconds of the Old Year and to celebrate and ring in the New Year.

It turned out to be quite frenetic as people tried to get onto their boats in time for the countdown. The marina was abuzz with action and excitement with the sounds and music coming from the town party on Jubilee Square.

By tradition the owner or the captain of a boat should be on board first to welcome whoever has been invited on her by saying "Welcome aboard". This is good traditional etiquette and I was just about to blunder it by being the last on board – but there they all were on the jetty, standing beside Tradewind.

'Sorry, sorry, sorry,' I said flinging myself ahead and onto the boat in a flurry. I then stood in the cockpit and invited everyone to "step aboard". Quite surprisingly, Bill and Allan's father seemed to have no trouble whatsoever stepping from the jetty, over the guardrail of Tradewind and landing nimbly into the cockpit where there was hopefully enough room for us all to sit – well, at least most of us. I saw that the cabin was open and lit up with glasses already out and plates of nibbles nicely displayed, and I hadn't done a thing… Yes, every home should have one, I thought to myself.

The final countdown came and the New Year was heralded in by the lone Scottish piper playing the bagpipes that drifted across the water, haunting, heart-wrenching and moving. Following at his close came the Navy fireworks and flares display with gunfire from every naval boat - each one decked with Christmas lights - in the harbour, sending a red smoggy hue over the entire marina. What a breathtaking sight it was. Twelve of us on board Tradewind raised our glasses and cheered in the New Year, revelling and marvelling in the goings on around us.

After the initial festivities had died down, we all sat huddled on the cockpit seats chatting away. Alex had been down in the cabin filling the glasses and passing up the food but now she came up and joined us, wedged herself in once again between Allan and myself, she raised her glass and clinked it against mine wishing me a 'Happy New Year.'

'Thought we'd done all that nonsense at midnight,' said Bill.

Bill had been helping Alex down in the cabin, I think mostly to get out of the cold, and he wanted to use the heads. 'This is a special New Year, Bill; I think our hostess deserves another toast, don't you?' said Alex.

'Alright then, here's to Christine and thank you for letting us be on this lovely yacht to ring in the year two thousand and three.'

'Thanks everyone. It's been great all being together letting in the New Year - nearly missed it though, if Alex hadn't dragged me from the dance floor... so here's to you, Alex, for rescuing me.' And I lifted my glass once again and we all cheered together.

'Who wants to come back to me for coffee and another glass of champagne or something else?' Lynn suddenly asked everyone.

Half of us said yes and most of them faced a long drive home. No one wanted to return to the club house and join in the festivities there, which would become increasingly raucous as the night wore on. Lynn was on a roll with her Hogmananny and who was I to burst her bubble.

Alex drove Sarah, Lynn and me back to the flat in my car as she was the only one who had had little to drink. Bill thankfully insisted on finding his own way back to Clovelly. Allan and Kathy along with Allan's father opted for home. I was impressed with the old boys being on board; they fared well and were unfazed by being cold on the water, cramped together in a relatively small boat. Allan's father has never stopped singing the praises of that evening.

Back at Lynn's flat, Alex was chosen to let in

the New Year by stepping over the threshold first... having very natural dark brown hair, she was the obvious choice to uphold this British custom (the darkest haired person should traditionally enter the home first). Lynn opened a bottle of bubbly then a couple of neighbours popped in to join us as Rod Stewart belted out in his gravely voice from the CD player. Later, drinking strong, fresh coffee in the wee small hours and making plans what to do for the first day of the New Year, we decided to let Alex choose as it was to be her last day... she chose to spend the day picnicking on Noordhoek beach together with Lynn, Sarah and me.

I finally fell into bed after a wonderful New Year's evening but I felt somewhat disturbed by a nagging feeling, and sleep evaded me for quite some time. Reflecting on the evening when we were all sitting in the cockpit of Tradewind, I am sure, absolutely sure that I felt a hand stroking the back of my neck and the only person it could have been was Alex. I went over and over the evening, remembering exactly how we were all huddled together, and no matter how I juggled in my mind I was certain it could only have been her. Sleep did finally succumb after assuring myself that it was not intentional, but merely the close proximity we found ourselves in.

It was a rude awakening when my mobile phone rang the following morning, shocking me out of a deep, champagne-induced sleep – I had forgotten to turn it off. 'Good morning,' I said groggily, not even bothering to look at the number.

'Good morning to you. How are you feeling today? Lynn has prepared the picnic and we're ready to go when you are.' It was Alex.

I thought, 'How could anyone be up this early sounding so bright and breezy after having had such a late night?' 'The phone woke me up,' I told her a tad harshly.

'So how long do you think you and Sarah will be ready?'

Alex had a good command of the English language with a slight hint of a German accent which was quite charming. I didn't bother to correct the grammar of her question.

'Well I can see Sarah already dressed and reading out on the balcony. It will take me about half an hour to get ready. Is that okay?'

'Fine, we'll wait for you.'

There was a fairly cool atmosphere about the flat. Sarah had hardly spoken since getting up. Tension filled the air and I had no idea why this was the case. I felt on edge myself and wished now that we hadn't made the arrangement to go to the beach – alas! It was done, too late now to turn back or feign a headache or such.

Sarah had also prepared a small cool box with drinks, nuts and some smoked salmon sandwiches. I was mightily impressed. 'You've done us proud.' I told her.

'Just leftovers really, threw them all together – hope you don't mind. We can't let Lynn do everything without some contribution.'

'You are quite right, my friend.'

'Dear Sarah, what was happening?' I wanted to ask. This was my dearest friend of many, many years and I felt I was behaving badly for some unknown reason. She was always welcome at the flat or to use it whenever I wasn't there; now I sensed that she would prefer to go home but was not exactly saying so.

Although the weather was warm, the beach was blowing a howler. The four of us battled through the flying sand to find an appropriate spot to picnic – thank goodness we had had the foresight to take two beach umbrellas for shade. We pitched camp as near to the sea edge as possible, though this proved not such a good move as the tide was coming in and we needed to "up sticks" several times – an unpleasant task in a sandstorm, but Alex was determined to spend as much of her last day as possible on that beach. Living in land-locked Malawi was probably as good a reason as any for this request.

Lunch was very good. Lynn, being the Nigella Lawson of Cape Town, provided a picnic lunch fit for a Queen and together with our contribution it turned out to be a gourmet feast, sand and all. Once lunch was over and the umbrellas safely secured, it was time for a horizontal nap. I made myself comfortable lying on a towel with my rucksack for a pillow and lay there dreaming, when suddenly I felt a weight on my legs. Looking up I saw that Alex had done the same, but was using my legs as a pillow. It would be an understatement to say I was taken aback and nervous - paralysed would be more to the point - even though it seemed as though Alex had made herself comfortable in the most natural way. I looked up and around to see if anyone had noticed this.

Lynn got up and said she was going for a walk and Sarah decided to go with her. Once they were out of earshot I edged myself into a sitting position, thereby having to move my legs away from Alex's head. She sat up. I didn't say anything.

'Tell me about your life in Germany, Alex, and what you did before going to Malawi,' I asked by way of distraction.

'Do you really want to know?'

'Yes, as a matter of fact I do.'

'Where am I to begin? I was born and brought up in the spa town of Bad Oeynhausen. Going to church as a youngster I knew that I wanted to eventually work in Africa. I studied food technology and worked in a factory. I spent some time living and working in India, then a spell in Cambodia before joining the VSO and being posted to Malawi.'

'Gosh! You seem too young to have done all of that.'

'Not really, a lot of VSO volunteers have done much more at my age.'

'And Malawi, do you enjoy living and working there?'

'Yes I do, but I'm not sure I shall enjoy to go back tomorrow,' Alex said, looking me straight in the eye whilst running a finger over the top of my bare foot, sending a lightning shock through my veins.

Listening to Alex was captivating. She obviously had talent, good looks, personality and a smile to die for. She was quite some gal!

We sat there shaded by the umbrellas though it was still windy and, quite frankly, uncomfortable.

I felt uneasy anyway being left alone with her; there was something very weird going on. With some relief I saw Lynn and Sarah in the distance making their way back to us.

'I think we should go when the others return. It's been a lovely few hours but time to get back, and I also need to take Harry for a walk,' I told Alex as I started to pack things together in the cool box.

'Fabulous walk, though I felt a bit like Lawrence of Arabia battling through that sand,' Sarah told us as they approached and were about to sit down.

'We're packing up now, hope you two don't mind but I need to get back to Harry and take him for a walk.'

Everyone agreed that it was too windy and hot – we had given it our best shot, enjoyed the lunch and spent New Year's Day on a beautiful white sanded beach... who could wish for more?

When we arrived back at the flat I suddenly felt "all in" and decided to go and have a rest once Sarah and I had unpacked what was left in our picnic box. It was too early and too hot to take Harry for a walk on Long Beach in Simon's Town and moreover, the Cape Malay community held their traditional New Year's Day on that particular beach in the Simon's Town area, and they would be there in their droves picnicking and enjoying the first day of the year together. They were usually afraid of the dogs and letting Harry out of the car would set them caterwauling with a million screeches – no, not a good idea on this particular day.

On really hot days I tended to leave Harry in the flat where it was coolest. He had plenty of water and the outdoor balcony to roam around on. During the hottest months in South Africa – between January and March – I tended to take the dogs for a walk on the beach in the late afternoon when it was cooler and there were far less people about. Harry loved to go in the sea. Although he was perfectly capable of swimming, he preferred, as a good Staffie would, to wallow in that cold refreshing Atlantic as far as he could without actually taking his feet off the sea bed. No tennis ball or stick could lure him further out than he felt safe to go.

Harry's walk today would have to wait.

I lay down on the bed with all the doors open to try and get a draught through, and hopefully some shut-eye. Sarah was in her favourite position, sitting out on the balcony reading when I heard a text message come through on my mobile. It was Alex, asking if she could come and help me to clear the rest of the stuff we had left on Tradewind – I replied 'no thank you', as it was my intention to spend the following day on the boat, tidy up and give it a hose down. Obviously not satisfied with my response, another text came through. This to-and-fro text conversation went on for about an hour until I got thoroughly fed up as it was all meaningless jargon, full of innuendos and suggestion. In the end I gave in and went over to Lynn's flat and suggested to Alex that she came with me to take the glasses, empty bottles and rubbish off Tradewind – no text message this time, straight to the source and in front of someone. I popped my head back into my flat and told Sarah what we were doing. It was early evening, around six-thirty pm, and I said we would be back around eight pm.

We drove together in my car down to the yacht club. I was feeling rather cross and we did the journey fast and in relative silence. Once we were on the boat I asked Alex to sit down as I needed to talk to her.

'What the hell is going on?' I asked.

'I leave very early tomorrow morning and I thought it would be nice to spend some time together before I go back to Malawi.'

'Alex, we have spent many times together between Christmas and New Year, why on earth do you want to spend your last hours with me? Lynn is your friend and hostess - you should be spending it with her. Or is there something you're not telling me, and all those text messages, what's it all about?'

'I like you a lot and I don't want to leave you and go back to Malawi.'

You could have cut the silence with a knife. I sat there speechless trying to take in what Alex had just said and, unbelievably, what it meant. I thought I was quite a bright spark but this confession hit me like a bolt of lightning and knocked me for six. Whilst regaining my composure as best I could, my mind was whirling round like a dervish thinking how to respond. It suddenly occurred to me that Alex thought I must be gay. 'I'm not gay,' the inner self kept telling me over and over, but there was definitely an attraction there and it was very frightening and unbelievably scary.

'Whatever it is you're feeling, forget it – there is not even an option on this one,' I told her angrily, and then went down into the cabin to start packing up the things we had left behind from the previous evening.

But why was I being so brutal? Alex was gorgeous, a good-looking girl with a nice athletic figure, a great personality, and plenty of spunk. I pondered over this as we passed things between us from the cabin up into the cockpit. Maybe I was reading her all wrong, the German intonation sending out a different message to what was really being meant? Oh dear, I could tell I had upset her, which was not my intention. I resumed a seat again in the cockpit sitting opposite Alex.

'I'm sorry, I didn't mean to sound so offhand,' I told her, now feeling guilty after all the help she had given over the last week.

'That's O.K. I've wanted to meet you for such a long time and now that I have, I don't want to go. I'm sorry if it upsets you but that is how I feel.'

'What do you mean you have wanted to meet me for such a long time, since when? You don't even know me.'

'Ever since Lynn told me about this person who was living in the flat next door to her, she made you sound so interesting and fascinating that I wanted to meet you. In fact, it was one of the primary reasons I visited Lynn this Christmas.'

Curiouser and curiouser – this was beginning to sound like something one only ever reads about. This was not happening to me sitting on my beloved boat Tradewind in Simon's Town,

South Africa on New Year's Day, in the year two thousand and three – but, alas it was… no hallucinations here. Should I have felt flattered? Decidedly not, and I dismissed it immediately.

Lynn bought her flat a few months after I purchased mine. Being away in Europe at the time, we never met until she moved in a couple of months later. Alex, I was later to learn, was the prime instigator to Lynn buying the flat, as they happened to be in Cape Town together at that time. Lynn was looking for a property and Alex was attending a conference. Six months later it would be a fair assumption to say that I knew very little of Lynn, and alternatively she knew practically nothing about me.

'So what did Lynn tell you about me that sounded so fascinating?' I asked her.

'I can't remember.'

'Well there you go. It was so fascinating you can't even remember. Why don't I believe you?'

'It was various things Lynn remarked about when she wrote or I telephoned her. Nothing in particular – you being a woman, owning and racing a yacht would be fascinating to a lot of people.'

'At least she told you I was a woman, but did she tell you what age I was?'

'Not in exact years, but Lynn inferred that you and she were about the same age.'

'We are the same age Alex, which is approximately twenty-six years older than you.'

'So, what has age got to do with anything?'

'I think it's got a lot to do with everything, the way you are, the way you feel, responsibility, maturity, and to put it quite bluntly – lifespan.'

'You don't look any older than I am. It's you, it's your lifestyle and the way you are, sporty and full of life.'

'This is not getting us anywhere. You must go back to your good job in Malawi tomorrow morning and forget about me and this whole Christmas and New Year episode. It has been great to meet you, let's just leave it at that.'

'You could come and visit me in Malawi.'

'Malawi! Why on earth should I want to visit Malawi? Frankly I could think of nowhere less I would like to go at this moment in time.'

'I could show you the development work that I am doing there and perhaps we could visit a game reserve.'

As luck would have it a distraction came walking along the jetty in the form of my fellow sailing buddy Lindsay, on her way back to Alec's boat Gladys May, moored a few berths past Tradewind, 'Hi Lindsay, Happy New Year to you and Alec. What happened to you both last evening? We missed you somewhere along the line.'

'Don't ask,' said Lindsay walking over to us. 'Better not to go there. I think Alec was pretty gone and in full throttle by about ten, we even missed supper. So much for our last New Year in South Africa.'

'Do you know, Alex, that after ten years of sailing around the world with Alec, Lindsay was 'head hunted' to work on the proposed new terminal five at Heathrow Airport – she's someone very high in electronics. With few people being qualified to do the job, she was made an offer she couldn't refuse. The airport's authority interviewed her electronically – impressive. Lindsay started the job in November with the proviso that she could return to South Africa for Christmas and New Year, which was accepted, and here she is. A clever girl is our Lindsay.'

'When do you go back to London?' I asked her.

'In a couple of days' time. Alec leaves shortly after that – as soon as Gladys May is a hundred per cent ready and the weather forecast and conditions are favourable, he will then head off, straight for St Helena.'

'Well, I think that's fantastic. We'll miss you of course; the yacht club will not be the same without you two amazing characters.'

'Och Chris, we've been here for nearly two years now, it's time to move on.'

As we were talking over the guard rail, I was standing on the cockpit seat which covered the lazarette. Alex was standing in the cockpit itself when I felt her hand stroking the back of my leg – this was intentional, I was very sure of that – not just a close proximity nudge, as the reaction and electric current that ran through my body nearly sent me catapulting over the guard rail. God knows what Lindsay thought as I hurtled unsteadily towards her.

'Fair enough, I totally understand,' I told her, then left Lindsay and Alex chatting and exchanging promises to keep in touch.

Once Lindsay had left we gathered the box and bags together and left Tradewind looking shipshape and Bristol Fashion. We deposited the rubbish and made our way to the car park. I was still feeling very nervous with Alex and annoyed that she was putting me in this ludicrous position. I chose not to mention the incident on the boat – I did not wish to justify it with a response. I drove rather fast, if not a tad foolishly, as we made the short journey back to the flat. Some instinct made me drive past the entrance to Sea View Heights and go straight on up around the hairpin bends to the top of Red Hill. From this spectacular vantage point you could see the entire sweep of False Bay with Simon's Town nestling in the crook of the Simon's Berg Mountain, which forms part of the Cape of Good Hope and Cape Point Peninsula.

'There,' I said to Alex pointing the car to overlook the Bay. 'Isn't that the most fabulous view of Simon's Town, I think it should be this view that you take back to Malawi with you?' And indeed the view was spectacular from so high up, the lights twinkled from the houses and glittered from the decorations in the town, while all the naval vessels moored in the harbour and alongside the bullnose were all dressed up in Christmas lights that made Simon's Town and indeed, False Bay, at this particular time of year, especially in the evening, a magical sight.

'It is beautiful, really beautiful, but I don't think it will be the view of Simon's Town that I will be taking back; it will be the memory of the time spent with you.'

'What rubbish,' I said, starting the car. 'What time do you leave in the morning?'

'We have to leave the flat around half past four in the morning to be at the airport for the early flight to Johannesburg… I change there for Ma-

Malawi.'

'And Lynn is happy to take you?'

'Unfortunately yes, otherwise I would have asked you. I know Lynn doesn't like driving at night or in the half light, her eyesight is really poor, but she was insistently adamant that she was taking me to the airport. Maybe she'll have a puncture, and then you will have to take me,' Alex said jokingly.

When we returned to Sea View Heights I parked the car and turned to Alex. Reaching over, I patted a friendly hand upon her knee. 'I think this should be goodbye. I will never come to Malawi – you must forget everything because it's never going to happen.'

Alex did not say a word; she just looked at me fully in the eyes, which I found exciting and unnerving. She then leaned over, gave me a kiss on the cheek and was gone.

I entered the flat where Sarah was just preparing for bed. She seemed annoyed and upset. 'I thought you and Alex were going to the boat to tidy up then coming back so that the four of us could have dinner together. Lynn eventually asked me in for a drink and we waited and waited, is anything the matter?'

'No, and I'm sorry it took so long, we got held up talking to Lindsay – I should have phoned. I'm off to bed now, I feel exhausted, see you in the morning.' I mumbled feeling extremely guilty. Sarah was a lecturer in philosophy with a brilliant mind to boot. Why was I being so deceptive and secretive with such a good friend?

Sleep evaded me for a while as I kept going

over and over the conversation with Alex and trying to rationalise what was going on. The tension between us was very powerful, so much so that I could feel it penetrating through the wall that separated us; indeed, there was a furnace burning.

I awoke the following morning after a deep sonorous sleep, it was 7am. Whilst brewing the coffee I looked out of the kitchen window only to see that Lynn's car had gone. This did not produce the sigh of relief that I had expected to feel; it left a rather dull and empty void.

Chapter Four

The Invitation

Life got back to normal and went on as usual. I spent the next few days of the holiday sailing, visiting friends and spending time with James and Elspeth, who were, after all, my guests. In fact I was busying myself as much as possible because I found my mind wandering off... thinking about Alex, reflecting on the entire surreal episode and wandering if it had really happened.

Alex was using Lynn's mobile phone when she text me on New Year's Day. She had not left a contact number and I did not ask for one, and quite frankly I did not expect to hear from her again. So it was with some surprise when a couple of days later my mobile rang and it was unmistakably Alex – I was pleasantly surprised to hear her voice. This alone was disturbing but I quickly discarded it, after all there was distance between us now – nothing to get nervous about. 'Hello,' she said sounding a bit stilted, or maybe it was the German intonation again?

'Alex! How nice to hear from you. Presumably you returned back to Malawi safely?'

'Yes, but I don't like it here now. Rusty, my landlady, is away and the house feels deserted. Lynn's car did not get a flat tyre, after all! And I had prayed all night that it would.'

'Well, that's not a very nice thing to think or say,' I told her, knowing it was said tongue-in-cheek.

'I miss you.'

It dawned on me there and then that I missed her too but could not bring myself to say so. 'You've only been gone a day, you can't miss someone in that short time. There's nothing really much to miss.' I replied, as nonchalantly as I could.

'You don't mind me calling you?'

'No, not at all, I presume you got my number from Lynn?'

'Yes. I took it from her mobile when she let me use it. Sorry, I should have asked you first if I could have your number.'

'Not to worry.'

'Where are you? What are you doing?'

'I'm flitting between Chelsea and Simon's Town, sailing and generally enjoying the holiday. Too soon it will be over.'

'No chance that you will visit Malawi?'

'I'm afraid not. I start work on Wednesday.'

'Can I have your e-mail address? I want to send you something.'

'OK.' And I gave it to her.

We said our goodbyes and rang off, a trillion things unspoken. It was not exactly true what I had said about starting work on Wednesday, this was my own choice. Being the financial director of a school I always liked to go into my office a couple of weeks before where all reigned in peace and quiet – allowing me to prepare and print the school fee statements without interruption before the start of the new term, which began in the third week of January. I loved this special time. Ambery House School, founded by Sarah, is a beautiful, converted Victorian house surrounded by lovely gardens, tranquil at all times, even with the children there.

James and Elspeth left to go back to Oxfordshire; they seemed to have had a good time and they looked after the dogs well. If the truth be told, what they really liked was to have Fleur to themselves and be able to potter about the village having lunch and dinner whenever they felt like it, and of course to be away from the cold English winter.

One morning I downloaded my e-mails whilst listening to Vivaldi's Four Seasons playing on the laptop, when I noticed an email from Alex. I opened it immediately and found to my surprise that my heart gave a flutter, and a tinge of excitement ran through my veins as I read it.

"Hello Christine, this is an official invitation for you to visit Malawi. I have looked into visiting Mvuu game reserve as I know how much you like seeing wildlife – would you let me know as soon as possible if you can visit Malawi around the 16th January, as I have made a provisional booking for the 19th – 21st. At this time of year Mvuu is inaccessible by road and we have to cross a hippo and crocodile-infested river to reach it by boat, it is a remote game reserve completely cut off from everything by a very wide river – but beautiful. I miss you; let me know soon. Love Alex."

I read it again and again. 'What a fantastic opportunity.' I kept saying to myself. This was really exciting, the chance to visit Malawi and a remote Wilderness Game Reserve all at the same time. Then I would have to ask myself if the excitement was the thought of seeing Alex again, or the idea of exploring another African Country and its wildlife. As these thoughts were coursing through my mind at an irregular speed, my mobile phone rang. I answered the call – it was Alex.

'Did you get my email yet?' she asked.

Sounding a bit flummoxed as I had not expected a call so soon after the email, 'I said yes indeed, I received it a few minutes ago. Mvuu sounds fascinating but unfortunately the school term starts on the 19th January so it would be out of the question.'

'Are you sure? I have to confirm with them as soon as possible. Its quite a trek, they have to take us by Land Rover for an hour and a half to reach the river, then take us across the river by boat – we are booked into a tented chalet on the banks of the river. Mvuu has the largest hippo population in the world,' Alex said making her invitation sound all too wonderful and convincing.

A tented chalet on the banks of a hippo and croc-infested river? Was this, the stuff of madness that I found so appealing? Still, work was work and this offer had come at a greatly inconvenient time. 'Much as it sounds like everything I would love to see and explore Alex, I really don't think I can make it. Sorry.'

'That's a great pity. Mvuu is not an easy game reserve to get into, they just happened to have this one chalet available due to a cancellation.'

I felt the disappointment in her voice as she told me this. My heart ached and a kind of sadness blanketed the moment. There followed a pause in the conversation as my mind whirred and juggled trying to find some perspective.

'Give me some time to think about it. A few hours to make some phone calls, then I'll get back to you as soon as I can.'

'Seriously? You mean there could be a remote chance that you would come?'

'Alex, I can't promise anything. Let me make a few calls first, please.'

'Fantastic! I can't wait.'

We ended the conversation with Alex sounding very cheerful now that she had a "ray of hope". We hung up. The handset was still warm in my hands as I held it like a loving cup.

Not for one moment daring to admit it, I was feeling very nervous and a bit crazy.

I dialled my favourite travel agent who gave me the price and availability of flights to Malawi. Once I knew what I was in for, I then phoned Sarah to tell her that Alex had invited me to visit the game reserve in Malawi and what were the possibilities of me taking the time off at the start of term.

'You always do your work before term starts anyway, so I don't see why you can't go. What a fantastic opportunity and experience. Take it while you can. I will look after the dogs as well,' Sarah reassured me.

'Thanks! I believe so as well. I might never be offered something like this again.'

My excitement was mounting. I had never done anything at such short notice before and the thought of visiting Malawi and a Wilderness Game Reserve was tantamount to derring-do. There was one last call I had to make before I finally made the decision to go – this was to a neighbour in Chelsea who was a bookkeeper. She agreed to work in my office at the school and be there in the mornings to greet and answer questions to parents old and new and also to receive and bank any school fee payments. This had been my greatest worry – now it was all taken care of.

I booked a return flight, leaving in the early morning of the 17th and returning in ten days. All was in order. I phoned Alex and told her the news.

'I'm speechless!' were her only words.

'So I'll see you on the 17th of January in Lilongwe?'

'I don't believe it! You're really going to come to Malawi?'

'Yes, it looks like it. My ticket is booked. The start of term is taken care of. I'm so looking forward to visiting Malawi; wild horses wouldn't keep me away.' If the truth be known, I was also looking forward to seeing Alex again but I was careful not to say this to her. My feelings about the situation felt like I was treading on egg-shells. Alex, on the other hand, and from what I had seen and heard, appeared completely natural and honest about how she felt.

We ended the call and life resumed to normal.

There followed moments of doubt in my mind as to whether I was doing the right thing. Too late now, the flight was paid for and Alex would have confirmed the Mvuu booking which was... a present for me! How lucky was that?

The ensuing days were hectic and I worked extremely hard to ensure that everything was prepared and ready for the start of the school term. I filled my spare time with catching up on some sailing. If there were three of us up as crew I would find myself, if the weather was calm, sitting on the side of the boat waiting for the wind – with my mind drifting off thinking about Alex and the forthcoming trip to Malawi.

One day I invited Lynn for supper at the flat. I class myself as a fairly good cook but Lynn knocks spots off me in the culinary field, so it's always somewhat of a challenge to cook for her.

'I'll make a tiramisu pudding then,' Lynn suggested. She knew I loved her galactic tiramisu puddings... could I refuse such an offer?

'Thanks, Lynn. I'm going to cook us a fillet steak with my special cream and crushed black pepper sauce, fresh English spinach and baby new potatoes, complimented with a fine bottle of Cabernet Sauvignon. I hope that will suit you?'

'That sounds fantastic, Chris, I'll see you later.'

Throughout the evening I found myself asking Lynn questions about Alex, how they knew each other and the time they spent together in Malawi, really asking her anything that would focus the conversation onto Alex. Poor Lynn, in hindsight I should really have been asking her about her work and family. From what I have since gleaned, she is such an interesting person... shame upon me.

The evening over, with both of us replete in our own culinary endeavours, Lynn bade me good-night and left. I sat there reflecting over the evening and how thoroughly selfish I had been. This thing was taking me over – what was happening to me? Was my invitation to Lynn just so that I could talk about Alex? On reflection, I believe it was.

Was I in love?

It hit me like a bolt of lightning out of the blue. I was in love with this girl as sure as eggs is eggs. This was what falling in love was all about – lightning running through my veins at the thought of Alex. This was devastatingly danger-ous ground I was walking on. A female twenty-six years younger than I was. This could not be hap-pening to me, but undoubtedly it was. 'Take stock,' I told myself, 'this can go absolutely no-where, absolutely nowhere at all.' The emotional pendulum swung as each day went by. One day I was a grown up, mature and intelligent woman, who was strong enough and needed to put a full stop to this growing attraction – the next day I would not be so strong and any attempt to cancel my trip flew out of the window.

I did confide some of my misgivings to Alex in numerous emails and phone calls but she just brushed it off and became more determined than ever that I should go to Malawi and that we would have this time together.

When I left Cape Town International Airport at some ungodly hour in the morning for the domestic flight to Johannesburg where I would catch a connecting flight to Malawi, there was still some fear and trepidation hovering and fluttering inside me. 'I could always turn back in Johannesburg,' I kept saying as I looked down over the dramatic Drakensberg Mountains.

It was all too late, I know that now. As soon as the plane taxied onto the runway ready for takeoff it was too late. I had every opportunity to bail out, but I had not done so. My destiny now felt as if it were in the hands of this magnificent flying machine that was carrying me gracefully above the clouds into another African country, Malawi.

Chapter Five

Love in Malawi

The plane circled down and I could see the airport buildings clearly surrounded by dry scrubby sand in the middle of nowhere. Most definitely an African country but it felt right, it felt right to be there. My back-up plan B – the coward's way out, really - was to see Alex, who would be waiting at the airport, tell her that this whole trip was a mistake, and wait for the return flight to Johannesburg without even going into Lilongwe. There was determination in my mind as we were hustled through passport control and customs, even more so as the customs officer appeared to view me with a supercilious snarl of suspicion – somehow I managed to get through without losing my cool. Feeling fraught with entering into the unknown and seeing Alex again was putting me on edge – superciliousness merely added fuel to the fire.

There she was, standing in front of a crowd of people who were waiting in the airport building to collect passengers from the flight. Her big bright smile shone out to me as we saw each other at last, and whatever thoughts I had been philoso-phising in my head throughout the journey merely evaporated as soon as I set eyes on Alex.

'I still can't believe it!' she said as we hugged each other.

'Well you can believe it because, here I am,' I told her stretching my arms out and upwards towards the clear blue sky as we made our way out of the terminal building and across to Alex's parked Pajero. 'The smell here in Malawi is ex-actly the same as Botswana. Once when landing in Gaborone and walking out of the airport building the pungent warm African air hits you, it's the same here – quite evocative.'

'What do you think it is? I mean, what do you think makes up the smell?'

'I'm not too sure really, a mixture of things. The scent of some shrub, hot dry sand, warm still air, dust, Africa.'

Alex put her head to one side as if contemplat-ing this analogy. 'You could be right; though having been here in Malawi for four years now I guess I don't recognise it anymore. Anyway, it's really good to have you here; welcome to land-locked Malawi.'

'It might well be land-locked but two thirds of the country is Lake Malawi, and in my estimation that is a mighty large piece of water.'

'You will soon see because we're booked to stay at the Livingstonia Hotel set on the banks of Lake Malawi. It's very lovely there.'

'Then I shall look forward to it with pleasure.'

We chatted amiably and were easy and relaxed in each other's company as we sped along the

Malawian roads towards Lilongwe. Alex had to go back to her office and finish off the rest of the afternoon until the office closed at five o'clock. We were met at the office by Chris, Alex's assistant, a tall, thin Malawian young man with an infectious smile from ear to ear. Chris had a good smattering of the English language and we got along famously together and soon became affectionately known as Chris1 and Chris2.

Alex dispatched Chris1 and Chris2 off to do some shopping at the supermarket and for me to change some South African rands into Malawian kwacha while she had a meeting with a couple of her team in the office. It was a whole new experience for me. Chris2 became my chauffeur with the Pajero and quickly proceeded to give me a whirlwind tour of Lilongwe, both fast and fascinating. I loved it, and the freedom of being on holiday gave lightness and a sense of fun to the occasion.

'What an exciting place Lilongwe seems to be, Chris, such diversity from one street to the next,' I remarked as we sped towards the supermarket.

'Oh yes, you'll see a lot more of it before your stay is over, believe me.'

'Do you like working for ICRAF (International Centre Research for Agro Forestry) and with Alex?'

'It's okay working for ICRAF but I do not like the boss, a Nigerian man called Festus. He's an unpleasant person to work for and has no communication skills with the staff. But I love working with Alex, she's a fantastic person. Here's the exchange bureau, I'll come inside with you.'

I changed some money with Chris2's good

help; otherwise I might well have been short-changed.

'Right, the supermarket next,' said Chris2 as he clunked the Pajero into gear and off we sped with a screech.

Honking cars, roadside markets, litter and music abounded. Lilongwe, in a sense, was what I had imagined a true African country to be like. It was buzzing with life and exciting. It was good to be there.

By the time we arrived back at the office Alex was ready to leave. We said farewell to Chris2 and the rest of the staff before heading out from the centre of Lilongwe and on to the house that Alex shared with her landlady, Rusty. The house was on the outskirts of the city in a rather suburban area. It was with some surprise that, on arrival at the house, I found the gates were all chained and padlocked; this was very disconcerting. Alex sounded the horn of the Pajero and eventually a man appeared running from behind the house, hot-footed by a couple of dogs, and ran towards the gate, whereupon he unlocked it and let us enter. Alex had a friendly chat to the man in Malawian Chichewa, the official language, and then introduced him to me as John. He extended his hand for me to shake and another enormous grin stood before me. I decided there and then that Malawians were extremely nice. Since arriving only a few hours previously, I had seen nothing but broad smiles from helpful, happy people... what a pleasure.

Alex showed me around the house and we put my bags into the room I had been given. Once unpacked, showered and changed, I felt ready for anything. Rusty, the landlady, had not arrived back from work when I returned to the sitting-room. Alex was in the kitchen getting dinner ready. My offer to help and, indeed cook the dinner, or at least the steaks Chris2 and I had purchased in the afternoon, was eagerly accepted. Alex would prepare a big salad.

'Why is the house all chained and locked?' I asked Alex as we prepared the food. It was some-thing that was bothering me and I felt compelled to ask.

She cocked her head to one side contemplating the question. 'It's theft mainly, to keep anyone from entering the property. Malawians call it borrowing. They can take a bike from your prop-erty and if you can find the culprit and ask for it back, they will give it to you. The same with money, mobile phones, should they still have it to return, then they will.'

'What an interesting concept.'

'Just the Malawian custom, but somehow I don't really think it works,' Alex added, laughing.

Rusty arrived home just as we were about to open a bottle of wine, perfect timing, so we were able to all sit outside and enjoy a glass of good Cabernet. Rusty was an interesting character to say the least - a person of the old South Africa who left the country because of its apartheid regime for which, clearly, she was adamantly against. Although having lived in other parts of the world, Rusty appeared to be spending her twilight years living and working in Malawi, a country in which she obviously felt at home. Aged late sixties, she still remained a child of the hippy era. Highly intelligent with an enquiring mind, she was fascinating to listen to and an avid listener to talk to, Alex warned me. Rusty was not opposed to having the occasional joint as a nightcap, but she never once smoked in my company… I think this was in case I smelt it permeating through the house.

Later, when Rusty made her excuses and went off to bed, I asked Alex what she had told Rusty about me and if she was curious as to why I was there.

'The first thing Rusty said when she arrived back in Malawi after New Year was, 'I think you have met someone whilst you were away in Cape Town. I can tell. It's in your body language.' Rusty is a very perceptive lady.'

'And what did you tell her?'

'Yes, I did meet someone. Chris, Lynn's neighbour. Then, looking her straight in the eye, I went on to tell her that Chris was in fact Christine.'

As she spoke about it, the way she explained me to Rusty, my fingers traced nervous patterns in the faint layer of dust on the wine bottle.

'What was Rusty's reaction to that?' I asked anxiously, thinking how I would explain Alex to my friends and family.

'Go for it,' she said. 'If it makes you happy that's all that matters for both of you. If neither of you are concerned about the age difference nor the fact you are both women, then it's not a problem.'

'That's pretty amazing. Rusty must be a very special person to have such understanding,' I told

Alex casually, whilst underneath a nervousness set in as realisation dawned upon me that this was no longer an electronic communication friendship. We were both there, at last together and about to embark or disembark upon a relationship, the likes of which I knew nothing about.

We were sitting together on the sofa discussing our trip to Mvuu. Alex had one leg laid casually across my knees – it seemed very natural and relaxed. I stifled a yawn; the tiredness was beginning to get to me as I had been on the go since before the crack of dawn that morning. Two flights later plus the excitement of being on holiday in a new country and seeing Alex again was taking its toll. 'I think it's my bedtime.' I suggested, trying to sound jovial… when in fact, I was as scared as hell.

'Let me lock the door and clear these glasses away - I'll be with you in a sec.'

I made my way to the bathroom and had a quick shower. When I came out and went to the single bedded room allotted to me, Alex was standing in there, looking amused.

'You don't have to sleep in here if you don't want to. You can sleep in my room. Come, I'll show you, then you can decide.'

I followed her across the hallway and she showed me her room, which was basically just a double mattress on the floor and not very much else. I realised then that she had given up her room for me and was camping in the less comfortable spare room. The ball was definitely thrown into my court. Back in my bedroom I put on a t-shirt and wrapped a kikoi around my waist, my mind in a complete turmoil as I stood there dithering and dathering - should I do this or should I not? Finally I took those few fatal steps that did indeed change my life forever.

From the moment I took those steps, everything fell into place. Getting into a strange bed with another woman who, I realised, I was in love with, felt natural and exciting. Alex was an exceptional and gentle lover, someone beyond my wildest dreams. Regrets? Not one little bit. There are moments in every person's life that remain special and significant. That first night spent with Alex would be the pinnacle of my entire existence on this earth thus far – very beautiful.

We spent another day in Lilongwe. Alex was working and briefing her staff before leaving for Mvuu the following day. She showed me some of the projects she was working on out in the field – this was fascinating, if not a bit daunting, as I found their Malawian relief programme difficult to follow with propagation, grain and trees all being essential areas that Alex was involved in. Whilst she was busy in the office, Chris gave me another recce of Lilongwe – he was a wonderful guide and passionately showed me around the poorer areas not usually visited by tourists, areas full of life, where bartering and begging are the norm, where shady looking shebeens' belted out African music and young girls danced in a stoned, sexy trance. Food stalls of all descriptions abounded the roadside and smelled wonderful.

That same evening Rusty, Alex and I went out for dinner to the local Chinese Restaurant where we met up with some of their friends, Marika,

Alfonso and colleagues... we had a great time. The friends greeted me like a long-lost relative and appeared to accept the situation as perfectly normal. Indeed, they were anxious to let me know how tedious life had become for them in Alex's company since she returned from Cape Town.

'She was forever attached to her mobile in restaurants, dinner parties, meetings, hiking up a mountain, no matter where, she made sure she was available. Heaven help us if there was no signal to be had – she would sure as hell-fire go in search of one,' Alfonso told me in the humour with which it was meant. They were all obviously very fond of Alex, but this "new" side of her was a complete anathema to them.

Alex and I spent another wonderful night together. We seemed to have such fun talking and just being close in each other's company. In the morning there was a shout from outside the bedroom door. 'Shut up you two, you've done nothing but giggle all night!' Rusty's guttural smoker's voice shouted out. Not quite true, but there you go, I don't think Rusty was awake for one little moment as witness. We laughed and told Rusty to get a life.

After Rusty had left for her early morning jog we got up, showered, breakfasted and, with the help of John, packed the Pajero ready to leave for Mvuu. The journey would take us down to the southern end of Malawi so Alex organised it such to incorporate visiting some farms that she was working with – these particular farms produced seedlings for the agro forestry programme and Alex, being an expert in the field, found this her particular speciality, all the more interesting as far as I was concerned. We would visit Zomba and the Zomba Plateau – wow! It was all so exciting. I'd heard from friends and in particular, my neighbour Lynn, who had lived in Malawi for many years, the relayed wild stories about Zomba and the steep hairpin climb up to the plateau. Hearing these stories I never believed for a moment that I would be experiencing this for myself.

Once outside Lilongwe, leaving the city behind us, we soon came upon rutted dirt roads which were normal in Malawi. Alex warned me beforehand that there were interminable road blocks along the way and that I should keep my cool if we were stopped because the guards could be very officious. Fortunately for us, Alex had diplomatic immunity in Malawi so when we did reach a road block we were more or less waved on – much to my relief.

'This is just fantastic.' I told her, sitting high up in the passenger seat of the Pajero. 'This really feels like being in Africa.'

'Is it anything like you thought it would be?'

'It's much, much better! It's a million times better,' I replied with a huge grin on my face. I was indeed a happy person.

Alex looked over at me with that wonderful smile of hers and the bright eyes sparkled in a mischievous way – she looked like the cat that had got the cream.

We were making good headway so we decided to stop for a break at a pottery that Alex was familiar with. It had a modest outdoor tearoom where we had a sandwich and something cool to drink sitting in the pottery's pretty garden – a welcome oasis after the pot-holed, dusty roads.

'Mvuu,' Alex started to tell me, 'is part of Liwonde National Park. It has the greatest concentration of hippopotamus in the world basking in the river surrounding Mvuu camp.'

'Then it would have to be a mighty big river – if there are huge numbers of hippo then surely there must be crocodile?'

'Plenty, plenty! We have to cross the river by boat to get to Mvuu,' she answered, making it sound highly dangerous, whilst licking her fingers and looking me straight in the eye with mock fright.

I was beginning to feel those butterflies deep within my stomach at the thought of being surrounded by hippos and crocs for a couple of nights, and at such close range. As Alex had told me, she'd booked a tented chalet on the banks of the river. The butterflies were excitement, well, at least I hoped they were; fear was not something that usually entered my psyche.

We finally reached Liwonde National Park and were asked to park the Pajero into an area reserved for us, as we would not need it again until our return. Alex got out of the car and stretched her legs. She then reached into the car to retrieve our paperwork and passports in order to complete the documentation with the park officials. We were then transferred to a Land Rover and driven one and a half hours until we reached an area along the river where the Land Rover suddenly, and thankfully for us, came to a bone-rattling stop. There was the boat that would take us across to Mvuu. We eagerly stepped aboard and regardless of hippo or croc the motor across that river was bliss in comparison to the kidney-shaking journey in the Landy.

The large reception lodge at Mvuu was awesome. We were greeted by the brightly-dressed and welcoming Malawian staff who showed us around the magnificent thatched building while explaining the rules of the camp. 'It's very important to know where you can, and cannot go without an escort or a guide,' explained Abdul, one of the Mvuu camp managers. 'Please remember that you are in dangerous territory at all times. Mvuu is not for the faint-hearted,' he said patting his hand against his heart. We were then introduced to an attractive-looking Malawian man called Marin, who would be our personal guide for the duration of our stay at Mvuu.

Marin escorted us to our tented chalet; it was like entering another world and yes, we were very near the river. 'At night the hippos tend to wander around and forage, they are dangerous and you must not leave your chalet,' Marin warned us. No sooner had Marin left when we turned around to enter the chalet - there before us were at least fifty monkeys sitting on our roof and the outdoor table and chairs, and they were already eating some of the fruit we had put down on the table.

'Heavens above, I've never seen so many monkeys,' Alex exclaimed, waving her arms and shooing them away amid our shouts of laughter.

We were amused at their audacity and fearlessness, but once we had staked our claim on the chalet we were never bothered by them again.

This was the first time I had stayed in, or even seen a tented camp. The chalet we occupied was built of stone to about knee height and the rest was green tented canvas – it gave an outdoor atmosphere in a luxurious kind of way, not exactly camping but as near to it with comfort. We unpacked, showered and rested. It had been quite a long journey all in all and it was good to be still. For the first time since meeting Alex at Christmas I was beginning to feel relaxed and happy. The peace and silence at Mvuu was overwhelming and it was not long before we both drifted off into sweet dreams.

The sound of djembe drums woke me up, or had I dreamt it? I shook Alex awake and we both realised that this was a call to let us know that dinner was served. We dressed hurriedly and once outside saw that a hurricane lamp had been placed by the tent – our guiding light. We retrieved the lamp and made our way to the lodge following a path that the guide had shown to us and which we were to follow and strictly adhere to – obviously a hippo avoidance route. We were greeted at the entrance to the lodge and then again as we entered the dining room, known as a boma – such chivalry and gracefulness from the Malawians, all beautifully dressed in traditional costume – we could choose any table we wanted, the waiter informed us. Well, this was not surprising as after an hour had gone by and no other guests appeared, we realised that we were perhaps the only guests in this entire remote camp a million miles from anywhere, surrounded by hippopotamus, elephants, crocodiles, lion and a bunch of smiling Malawians. Thank goodness Alex could speak Chichewa.

'I wonder where all the people are? I remember you saying on the phone that they had one chalet left and that was only due to a cancellation,' I remarked in puzzlement.

'You're right, it doesn't look or feel as if anyone else is here – how strange.' Alex replied, looking somewhat perplexed.

'Well, I'm sure we'll soon see one way or another.'

You could not have found fault with the food served at Mvuu, and that first evening it was delicious and plentiful. We were waited upon like royalty. Oh yes! I could get used to this, I thought to myself. It was difficult for Alex and me to have any serious conversation with six pair of eyes watching our every move and not another person in sight to distract them, so we ended up chatting to the staff and asking them what life was like working for Wilderness Safaris and being based at Mvuu. We had a great evening and when it was time to return to our chalet, Marin escorted us and waited until we were safely zipped in. We slept fitfully with the sound of the snorting hippos trudging around outside and something else I could only imagine might be monkeys, bounding around on the tented roof. A cacophony of sound for this wilderness camp, but that's Africa.

Djembe drums serenaded us to the breakfast table the following morning. The same courtesy presided as the previous evening – all exactly the same, only with eggs, bacon and a wide variety of everything anyone could possibly wish for to start the day – smiles abounded.

Mvuu offered a variety of game drives and river trips into the wilderness. 'What would you like to do today, my darling?' Alex asked.

That was so nice to hear, being called 'her darling'. 'I think my priority would be to go on the river. It's what Mvuu is famous for, so let's do that first.'

What a fantastic experience it was, just the two of us, and Josef, our knowledgeable Malawian river guide. As informed, the river was an abundance of wallowing hippos peering lazily above the water with arched brows and in parts quite densely populated with large, medium and baby hippos cavorting in all sorts of fashion, ungainly copulating at times, seemingly unaware that human eyes were near and watching them in wonder. Josef would point out the silent and predatory ridged pattern gliding silently through the water... a crocodile, completely unnoticed except to the trained eye. Cormorants and Jacanas strut and wade between banks of crocodiles lying immobile as if touched by magic, petrified in their stillness. The bird life was exceptional from kingfishers to hawks, falcons and the amazing fish eagle. Josef would glide us into secret rivulets to get better views of the birds and at times to go up close and personal with an army of hippos.

The river was huge and very wide. Josef explained to us that it was a tributary of the Great Rift Valley – and I quite liked the fact that this was the case... a memory of my favourite novel, Karen Blixen's book "Out of Africa" set in Kenya where the Great Rift Valley plays an integral part. Being at Mvuu in the Liwonde National Park was a timeless and special place.

Dinner the second evening brought Andrew, one of the owners of Mvuu camp, to the dining-room, together with some guests. We were invited to join them for drinks after dinner, which we accepted, and enjoyed a pleasant evening chatting and learning more about Wilderness Safaris, which had game reserves throughout Africa. Andrew, a tall dark and rugged-looking man in his fifties, had a rather dour looking face and hangdog expression which looked out of place at Mvuu.

'I'm from Norwich,' Andrew told me as we sat around the warm boma fire.

'And I'm from Manchester. What brought you to become a part owner of a safari company in Africa?'

'Circumstances really, I've always wanted to work and live in Africa and when the opportunity presented itself, I jumped at the chance. And what, pray, dragged you from Manchester?'

'I was made an offer I couldn't refuse. My bosses in London sent me to investigate an elephant and rhino poaching syndicate operating in South Africa.'

'Wow! That's pretty impressive if not a bit scary. And, did you find the buggers?'

'Yes, and that's all I'm at liberty to divulge. But rest assured that the top dog sitting behind his grand façade in England will not be operating in horn and ivory poaching any longer.'

'That's fantastic to hear. Our Wilderness Safari business solely thrives on African wildlife and if poaching is not eradicated there will be no wild-life left. No safari business and no work for the Africans,' Andrew remarked shaking his head.

'I agree with you completely. Unfortunately I'm a bit long in the tooth now to be active in such assignments. That last one was quite a long time ago.'

'Pity about that, we need people onto those bloody poachers on a full time basis – twenty-four-seven. It's something the government of each country should be monitoring but there's so much corruption going on at government level that they feign lack of funding for not monitoring their own country's greatest asset.'

I could sense Andrew was getting angry. Poaching was something he abhorred and it was a threat to his livelihood and that of his African staff. The warm fire, good food and rather robust red wine were making us loose-tongued and tired. It was time for bed.

The following morning after breakfast we got ready to leave Mvuu. This time we would be taking the boat all the way back up the river to the base camp where we had left the Pajero; this would take a good hour. On board the boat were the previous evening's guests and another couple whom Alex knew and who told us that they had been there as long as we had. Surprise! Other people were there at Mvuu as well as us, obviously holed up in their tented chalet from the lovey-dovey way that they behaved towards each other; still, they were fun to talk to on the return journey and when the young man, an English doctor, told me he was leaving Malawi at the end of the month to take up an appointment at a Glasgow hospital in Scotland, I quite understood their reluctance to leave the tented retreat.

We left Liwonde National Park with wonderful memories of our time at Mvuu with its abundant wildlife, our glorious trip on the river and the charming staff who had made us so welcome.

From Liwonde we made our way to the town of Zomba. Alex especially wanted to show me Zomba Plateau, a great slab of mountain rising to 6000feet covered in forest and one of Malawi's better known forest reserves. There is a hotel almost at the top Alex told me, where she wanted us to have lunch. Once we reached the town we made our way up the precarious hairpin bend road, around and around as Alex's expert driving and concentration kept us clear of the many pot holes. It seemed to go on forever.

'This is where we were attacked last year. Lynn and a few of us volunteers came on a hiking trip for the weekend and we were attacked by two Malawian men swinging panga's,' Alex casually announced as she was manoeuvring a particularly bad hairpin bend.

This took me somewhat by surprise. 'Attacked? What on earth happened? Robbed or raped, I thought it was pretty safe in Malawi.'

'They stole on demand, three rucksacks from our group of seven, and then made us run away, which we did - into the bushes where we armed ourselves with big sticks and stones ready for any other incident as we made our way back to the campsite we were staying in.'

'Did you see them again and report the incident to the police?'

'Yes, we did when we went back down to Zomba. Can you imagine? We had to supply the policeman taking our statement with paper! I'll leave the rest to your imagination.'

'Obviously nothing ever came of it?

'Exactly, we never heard another thing.'

'Is that typical of Malawian police?'

'I'm afraid to have to say that it is.'

We reached the top of the plateau and there before us was the luxury hotel, Sunbird Ku Chawe. Sitting on the hotel's terrace overlooking the plateau we relaxed and enjoyed our delicious and refreshing ice-cold Malawian rock shandies. Alex had arranged for us to visit and stay overnight with a male colleague of hers who lived with his wife in Zomba. I felt somewhat reluctant to go and be with other people who I didn't know. My time in Malawi thus far had been quite magical and I was reluctant to break the spell.

'Let's stay here tonight. Would your friends mind awfully if we didn't go there?' I asked tentatively, as I did not want to hurt her feelings in any way.

'What a brilliant idea. Let's see if they have a room first then I'll give Pierre a ring and tell them we just cannot make it. It was a pretty loose arrangement anyway, as I was never really sure that you would turn in Malawi in the first place.'

'Ah! She of little faith!' I told her as we set forth to the hotel reception in search of a room.

Much to our delight the Sunbird Ku Chawe did have a room for us. So that afternoon we took a leisurely drive around the top of the plateau which was covered in criss-cross streams, tumbling waterfalls and still lakes.

'There are leopards up here.' Alex said, as we gazed about us looking at views of such splendour.

'Well I'm sure there are, it's most definitely leopard country up here, I'm so glad we decided to drive and not walk after what you told me about being attacked and with the odd elusive leopard about… I think we made the right decision, though I would dearly love to see a leopard.'

'Look over there,' Alex whispered pointing to a lone, rather dead-looking tree. 'That's a long-crested eagle.'

Looking through my cameras zoom lens, I managed to take a super photograph of the splendid eagle perched imperiously on the branch of the tree a second before it swooped down and plucked something from the ground.

We left Zomba the following morning and made our way back to Lilongwe, where we would stay for an evening before making our way north to stay at the Livingstonia Hotel on the banks of Lake Malawi. As we enjoyed supper that evening at the local Chinese restaurant we regaled Rusty with every detail of our journey south and of the Wilderness Reserve. We had the greatest fun. Alex and Rusty said 'hello' to a thousand people, and one or two joined us at our table as we married the night away talking of fellow USAid workers or VSO volunteers who appeared to be in abundance in Lilongwe – quite frighteningly so, in my opinion. When, some years later, I read the book Last Orders at Harrods by Michael Holman, depicting the amount of aid workers in Africa, I completely empathised with it.

Journeying north the following day was as interesting, if not more so, than the journey south had been. At lunchtime Alex was really keen for us to stop at a restaurant, or should I say a café that, she assured me, cooked the most fabulous local fish, a speciality of the area we were in. The café was unbelievably primitive, but I quite liked that. The guys running it were friendly and unpretentious - laid-back would probably be the right description. Yes, they did have this fish fresh from the lake and would cook it for us there and then they assured us with amusement, obviously not too used to seeing two white women alone together in their macho café. We waited and waited, then realising that no chef would take that long to cook some fish, I suggested to Alex, 'Perhaps they have gone to fish for it in the lake.'

She pondered on this for a moment. 'You know? I think you are absolutely right.'

'Well, I suppose you couldn't get fresher than that, could you?'

'I suppose not, but they could have told us we would have to wait.'

Frankly, I was in such a relaxed mood I wouldn't have minded waiting all day. Everything in Malawi moved at such a slower pace than in South Africa – we were in their space and that's how it was.

'We're not in any hurry are we?'

'No not at all. I just thought you might be hungry.'

'I am, but it doesn't matter. I'm enjoying the

vibe of this place, it's obviously where all the locals come to eat, not a white face in sight.'

'Not on the tourist route that's for sure, one of the reasons I wanted to bring you here, as well as to taste the succulent rare Chambo fish.'

The words had hardly left Alex's mouth when there placed before us was the famous fish resplendent in garnish, most decidedly fresh and smelling wonderfully of herbs and spices. It tasted as delicious as it looked. If we had waited for an hour or more, so be it; the result was worthwhile, and I do believe they did go and catch the Chambo as it was ordered.

Lake Malawi is an enormous lake that takes up two thirds of the country. Affectionately known as the calendar lake – because of its size in length and breadth to a calendar year – when you first set eyes on this lake it quite takes your breath away. Its sheer expanse gives the illusion that it's the sea, and it's even harder to imagine that it is completely land locked. The Livingstonia Hotel sits right on the edge of Lake Malawi and the cottage we were given was on the beach – a thatched rondavel (round) cottage with three steps leading directly onto the sand with the water a mere fifteen metres away – how very beautiful it was.

We could not wait to take our clothes off, don our costumes and get into that water, which we did within minutes once the hotel porter had left, after carrying our bags to the cottage. The lake water is not clear like the Atlantic sea water around Cape Town. It had a lot of soft-floating reed which made one automatically want to clear it out of the way until you realised it was an end-less and thankless task, and the water was warm, quite unlike the cold, cold Atlantic, so we enjoyed it and revelled in being able to swim to our hearts content from our very own private beach.

The last evening at the Livingstonia became quite emotional for me and I tried my very best to hide this from Alex. My time in Malawi would soon be coming to an end and in my heart of hearts I thought it would be best if Alex and I did not see each other again. She was young, beauti-ful, intelligent, and full of fun, with a whole life ahead of her; it would be unfair and remiss of me to allow it to be otherwise. What we had shared together already was very special, so special that I wanted to put it in a box and keep it forever. Already the thought of never seeing her again was breaking my heart.

'What would you like for your birthday?' I asked Alex as we sat having dinner in the hotel courtyard. Her birthday was on the 6th February, about two weeks away.

'I would like you to be here with me in Ma-lawi.' She answered so spontaneously it took me by surprise.

'Well, I doubt that could happen, much as I would like it to.'

'You asked and that is my answer. I don't want anything else.'

Any thoughts about having a discussion with regards to our future flew away on a breeze. I neither had the courage nor the heart, to tell Alex what was on my mind, especially not now after hearing what she had just said. Like a coward I would take it away with me. Suggest over the phone or in an e-mail that it would be the stuff of madness for us to carry on this relationship. I was far too old and it would be inappropriate of me to allow it to continue.

All too soon the fairy tale visit to Malawi and Alexandra came to an end. Ten magical days imprinted on my mind forever. At Lilongwe airport it was the hardest goodbye I have ever had to say. Alex and I waited until the very last minute before I went through passport control, and it was all that I could do to stop myself crying. Every being in my body controlled the flow of those unshed tears. We were both trying desperately hard to be brave.

The aeroplane took off and circled above Lilongwe before winging its way towards Johannesburg and at last the tears fell. I looked down to see if I could see the Pajero heading back to town, but I couldn't. I sat at the rear of the fairly empty plane all by myself. I had asked the air hostess on boarding if I might do that, there was no way that I wanted to sit next to someone. I needed to be alone with my broken heart.

At Johannesburg airport I had to change planes for a domestic flight to Cape Town with a couple of hours to spare in between, so I switched on my mobile phone, which immediately started to ring. It was Alex and my spirits soared.

'I miss you already. Did you have a good journey?' she asked.

'Yes, the flight was good, that's all I can say.'

'Thought I'd just check that you had landed safely, I couldn't wait to hear your voice again.'

With the biggest lump in my throat I could hardly answer – completely choked up. What on earth was happening to me? It was as if my body was going through the motions but my heart and head were somewhere else. This was not good news, 'I miss you too. Must rush now to catch my connecting flight,' was all I managed to blurt out before switching off the phone. The flight to Cape Town took two hours, during which I had a light supper and downed a small bottle of in-flight wine.

Chapter Six

Magic Moments

My life had changed immeasurably. All the philosophising in the world I handed out to myself went nowhere. Rhyme nor reason slipped away from me when I heard Alex's voice on the phone. From day one after arriving back in Cape Town it was my intention to break this relationship off, yet I felt powerless to do so. Her resolve for it to continue never wavered, so what was my problem? I had entered this with eyes wide open; was I afraid of the age difference or the homosexuality stigma? On rationalisation, being the same gender did not bother me nearly as much as the age difference did.

One day a surprise awaited me in my e-mails. Rusty telling me that life was too short, and to get on a plane as she was arranging a big party for Alex's birthday and it was imperative I was there.

Without preamble I soon found myself looking up an air ticket again. My plan was to fly to Malawi on Thursday, Alex's birthday, and return on Monday morning which would give me four days there. Heavens! I was being weak.

I mentioned to Sarah and Keith that I was going off to Malawi again. Sarah was curious to know why I was returning there so soon after arriving back – I told her I had been invited to Alex's birthday and there was to be a big party – all true, but even Sarah knew that I would not travel all that way just to attend a party.

'What exactly is going on?' she eventually asked me.

'Alex and I have grown very fond of each other and I would like to be with her on her birthday. Her landlady, Rusty has just sent me an invitation for the party she is giving for Alex,' I answered, sounding as pathetic as the feeble explanation was. But Sarah is extremely perceptive and read between my lines as transparently as I tried to cover them.

'Chris, it was blatantly obvious that Alex was attracted to you as soon as I saw you two together. So this is not exactly a surprise.'

'Oh!' I was taken aback. 'Well, it has been a surprise for me, I can tell you!' I was quite shocked that it had appeared so obvious to Sarah.

'Quite a difference in your ages, wouldn't you say? Maybe Alex desperately needs something in you at the moment, and you need something in her.'

I was not sure about that remark or indeed if it justified an answer. Sarah was my best friend after all and I wasn't confiding in her, she probably felt miffed at that, and no doubt felt that I was making a fool of myself. Nothing on earth would make me hurt Sarah but I was not even sure where the situation was taking me, therefore it was impossible to discuss or comment about.

Keith, my fellow yachtsman, skipper and friend, was not altogether delighted that I would be taking off again… as he put it. The racing season had started and we needed to be in the start of the series for the mid-week or for the weekend racing. Keith was a twenty-three year old natural sailor and I had learned a great deal about sailing from him – we were buddies. I suggested we enter the twilight series held on a Wednesday evening and if I was unable to make it he would easily 'make a plan'. Keith agreed eagerly to this. He could then helm Tradewind and, with his young friends for crew, sail her to her capacity instead of having me on board to dampen his sailing ardour.

So it was, that with everything organised and in order, I set off for Malawi on the 6th February 2003 to visit Alex once again. Between my last visit and this one Rusty had moved houses and Alex had moved with her. The house was in an area that Rusty preferred, nearer the centre of Lilongwe. Alex told me in one of our conversations that when they moved into this rented house it was in a pretty disgusting state, really awful, and Rusty made the landlord paint and clean the place thoroughly before they would step inside. This was all done in a huge hurry before I arrived and it was to the new house that Alex took me.

I suppose when you're heady and in love you don't really notice your surroundings. For someone as meticulous as me, this was a first. The town house was in a rough, grubby area and the house itself much smaller and shabbier than the previous one.

'Welcome to our new home! What do you think?' Alex asked taking my bags out of my hand and leading me to the bedroom to unpack.

Dogs barked and serenaded me as I showered while feeling utterly happy to be back in Malawi with Alex. 'I think it's got character, a little rustic maybe, but I prefer it to the other house most definitely.' I told her as I stepped back into the bedroom.

The house did have its charm and I grew to quite like it. We were in the buzz of things; noise abounded, dogs barked, people shouted. John, the houseman, had also moved with them and he kept the house clean and tidy as well as doing the washing and ironing – what a gem John was – I enjoyed him being around.

Rusty had most certainly arranged a big birthday party. The party was to be held in a friend's house somewhere on the other side of Lilongwe. Alex did not seem too keen to go out, she just wanted us to be alone – so did I, if I have to be honest. But Rusty had gone to a lot of trouble and people would be waiting, so I got the ball rolling and gave Alex her birthday presents.

'Wow!' she exclaimed, opening the first one. 'These are fantastic, look how beautifully they fit.'

I had given her a pair of blue two-tone traditional sailing shoes, and yes, they did look lovely on her, and a perfect fit to boot! A bottle of her favourite perfume and an antique silver chain were in the birthday parcel as well and she insisted on donning it all for the party.

'Let's hope the sailing shoes are a good omen

that I shall soon be learning to sail with you in Simon's Town,' Alex remarked mischievously.

'That would be good, very good indeed.' I told her jokingly.

She gave me a knowing look. 'It might be sooner than you think.'

'Are you planning to come to Cape Town for a visit?' I asked, trying to sound nonchalant.

'Definitely. I might even come to live there.'

If any remark could stop me dead in my tracks, that certainly did. I was about to ask Alex to elucidate but quickly changed my mind. These were very early days of knowing someone – it could end tomorrow. I accepted the relationship as a brief encounter, the logistics, the age difference, the same-sex gender. All the odds were stacked highly against it becoming more than a passing flight of fancy, and, let's face it; I was flattered, attracted and more than extremely happy. I loved this girl and if it should end tomorrow – so be it! Living in the here and now was all that mattered. Tomorrows would have to be faced when they happened.

The birthday party was a great success. Rusty had invited a lot of Alex's friends and colleagues who arranged all the food and drink, while a friend of Rusty's together with a few other musicians provided the live music. Alex introduced me to all the people she knew. There was no self-consciousness about her relationship with me and she proudly showed me off to each and everyone there. God knows what they thought, God knows what anyone thought, but I was welcomed wholeheartedly by all. Perhaps in hindsight, it was indeed Alex's openness and transparency with our relationship that was the true test and which gave me the confidence to face, in the future, my own family and friends with our relationship.

Another part of my birthday present to Alex was a stay at The Livingstonia Hotel. I had arranged for us to spend the rest of the weekend there, in our own apartment on the beach. We left the following morning after the party and made our way north. This time we did not stop for Chambo but made straight for the hotel. The apartment we were given was not far from the little cottage we had stayed in ten days previously, but this one was larger with a generous terrace and a whole expanse of beach, seemingly to ourselves as no one else appeared to be using it. We luxuriated in room service, took long walks along the beach to a small Malawian settlement which fascinated us, swam a lot in the lake and watched the abundance of fish eagles swooping off the rocks to accurately catch their prey.

Too soon again the short visit came to an end and I found myself once more circling up and off over Lilongwe as the aeroplane took me sadly back to Johannesburg. When we were together, Alex and I never really discussed the future or if we would see each other again. Our partings were painful enough and to discuss if, where and when we might be together again made it all the more difficult, so we parted with goodbye and no promises.

Working at the school was always a pleasure and never a chore. I had my own office and for most of the time I was left to my own devices. The entire staff worked together as a team and a jolly good team at that. Started by Sarah in 1984, it was one of the first multi-racial schools to open and function within the South African apartheid regime. Pupils there ranged from three to twelve years old. My brother Geoff, from England, on holiday for three months, came to do some odd jobs at the school. He commented, 'In all the time I have been here I have never once heard a child cry or a voice raised. It is the most peaceful school I have ever come across.' With an ex-wife as a teacher and two daughters teaching at schools in Lancashire, plus ten grandchildren, this was fair compliment indeed from Geoff.

Pride in my work and the success of the school was paramount. I put my head down and tried hard to concentrate on the business at hand without my mind wandering off into Malawi. The days since arriving back passed uneventfully with the odd text messages exchanged between Alex and me. The Friday of that same week was Valentine's Day so I decided that I would take myself off to the flat and spend the weekend in Simon's Town and try to get some sailing in. There would be racing on Saturday afternoon and a medium distance race starting on Sunday morning – we would do one or the other, but I doubted both.

After work finished early on Friday afternoon I went to the house in Chelsea to pack a few things for the weekend. Frances the housekeeper was there, finishing some ironing with a knowing grin spread across her face. It was always a joy to see this wonderful lady from Mitchell's Plain, with her brown twinkling eyes, warm heart and smart appearance. I wandered into the sitting room and there was the largest bouquet of ivory white roses I had ever seen – a spectacular sight, I can tell you! My heart soared as I read the accompanying card, which simply said, 'I love you.' Feeling overwhelmed would be an understatement.

'I wonder who sent you such beautiful flowers?' Frances asked mischievously.

'Well Frances, that is the point of Valentine's Day – to secretly declare your love for someone without the recipient knowing who it is.'

She looked at me as if I had fallen from the moon. 'So you have no idea who sent them?'

'No, I don't.' I half-lied simply because I couldn't be one hundred per cent sure who it was.

Frances gave me a knowing look, disbelieving me totally. She was aware of my every move and looked after me like one of her own. Jonathan Hall, Sarah's brother, once told a group of people that if anyone ever wanted to know where I was or what I was doing, they had only to ask Frances. Going away to Malawi, or to anywhere twice in the space of three weeks was bound to arouse suspicion in my dear and trusted friend, who, I might add, was also the housekeeper at the school. So not a lot slipped past her where I was concerned.

'Why don't I believe you?' she asked, putting her arm around my shoulder and laughing.

'Because Frances, on this one, you are just going to have to,' I replied with a teasing wink.

So, with a lightly packed weekend bag and the enormous bouquet of flowers standing in a bucket of water behind the drivers' seat of the BMW, with the dogs sitting happily ensconced on the back seat, I waved Frances a cheery farewell as I took my leave and drove speedily off towards Simon's Town. The first stop was the flat as the weather was hot and the flowers needed to get into a cooler place. I arranged them in a large plain glass vase – in fact it was a cookie jar without the lid – and they filled the room and my heart with their beauty. Next stop was Scarborough beach. The dogs loved running and sniffing along the sand then taking short swims in the ocean. Harry could swim alright but he obviously felt safer as long as his tippy toes could touch the sand beneath him. Scarborough, a small cove on the Cape Peninsula adjacent to Cape Point Nature Reserve, is home to a well established artistic community and is a surfer's paradise. Its white sandy beach stretches a kilometre from the village to the nature reserve fence, wild and rugged with a turbulent sea spewing up surf, Scarborough is ten kilometres from the flat and one of my favourite places.

Striding out barefoot along the seashore, enjoying the cold waves splashing against my legs, the dogs and I managed to walk the entire beach and even further toward a rocky promontory that held large rock-pools where Harry could immerse himself completely without any fear… and boy! Did he love those rock-pools. Round and round he would go, soaking in the cold water up to his ears to cool his body after the heat. Hettie and Josh preferred the lapping waves of the ocean. We would find a suitable rock form to sit down upon and from there Harry would rest before exploring another cool pool. Mesmerising stuff watching Harry, I wanted badly for Alex to be there to share this lovely afternoon with us. The thought that I had done nothing for her for Valentine's Day left me feeling a bit embarrassed. The antique silver necklace I had taken to Malawi for Alex's birthday was meant to double up as a Valentine present, but somehow I had forgotten to tell her – not surprisingly so at the time.

Back at the flat I bumped into Lynn, who kindly asked me to join her for a glass of wine and a little supper, which I gratefully accepted. Much as I wanted to be on my own, another part of me needed to be distracted from my own turbulent thoughts. Lynn knew that I had visited Alex in Malawi but refrained from asking or commenting about it, which was unusual as Alex was her closest friend and ally – best not to go there. I had the distinct feeling that Lynn would not approve of our relationship one little bit.

Later when I opened my emails there was one from Alex, a singing valentine card. Not six weeks earlier I would have automatically deleted such nonsense from my computer – like Christmas cards sent electronically. I find this mode of communication invasive and a bit kitsch, now, here I was, a changed person opening up this electronic valentine message like a lovesick teenager. 'I had better get a grip.' I heard myself saying.

'Hello,' said Lynn as she tapped on the open front door of the flat. 'I've opened the wine, what time do you think you'll be over?'

'In a few minutes, just checking my emails, then a quick shower and I'll be with you.'

'What a fabulous display of flowers! Where on earth did you get those from? Not in Simon's Town that's for sure.'

Simon's Town was, unfortunately, not blessed with any flower shops, so the display such as it was would have had to have come from elsewhere and although I often had St Joseph lilies in the flat, Lynn knew that I would not buy myself such a display of ivory white roses.

'They were sent to the house in Chelsea and it seemed such a pity not to have the pleasure of them over the weekend, so I brought them with me.'

'Aha! Are they from a secret admirer?' Lynn asked curiously.

'I have absolutely no idea. I am going to have a quick shower then join you for that welcome glass of wine – I'll only be two ticks, I promise.'

Twice now I had denied knowing who the flowers were from and I had to ask myself why? Was I embarrassed about the relationship being with a woman or the fact that it was someone twenty six years my junior? Or was it the reality of the affair being very new and it could all end tomorrow? I actually felt chuffed and flattered that someone had sent me flowers at my age, but I seemed disinclined to share who the flatterer was. Would I behave in the same manner if Keith had sent me the flowers? I doubt it.

Supper with Lynn was as delicious as always. She is incapable of making a "quick" anything, it was a faultless full-on dinner down to her great speciality – Tiramisu pudding. We talked a lot and I told her a bit about where we had visited in

Malawi. She was interested to know how Alex's new job was going and what it entailed, so I enlightened her as best I could with what little knowledge I had. After a while, I feigned tiredness and made my excuses that there was a yacht race the following day and the need for a good nights sleep was essential. Thanking Lynn profusely, I left and went back to the seclusion of my own flat.

It saddened me that I could not be open with Lynn, I felt deceitful. She was Alex's friend and I felt strongly that if she was to be told anything about our relationship, then it should come from Alex.

I phoned Alex on her mobile as soon as I got inside. It was around ten in the evening and the possibility of her being out on a Friday night was as great as most peoples would be at that age... she answered on the first ring. 'I knew it was you the moment it started ringing,' she told me excitedly.

'Where are you?'

'At Alfonso's having dinner with Rusty and Dampa and a few of Alfonso's friends. I wish you were here with us'.

I'd met the Spaniard Alfonso and his Malawian boyfriend, Dampa, at Alex's birthday party. Alfonso worked for the European Union, and he was very amusing in a camp way. Dampa, quite a bit younger than forty-year-old Alfonso, was one of the musicians.

'Me to, or better still, I wish you were here in Simon's Town with me.'

'Have you had a nice day?'

This was not as much a question as curiosity. 'Yes I had a really good day, walking on the beach with the dogs, having dinner with Lynn, perfect in fact. Now I'm off to bed as we're racing tomorrow.'

'Nothing else happened?'

'No. Nothing happened worth mentioning.'

I could feel across the airwaves that curiosity was getting the better of her.

'Nobody sent you anything for Valentine's day?'

'A bouquet of flowers arrived but it didn't say who they were from.'

'Oh! How nice! What sort of flowers?'

'Ivory white roses, my favourite most beautiful ivory white roses.'

'You must have a secret admirer.'

'Well, I don't know about that. They're probably from Keith or Graham though I doubt that either one of them would send anybody flowers, still, you never know.'

'How many roses are there?'

'About two dozen... twenty-four, though I haven't exactly counted them. I brought the roses here with me to Simon's Town so I could enjoy them.'

'Someone must love you very much to send such a gift.'

'Yes, I think they must.'

'Be careful, I could get jealous you know!'

We carried on chatting for a while, rather nonsensically as neither one of us wanted to end the call, but needs must and I knew that Alfonso would be champing at the bit waiting for Alex to return to his dinner table, and I did need to get to bed if I was to be of any use racing the yacht the following day. 'Goodnight and sleep well. Oh, and by the way, thank you for the beautiful flowers. I love you too.' And with that we ended the call.

Three weeks later, at the end of February, Alex came to stay with me in Simon's Town for a long weekend. I met her off the plane at Cape Town International Airport on a Thursday evening and we returned to stay at the flat. That meant we had managed to be together three times in two months, not bad going considering we lived in different countries. I mentioned to Lynn that Alex was coming to visit. She seemed pleased but refrained from commenting any further or asking me where she would be staying… for which I was grateful. Ducking and weaving around things is not at all my style and it bugged me that some form of cowardice was rearing its ugly head in my inability to shout out loud, 'I love this girl,' to everyone. I also felt I was withholding the truth from my friend and neighbour. But, in my heart of hearts Lynn was Alex's friend and therefore any explanation about the two of us should come from her.

Sailing was something that was high on our agenda that weekend. So Alex, kitted out in her new sailing shoes, joined the crew on Tradewind as we raced around the cans in False Bay. And what a fantastic sail it was – we won. The weather and wind conditions were conducive to a beginner's first sail – otherwise I would not have allowed Alex to join us if the wind had been any

103

stronger. As it was we were lucky on all counts and her first initiation onto a racing yacht was exceptional; better still, Alex took to it 'like a duck to water', no fear, no seasickness, she just worked the winches as she was shown. What a star, I felt enormously proud of her.

After the racing most of the racing crews usually converge on the yacht club bar "The Crow's Nest", where we drink, discuss our various tactics used in the race that day whilst waiting for the race results – this gathering of yachtsmen happens every time and is an integral part of the racing scene and one I would not miss for anything. That evening Alex was being hailed as "the new kid on the block", with all the guys asking her questions as well as receiving plenty of offers to crew on other boats. A resounding success, I would say.

It was something of a relief that Alex had taken to sailing as she did, I must admit. There is nothing worse than having a hobby that completely excludes the person you want to be with and not be able to share your passion with that person. Sailing is not everyone's cup of tea, mainly due to fear of the water, seasickness, let alone the boat heeling over – tantamount to madness, most people call it. But sailing is my love and my passion and I feel truly blessed that I fear nothing. For me, it's sheer exhilaration being on board a sailing yacht.

The weekend was quickly over and on Monday morning I found myself driving Alex to the airport for her flight back to Malawi. We had not seen much of Lynn during the weekend though Alex went over to Lynn's flat and had a chat with her. Nothing apparently was asked so no explanation was given as to why Alex was there in Simon's Town so soon after being there for Christmas, and nothing was mentioned about her staying with me. The situation was left unspoken between them and perhaps for the time being, it was best kept that way.

Life went on pretty much as usual, though in my deepest conscience I knew it had changed irretrievably. So who was I kidding? My job at the school continued in the same vein but somehow, the staff, especially Frances, knew something was afoot. Do our actions actually change that much? Obviously they must and yet we think we are in complete control of the situation when we most certainly are not. The constant text messages bleeping on my mobile, two trips to Malawi, a visitor from Malawi to stay, my happier demeanour and lightness of step, all in the space of two months – yes, they knew and were curious to know who.

Out of the blue an email arrived from Rusty inviting me to join her and Alex to stay for Easter at a pottery she loved on the banks of Lake Malawi called Nkotakota. Rusty is an amateur potter and spends many happy times at this particular spot where you can rent a chalet or camp for as long as you wish. Pottery lessons are provided or you can use their facilities to do your own thing including glazing and firing – a potters dream, in fact. How could I refuse such an invitation?

Of course I went scurrying off to Malawi for Easter. I was beginning to know the country quite well by now. The three of us took off for Nkotakota the day after I arrived. Driving north from Lilongwe, it took us about two hours to reach the pottery, and it was not a disappointment when we did finally arrive. What a beautiful place it was – situated right on the edge of the lake. From the throwing workshop you could sit at a potters wheel and feel as if you were on the deck of a boat as the water came up to the ever open door – I defy any potter who could not produce a master-piece in a setting such as Nkotakota. Though rustic to some extent, it was peaceful and relaxing to be in such a wonderfully productive, artistic space. We found our chalet some distance away from the pottery on the sand by the edge of the lake. Rusty insisted she wanted to sleep outdoors and swiftly pitched her tent on the sand next to our chalet – no good arguing, her mind was made up.

Rusty would go for her usual early morning run every day before going across to the pottery to do some slab work in clay, or attempt a jug or a bowl, paint, glaze and help with the firing. Rusty just loved being there and literally pottering around – to her, this was a second home. We all breakfasted together and would meet up again for lunch. In the evenings we barbecued. Alex would build a fire on the beach, we sat around as we cooked our food, drinking and talking to our hearts content. Rusty enjoyed her Malawian gin and the odd joint in the evenings and I often wondered how she managed to get up so early in the mornings and go for a run having partaken in such indulgences – far be it from me to wonder. Alex hated smoking of any kind and only occasionally enjoyed a glass of wine. Odd this land-lady and tenant bit, such opposites in every way - but the greatest of friends. I asked Alex if Rusty had a boyfriend. 'She has a Malawian boyfriend who is married and lives in the north of Malawi, I haven't met him yet,' she told me.

'I thought she must have someone. Rusty does not look the kind of person to be without a lover.'

'She thinks it best to have a married lover than a single boyfriend – no attachments.'

Through the marijuana-fuelled smoke, sitting around the fire, Rusty would enthral us with tales about her twenty-five year old daughter whom she hardly ever sees, and about the love of her life, a coloured man with whom she had an affair some thirty years ago – illegally of course – as this was in the apartheid era in South Africa. He left her and she had never really got over it - such a long time to hold a candle. 'No one ever came close to him,' Rusty sighed wistfully as she related her story. Sitting there on the sand around the fire reminded me fondly of my own halcyon flower-power days when living in St Ives, Cornwall some forty years ago – Rusty still remained a child of that time.

After that Easter visit, Alex returned once again towards the end of April to stay with me in Si-mon's Town. In several emails and phone calls she expressed to me that she was not exactly happy with her position and her work in Malawi. There were times when she travelled alone to the border post with Mozambique to meet farmers. I person-ally thought this was extremely risky, if not out-right dangerous. But this was not the root cause of her discontent, her rather obnoxious Nigerian boss; with his unpleasant manner was the underlying cause as Alex and the rest of the team found him so impossible to work with.

'I want to move on. I've been thinking of doing an MBA (Master of Business Administration) in Cape Town, it's something I have always wanted to do, I feel now is the right time to do it,' Alex suddenly blurted out as we sat having breakfast in the flat the morning after her arrival.

Words escaped me literally. This was a shock, a big shock because I could tell she was deadly serious. When I did eventually find my voice I said, 'Alex, I think you should think about this seriously. Don't do something you might regret, something on a whim or an emotional decision,' I told her.

'I have tried with Festus, we've all tried, but it's not getting any better. He is impossible. Why waste my time? I would love to do an MBA, so why not now?'

'You earn a lot of money, dollars in fact, in Malawi, if you came here to South Africa how would you live and do an MBA at the same time?'

'Quite easily you see – I have done my sums. With what I've saved in my account in Germany where my salary in deposited, I can pay for the MBA and keep myself for approximately eighteen months. It would be my intention to come here to South Africa in June or July and prepare myself for the one year intensive MBA course that starts at the Graduate School of Business in January 2004.'

'You have it all worked out, haven't you?' I

said quite dumbfounded.

'Yes I have. The GSB sent me all the details and requirements needed for the course, so I believe I qualify.'

'Wow! You really have been busy. Regardless of how convincing you make it sound, I think you should give it some serious thought my darling. To give up such a good salary so soon would be crazy, you can do the MBA anytime you choose.'

'My contract with ICRAF finishes at the end of June, I can extend it for another year but I don't want to and I certainly have no wish to remain in Malawi while you're here in Cape Town.'

'So that's it. Because of me you will not extend your contract, give up a good salary and move here to South Africa?'

'Not the entire reason but a big part of it. If I do the MBA there will be a couple of examination papers to do in October or November before the course starts. A fifty per cent pass rate for these exams is required for me to qualify, so I will need to do masses of revision beforehand.'

'Quite honestly, Alex, the burden of letting you do something like this is far too great for me to comprehend.'

'You don't have to; I'm doing it for us.'

'We're not going to spend the entire weekend discussing this. You seem to have an answer to everything. Let's enjoy your weekend here and you can rethink it all seriously when you return to Malawi.'

'You don't want me to come and live here?'

I was beginning to get cross and frustrated. 'We are not talking about me; we are talking about you and your future. What I want is irrelevant; you are young with your whole future ahead of you. As for me, I've had my life.'

'But it is you I want, you are my future.'

'I'm sorry, I cannot listen to this. I love you very dearly but I won't let you throw away your future. There can be no future with me. You will find a good man, get married and have beautiful children.'

'I can have beautiful children with you,' Alex replied as a matter of fact.

That was definitely the end of our conversation as I refused to listen to anything further on the subject. This was scary stuff and way above my head. It would ruin the weekend to allow it to continue. The weather was glorious and that afternoon we were going to race Tradewind around the cans, so peace reigned and we went shopping and pottered about Simon's Town until it was time to set sail down to the yacht club.

My family invited Alex and me to Sunday lunch at the farm the following day. I was looking forward to the trip through the Hottentots Holland Mountains, over Sir Lowry's Pass and on to Elgin, showing Alex the breathtaking view from on top of the mountain pass looking down across the entire sweep of False Bay. The day heralded sunshine and fine weather so we left at a reasonable hour in the morning, enabling us to enjoy the scenic route at our leisure. Alex was included in the lunch invitation because I mentioned to my niece when she phoned that there was every chance of me having a visitor from Malawi staying at the time. 'Then bring whoever it is along with you,' she told me cheerily.

As we were approaching the farm it suddenly occurred to me my family would be wondering who I could possibly be bringing. They would size Alex up between them and spend the entire lunchtime trying to figure out how and where she fitted into my life. Let's see their reaction.

No sooner had we parked in the driveway when Leigh and Rory – my great niece and nephew – rushed out to greet us. This was not unusual, they were smashing teenagers and both excelled in good manners. When the hugs and kisses of greeting were over, we all went into the house where the rest of the family were waiting for us. I introduced Alex to everyone and she charmed them instantly with her big smile, good looks and easy manner – no worries there. Alex had a habit of being a success wherever she went, so leaving her in inquisitive hands, I took off for a long and welcome swim in the pool.

The shouts for lunch in five minutes rang out across the lawn so I left the pool and hurried back to the house to shower and change. I later found Alex in the kitchen helping Ali and Leigh who were all chatting away to their heart's content as they set out the serving dishes. Out on the terrace my nephew Jonny and Justine, his rather glamorous girlfriend of the moment, and Ali's husband Chris were busy with beers in hand, barbecuing a leg of lamb and discussing how they would change the world; the atmosphere was relaxed and happy. Chris offered me a glass of wine, which I readily accepted, and I contentedly joined the gorgeous Justine and the boys.

Lunch was a huge success. The dining table was moved under the trees, where we would be beautifully shaded. It was a perfect setting, the food, as always, superbly delicious, the fine wines flowed freely and fast – heaven knows what Alex thought of us all but I could tell quite clearly that they liked and enjoyed her company a lot. We all chatted amiably, Jonny talked and discussed about his forthcoming Channel swim which he was intending to do in August – the English Channel swim to the coast of France - together with a couple of his friends.

'Why don't you come over to England with us and be my supporter, Aunty?' Jonny asked me from across the table.

Jonny, an excellent swimmer, surfer and water polo player was a favourite nephew, and something in his enthusiasm about swimming the Channel sparked a flame. 'That sounds a fantastic idea. I think it's something I'd really enjoy. Thanks, Jonny – let's discuss it sometime next week.'

I felt really chuffed that Jonny had asked me to join him in the Channel swim. It would be a great privilege to support and watch him achieve this remarkable feat. Driving back to Simon's Town replete and content, I asked Alex what she thought of my family.

'They're really great, I have to say. Easy going, fun to be with, and every one of them made me feel so welcome. Wow! What a good-looking bunch they are,' she replied.

'Well, I am pretty proud of them, I have to admit.'

'You have every right to be, and oh! Are you serious about going to England for that Channel swim?'

'I'll think about it. If Jonny's serious about doing the swim, then I just might.'

'If you do go over to England I would love to come with you.'

'We'll see.'

What really signifies a magic moment in one's life? Well, I will explain one right here. I was invited to my friend Kim's birthday – nothing unusual in that. The birthday party was held at Plankhuis, Kim's family's retreat – a stretch of unspoilt pristine coastline just outside Hermanus about 125 kilometres from Cape Town. I took Alex along as my partner. Once on the property we had to drive down a private dirt track that was clearly meant for 4x4 vehicles, but the BMW made it without us knocking off the oil sump. When we reached Plankhuis – an old wooden house nestled literally on the beach – I knew the treacherous road had been well worth it. Lots of relaxed people scattered the cove, wearing kikoi's or beach clothes, swimming costumes. Some gorgeous hunky young men were diving for crayfish which they then cooked in large pots of boiling water immediately as they came out of the sea. We swam in the cold bay to cool ourselves, we ate the crayfish lavished with mayonnaise or garlic butter, salads of every description were plentiful and the monumental cheese board sagged. There was champagne and wine aplenty to wash it all down – manna from heaven.

Jonny was at the party – well, he would be as

he was Kim's very best and long-standing friend –
with lovely Justine looking outrageously gorgeous
in a bikini made of nothing. Luckily for us he and
Justine were leaving at the same time as we were,
so Jonny suggested we follow him back up the
rough road as he knew it extremely well. We did
as bidden and returned home safe and sound, if
not a teeny bit inebriated on the sheer beauty of
being together in such a breathtaking place as
Plankhuis. Beautiful people, outstanding food
along with gloriously good wine, puts that day as
one of my special 'magic moments'.

After those few wonderful days together, Alex
reluctantly returned to Malawi. I left her at the
airport still pretty hell-bent on relocating to Cape
Town as soon as her contract ended. I listened to
her reasons, her for and against arguments without comment. By this time I was becoming philo-
sophical about the whole situation and merely felt
that what would be would be – not to fight against
it, to take each day as it came, sort out the if, whys
and how as they presented themselves, and take it
from there.

During the following week, Jonny telephoned.
'Hello, Aunty. I'm officially asking you to second
me on my forthcoming attempt to swim across the
English Channel,' he said jauntily.

My nieces and nephews nearly always call me
Chris – they sometimes say Aunty just to tease
me.

'Of course, Jonny, I'd love to,' I told him. Not
only chuffed, I was seriously flattered that my
nephew had asked and wanted me to be there.

'Two other friends will be attempting the

swim, albeit on different days, and the plan is to all be in Dover together for the week of the swims. How does that sound to you?'

'It all sounds great.'

'Good, then I'll arrange a get-together for supper one evening soon so that we can meet each other and discuss plans from thereon.'

I was soon to learn how hugely professional the Channel Swim Organisation is, the training that goes into it, the technicalities and sheer guts it takes to achieve this tremendous swim - but more of that later.

I heard from Alex almost every day by phone or e-mail. Sometimes she would call from the top of a hill somewhere in a far flung area of Mozambique in order to get a signal. I once phoned her from the Kalahari atop a massive sand dune which I climbed to get that illusive signal. Yes, mobile phone masts have reached the remote Kalahari. Alex was still set on terminating her contract at the end of May regardless of how I tried to persuade her differently, and this she reminded me of at every available opportunity.

Our next time together was in Johannesburg during the middle of May. We stayed in a German guest house in the Fourways area and enjoyed it thoroughly. This sojourn into the Transvaal gave me an opportunity to do some investigation into the plight of some Bushmen girls who were being used as an exhibition to show visitors how they lived in their natural, Kalahari environment. These girls were transported away from their families and life in the Kalahari by an Afrikaans farmer, with promises of financial reward – to be put on show and ogled at by tourists, as one would animals in a zoo – at a set-up near Hartebespoort Dam. I found this sort of display a disgraceful abuse of human rights. At the end of the day and the last show over, the farmer would whistle for the girls to get over to his pick-up truck whereupon they were herded into the back like cattle and taken away to his farm where they were staying. The girls knew me and I had to get the message across to them not to show it. I was photographing the situation and this would be used against the farmer at some point or other should an investigation be required. I found out from the girls and their parents that the farmer gave them absolutely nothing (a percentage of the show's takings were part of the deal, I was told by the museum's staff) as he charged board and lodgings plus transport to and from the Kalahari for the girls, which amounted to the pay the girls received. Injustices still go on.

This episode with the Bushmen girls was a complete eye opener to Alex and one which would culminate in her and a colleague doing their dissertation on the plight of the Southern Kalahari Bushmen for their MBA.

We met up with good friends of mine, Pierre and his wife Hilda, whilst we were in Johannesburg. They invited us to have dinner with them at a restaurant in Monte Casino – what a place! Monte Casino was a village all by itself; it had everything you could wish for under one roof. The restaurant, whose name eludes me as I write, was Asian, providing all sorts of dishes, including sushi. We sat on the floor with our legs dangling down somewhere beneath and you could have your body massaged before, during or after eating your meal – depending on your bent. Well – it was certainly different, that's for sure! Johannesburg will always have a soft spot in my heart for being the first place I landed in after leaving England.

After a good and productive weekend, Alex and I left Johannesburg International Airport together, flying in opposite directions. This would be our last meeting before Alex finally got her own way and came to live with me in Cape Town.

Chapter Seven

A New Life

Fleur was all ready and waiting when Alex finally arrived to live in Cape Town, July 2003. This was the start of our new life together and enabled Alex to concentrate on her preparation for the GMAT – Graduate Management Admission Test - the exam necessary to pass in order to do her MBA. Life carried on much as if nothing really different had happened, only that it was a great deal more pleasant to have someone to go home to, share cooking with and just generally enjoy each other's company. It was working out a lot easier than I had anticipated.

One Sunday morning, not long after Alex had moved to Cape Town, I had the newspaper spread open before me. Perusing the property pages, I happened upon an interesting looking property for sale in a village on the other side of the mountain called Hout Bay. I showed it to Alex.

'Let's go and have a look at it. We can have a leisurely lunch at Luigi's first. The house is on show between three and five this afternoon, which will give us a chance to do a recce of the area beforehand,' I suggested in a sudden burst of enthusiasm.

'That's okay by me. Why not, there's nothing to lose by looking.'

So off we went, stopping as planned to have lunch at Luigi's Trattoria in Hout Bay. Replete with good Italian food, we then took the dogs for a much-anticipated walk on the beach. After locating the area in Hout Bay where the house was situated, we proceeded to do a quick tour around to see if we liked it.

We did like it. The house was a charming split level artistic home with a delightful garden, an added Zen garden, a dining room with a glass floor and sitting room with a big fireplace. It was a smaller house than Fleur but with a much larger garden for three dogs to have free range in. To buy it felt the right thing to do. Fleur had been my beloved home for the last twelve years, it was a lovely house in a historical village with friends and neighbours around, it would be a wrench to sell it; but I felt in my heart that Alex would always feel that the house was my territory and a new start in a new home together should bode well. I put Fleur on the Market.

It was August and the intended Channel swim in Dover was looming. By this time there would be Jonny, plus two of his friends from Cape Town, all going over to do the swim during the same week. It was decided over a pre-Channel swim get-together one evening at Fleur that we should all stay in the same accommodation, and, by the time we added wives and partners, there would be ten of us. Having far less to do than the others in the planning of this trip, I volunteered to try and find a house large enough for us to rent for the period we would be in Dover.

We all travelled independently to England as each person had plans besides the Channel swim – we all agreed to meet up on the Saturday before the week of the swims at the house I had booked on top of the 'white cliffs of Dover'. I prayed that it would be suitable and everyone would be relaxed and happy there. Alex and I went to stay with my best friend Flo in her lovely house in Devon for a week when we first arrived in England – I had told her about Alex and our relationship beforehand so there were no big surprises for her. Flo's daughter is my god-daughter and her two sons are like my sons as well. We all got on famously and had a fabulous time. They thought Alex was great and loved her bright sparkling personality.

After our halcyon time in Devon was over we made our way along the south coast of England to Dover. It would probably have been a lot quicker ducking and weaving on the motorways to get there, but I thought the scenic route would be a tad more pleasant for Alex so that she could see a lovely part of England that she might not have the opportunity to see again.

We arrived at the gate of White Cliffs House in Dover on Saturday afternoon, and my heart sank. The rusty gate was leaning open - just about hanging on its hinges.

'And this was what we have paid a fortune for? No wonder none of the others have been in touch,' I dismally said to Alex.

'Let's see what it's like inside before you start making overtures,' she suggested. So onward we marched like good Christian soldiers brave and ready for battle to face the chagrin of the others should they have arrived before us. 'Withering Heights,' I thought to myself as we entered the rambling old house – but there before us were our friends already settled in, and the house was all but perfect and exactly what we wanted in the spacious rooms, sweeping staircase, massive kitchen. It was a large house, its former glory gone slightly to seed – but it was clean. The best prize of all: Withering Heights, as it became affection-ately called, perched literally on top of the white cliffs of Dover, the garden reaching to the edge with nothing else around except an uninterrupted view of the English Channel. Everyone was de-lighted and I felt pretty chuffed with myself now at having found it.

In order to do a Channel swim each competitor has to book well in advance, as much as a year sometimes, and it is not inexpensive. A swimmer is required to have a registered Channel-swim boat with crew supplied by the organisation – these people are very experienced. Each swimmer has their own support team on board who will feed the necessary liquids, energy bars, bananas, that are required by the swimmer during the attempt to swim the twenty two miles across to France. Of course the distance depends on the current, as this can move many times from side to side as the tide ebbs and flows. Hence the need of an experienced skipper who knows the Channel changes like the back of his hand.

There was a wonderful camaraderie in the house. Sabine, the wife of JD, one of the swimmers, had her communications set up on a big table in the vast hallway where she would be relaying all our news, race conditions and results across the airwaves and cyberspace to newspapers, radio, TV, family and friends. We each took it in turn to cook an evening meal. It was important the swimmers ate a lot of carbohydrates – so pasta was prevalent on the menu. A couple of evenings we barbecued in the garden and drank champagne – heady stuff to be having six inches from the edge of those white cliffs with a sheer drop below into the English Channel. There was a suicide whilst we were there – quite a famous spot for it we later learned, only a few metres outside the grounds of Withering Heights - not to bear thinking about.

Each of our swimmers had been allotted a different day for their swim but this was entirely dependent on weather conditions, which made the boys slightly anxious. They were on their mobiles with the skippers constantly waiting for the all-clear. JD's swim was to be first. Alex and I decided to join Sabine on the boat that would be supporting JD – we would get to know the ropes and it felt the right thing to do, Sabine would be there for us. So off we went across the Channel. JD achieved his swim in fairly good time, but he was frighteningly exhausted afterwards. When we got back to Dover that evening, JD took us all out for dinner to celebrate and we had a most fantastic time.

Jonny's day had been put off twice but got

OK'd for the following day. We were up and ready to go at 3.30am and drove into Dover to the jetty from where our boat would be leaving. The swimmer is not allowed to wear anything other than a pair of swimming trunks, cap and goggles, but can grease up the body as a protective coating against the cold and polluted water – which Jonny did before the boat dropped him off on a narrow spit of beach somewhere beneath those towering white cliffs.

At a signal from the skipper, Jonny was in the water just before dawn and began his swim. Alex, Sabine, Jonny's best friend Grant, who had flown over from Switzerland, and I were his support team, and we never let him out of our sight for the entire trip. We fed, watered and encouraged him all the way. As permitted in the race rules, Grant swam with Jonny periodically. The accompanying swimmer has to keep a certain distance behind the challenger – one finger over and the Channel swim attempt is disqualified. As with the drink or food, you cannot come into contact with the challenge swimmer, everything has to be thrown to him or swung on a string – hairy stuff after several hours in the water. It's blatantly clear the moment the swim begins how important it is to have a qualified skipper with a good reliable boat. Channel traffic is horrendous. At one point I saw what I can only describe as a massive, floating multistorey car park passing in front of our boat – no fore or aft, but definitely on a course. We saw Jonny look up out of the water and, as he told us afterwards, he completely freaked, thinking it was a mighty brick wall. We never did discover what it was; it even flummoxed our skipper who, in his thirty odd years in Dover, had never seen anything like it before.

Nine hours twenty six minutes after we had set out from Dover Jonny reached the coast of France in an emotional, exhausting and brave-hearted swim across the English Channel. He had 'done it'; we were all very thrilled and proud of him. Many phone calls of congratulations from family and friends in South Africa followed Jonny on the fast boat ride back to Dover.

Hugh, our third swimmer, had not been feeling well and although later in the week he made an attempt to do the swim he abandoned it, and finally completed his challenge the following year.

During the swim I received a phone call on my mobile from the estate agent in South Africa informing me that an offer had been made for Fleur – the entire house situation had completely been blown out of the window during our trip to England, so I was taken aback somewhat by the call. However, the offer was not acceptable and I told the agent so with a touch of relief – I knew I was avoiding the inevitable. Alex really did want to move to the house in Hout Bay away from Fleur and have a new start. I was simply procrastinating.

Those Channel swims, Withering Heights and the wonderful people we shared it with during that week, have to be another one of the 'magic moments' in our lives. The fun, the laughs, the successes and everything about it was brilliant. A few weeks after we all returned to South Africa, Hugh's eighty-five year old mother gave a party for us at her home in Cape Town. Seven years later we still talk about our time in Dover. We remain good friends with Hugh and his wife Fran to this day. Personally I would not have missed the experience for anything. What made it particularly special to Alex and I was that no one made us feel uncomfortable in any way whatsoever; in fact, we were embraced and accepted wholeheartedly.

After Dover Alex, Jonny and I drove up North to drop Alex at Stanstead airport where she was flying off for a quick visit to see her parents. Jonny and I went to visit our families spread around Manchester. I would pick Alex up on my way back to London and together we would return to South Africa.

An acceptable offer came in for Fleur that I had to take, as the sellers of the Hout Bay house were champing at the bit as they had bought somewhere else in Hout Bay subject to the sale of their house. I would like to make a point here that I am forever grateful for the South African way of buying and selling property in that once an offer has been made and accepted, this is legal and binding – no disgraceful gazumping – none of the heartbreak and interminable expense that goes into buying and selling a house in England. But to England's defence, the estate agents in South Africa charge a mighty 7% commission which is negotiable, against English estate agents who, at the time of writing, charge 3% commission. In South Africa it is the purchaser who pays all the conveyance fees.

At the end of November 2003, Alex and I

moved into our new house in Hout Bay, which we named Zennor. Careful Ken, the removal man, had parked the lorry outside the gate of Zennor to enable them to unload, blocking the way for me to park my car inside the garage area – so I parked in the road until they were finished. I had not been in the house for five minutes before I heard the alarm of the BMW sounding, I rushed out only to find the driver's window smashed and my wallet stolen. A sense of foreboding set into me from that moment, and did not leave until we left Hout Bay.

Chapter Eight

Spark to a Flame and the MBA

Alex started her MBA at the Graduate School of Business at the beginning of 2004. Living in Hout Bay made her daily trip to and from the V&A Waterfront in Cape Town a scenic pleasure, as you drive along with the Atlantic seaboard on one side and the mountainous range of "The Twelve Apostles" towering majestically above you on the other. GSB is part of the University of Cape Town, but housed some kilometres away in the now converted Breakwater prison – this has to be one of the most beautiful positions in the world for a prison, situated slap bang at the waterfront over-looking the entrance to Table Bay. This, of course, would have been lost on the prisoners who were incarcerated in cells beneath the ground. Once upon a time, this prison played a large role in Cape Town's history by being the first prison to affect segregation due to the increase of "white" IDB (illegal diamond buyers). This prison housed most of these offenders.

Life settled nicely in Zennor though I still car-ried a sense of foreboding about the house, something I had never felt before in a home. I now drove a distance of seventeen kilometres to my job at the school - from Fleur it had been half a kilometre. Still, the drive was pleasant enough, though after about a month I had witnessed approximately six serious car accidents on the road I travelled everyday between Hout Bay and Constantia Nek, a distance of seven kilometres – that's a pretty high statistic in my estimation for a country road. I added that to the foreboding.

Weekends we spent at the flat in Simon's Town, as the racing season takes place between September and June. Alex loved it, and was learning the ropes fast, as you have to do in order to get anywhere in competitive racing. Some Saturdays if the racing was cancelled or the weather not conducive (too windy or no wind), we would go to the tennis club and batter out a few sets and have wonderful afternoon tea with our friendly fellow members.

Our relationship was blossoming as we settled into our life together. I constantly kept reminding myself that it was 'we' now and not just 'me' there to think about; impossibly difficult at times, but Alex seemed to take everything in her stride and accepted my sometimes selfish ways. She, of course, was just a complete pleasure and a breath of fresh air to be with, always happy with that wonderful "bright smile". Alex, I was beginning to realise, gave her absolute everything to whatever she takes on, and the MBA intensive course was no exception.

From the very outset she had made no hidden secret of her relationship with me to her fellow colleagues at the GSB – she was proud of it and never mind who didn't approve. There would be many occasions when I would be expected to join Alex for a GSB reception, a lecture, a party or a group meeting, some optional, some mandatory. As a couple we were often invited out to one of the group's homes, for dinner, a Sunday lunch or a casual party, or sometimes they came over to us. Everyone I met was charming and friendly. This was a completely new world, and for a start these people were twenty-five years younger than me and more. Still, this came with the turf, something I had to come to terms with and accept.

Alex's birthday is on the 6th February. We decided to have a party at home for family, friends and her colleagues from the MBA course – our pals from the Channel swim were also invited. This was also a combined house-warming so a few neighbours clocked in as well. Everyone turned up and we had one heck of a birthday bash. Alex was delighted all her crew pitched, really making it a special birthday – but it was not to be a happy ending. At sometime in the early hours of the morning I felt Alex shaking my shoulder shouting at me to 'wake up and get out of bed quickly, there's a fire raging within metres of our house!' I stirred, thinking I was having a bad dream, but no – It was all too clear, seeing the fear in Alex's face, that this was no joke, and I threw myself off the bed and into some clothes.

'Quick get outside,' I heard somebody shouting. I was clearly worried about the dogs and frenzied about searching for them, but I could tell the voice was urgent so I hurried outside to find a crowd of people watching the fire blazing, while others were spraying the roofs of our house and next door's with the garden hose.

'Where are the dogs and Toby?' I asked Alex when I eventually found her helping with the spraying.

'They're fine; I've put them in the car and parked it down the street away from here'.

The Cape of storms definitely lived up to its name that night. I was later to learn that, just after midnight, a howling wind came out of nowhere and obviously caught a smaller fire that had started in the squatter camp, whipping it howling and raging through the narrow forest of trees separating us. As fortune would have it the fire was extinguished before it did any damage to our property and that of the neighbours – but it was a close and very frightening call.

Once we were assured the fire wouldn't flare up again and it was safe, with huge relief we went to collect the car where Hettie, Harry, Josh and Toby the cat were fast asleep, oblivious to anything, bless them. The animals were always my ultimate concern.

A month after the fire we were relaxing in the sitting room at Zennor when Alex heard a noise outside in the garden and went to investigate. When I heard her talking to someone I followed, knowing that no one had rung our doorbell and therefore there shouldn't be anyone in our garden. Outside I saw three African youths scrambling away over our fence from whence they came, the dogs barking furiously at their feet. Alex had caught them coming over our fence, encouraged by an older youth who stayed on the other side in our neighbours' garden. The intention would have been robbery or even worse. Dear brave Alex confronted them nonchalantly and they hot-footed away like headless chickens. No nonchalance on my part. I quickly grabbed Harry, put on his lead and ran after them through the woods towards the squatter camp. Once they realised I was on their tail and quickly catching up they did an about turn and started hurling stones at Harry and me, and I hot-footed back from whence we came with the four youths on our tail – wham! As I reached our road a police car smacked straight up in front of the offenders and caught them while I puffed and panted back to the house and a mortified Alex. Apparently a neighbour living behind us had seen me chasing after the guys and phoned the police.

Alex was not best pleased at my actions. 'That was an idiotic thing to do,' she told me in no uncertain words.

'I'm sorry, but I can't sit back and let these people just attempt to rob or injure us without doing something about it, I just can't.'

'It was terribly funny watching you chasing those guys and then running away with stones raining down. Lucky one of them didn't hit either you or Harry, it could have had dire consequences.'

I'm well aware it was a stupid thing to do but instinct kicked in before I really knew what I was doing – thank God the man in the elevated house behind us saw it all happening and acted swiftly. We laughed about it after the event, both of us knowing it was another serious omen.

For such a short time living in Hout Bay a lot of unfortunate and quirky "happenings" kept creeping into our lives and I was feeling very spooked about the house itself, and so was Alex. If we went away at weekends or even for a night, we had the dog-sitter staying there not only to look after the dogs but to protect the property – this was not right. Some of our neighbours were also worried, not only about their own safety, but the depreciation of the properties – our lifetime investment.

'Let's have a meeting with one or two of the neighbours, a Sunday brunch, and discuss this security problem,' I suggested to Alex one evening shortly after the fire.

'What a brilliant idea,' she enthused.

Back in England the previous year, a cousin of mine, Derek Redford, had died sitting on a sofa in the home he inherited from his parents, my paternal Aunt and Uncle. Derek was fifty nine years old; single – due to a broken romance when he was a teenager that he never got over. He died intestate, leaving the terraced house that had not been upgraded for the past forty years and thirty odd feral cats that lived there with him. Needless to say the social services were called in; whereupon they cleared the house of everything including the feral cats, fumigated the place from top to bottom, then locked the front door behind them. As the only living next-of-kin my brother, sister and I became the proud owners of Les Miserables house. In a nutshell I paid my siblings a third share each and kept the house, the intention being to renovate it together with my brother Geoff, as he only lived fifty yards away. He would be the project manager and I would pay the renovation costs. The best laid plans of mice and men were not to be. Logistically it was difficult, with me being in South Africa for a start. Not long after the renovation work started Geoff's eldest, much-loved daughter Deborah, died of a stroke, aged forty-two. This gutted Geoff completely and when I went over to England to see him and check on how the renovations were going I knew he had lost heart in the project. When I returned to South Africa I promptly sold the house to the builder doing the renovations and popped the money into the bank for a rainy day.

One of the teachers at our school was looking, together with her boyfriend, to buy their first house, and asked my advice. I thus started to look out for suitable properties for them and in so doing came upon an advert in the property pages of The Cape Times for Wisteria Lodge a charming, newly built cottage in the Victorian village of Stanford, a two hour drive from Cape Town.

This must have been fate playing a part here. Friends of mine Judy and John have a property on the Klein Rivier – being the river running from Stanford to Hermanus lagoon, then hence across the sand bar into the Atlantic Ocean, an idyllic and beautiful spot. Whilst staying with them one weekend, John took us for a jaunt up the river one early evening for sundowners and bird spotting on his motor boat. We went up river towards Stanford and as we approached I remarked how attractive it looked from the river – in fact, it had a Tuscan look about it that I found appealing and thought perhaps the following day I would drive there and take a look. But I never did.

Curiosity was getting the better of me so I made an appointment with the estate agent advertising the property in Stanford, and duly set forth a few days later. Wisteria Lodge from the onset captured my heart. The agent, quite rightly, insisted that I look at other properties "For Sale" in the village to have a comparison, which we did, and all paled into insignificance. Wisteria Lodge, which was brand new and delightful – designed and built by an architect - was made for Alex and me.

Buoyed with the idea of buying Wisteria Lodge we went ahead and made a Sunday brunch for our neighbours on either side of Zennor to discuss our situation in Hout Bay. Each person was concerned about the danger and impact the squatter camp was having on the area – each one petrified the price of their property would plummet. Would there be people out there who would still buy property in Hout Bay as the already massive squatter camp was growing larger every day with illegal immigrants? – No one was sure. 'I'll put our house on the market to test the response,' I blurted out. 'We do at least have a flat in Simon's Town to go to if it does, by any chance, sell.' This was followed by a stunned silence around the table.

'That's a pretty drastic measure,' Mandy our new next door neighbour commented. 'Anyway we don't want you to leave here, we love having you and Alex as neighbours.'

'We love having you and Jonathan as neighbours but we all feel we have to do something, so let us go ahead and do what Chris suggests. An estate agent will tell you your property will only sell at half the price its worth to get a deal out of it,' Alex told the assembled brunchers.

Good on her I thought.

The estate agent I phoned came around to look at the Zennor property during the following week. Much to my huge surprise she gave a market value price of two hundred thousand rands more than I had paid for it. 'Go ahead and put it on the market,' I enthused without thinking it through. That same evening I informed the neighbours, who were highly amused at my spontaneity and told me they would look forward with bated breath to see what transpired. In the meantime I had put an offer in for Wisteria Lodge which had been accepted, much to our delight.

The week after putting Zennor on the market I had to do a First Aid course near Simon's Town for three days... this being part of the Coastal Skippers ticket requirement that I was studying for. I opted to stay at the flat in Simon's Town for convenience and concentration – much needed at my age to pass tests. Second day into the course I received a text message to phone the estate agent in Hout Bay. During the lunchtime break I did so, only to be excitedly told that she had sold Zennor for the asking price and could I sign the offer that evening if she came over to Simon's Town. Speechless would probably be the correct adjective to describe my initial shock at hearing this fairly sudden news. 'I'll phone you back.' I stalled and promptly tried to get hold of Alex who, when

I did track her down, was as surprised and delighted as I was that the house had sold so quickly, 'It's the right thing to do,' she assured me.

The "Offer to Purchase" for Zennor was counter-signed by me that same evening, making the sale agreement final. The conveyance would take another couple of months, and then we would be free of Zennor and Hout Bay. The neighbours will be delighted, I thought.

As I write - seven years down the line - each neighbour at the Sunday brunch that live either side of Zennor, have not sold their houses. They did not put their houses on the market, and are now having the greatest difficulty selling their properties. To this day we remain good friends with Jonathan and Mandy who rent out their Hout Bay house and have moved, job-wise for Jonathan, to Durban.

Wisteria Lodge purchased and Zennor sold; we were now based in the Simon's Town flat, which was small. Alex had to commute quite a bit further, which she didn't seem to mind, and I continued at Ambery House. We spent the odd weekend in Stanford and enjoyed it very much. One day Alex informed me that she and her friend Rachel, also doing her MBA on the same course, wanted to do something completely different for their dissertation.

'Have you anything in mind?' I asked.

'Yes, we would like to do a study and sustainability thesis on the Bushmen. Nobody has ever done anything like it before on the MBA course. What do you think?'

'What a brilliant idea. As you well know I've

been involved with the Kalahari Bushmen since arriving in South Africa, so who better to point you in the right direction? I have reams of documentation in connection with their land claim from the South African Government. You'll have to make a couple of trips to the Kalahari to spend time and experience being with them at first hand… what a fantastic subject to take on, what on earth made you and Rachel decide on the Bushmen?'

'When your family came over from England and we briefly made the trip to the Kalahari with John, Rachael and Lewis, remember? Well, I was so captivated by the Bushmen that I was telling everyone in our group session the other day how fascinating and unspoilt the last Bushmen of the Kalahari remain. There and then we decided to go for it,' Alex explained enthusiastically.

The last remaining Bushmen of the Southern Kalahari have been my passionate project whilst being in South Africa. In my early days at Ambery House a request came from Dawid Kruiper – the leader of the Bushmen group - that he would like the Bushmen children to learn maths, to read, write and be able to speak English. This request came via a woman called Cait Andrews, also known as "The white Bushman". Cait was an ethnomusicologist and for years studied and lived with the Bushmen learning their trance dance, chanting, emanating haunting sounds from the large seed pods strapped around their ankles. Only the men do trance dancing that can go on for many hours, until the elder woman of the group stops it whenever she chooses, and only she can do so. Personally my involvement came in the guise of helping the Bushmen to get their land back... They were thrown out of the Kalahari Gemsbok Park by the National Parks Board during the apartheid era. Together with human rights lawyer, Mark Reynolds, Minister of land affairs, Derek Hanekom, myself and others, we did achieve our goal and the Bushmen were eventually given six re-appropriated farms and state land covering a vast area of 25, 000 hectares - not in the Gemsbok Park itself, but on the outlying area surrounding the park. The South African National Parks (SANP) made available 55,000 hectares of land in the Kalahari Gemsbok National Park to the San and Mier communities to be used as a contract park.

Being involved with the Bushmen over a span of twenty years has given me invaluable experience. It is a privilege spending time in their company around the campfire listening to their stories fuelled with nonsense, alcohol and home-grown joints, with jackals waiting in the wings for a discarded bone of a bird or a donkey, which is a Bushmen delicacy. These small statured people, perfectly proportioned and as lithe as a springbok, had been worth fighting for, and if I came to Africa to do one good thing, then being part of the successful re-claiming of the land for the Bushmen was it.

'Well, Alex, I have to say quite selfishly that doing your dissertation thesis on the Bushmen can only be the most interesting of subjects – and from my part I'd be happy to tag along whenever you go to visit them.'

'Good, as I have no intention of going without you. Also Rachel and Kevin want to go together… they intend to carry on after we've spent some days with the Bushmen, and trek north into the park as far as Nossob. They've got a fully equipped, rather old Land Rover which they love, and can't wait to get going. Kevin can also be the interpreter as he speaks fluent Afrikaans.'

'Then, my darling, I suggest you get the show on the road, and see what bookings are available for Twee Rivieren (southern camp of the Kalahari Gemsbok Park) as soon as possible so that we have dates to plan accordingly. This is imperative for Kevin. Being a doctor he'll need time to make arrangements, especially if they're going further north into the Kalahari.'

Chapter Nine

In The Beginning

Christmas Eve 1943, my mother Alice was rushed into the Bealey maternity home in Radcliffe, Manchester. Several hours later she gave birth to a seven and a half pound, healthy baby girl and named her Christine Anne. My father, Robert, had been called away on urgent fire duty – the war was on and his contribution to the war effort was being a volunteer. He knew nothing about my mother going into labour and subsequently giving birth, until he arrived home the next day to be presented with a baby daughter.

What a shock it must have been for both my parents to suddenly find themselves with a third child at the age they were – my father forty-one, my mother forty-two, some Christmas present! Their two other children, Brenda, thirteen and Geoffrey William, eight, were of course, delighted with their new sister, well, at least until the novelty wore off.

We owned a shop and lived above and behind it in Water Street, Radcliffe; the town were both my parents were born. The shop was my mother's where she designed, made and sold fashion clothes. It was a pretty high class establishment for its time. It also covered as a meeting place were her friends would drop in and out all day long chatting and drinking tea, whilst mother peddled away on her Singer sewing machine in what we called the back room at the rear of the shop. Mother was very popular and much loved by everyone. She had a wise head upon her shoulders and I think she doubled up as advisory counsel to the needy women in the neighbourhood – it was a bit like a tea club. Very convenient, of course, that the butcher and the fish and chip shop were almost next door, with the pet food store a few doors down. Our shop was on the main drag and hopelessly convenient for that welcome cuppa.

Father, on the other hand, worked as a power-loom overlooker at a massive cotton mill which dominated Radcliffe at that time. Pioneer Mill was straight out of an L. S. Lowry painting, matchstick people and all. Perhaps that's why I came to love and appreciate Lowry's work; no one could have depicted the mill town scenes and the Northern industrial area better than he did. To this day I can still smell the inside of Pioneer Mill with its huge cotton looms cranking back and forth and the heavy pungent smell of loom oil and imported Indian cotton. At a very young age, father used to take me to the mill with him on Saturday mornings when it was empty. We would go up onto each floor in one of the ancient open lifts that were a bit like a cage. I loved it. He would check that everything was as it should be then we locked up and left. Usually he would take me home via a walk along the canal, telling me wonderful stories of how the canal system worked and about the heavy dray horses that were used to pull the industrial barges along and, very best of all, that people actually lived on the canal in narrow boats. If that doesn't capture the imagination of a child, I'll eat my heart out.

One Friday evening when I was five, my mother was bathing me and gawped in shocked horror at a strange rash decorating my body. I was soon diagnosed with scarlet fever and before you could say 'Jack Robinson' I found myself plonked in the isolation ward of a sanatorium – with no visitors allowed. Sad though it was, that's how it had to be. Not only banished from home and the family, but, also I would not be starting the ballet lessons I had been so looking forward to with unbridled excitement. I was due to have my first lesson the Saturday morning following the bath and the discovery of the dreaded fever. I thought life was really unkind. However, after a few days of isolation, apart from doctors and nurses, I started to receive presents; this cheered me up no end. They arrived in the late afternoon, where-upon I would open them with relish as if every day was Christmas Day – the presents of course, were from my parents, Brenda, Geoff and the many friends, neighbours and habitués of the shop's back-room, as I was somewhat of a star in their eyes.

This star status was well-earned; I was later to learn, being one of the amusing highlights in Radcliffe during that rather dismal time after the end of the war. The story goes that my parents had to go to a meeting one evening when I was three years old. Cora, a family friend who often took care of me during the day, was looking after me that evening. Suddenly I went missing and Cora could not find me anywhere. Eventually and in desperation she went to look outside, only to see a gathering of people looking in the shop window and laughing. The lights in the shop window were always left on in the evening to show off the mannequins dressed in mother's latest creations. That particular night, it was me. I had hoisted myself up onto the platform of the shop window and was wobbling around on the high-heeled shoes, a scarf slung around my neck and whatever other accessory was available for me to try on. I would not come out of the window so Cora, in her despair, got hold of my parents and told them, 'Christine's in the shop window and I can't get her out.' It became an evening of amusement to all that watched, and "The Little Star" became a talking point in Radcliffe for some years after.

I had great anxiety during my stay in the sanatorium that we, our family, were moving from the shop and our home to somewhere far away. I was petrified they would move without me and I'd be left in the sanatorium forever. That was not to be. After three weeks I got the all-clear from the doctor and my parents arrived and took me to our new home in Whitefield, five miles away from Radcliffe, but a whole new world away from the mill town.

Posh is how one would describe Whitefield.

Our new semi-detached house in Grosvenor Avenue, sat between the towering domination of Stand Church, Whitefield Park and Stand Cricket Club. This was a whole new ball game from life in Radcliffe – the Barrington family had moved up! I was enrolled into Higher Lane Primary School. I attended confirmation classes at Stand Church, which I enjoyed, and played tennis every God-given moment possible on one of Whitefield Park's eight clay courts. The tennis pavilion became a refuge not only from the rain but from home, I realise now.

Life changed quite dramatically with the move to Whitefield. I could not put my finger on anything in particular, just a general, uneasy feeling. Mum did not appear to be the happy-go-lucky person that she had been in Radcliffe, but then, all her friends and cronies were not around and she hadn't the shop to run. One cold Saturday morning she took me shopping with her to Bury Market. I loved the busy market and its larger-than-life buzz of people. This is the very market where I tasted my first black pudding lashed with Colman's hot mustard. It warmed the cockles of my heart and kept the cold at bay. We were crossing the road to a shop mother needed to visit when she fell rather badly – tripped on the cobbled road in between the tram lines. It shook her up quite a bit though nothing seemed to be damaged. I managed to get her to the shop where she was offered a seat and a cup of sweet tea.

My beloved mother died of cancer when I was eleven years old. She spent a good deal of those eleven years of my life in hospital, where I saw her with tubes dangling from her nose and mouth and with drugs being fed intravenously into her body. When she was at home I saw her suffer miserably, bent double in pain and agony. There was nothing I could do to help her. Through all that pain she was a wonderful and remarkable woman who instilled a lifetime of philosophy into me in those few short years we had together.

The time we spent in hospital at my mother's bedside and especially over several Christmases never made me feel sad. She was a happy and intelligent person whom the nurses loved and admired. The hospital wards at Christmas time were always festooned with decorations and a cheery air. When she did eventually die I was well-prepared. Heartbroken yes, but the wise words of my mother, when I used to snuggle into bed with her after father went to work, helped me through it and set me up in fine form to face the future.

At first it was a bleak future I had to endure. Brenda and Geoff were already married and in their own homes, so that left my father and me alone to get on with things. Ours had been such a happy household even during my mother's illness. At the time we belonged to Radcliffe Amateur Operatic Society and we children were more often than not in one of the productions, which meant that at home there would be costumes to be made or altered and songs to be learned. Mother was a fairly good pianist and we would all gather around the piano with her and have wonderful sing-songs. Autumn Leaves was her favourite, which she played and sang so beautifully. To this day, after all that time, whenever I hear someone playing or singing Autumn Leaves it brings tears to my eyes.

My parents had not wanted to send me to the local comprehensive school, which is where I desperately wanted to go...comprehensive schools were a new type of school in those days. Instead, I was sent to Hope Park School for Girls in Prestwich, quite a distance away, by school standards. Hope Park was alright but I was not with or near my friends who were at the comprehensive in Whitefield. Hope Park was predominantly Jewish and I'll never know, as fairly strict, High Church of England Anglicans, why my parents insisted I go there. I never really found out but I believe, as I was sent to private elocution lessons, my parents – especially my mother – seemed adamant that she did not want me to have a broad Lancashire accent. She thought Hope Park a better place of achieving this than the comprehensive school.

Margaret, Geoff's wife, and their baby daughter Deborah, came to live with us for a couple of years after Mother's death. There was still conscription in those days so Geoff was away serving in the merchant navy. Much better all round for us to have each other's company. It was great having them there and life became happier. I enjoyed my beautiful little niece Deborah, Margaret had a brilliant mind and became more of a teacher to me than any of the teachers at Hope Park. I learned a lot from her. Later in life and after having five children, Margaret won a scholarship to Manchester University where she graduated with honours in English literature and drama, and eventually became a successful teacher.

Christopher Lowe, Pat Miller and the Geddes sisters were all neighbours and good friends. We spent our time at the tennis courts, playing in Christopher Lowe's cellar, befriending Alison Hall, whose father owned the one and only industrial building in Whitefield, HALLS MENTHO-LYPTUS factory. This was a great bonus as we were allowed to go into the sweets' factory on a Saturday morning (they produced tons of different sweets other than their famous mentholyptus) where we were each given a brown paper bag and allowed to fill it up; we always did this before going to the matinee film at Whitefield Odeon.

Our group's only bad habit way back then was to smoke roll-up cigarettes behind the bushes in Stand cricket ground - I think these were produced from dog ends of cigarettes discarded by grown-ups and the price of a pack of Rizla papers. Heavens! Those were daring days! By that time I was showing a sign of promise, playing tennis quite well, and was approached by the coach of Stand tennis club to play in a junior event in Buxton, Derbyshire. Yvonne, the coach in question, would take me in her car and bring me back. I was delighted and honoured because Yvonne drove a bright red open-top sports car.

On the Saturday morning we set off and made our way over the Cat and Fiddle, the high mountainous road winding up from Macclesfield to the Derbyshire Dales and thereon to Buxton. The ride itself was a complete revelation. Having never before left the industrial north, seeing the lovely dry-stone wall fields of the Derbyshire country-side bathed in a myriad of wildflowers, especially viewing it from the seat of the MG, felt like being transported into another life. The historical town of Buxton was also a sight to behold with its unique glass-covered pavements, its spa and opera house set high atop the Peak District. What an eye opener it all was; so much so that for the life of me I cannot remember what happened in the tennis. The next thing I do clearly remember was taking piano lessons with Yvonne, who happened to be a music teacher as well – maybe everyone thought I held more promise tinkling the ivories!

Some months after mother's death, I began to notice a change taking place in my father's appearance. He no longer looked haggard, his demeanour became lively. Above all, he looked smarter, cleaner and even quite handsome. This was a great relief as mothers' illness over the years had taken its toll and despair dragged him down. He once again became a father – alive, a refreshing sight, with new clothes, well-trimmed hair and freshly shaven. This was a father I had never seen before.

I was remarking on this new appearance to Margaret one day after father had left the house to go out somewhere, leaving a faint whiff of eau de cologne in his wake. 'He's got a fancy woman,' she replied matter of factly. 'He's got a what?' I asked not quite grasping the meaning. 'You know – a girlfriend.' You could have cut me dead with a knife hearing this unbelievable news. 'How could he? How could he have a girlfriend when my mother is not even cold in her grave?' I indignantly retorted. From then on, I told myself, I would keep my eyes and ears open for any signs to substantiate Margaret's remark. When I knew for certain, I decided I would confront him about this betrayal of his late wife so soon after her demise. For betrayal it was in the eyes of twelve-year-old me.

All observed signs pointed to what Margaret had told me. It became clearly obvious and I felt a fool for not seeing the signs myself. Then one day, bold as brass, my father asked if he could talk to me. I had a sinking feeling as I knew what might me coming. He was pre-empting me and I didn't like it one little bit. It was I who needed to talk to him. 'Sure.' I answered grumpily; feeling miffed being pipped at the post. He then proceeded to tell me about meeting Lily in the bakery shop in Radcliffe. Lily had worked for him at Pioneer Mill many years ago. She had left to get married – and quite soon had three children, all girls, when her husband died. The three girls were still quite young. Poor Lily had to bring them up by herself. He'd braved asking her out, she'd accepted, and as sure as Bob's your uncle they were courting. It was serious.

I burst into tears shouting, 'How could you? So soon after mother's death!'

'Your mother was ill for a very long time. It's been painful for me seeing her suffer as she did, and then worrying about you not having a mother. Lily came into my life when I was in despair and at my lowest; she has cheered me up no end since, bringing new vigour into this old dog. She herself has had it hard so I think we both deserve a break and to see if it can work.'

Still sobbing, I remonstrated, argued and reminded my father that mother was not yet cold and he already had a fancy woman. There was no consoling me. Instead, he suggested that Lily and I meet each other and see how I felt after that. We met the following week. I didn't like her much; she was a good bit younger than father but absolutely nothing compared to my wonderful mother, whom she had known and, I was later to learn, had been extremely jealous of. The burden of losing a husband whilst her children were still young showed clearly upon her face, with the down-turned mouth, resentful eyes and a chip on her shoulder the size of a boulder. Lily had attitude.

Robert and Lily got married one year after my mother died. It was a church wedding at St John's church in Radcliffe. Well at least they did not have the effrontery to get married at the same church, St Thomas's, where my parents got married. Neither Brenda nor Geoffrey attended the wedding; only myself and Doris, Lily's remaining unmarried daughter, were there to witness the nuptials. As they knelt together before the vicar, the new shoes my father was wearing, bought for the auspicious occasion, still had the large price labels stuck on the soles.

Decisions had already been made without any consultation with me. The house in Grosvenor Avenue was to be sold. Father and I were to move into Lily's council house in Radcliffe, a fait accompli. How dreadful was that? Going back from where we came? Still, one day at a time was my modus operandi, I decided to give father the benefit of the doubt and see how things went. My step sister Doris was a couple of years older than me and basically we got on, other than being a zillion miles apart in most respects. Life in the council house was alright until one day when I arrived home from school to find my mother's piano, which she had bequeathed to me, was missing.

'Where's the piano?' I asked Lily, as even-tempered as I could.

'I've sold it.'

'You've what?'

'We've got rid of it. I couldn't bear to hear you practicing anymore and it took up too much space, so we've sold it.'

I was just thirteen years old when Lily uttered those words. If there is ever a moment in one's life which culminates in altering it in any way, the moment Lily spoke those words to me, my destiny was sealed.

It was obvious all too soon that my father was under Lily's thumb from the word go. He became meek and mild under her roof. Brenda and Geoff were not made welcome at the house and stopped visiting. Father Moorefield, with a rodent ulcer eating into his nose, practically lived with us – he was Lily's father. Her sister lived next door. Between them they looked after the old man. Step-sister Doris became a nightmare. One evening when we went upstairs to bed, she insisted that I sleep in her room; it was warmer and would be more fun she insisted. It was not fun – it was evil.

Each evening she would be waiting for me, trying to entice me into her bedroom threatening to tell Lily something awful about me if I didn't. This lasted for some months though I couldn't for the life of me think what Doris could possibly know about me to threaten blackmail in this way.

Lily's sister Annie got taken away unexpectedly in an ambulance one evening amid a flurry of action going on between the two houses. 'Something's wrong with her brain,' Lily bluntly told us in her dismal overtones the following morning. She was alive but in a coma and not likely to recover. This news would indeed have dire consequences as Lily now had the added responsibility of looking after Father Moorefield as well as Annie's pitiful husband, Fred.

Mighty relief from the unbearable life I now found myself living came in the guise of my friend Rhona. I was invited to join Rhona, her brother Roy and their parents on a holiday to Newquay in Cornwall. Miraculously I was allowed to go, and I thank God to this day. Newquay will remain a special place for me. Our hotel sat above the old harbour and was lovely, we spent most of our time on the beach, learning to surf and enjoying the wonderful freedom of being away from depressing Radcliffe. I can honestly say that I fell head over heels, for the very first time, with a gorgeous blonde boy called Jacques, a local boy despite his French name. It was a true holiday romance, innocent and eye-opening, when passionate kissing was our only sin. On the last day of our holiday Jacques told me he had a steady girlfriend who was away during our brief encounter. He was honest, I admired him for that. The holiday came to an end and memories did fade, for they were too sweet to last.

Chapter Ten

Bus Stop to Freedom

Leaving school with no sparkling honours other than a great aptitude for maths, it was decided, mostly by my father, that I should study to become an accountant. Perish the thought that this was my wish but, in hindsight, it has stood me in good stead and became the base for a dazzling future.

I was attending an accountancy course in Manchester at the same time as doing an apprenticeship at Walmsley's Pulp and Paper Mill in Bury in the accounts office, where I actually loved the work and enjoyed the massive Burroughs accounting machines we used to do all the wages and salaries on. One Saturday morning whilst working there in the office alone, a pain in my left side flared up and I was doubled over in agony. When someone from another office dropped in he could see I was in a state and suggested I go home immediately and offered to give me a lift; in the meantime he phoned Dr Kiernan, our family doctor, who advised him to take me straight to the surgery before it closed at lunchtime. On examination, Dr Kiernan had no idea what was wrong with me, and by this time I now had a raging headache. He advised I went home to bed and rest, which I duly did. By Saturday evening the headache had turned into a screaming rage and I was banging my head against the bedroom wall in agony. Sunday morning my father was at his wits end not knowing what to do, the locum doctor arrived and suggested I had pleurisy, then something else, but he also smelt of alcohol. Father, now beside himself with fear, decided to call the consultant, Dr Savage, who had attended my mother during her illness. Dr Savage came at once, and without hesitation sent for an ambulance and a nurse. I was to go into hospital immediately with suspected meningitis.

Hell's bell's that was quick thinking on father's part, another couple of hours and I'd have been a goner! Safely in the ward of Bury General Hospital I was given sickening lumbar punctures, constant attention, then peace and quiet. I was never a child with the sickly diseases of chicken pox, measles, colds and tonsils like the myriad of illnesses that other children seemed to contract. Mine were few but highly dramatic, to say the least. I was dangling on the edge of darkness one moment, returning to life like a miracle the next.

This unfortunate life threatening illness of mine coincided with father and Lily's scheduled holiday plans to go to the Isle of Man. After discussions with the doctor in charge they decided to go anyway - there would be plenty of people to visit me, was their weak explanation. My sister,

Brenda, came to see me during this time in hospital; it was great to see her and a huge and refreshing relief. When my father and Lily returned from their holiday they were met at my bedside by Brenda, whereupon a monumental argument started as Brenda gave them a few words of her mind for selfishly leaving me to go on holiday – they had to be stopped by the sister-in-charge from arguing over my bed, and were asked to leave the hospital.

Recover I did, slowly but surely. To this day I have no idea what the pain in my side was that started the meningitis, it seemed to disappear the moment the headache started. A touch of drama in the hospital by the Barrington's of course added spice to the hospital ward. The nurses and other staff told me when Annie, Lily's sister, had been admitted she was put into a room by herself at the end of the ward where she sang hymns and arias in the most beautiful voice up until she died. Funny really as Annie hardly ever spoke, let alone sang. Poor soul must have been a suppressed opera singer, a sad end indeed, but at least she left her mortal coil singing.

'How would you like to go to London?' Father asked shortly after my discharge from hospital. 'By train would be a good idea,' I wanted to reply in slight mock to his question but thought better of it. Lily was in the room and she already resented my accent, the result of my mother's insisted elocution lessons followed by the years at Hope Park School. 'What do you mean, go to London?' I succumbed to ask.

'Kenneth and Irene are there on business and

they've invited you to go and join them, give you a break to convalesce.'

Wow! This was a wonderful chance to go to London, another world. Be away from the claustrophobic home environment of father, Lily and Doris. 'I'd really like to go,' I told them. Irene was Lily's eldest daughter and the best of the bunch, Ken, her husband, was a nice enough chap, worldly and way out of the Radcliffe syndrome where he was born.

'Good. We'll get you to Victoria Station tomorrow and on a train to London, they'll meet you there and take you to Richmond where they're staying. '

This was probably a great relief to my father, as the atmosphere at home you could cut with a knife. Since the row in hospital with Brenda, Lily became more lemon-lipped than ever and her resentment towards me now was paramount. I was later to learn that Lily had been very jealous of my mother before and after her death. She had resented her popularity in the town, her striking looks, talent and above all, her personality. Many people at every opportunity said I looked like my mother and this was what Lily could not tolerate… the appendage of her jealousy living under the same roof. Unfortunately Lily had no redeeming features, no personality whatsoever to even begin to compete with Alice Barrington.

Richmond was wonderful. I was given my own bed-sitter in the same guest house as Kenneth and Irene. We ate in a local Italian restaurant that made mouth-watering fluffy cheese omelette and chips, not very Italian but so, so delicious. The smell of herbs and garlic filled my senses, making me a lifetime slave to Italian food. We walked along the river Thames, over Richmond Hill. Sometimes I heard an orchestra playing in a hotel somewhere near the river where chandeliers glistened and people danced. No L. S. Lowry look-alikes in Richmond, this was wealth and fame country and I liked the feel. My life was a million light years away from this; how would I ever know then, that in the not too distant future I would own my very first house somewhere close.

The convalescent period spent in Richmond gave me plenty of time to think. There was a big problem with Doris which, I believe, culminated in my becoming so ill. I knew deep down that if I did not move away, my sanity would be in serious danger or, alternatively, I might well end up killing her. It was definitely time to move out. I just had to.

'I'm leaving,' I said to my father one day shortly after my return from Richmond. The atmosphere in the house when returning to Radcliffe became intolerable. Doris now had a boyfriend, David, who was in fact, very nice. I could never understand what he saw in Doris other than them having it off together at every conceivable opportunity when the folks were not around. She was going to nab him for sure, I thought to myself. Get pregnant and weave him into her spiders' web.

'What do you mean you're leaving, leaving to go where?' asked father, following me up the stairs and into my bedroom.

'I haven't decided yet, but anywhere is better

than here. Lily has you wrapped around her little finger. Doris behaves like a dog on heat and between the three of you, I don't really exist. Brenda and Geoff are not welcome here or for that matter any member of our, your family. Lily will fleece you of every penny you have ever had and whatever you are likely to make in the future, mark my words,' I told him furiously as I packed a suitcase.

'Lily's not like that,' he spat back, now realising that I was seriously going to go, and the pent up emotions of the last few years had finally reached breaking point for me.

'Lily is like that, Dad. She has made you sell our house to move into her council house. She gives you spending money out of your own wages which you hand over to her. She despises me and any other member of our family. You are not even allowed to go and visit your own sister – Auntie Janie is devastated. Lily is cutting you off from everyone; even me and I cannot sit here and watch it.'

'Well, here you are then if you must go,' he said, throwing a wad of pound notes onto the bed next to my packed suitcase and bag - most probably his month's spending money from Lily.

Not one little bit too proud I took the notes and stuffed them into a pocket, picked up the case and hurtled down the stairs with father following, carrying the bag. I opened the front door, whereupon Lily appeared from the sitting room to see what the commotion was. Walking down the path and out of the gate to freedom with the last words I ever heard again from Lily, 'If you leave this house you'll never be allowed back!' floating off into the breeze.

As I took a long, amazing walk to the bus stop on Ringley Road, it felt as if a massive weight had left my body, I was fifteen years old. From that moment on I vowed that I would never set foot in their house again, and I didn't. It would be twenty-two years before I saw my father again.

There had been no plan and I even surprised myself. Brenda assured me on the few clandestine meetings we had had together since the hospital incident that I could always escape to her and Neville, her new husband, anytime that I needed to. So off to Whitefield and Brenda I went. No surprises there when she opened the front door of their new house. In fact, she would have been more surprised if I hadn't escaped, it was only a matter of time she and Neville assured me. Not too proud to take my father's money but I was too proud to stay with my sister for long. She was married with a new baby and not much room. The following day, a Saturday, I went to visit Auntie Agnes who lived in Radcliffe, the other end of the town from father and Lily. Auntie Agnes lived alone; she had a sister Auntie Nellie and her husband Uncle Ernest who lived next door but one. They were not real aunts but friends of my parents, whom I had known all my life, and both Aunts had looked after me as a child. Auntie Agnes had a spare room so I asked her if I could go and live with her. She was delighted and I moved in the next day. We agreed on a small rental which included supper, and we were both highly satisfied and content.

Brenda and Neville informed me that father

had been to their house looking for me. Brenda had given him short shrift, asked him what he intended to do for me financially… nothing, apparently, and sent him on his way. Not long after, I learnt that Doris had indeed got herself pregnant and was to marry David. Father, with no choice, distanced himself from our family as they ostracised him for allowing Lily and Doris's behaviour towards me to continue as it did for so long without lifting a finger to do anything about it. I believe to this day that the meningitis I suffered was caused by the distress and unhappiness I endured during the time spent with that family. My father seemed happy and that's what mattered to me, after watching him suffer through my mother's illness for so long I believe he deserved it. He'd made his choice; he had to live with that. I had my whole future ahead of me. I was free; I would succeed and make the very best of it.

Auntie Doris, mother's younger sister, had been a great comfort to me during Mum's illness. Doris was married to Stanley, Chief Inspector of Police for Cheshire and based in Neston on the Wirral, where I spent my school holidays. They had only one child, a son called Billy who was quite a bit older than me, whom I adored. I loved Auntie Doris; she was a short, sweet smiling woman with a lovely face who adored her sister, my mother. They were quite different to look at as mum had been tall, elegant and handsome as opposed to beautiful. They were born actresses both and often appeared together in local amateur dramatic productions. I still have a treasured photograph of them together dressed up for their parts in the Mikado. Uncle Stanley was married to his work at police headquarters in Chester. Even off duty he listened in to the police radio all the time. My holidays were spent cycling around Vicar's Cross and Neston when I wasn't feeling sorry for the stray dogs being held in the police kennels. I was well fed and looked after like the daughter they never had, and dear cousin Billy – a lookalike Elvis Presley - was always taking me for special treats, like boating on the river Dee. Proud moments came when we went on a car journey with Uncle Stanley who drove not a jot more than twenty miles per hour – earning the nickname "Steady Stan" - and was saluted by every police-man on duty as we drove along. I did not really know the protocol in those days; I just thought that Uncle Stanley was someone very important, which I suppose he was. He had been highly commended for the capture of several murderers during his illustrious career.

Since leaving Whitefield, after father sold the house and moved back to Radcliffe, there had been little time or enthusiasm to keep up with the friends I had made in Whitefield, the comprehen-sive crowd I affectionately called them. Now that I was free I made a concerted effort to go and ex-plain to Pat Miller and the others what had hap-pened. Everyone seemed delighted to see me and our friendships resumed and on a much better footing.

There was to be a dance one Saturday evening at Whitefield comprehensive school. This was held for the students who had left the previous year. Pat invited me to go and I happily accepted.

It was a shimmering affair if you consider it was held in the school assembly hall, but I enjoyed it, especially towards the end when the lights were lowered and the band started to play "Save the last dance for me" and a tall handsome young man stepped forward. 'Please may I have this dance?' he asked, and then before I could even think about it he whirled me onto the dance floor for the last smooch.

He smelt good, dressed well, and I felt I had landed in heaven. 'What's your name?' I asked.

'It's Kenneth, Ken for short, and your name?'

'Christine.'

'That's a nice name. Where are you from? You don't sound as if you're from around here?'

'Yes, I come from Radcliffe and Whitefield, I've lived in both. And you, where are you from?'

'Whitefield, Besses o'th' Barn, I've come with Melvyn over there, dancing with your friend Pat.'

Then the dance was over and the evening at an end. I was staying with Pat for the night and Ken asked if he could walk me to her house. Pat would be going with Melvyn in his car. This seemed a bit strange to me but when we got outside and I saw the gorgeous green MG I understood, there was no room in that two seater sports car for Ken and me. When we arrived back at Pat's house there they were sitting in the car, canoodling. We said our goodnights to the boys and agreed to meet them the following evening for a trip into Manchester. We went to bed that night excited and thrilled with our newly-acquired dates.

It was always great staying with Pat, her parents were always welcoming and they lent an air of sophistication to Whitefield. These were people who spent a great deal of time in Spain and drank wine with their lunch. Pat herself was turning into a beauty with her blonde hair, blue eyes and stylish dress sense, she stood apart from anyone else – the boys certainly flocked after her in droves, which she appeared to be completely unaware of.

My first time in a bar – other than an occasional ham sandwich affair after a funeral in the local pub function room - this fairly sophisticated bar in central Manchester was something else. 'What would you like to drink?' Ken asked as he and Melvyn escorted us to our seats. For the life of me I couldn't think what to ask for, trying desperately hard to think of something, 'sherry, please,' I said, being the first thing that came into my head whilst trying hard not to look a total ignoramus in front of our two attractive dates. For some uncanny reason I had the distinct feeling that asking for a Babycham would not go down too well in the present company.

'Have a glass of red wine?' Pat suggested.

I'd tasted wine from father's Burgundy bottle kept in the front room cabinet, it was revolting and I couldn't imagine anyone wanting to drink an entire glass of the stuff. 'No thanks, I'll stick with the sherry if you don't mind.'

'Would you like dry, medium or sweet?' Ken asked.

This was getting embarrassing as I thought hard to capture the taste of the occasional glass I was allowed at Grandma's when we used to go there on a Sunday afternoon in the far distant past. 'Dry sherry please, Ken,' I replied, throwing him a look that implied there should have been no need to ask as the "right" people from Whitefield only drank dry sherry.

After the drinks it was then onto the Odeon to see a film. Manchester Odeon usually premieres new films and tonight was no exception. Ken and Melvyn went off to buy the tickets while Pat and I stared round the Odeon foyer, looking at the crowd of people dressed up smartly and chatting amiably together, before going in to see the film. This was what life was all about I told myself - a smart bar, a clean and elegant cinema, not like the fleapits that we called Radcliffe and Whitefield Odeons.

The men arrived back with tickets in their hands. 'We only just managed to get these, and they were the last four,' Ken informed us enthusiastically flicking the tickets in the air for us to see.

'Well done,' Pat and I told them in unison.

'We're up in the mezzanine so we'd better get going, it's at the top above the balcony seats,' Melvyn said, ushering us towards a staircase.

My! How impressive was that, having seats on the mezzanine floor of Manchester Odeon. I was suitably thrilled and delighted, and this was our first date. Little was I to know then that seats in the mezzanine were the cheapest and considered the worst for being so high and away from the cinema screen – but hey! Ignorance was bliss then and I never considered Ken a cheapskate for it.

Our romance, as it was, blossomed. Ken and I became an item; as they say in easy speak. Pat and Melvyn were courting quite seriously, well at least seriously on Melvyn's part. The four of us went off at weekends whizzing around the Yorkshire moors in sports or other cars, usually borrowed from either Ken or Melvyn's father. We would go dancing on Saturday evenings at Rivington Barn or Bellevue. It was a magic and fairly innocent time for Ken and me, though I expect he would have preferred it to be less innocent than I insisted upon.

After two years with Auntie Agnes I decided it was time to move on and get my own flat. I now had a job in the accounts department of a clothing manufacturer near Strangeways prison on the outskirts of Manchester. I also had a most unusual part-time job in the evenings, working the tote Tuesdays and Thursdays at Salford greyhound track. Pat's mother was in charge of the totes at the racetrack and one day asked me if I would like to earn extra money by working two nights a week for her there. I jumped at the chance because I knew Pat did this and earned quite a bit on top of the salary she was earning in the model agency office.

What an eye opener that was to the world of greyhound racing. It was non-stop from 7–9 pm. At my tote window I would be given numbers and the money placed by the punter, and punch each number into the machine which gave them their bets in an allotted time for each race. It was a hectic frenzy watching them getting the bets on in time, but still, I earned a tidy sum for those days - and the best part being I would have supper before going to the race track with Auntie Doris and Uncle Billy Ashworth, cousins from my mother's side of the family who lived nearby. Rotund and larger than life, Uncle Billy was also in the police force like Uncle Stanley but not nearly as important, Auntie Doris was a small, petite, busy lady with sparkling and mischievous eyes who cooked, cleaned and kept a good house for her husband and their practically deaf son, Peter. So I was guaranteed a good meal in warm, familiar surroundings for two nights of the week whilst I learned and earned for a couple of hours after.

Although greyhound racing was a shade on the seedy side it was exciting. The race track was in down town Salford, not the most salubrious area of outer Manchester. Fascination came in the way of the punters who habituated the races – Asian, Indian and Chinese men flocked to the tote booths brandishing large wads of money. There were of course, Englishmen but in the general rush of faces they seemed few and far between. It was the first time I had seen so many foreigners, as we called them, en masse. After the racing was finished I would catch a bus back to Whitefield which would be filled to bursting with these foreigners with their smell of garlic, betel nut and not-too-clean body odours permeating in the most obnoxious way, sure that the bus could have been fuelled from human fumes alone.

It was hard to tell Auntie Agnes that I wanted to leave. She had been very good to me, providing my much loved steak and onions most evenings with the odd sausage thrown in on other days. The room had been adequate and my laundry washed and ironed. I think the rent I was contributing each week could have only covered the food, but that was what she wanted. We had muddled along together enjoying the moment, both being fully aware that I would one day leave.

Auntie Doris Finney was very shocked when I told her I wanted to get my own flat. 'You can't live alone, and anyway how could you afford it?' she retorted at this sudden news.

Something called a flat would have been anathema to Auntie Doris who was strictly a two up, two down, kitchen and bathroom lady, bungalows were only just appearing and even these were hard for her to grasp. A flat was from another planet.

'I've got my wages from Doniger's and the money I make at the greyhounds, that's more than enough,' I informed her. She had no idea I worked on the tote - I most probably told her I worked in the office, which wasn't entirely untrue.

'What do these flats cost?'

'I've no idea yet as I haven't even looked. Thought I'd tell you first before seeing what I can find.'

'Then how do you know you can afford one if you haven't looked?'

'Because I first have to decide how much I can spend, then look for a flat in that price range.'

'Sounds dodgy to me,' she said puckering her lips in distaste. 'Where do they have these flats anyway?'

Exasperation was about to kick in. 'Flats, Auntie, are all over the place. Manchester, Salford, Bury, they're not just together in one area. Some of those large Victorian houses in Cheetham Hill, where Brenda and Neville lived when they first got married, have been converted into flats. I'm looking in that area as it's between work, the racecourse and Whitefield, so I won't have too far to travel.'

'Well your mind's obviously made up. I just hope you know what your doing and can afford it. We don't want you starving to death now do we?'

'Thanks Auntie,' I said jubilantly throwing my arms around her and giving her a big hug. 'I promise I'll look after myself, eat properly and pay the rent.'

'You are your mothers' daughter alright. You can look after yourself. I'm going to give you some money every month towards food and things until you get on your feet,' she said, with a tear running down her cheek.

Chapter Eleven

An Engagement of Sorts

It wasn't exactly a flat, more a bed-sit, but whatever; it became my very first home and I was
thrilled. The top floor conversion of the house – in
a row of tall Victorian houses – comprised a large
bed-sitting room with separate kitchen and bathroom in one of Cheetham Hills' nicer tree lined
roads. My claim to fame living there was that
Britain's famous, well-loved and most unusual DJ,
Jimmy Savile, lived in the house next door. Jimmy
Savile had some nice classic cars and more often
than not one of them would be parked in the road
outside my house, which always thrilled my
friends and family whenever they came to visit; in
fact I think they visited more than they normally
would in the hope of catching a glimpse of Jimmy
himself. If not, then seeing one of his cars, especially the E-Type Jaguar, would suffice.

Ken, of course, was delighted now that I had a
place where we could be alone together. The first
night I cooked him a meal at the flat we sat in
front of the little fire I had made in the small but

very adequate fireplace. In Manchester, being famous for its cold wet weather, this fireplace was a smashing added bonus. Ken thought the double bed was a better idea and bounced on it to try. 'Wow, this is great, why don't you come and join me,' he suggested, patting the empty space beside him.

I was feeling a bit vulnerable being alone with Ken and I did not want to get onto the bed with him. Whatever our relationship was I was not ready for anything more than the odd kiss and cuddle; getting onto the bed might encourage him and we would be into it before I knew what was happening. 'No, I don't think it's a good idea, its warmer near the fire and you'll have to be going soon.'

Ken's face dropped and I could tell he was hurt, I sounded like a prissy old housewife even to my ears. Dear Ken with his Ivy League look, blonde hair and tall gait, a good, kind person going nowhere, especially with me.

'Let's get engaged,' he suddenly blurted out of the blue.

At first I thought I misheard him. 'Sorry, what did you just say?'

'I thought it might be a good idea to get engaged, we've been going out together for quite a time now so I thought we should get serious.'

'Like getting married?'

'Eventually, I hope we'll get married.'

I did not want to burst Ken's balloon, but it was quite a shock to hear him uttering such thoughts. Engagement and marriage were not on my agenda. 'We can be informally engaged Ken, between you and me, but not such as to alert our families - we're still quite young and I've hardly been outside Manchester, let alone travelled the world. Your job in Pete Waterhouse's car show-room in Prestwich isn't going to keep us very well.'

'You told me you went to Newquay in Corn-wall some years ago. Cornwall's a long, long way from Manchester.'

'That's hardly travelling the world, Ken. I want to see somewhere other than England before I settle down and have children.'

'We can do that together; take a trip round the world once we're married. There's no rush to have children.'

'I've had enough of this talk, Ken - it's high time you went home.'

He rolled off the bed looking dejected, put his coat on and started down the stairs. 'We can go and look for a ring on Saturday if you like, we can take a trip into Manchester and you can choose one.'

'Oh! That would be nice,' I said blowing him a kiss as he turned the corner to descend the next set of stairs.

My God, what was the matter with me? I kept asking myself. This lovely guy wanted so despe-rately to be my boyfriend in every sense of the word yet I always seemed to be pushing him away. He wanted a proper relationship, I didn't. This was not the stuff of fluttering hearts and breathless moments that I heard my friends talk about, still, it might happen.

Saturday arrived and we went into Manchester

as Ken had suggested. The thought of a sparkling diamond on my finger had bucked me up no end and made me realise Ken was such a nice guy that I should make more effort with our relationship. Also Pat would be green with envy when she saw my ring. I don't think Melvyn had such aspirations towards Pat, he was a handsome hunk himself with plenty of other girls aflutter around him and with a sports car thrown in he had the pick of the field.

'I like that one.' I said to Ken pointing at a ring bearing a nice looking diamond in the showcase of H. Samuel the jewellers'. The assistant took out the ring to show us, after taking great pains to unlock the case. I picked it up.

'How much is it?' Ken asked the assistant.

He said a figure that made me go white, and Ken nearly faint.

I put the ring down as if it were red hot molten, grabbed Ken by the hand and fled from H. Samuels as quickly as decency allowed. Once outside and away from the shop I told Ken that there was no way I wanted a diamond. 'Good,' he said with a sense of relief, 'I hadn't thought we would go for a diamond as it wasn't an official engagement, more a dress or costume ring or whatever you girls call them.'

Eventually I plumped for a cameo set in marquisate and silver. This was the cheapest ring we could find that did not look gaudy and had a touch of class about it. Poor Ken, he must have been at his wits end wondering what I would choose, as he had very little money to spend on the ring. I soon worked this out for myself in our search, so there was no reason to embarrass him.

That evening we went out for dinner and celebrated our unofficial engagement. Later back at the flat I allowed Ken to stay for an hour longer than usual as we kissed and canoodled on the bed. There was no fire that evening and there was no fire in me for Ken at all and I felt like an eel; he wanted more of which I didn't want to give. My body was taboo and I realised then that there could never be any intimacy between us. I loved him as a friend but Ken touching me felt repugnant. He smelt nice, looked nice, but I had no desire to see him without his clothes on, or touch him other than holding hands and the occasional embrace. Maybe I was frigid? I didn't know about that sort of thing in those days.

Then the nightmares began, well not exactly nightmares. I repeatedly dreamt of my wedding day, walking down the aisle in Stand Church amid a huge congregation of family, cousins, friends and neighbours, all gathered together to bear witness of our marriage. There was Ken standing proudly up at the Alter with his best friend Pete Waterhouse in attendance. When I get halfway down the aisle with the sound of the wedding march ringing in my ears, I suddenly freeze, and then turn around and run like the wind out of the church and far away. This began to happen quite frequently and I would wake up in a panic.

Time to face the truth, I told myself when Ken and I were next together, which happened to be on a drive across the Yorkshire moors. 'I'm sorry, Ken, but I can't marry you,' I told him, completely

174

out of the blue, as we sped along through the emerald green dales. I tried to gauge what his reaction might be to this sudden announcement. The silence was deafening.

He slowed the car down and pulled over to the side of the road. 'Why, have I done something wrong?'

'No Ken, you've done nothing wrong at all, it's me, I am just not the marrying type, that's all. I want to be free.'

'Is there someone else?'

'No, no, no it has nothing to do with anyone else. I don't want to get married and I think we should stop seeing each other, our relationship is not going anywhere.'

'But we're engaged, damn you.' He shouted banging his clenched fist against the steering wheel. 'Why have we wasted all this time going out together if we're not going to get married?'

I was beginning to get a bit alarmed at this first ever sign of aggression from Ken. 'People do go out together without getting married, Ken. If you're attracted to each other you have to give it a try and if it works out, that's wonderful; if not, you split up and go your separate ways.'

'And that's what's happened to us?'

'Not once have either of us said that we love the other, don't you think there is something wrong with that for a start. You don't really love me and I realise now that I'm not in love with you.'

At that Ken turned the key in the ignition and the engine roared into life. We drove back to Manchester is stony silence at a speed that defied a sense of gravity. In hindsight it was a stupid time to have told Ken our relationship was at an end on those remote moors. He could well have turfed me out of the car and left me to walk, which would probably have taken me a week.

Very much relieved and now fancy-free, I occasionally went with Pat to a couple of nightclubs in Manchester where we would dance and have some fun. We frequented the Ambience and the Jungfrau where we would see groups like The Hollies, The Beatles, Gerry and the Pacemakers perform in their very early days, the start of the sixties. What a time it was... fairly innocent by today's standards but exciting and carefree. Moira, one of the girls in our office was dating the owner of the Jungfrau, Alan, so we got concessions to go there in the evenings free of charge. During the day the Jungfrau served coffee and light meals. One day I met and took Auntie Doris there for lunch. She thought she had entered a den of immorality when we went downstairs into the cellar which was the Jungfrau, dark and cosy. 'There must be some goings on down here,' she remarked looking suspiciously around her before taking a seat at our table. Lyons Corner House was more Auntie Doris's cup of tea, not the bowels of the earth in Manchester. She did confess to enjoying her lunch in the most unusual surroundings once she realised she hadn't been assaulted and murdered.

My favourite times were spent visiting Geoff and Margaret and their fast-growing family in Radcliffe. I often kept Margaret company in the evenings when Geoff was out at work on night shift. Sometimes I baby-sat if she had something special to do. I loved the children, my nieces and nephews, and the atmosphere in their home, relaxed, comfortable and friendly. I would go to Brenda and Neville's occasionally and spend time with my nephews and niece at their new house in Whitefield, which unfortunately was not on the public transport route; it was quite a hike to walk from the nearest bus stop, hence I did not visit them as often as I would have liked.

We got friendly with the receptionist at the nightclub Ambience, a young lady from Ireland called Olivia Falls, who asked me one evening if I wanted to share a flat with her. She was moving and wanted a larger place and I knew that my time in Cheetham Hill was fast coming to a close - all those stairs and being alone was beginning to take its toll. The idea of sharing somewhere nicer that we could both afford appealed. Olivia was in her mid-twenties with a lovely, lilting Irish accent. She worked for a firm of accountants during the day and her job at the Ambience was part-time a couple of evenings a week. One day she phoned me and said there was a flat advertised for rent in Didsbury which sounded nice and could I go to see it that evening as she was working.

I went to the address given by the landlord whom Olivia had phoned in advance to make the appointment, the address being number four, Lansdowne Road; I eventually found number four, and pressed the bell. A kindly-looking gentleman answered the door but we soon realised I had the wrong house, I was at number 4A. I proffered my apologies and started to walk down the down the path when he called, 'What kind of accommodation are you looking for?'

'I'm looking for a flat for two ladies and not expensive,' I told him. Didsbury was an upmarket area of south Manchester and you paid through the nose to live there, so I wasn't quite sure why we were looking there.

'Well if you are interested we have just converted our first floor into a flat, would you like to have a look at it?'

Nothing ventured, nothing gained. 'Sure, why not,' I told him, walking back to the front door. He introduced himself as David.

I followed David up the flight of stairs in the warm and comfortable house which smelt like home. He explained on the way that he and his wife had converted the self-contained flat in their house for his mother, who, unfortunately died before she had spent one night in it. They had talked about letting it but never got round to doing so.

Gobsmacked would be the only way in which to describe my surprise when David unlocked the door of the flat and ushered me inside. It was perfectly lovely. The sitting-room was very spacious with two large Victorian sash windows looking out onto trees and the road below, tasteful and modern. The bedroom, bathroom and kitchen followed through. Everything looked brand new.

'Wow! This is something very special, what a fabulous flat. We would love it, at least I certainly would, but I doubt we could ever afford it. I dare not even ask what the rent is, David.'

'What kind of budget do you two young ladies

have to pay for a flat?'

I told him our maximum and felt feeble doing so. This was a luxurious apartment, the type of place the rich and famous stay in, not Christine and Olivia from Manchester and Ireland working in the evenings to earn extra bucks. It was film star territory – the flat and Didsbury.

'I'll speak to my wife and get back to you. I am sure we can work something out.'

In a state of euphoria and on cloud nine, I caught the bus back into Manchester to tell Olivia all about the amazing apartment. Not a thought had entered my head that perhaps I should have gone to look at number four as well or at least kept the appointment. No, I would take my chances on this one, anything else I saw would pale into insignificance. Going to the wrong house was fate, I'm sure of that now.

Olivia was as excited as I was when I told her the story, though being a bit more reserved than myself she held council until we heard something positive from David. Olivia herself only lived a hop, skip and jump away in East Didsbury so she would be in familiar territory. In the mean time she phoned the landlord of number four and apologised.

We got the magnificent flat and moved in – and up – into another world. South Manchester is so very different from North Manchester, like chalk and cheese. Didsbury is not too far from Wilmslow where I stayed with Auntie Doris – when Uncle Stanley was stationed there at some point – during the school holidays, so it wasn't totally unfamiliar turf and I liked it. Our landlords the

Barnett's were happy, we were happy.

Accountancy study was becoming tedious. The work at Doniger's I loved, as we all became firm and close friends in the office. Mr Briggs the chief accountant was a whiz at figures and I had great admiration for him. A peculiar looking young man, short in stature, with straight mousy hair and round horn-rimmed glasses, he looked like someone from the pages of Dickens. Mr Briggs' hobby was collecting traction engines – unusual to say the least. He fascinated me. Moira headed reception and was dating Alan, the owner of the nightclub Jungfrau (named after the mountain Alan had once climbed). Elegant Jean Murray was dallying about with her Paul who appeared to specialise in unusual sports cars. Angela Collins, the boss's daughter, came in at very busy times when she was visiting her parents, to help me with the end of month accounts. Angela would sit next to me at the accounting machine with her beautifully long and manicured nails, making mine look like cigarette stumps, and tell me about her husband who travelled the world as a lieutenant on Ark Royal, the British navy's famous aircraft carrier. Hearing her stories so passionately told, made me long to visit Ark Royal and sail away in her. One fine day many, many years later I saw her Moored majestically in Plymouth and the longing returned.

Boyfriends came and went with nothing too serious. Ken and Pete Waterhouse drove over to West Didsbury to see the flat. It was always nice to see Ken. I fell for Alan's best friend, Geoff, and we went out together for a while. Geoff was a racing car enthusiast with red hair, a slight boyish figure; not exactly good-looking, but Geoff had a fresh country charm, and it was he who took me to my first big car race at Silverstone near Northampton. He was a different breed altogether than Ken, Melvyn or Pete, or anyone else I'd met for that matter. Corduroys, tweed jacket, sports shirt and brogues – that was Geoff, quiet and gentle with a punch coming in the form of mountaineering with Alan, and racing cars. He kept warning me that he was waiting for delivery of a brand new car, a really fast one, so with much anticipation and eagerness I imagined myself being whisked around in an E-type or something of similar status.

'I've just collected my new car from the garage; can I bring it round to show you?' Geoff asked enthusiastically on the phone one Saturday morning.

'Please, come over now and have coffee, I can't wait to see it, Olivia's here, perhaps you can take us for a spin if there's room?'

'Coffee would be great. Then we can head off for a drive towards the airport. Of course Olivia must come, there's plenty of room.'

Well that was interesting, I thought to myself. It can't be a two seater sports car if there is room for someone else to fit in... my hopes dashed off the E-type in a second. I didn't have to wait long to unravel the identity of Geoff's mysterious car as I saw him parking a smart navy blue Mini outside our house half an hour later.

'I thought you were getting a fast car,' I said as he entered the flat, trying hard to keep the disappointment out of my voice.

'It is fast, it's a Mini Cooper S.'

I must have looked blank.

Olivia, peering through the window took charge. 'It looks very smart indeed if you ask me.'

We were not asking her but my disappointment must have been as transparent as all let loose, when, after all, she was only jumping to the rescue and saving my face. 'Lets have that coffee; the sooner we do the sooner we can be out on the road,' I extolled cheerfully.

The Mini Cooper S was very fast and ignorant old me soon had to learn that this was a particularly special car designed by John Cooper. Geoff was not a flashy sports car person; I should have known that, it was just my own imagination running away with me and the fact that Geoff's love of racing cars, and the secrecy behind what he was getting, led me to believe it would be a classic sports car.

Not long after that I was to learn that Geoff's attention to me was being diverted into another direction. He fell for Olivia and she fell for him. They were well suited together and they're relationship blossomed. It was no great loss, though a surprise at the time.

The next boyfriend was a relative of Oswald Mosley... which I was unaware of when I first started dating him. Matt, as we shall call him, invited me to join him and his parents for dinner one evening at a popular Indian restaurant in Manchester near the university. I loved Indian food, and curries I could eat forever. So with some anticipation I ventured forth and agreed to meet them there. It was during the introductions that I realised they were the Mosley family but they appeared charming enough. At that time in the sixties there were passionate anti-fascism groups and Oswald Mosley, the fierce fascist leader in the UK at the time, was not the kind of person I felt I needed to be associated with.

Fate has a way of dealing with things in its own peculiar way. After the first course during that memorable evening, I started to feel very sick and the restaurant swirled round and around. Every sense of my being was trying so hard to concentrate on what Matt and his parents were saying; I could hardly eat anything and could only think of having something refreshing like lychees and water. In the end I had to ask Matt to take me home, he had hoped we would go on to a club after dinner, but nothing on earth would have got me to one. Death felt an easier option.

Food poisoning, acute food poisoning was the diagnosis. I spent three days without moving from the bathroom when even water would not stay down. I was off work and no studying for two weeks. One good thing came out of it, I never saw Matt again; one bad thing, I could never face curry again. It would be thirty years on before I could face eating rice.

Olivia told me one day that she was going away on holiday to Cornwall and suggested that I might like to join her.

'Where were you thinking of going?' I asked, remembering my last holiday in Newquay some years before.

'I'd like to go to St Ives. Look at the brochure,

this little guest house does bed and breakfast and seems reasonably priced, what do you think?'

I leafed through and saw that St Ives looked incredible, small with narrow lanes, a harbour, quaint shops and Inns, beaches with white sand and sea that looked blue, not grey like Blackpool. 'Yes, I think I could quite like St Ives. When are you planning to go?

'In August, it's the height of the season of course but we need to book now or we'll never get accommodation.'

'Count me in. St Ives here we come,' I told a triumphant Olivia.

Chapter Twelve

St Ives

St Ives was my destiny; I knew that the moment Olivia and I stepped from the train that August holiday at the start of the sixties. It became a large part of my life and future for the next twenty odd years. I loved it passionately and always will.

We found a taxi on the little slip road by the railway station waiting patiently for passengers and found ourselves a handsome rogue Cornishman, with an accent thicker that pea soup, to take us to the Kynance Guest House. I gazed in awe as the driver obviously took us the scenic route as we traversed St Ives from every angle. I was smitten. The quaint Cornish fishing village captivated me completely. It was so unlike anywhere I had ever seen apart from Newquay. Blackpool, Cleveley's, Bispham - these places had been our holiday destinations and hotspots as a family. Grey sky, grey sea, grey sand and rain.

'This is fantastic,' I told Olivia as the car wound its way along the very narrow Fore Street and down onto the little harbour, sitting there pretty as a picture with its smattering of fishing boats bobbing on the water and a bench where a few, old weathered fisherman sat chattering away next to the slipway. Warm sunny skies abounded and casually dressed people strolled leisurely along the harbour-front.

'Rather lovely, don't you think?' Olivia muttered in a manner indicative of being impressed and proud at having chosen such a place as St Ives.

Kynance Guest House was up a narrow lane called The Warren and it was enchanting. In fact it was not a stone's throw away from the railway station but not accessible by car because of the steep slopes and narrow steps leading to it – walking there with our suitcases would have been an almighty mission, though I was to climb those steps in The Warren on many occasions during our two week stay there. With exciting anticipation we showered, unpacked and changed into appropriate holiday clothes - shorts, t-shirts, a gay abandon of colourful, casual and exciting outfits. Taking our newly-bought bathing costumes and towels, we went out to explore the narrow lanes, cobbled passages, shops and beaches that made up this little piece of paradise.

Virgin Street, Salubrious Place, The Digey were just some the names we came across in our meander through the lanes, the steps and alleyways of fisherman's cottages full of character and charm, each and every one of them. Shops bursting at the seams with tourists, windows full of Cornish pasties, freshly baked bread and saffron cake, their smells permeating Fore Street as we strolled along breathing in everything around us in wonderment.

'This has to be something else,' I said to Olivia as we finally came upon Porthmeor beach. 'I never believed that somewhere like this existed. Look at the pale blonde colour of the sand and that turquoise blue sea.'

'The bodies on the beach don't look too bad either. Come, let's get ourselves into the water and have a good swim, after the long train journey we need some exercise, then we can languish on the beach to our heart's content.'

'Good idea.'

The magic of St Ives enveloped us completely. We swam, sunbathed, visited the art galleries, potteries and ate in the numerous coffee shops and restaurants. We explored and came upon old working sail lofts, delved into every nook and cranny of the artistic and enchanting little town like two Alice's in wonderland. During our holiday the sex scandal starring John Profumo, Christine Keeler, Mandy Rice-Davies and Stephen Ward exploded across the country and became front page news in almost every daily tabloid. Our books were abandoned as our reading time became a habit of going to the beach each morning with the newspapers and devouring every morsel of the juicy scandal we could find.

It was at the Copper Kettle Coffee Bar that I met Patrick, a local Cornish farmer. Patrick was a taller version of Geoff with his cords, tweeds and brogues, only Patrick had a stutter and played a mean game of squash. He seemed totally out of context in St Ives – which was bordering on the beatnik era and about to erupt into its Flower Power period. My Cornish farmer did not fit in. Patrick was nice, and so started a holiday romance. On our first date he took me to Tregenna Castle to watch him play squash with a friend. This was the first time I had heard of the game, let alone watch it being played. After showering and changing, he did take me out to dinner. Patrick was not exactly the Australian life-saving hunks we saw on the beach and ogled after, but there was an innocent charm about him which I liked. Olivia had met someone she knew from Ireland so was well-occupied. Geoff was never mentioned, I think he was the furthest thing on her mind during that memorable holiday.

I wish I could indulge some passion into the romance with Patrick, but it was not like that. No star-lit skies and dark sandy beaches where groups of hippies met and played their haunting guitars well into the night. It was a polite relationship and Patrick was a gentleman, boring as that seemed at the time. On our last evening together, sitting in his car, he did profess his attraction to me and presented me with a box of After Eight chocolates as a parting gift. I was duly impressed, having never seen such a box of terribly thin, delicately square chocolates before, and presumed that they must have been expensive. So with goodnight embraces and kisses taking in the clean, fresh smell of Patrick's neck, we promised letters and phone calls to each other, fully aware that they were empty words.

I sat forlornly on the train taking us back to Manchester. The holiday was over and reality loomed. 'I'm going to go and live in St Ives,' I blurted out to a startled Olivia as her head shot up from the book she was reading. 'You are going to do what?'

'I'm going to give everything up in Manchester and go to live in St Ives. It will take about six months but I want to live in beautiful Cornwall away from the North where it always seems cold, grey and miserably wet. Live somewhere warm with blue skies and palm trees.'

'You're completely mad. What on earth are you going to do in St Ives - the accountancy and becoming a chartered accountant - you have a good position at the moment, why give that up?'

'Life's too short. I want to live amongst people who write poetry, painters, potters, writers like D.H. Lawrence, he once lived in Zennor out on the coast road between St Ives and Lands End.'

'You are totally bonkers, you'll change your mind once we get back and settled down, you'll see.'

'I never did want to do accountancy, you know. It was my father - he wanted me to become "something important" and as I excelled at maths and love financial figures, accountancy seemed the appropriate way to go. I will find being a CA boring as a full time profession. I would prefer to use my skills in another direction.'

'You'll see, when we get back into our mundane routine in Manchester these notions of yours will fly out of the window, soon forgotten.'

'There you go, mundane! That's exactly why I want to move to Cornwall. My life at the moment is mundane and I know yours isn't exactly exciting either. If I have to live and carve out a career, why not do it in beautiful surroundings. Our flat is lovely and the highlight of my life at the moment, but I can't live by that alone.'

'Well we'll see, to be sure,' said an assured Olivia, and promptly returned to her book.

On Monday morning, my first day back at Doniger's after the holiday, I gave them six-months notice which, I thought at the time, was the correct thing to do. This gave them plenty of time to engage another articled employee and it gave me time to plan my return and new life to Cornwall. The family were taken aback on hearing my news and not exactly encouraging. Auntie Doris was fraught with worry as to what I would do for work in St Ives; a white lie came in here and I told her that I would be doing accounts for a pottery, to ease her mind. Geoff and Brenda were busy with their own lives and children; they thought my move to Cornwall was a brilliant idea. In the meantime I wrote off to several places to try and get some employment, it did not matter to me what it was as long as I earned enough to get by on. An advert in the Cornishman Newspaper I had brought back with me caught my eye. 'Manageress/waitress required for season starting April – September, accommodation included. Please apply in writing to: The Copper Kettle, St Ives, Cornwall' – the very place where I had met Patrick. This would be perfect, I thought, and duly wrote off for the position.

The following March I arrived in St Ives on a cold stormy day, and it was not the St Ives we had left the previous August. My spirits dropped as I stepped from the train and battled my way in the pouring rain along the promenade to the Copper Kettle, a coffee bar and afternoon tea restaurant, one of St Ives' oldest and famous with a lovely view across the harbour. I had been summoned to start in March in order to help get the Copper Kettle ready for the season. What a great place it was. The owners, Henry and Joan, a well-known Cornish family, lived on the premises and had two sons, John and Robert. Robert was my age and we got on famously. My accommodation was a small, clean, perfectly adequate room above the restaurant itself, and very cosy. I was shown all the ropes and pretended to be quite knowledgeable managing to take on the persona of having worked in such a place before, which I had not. Some days Henry and Joan went and spent the night at their other house in Lelant, leaving Robert and me to our own devices, which usually ended up with us going to The Sloop Inn for a drink and a pasty. Here was the first time I ever drank beer. I listened to what other people were ordering then asked for half a bitter, nearly spitting it out after the first gulp. Forty-five years on and half a bitter is still the only beer I drink.

After an evening in the Sloop we would go back to the Copper Kettle. Pop Short, Robert's grandfather, kept a wonderful wine cellar there and Robert would raid it on more evenings than I care to remember when he was three sheets to the wind, and glug it from the neck of the bottle sitting at the kitchen table. One memorable evening he performed this same ritual, creeping down to the cellar and returning with a bottle which he opened, took one mighty mouthful then spat it all out in horrific disgust. Father or grandfather had cottoned onto Roberts wine pilfering and caught him out by urinating into a few empty bottles, corked them, and left them in a convenient place. I laughed all the way to bed that evening. Robert never took another bottle.

The season was balmy and I savoured every minute. Managing, waitressing and general dogs-body was immensely hard work but I took to it like a duck to water. Meeting lots of people, tourists and locals was fascinating and I became an entertainer revelling in the holiday mood and chatting to people who came back time and time again. I had one full day off a week and some hours during each day depending on shifts. By myself or with one of my new local friends this precious time off would be spent on Porthmeor or the little harbour beach, sunbathing and swimming... idyllic.

'Seth thinks you're handsome,' Robert announced to me one morning after we'd been for a drink in the Sloop the evening before.

'Who's Seth and why does he think I'm handsome, I'm a woman?'

'Seth is the fisherman I introduced you to last night. Handsome is a Cornish expression for liking you – so I'm telling you that Seth likes you.'

'And in what way does Seth like me?'

'He wants to go out with you.'

'Then he should ask me, anyway I don't want to go out with a smelly Cornish fisherman who looks like a Spanish pirate and smokes Gauloises.'

A few days later Seth did ask me out and we

went for a drink, then on to the excellent fish and chip restaurant up behind the Sloop which was delicious. I romanced for a whilst with my rough Cornish fisherman who already looked as if he was steeped in history, rollicking on the beach. Groping in the sand dunes in the dark night was Seth's idea of a date, but I enjoyed the ride while it lasted, always reminding me of bygone days of pirates and wenches.

The Copper Kettle closed at the end of September for the season and would not re-open its doors until the following April. It had been a great experience and I would miss the wonderful smell of fresh coffee, the baking of warm scones and the general buzz of the place. It had served me well and I earned enough money in wages and tips to buy me some time for several weeks.

An amazing change descended over St Ives once the season had finished and it transformed itself back into a small local village again. Darker nights and cold weather set in and the atmosphere took on a completely different persona. One or two little cafes remained open along the seafront and we locals, as I now classed myself, often met up for coffee or cheese on toast with crispy bacon at the Italian cafe Luca's down on the harbour front, dressed in the fashionable attire of the time, a fisherman's sweater and Levi's to discuss art, literature, Freud and Jung – such wise philosophers, all of us.

My new home became a house called Trewyn. This was perhaps the largest and most beautiful house in the centre of St Ives owned by the artist, sculptor John Milne. If you had to fall with your bum in the butter, then I fell hook, line and sinker into this one. I first met John at the opening of an exhibition held at the Penwith Gallery – St Ives's contemporary art gallery. It was a marriage of souls on first meeting, and eventually John offered me his house to live in – he had a studio at the bottom of his lovely garden, and spent long spells in London, Morocco and other parts of the world. John was a sophisticated man a bit older than me and came from Eccles, a suburb of outer Manchester. He was always beautifully dressed in a casual way, with closely cropped blonde hair and a suntanned body. His superb taste in décor, food, and art was well known as was his wicked sense of humour, which kept me constantly amused. My role would be to keep an eye on the house and if any of his London friends wanted to stay I would see to it that rooms were ready and breakfast served. This was a pleasure beyond dreams.

The following season brought the advent of Flower Power to St Ives and we all revelled in it. Everyone seemed cheerful and happy with flowers in their hair and light-hearted flippancy abounded. It was fun; it was harmless when the largest crime was to steal a bottle of milk from the doorstep step of a Fish Street cottage early in the morning on the way home from a beach party. There was hash and no doubt other drugs around, but this never touched or affected me. It was there if you wanted, there if you didn't. We partied to Jim Morrison and the Doors, Bob Dylan, Joan Biaz, sympathised with Leonard Cohen and danced the night away with The Beatles and surfed to The Beach Boys. The sixties at its zenith in St Ives

194

exuded pure magic.

Needing extra money to buy myself a car, I worked at The Garrick Hotel in the still room during the evenings and at weekends. I worked through the whole season, earning myself an unexpected and thrilling bonus, and that added to what I had managed to save bought me my very first vehicle, a Mini van. All I had to do now was get a driving licence. No car thereafter would give the thrill – having worked my butt off – as I got when I bought and paid cash for that Mini van. The Passion Wagon – as it was fondly named – was a popular vehicle and a few months after buying her a friend's husband, Jack, asked if she was for sale as it was just what he was looking for. I said no. Two days later I bumped into another friend of mine, Brandon, at the local garage where we were both getting petrol. I was admiring Brandon's little sports car when he told me it was for sale. 'How much do you want for it?' I asked inquisitively. Brandon mentioned a figure; I did some quick calculations and before you could say Hey Presto! I was the prospective new owner of a British racing green, frog-eyed Sprite. Jack did buy the beloved Mini van and a few days later I was whizzing around St Ives in my newly-acquired sports car.

Heather, Rob and Owen, Betty Thatcher, Boots Redgrave were all friends that I made during this time and diverse as they all were, they each presented a special quality and presence in my life. It was time to get on my bike and start to do something career-wise. My family would be having a fit if they knew what I was doing – my mother would have been delighted. Boots Redgrave announced one day that someone was starting to give jewellery classes at her house in Nancledra, about ten miles inland from St Ives. The lessons would be one evening a week with a maximum of four people, throughout the winter. I jumped at this chance as the classes were being given by a well-known St Ives goldsmith/jeweller Bryan Ireland. This, I knew, was a rare opportunity, though I knew little about jewellery other than the cameo ring which Ken had given to me and insisted I keep. Learning to do goldsmithing was to be in a different class altogether.

Heather Cottage was a typical Cornish stone cottage, long and low set in an acre of garden with a stream running through it. A large kitchen with the warmth of an AGA, a big round table from where the hub of life in the country existed and a pack of Bassett hounds to finish the perfect picture of rural Cornwall. The lounge had a massive fireplace where logs burned merrily and threw out tremendous warmth to the low-beamed room with its soft enveloping sofas and armchairs. Boots appeared to live there alone.

A room leading off from the lounge was to be our workroom. Partly set up as something before with workbenches, it was perfect and just about enough room to fit us in without being squashed. Theresa, Nick and Jackie were the other three enrolled for the classes. So began our world of goldsmithing and jewellery making, in our case, silversmithing. Due to the colossal cost of gold which none of us could remotely afford, we had no option but to plump for the cheaper precious metal. It was fascinating to feel and get to know the tools of the trade. Miniature hammers, cutters, files, tweezers and steel anvils were the basics, together with silver sheet, wire, solder and a torch burner, and these fine precision tools – usually made in Germany – became a great pleasure to work with. Basically it was like being a smaller version of a blacksmith.

Weeks and months went by and I became completely engrossed in the jewellery classes, putting my heart and soul into it and producing some pretty impressive pieces. Looking over my shoulder as I sat in concentration over a silver bracelet that I was working on, Bryan would comment. 'You're doing very well, keep at it and we'll make you into a jeweller one of these days.'

That of course was encouraging from the master and spurred me on to concentrate and work harder. 'Do you seriously think I could become a jeweller?' I asked Bryan during one of our class evenings.

'I'm sure you could, you have a lovely touch and eye for welding, you just need to concentrate on the design and accuracy of links in bracelets and necklaces. I would like to see how you manage setting a stone when we get to that.'

'Perhaps we could have an extra class each week?'

'I don't think so. Theresa and Jackie have already lost interest, it would not be worth my while to drive out to Nancledra for an extra class and I do have a family who like me to be there in the evenings. We are snowed under with commissions at the studio but you might like to come and watch and see how it's done, get a few tips, or ideas?'

'Wow Bryan! That would be great. I won't get in anyone's way.'

Staying at Trewyn was glorious. John's friends were invariably sophisticated people from all over the world, but mainly from London. There were film directors, actors and actresses, artist's and writers. Some were personal friends, others were paying guests. There was an Italian chef and housekeeper, Ivaldo, who cooked the most delicious dishes imaginable. The music of Mozart, Handel and Puccini always rang through the house. Opera was played and I learned about singers such as Leontyne Price, Joan Sutherland and of course, Maria Callas. I was not altogether ignorant of opera as my mother loved Kathleen Ferrier and Paul Robeson with their deep resonant voices which we heard frequently in our home. Now, listening to opera or better still, seeing a performance, is tantamount to paradise in my music repertoire.

An invitation to have dinner with a table of guests staying at Trewyn culminated in the first sale of my jewellery. It was a long silver necklace of hammered discs I was wearing for the occasion, when one of the female guests asked where I had bought it. 'I made it myself,' I told her proudly.

'I love it. Is it for sale or could you make me one?'

This took me by surprise and I was about to harp and stutter my way to saying it would take quite some time to make another necklace, when common sense took over in the nick of time. 'I'm sorry but each piece of jewellery is individual, designed and made by me. I will not duplicate a design. I can make you one fairly similar which will take quite some time, or you can buy this one,' I heard myself saying, trying for the world to sound professional.

'Well we don't have much time as we leave at the end of the week and I'm sure you cannot design and make me one at such short notice. How much do you want for it?'

This was well beyond my limit. I detected a hint of American in the lady's accent and how inappropriate it was to be discussing this at the dinner table in front of other guests, but quickly - quickly - what price should I put on my first piece of jewellery. 'This particular piece is three hundred pounds,' I heard myself saying, it was the first amount that came into my head. 'It's solid silver and one of my early designs.'

'We'll take it,' boomed a male voice, it was the gentleman purporting to be her husband.

I was pretty speechless. Three hundred quid - how many days at the Copper Kettle and nights at The Garrick would I have to work to make money like that, I thought to myself. 'Great, I'll give it a quick polish, wrap it nicely and let you have it tomorrow.'

'No, don't bother with all that, give it to her now.' Reaching for his wallet, her husband handed the three hundred pounds to me across the dinner table.

Three hundred pounds was a fortune then. How on earth I pulled it off, I have no idea. Wealthy Americans, two bottles of wine down the hatch, who cares; I got my first sale and I was thrilled. This episode was to stand me in good stead as it gave me the confidence to steer myself into the future as a goldsmith–jeweller. When I told Bryan about the sale he was delighted. Dear Bryan with his soft sensuous voice and shock of black Romany hair sweeping over one eye, his gentle but firm manner made him a charming and irresistible young man whom I admired a lot. Bryan had guided me well to get to this point.

'That was a one-off Christine, you have the winter months to go through here in Cornwall, if you really want to succeed in this field then you should go to London, apply for a gold licence and buy your own metals from Johnson Matthey, and apprentice yourself to a workshop in Hatton Garden. Go and talk to the director of Goldsmith's Hall, do whatever it takes.'

Chapter Thirteen

Streets of London

Leaving Cornwall was not easy. I had found a new home there and lived a life beyond my wildest dreams. Living at Trewyn with John and meeting such interesting people was a tremendous wrench. Spending time trying to surf and swim in the cold Atlantic ocean from Porthmeor beach I would miss passionately, and those Australian life-savers, well, best not to go there. But life had to go on. I would be giving up a fabulous lifestyle, and like Dick Whittington, I would find out if the streets of London were indeed... paved with gold.

John suggested we spent a day on the Helford River just before I left. Helford village was one of my favourite places in Cornwall and I loved the river and the Falmouth estuary much steeped in history and romanticised by Daphne Du Maurier in her book, Frenchman's Creek. We lunched at the Riverside Restaurant, sitting out on the terrace overlooking the creek surrounded by an Old English rose garden. Later we took a walk to the end of the little estuary and stood admiring a couple of yachts each tied to a swing mooring out on the water.

'How sleek and graceful that yacht looks,' I murmured dreamily to John. 'I'll have a yacht like that one of these fine days,' I declared, pointing to the sleek dark blue and white hulled one.

'In your dreams my friend, in your dreams,' he retorted with a wry smile.

'Well, at least I can do that.'

It had been a wonderful day and a fitting end to our excursions which John and I often took exploring and discovering a part of Cornwall that we particularly liked so much. Kynance Cove, Gweek, Cadgwith Cove and St Mawes, evoke, still, a stirring within me when I hear or see these names.

A couple of weeks before I was due to leave Cornwall I met Sarah Hall and a friend of hers who were in St Ives to collect some items from a pottery. It was a chance meeting, in Fore Street, at the end of The Digey - in fact, we were introduced by Rob and Owen who turned out to be mutual friends of Sarah and myself. We all arranged to meet later that same evening to have a drink and something to eat in The Sloop. Sarah turned out to be an interesting person; she was beautifully spoken and boyishly attractive with a vivacious personality, and she lived in London. I told them that I would be moving to London and the reason for doing so. 'We can give you a lift there if you can arrange to leave St Ives sooner, we'll be leaving in the middle of next week. We can put you up for a while if you like, at least until you find somewhere.' Sarah offered, as her friend Sandy nodded in agreement.

This was an offer I could not refuse. 'That's fantastic. I'd love to travel up to London with you. I'll make arrangements and be ready – thanks, I really appreciate it.'

Sarah's offer was better than I could ever have hoped for. It would take the sting out of leaving. Travelling to London alone on the Cornish Riviera train was not something I had been looking forward to, and the offer of somewhere to stay was the icing on the cake. Although I had been to Richmond on the outskirts, I had never been into London itself, so I felt this opportunity was a huge blessing.

I wrapped the frog-eyed Sprite into cotton-wool for a well earned holiday and parked it lovingly into John's double garage at Trewyn, where I knew it would be safe until I decided what would be best to do with it.

'This is wonderful.' I told Sarah and Sandy as we arrived at Elgin Crescent, West London, where they each had a flat in the converted house which belonged to Sandy's parents who lived on the sprawling ground floor. Her father was Jamaican and her mother was Austrian, Sandy was the stunningly lovely product of this combination of parents. With her hair cropped dangerously short it framed her face like a piece of sculpture, showing off her liquid brown eyes, perfectly proportioned nose and sensuous lips. I think it would be a fair assumption to describe Sandy as being very sexy, of which she seemed totally unaware.

Waking up in London was a far cry from the silence and peace of Cornwall. A cacophony of sound orchestrated the early morning hum of traffic, police sirens, busses and people. It was exciting and I couldn't wait to get out and explore the area. I knew we were practically next to Portobello Road but having arrived late the previous evening it was too late to go out again.

'I'll give you a quick whizz around this morning if you'd like, help you to get your bearings. This part of London is buzzing with Portobello Market on one side of us, Ladbroke Grove on the other and Notting Hill and Holland Park only a stone's throw away. How would that suit you?' Sarah suggested as we sat down to coffee and toast.

'That sounds great to me, but what about your work?'

'No problems there, I work for myself. I spent the weeks in Cornwall doing work, collecting different crafts, pottery etc for our showroom, so I'm my own boss. Sandy won't be joining us; she has to work today at the hairdressing salon. She's a super hairdresser and much sought after.'

'Does she work for herself?'

'Technically, yes. She uses a top hairdressing salon but has individual clients who pay her, Sandy then gives the salon a percentage of her takings to cover rental and overheads.'

'That sounds a bit precarious to me.'

'It works very well. Sandy makes a lot more money than if she just worked for a salary, I can tell you. She brings in a lot of well-known clients who pay a fortune to have their hair done by her.'

'I'm sure that makes good business sense. Her prices, I'm sure, will be a bit out of my league to have it cut by Sandy?'

'No, she'll do your hair for nothing – she likes practising on friends.'

'I shall look forward to that.'

Portobello Market was our first destination; it was a mere two minute walk from the flat and buzzing with activity. Fresh produce stalls crammed with fruit, vegetables, cheeses and flowers in colourful display, the stall holders shouting across at each other in merriment, carrying round mugs of coffee and eating bacon sandwiches. 'The famous antiques end of Portobello Road won't come into its own until the weekend,' Sarah told me, 'then you'll see why it's so famous.'

'I can't wait.' All the activity and camaraderie in Portobello was intoxicating.

We went on to Notting Hill Gate, down Kensington Church Street as Sarah pointed out well known shops like Biba and Bus Stop… iconic in their day. On along Kensington Gore towards Harrods, past The Albert Hall, through Hyde Park, back down Bayswater Road into Holland Park Avenue. Whirlwind indeed this tour of Sarah's but what an eye opener. I would come to know the area we had travelled like the back of my hand.

Goldsmith's Hall, one of London's architectural treasures and one of the Twelve Great Livery Companies of the City of London, receiving its Royal Charter in 1327, is responsible for testing precious metals and hallmarking. It promotes contemporary jewellers and silversmiths, including an annual exhibition, Goldsmith's fair. I had a meeting with the Director and felt nervous once inside the magnificent Hallowed Hall. There was no reason to be nervous as the Director, David James, a tall, good looking forty-year-old wearing an elegant dark grey pin-striped suit, put me at ease instantly with his quiet reassuring manner. I explained to this kindly gentleman, in great honesty, what little experience I had, the move to London to try and gain experience being apprenticed to a professional jeweller, perhaps someone in Hatton Garden. I asked David James if he could offer any advice, what would be the correct procedure to approach the Hatton Garden Jewellers.

He put his hands together on the large desk in front of him as if in prayer and looked in deep thought. 'I don't think you should go and apprentice yourself to anyone, the pay would be pathetic and you end up doing all the dirty work and not really getting anywhere fast. My suggestion to you would be; set up a workroom somewhere as best you can, make jewellery through trial and error, get it into galleries, shops, sell to friends. You will learn a lot, lot quicker and gain huge experience faster that way than wasting two or three years working for someone,' David James told me in a very deliberate manner.

This advice took me somewhat by surprise, not at all what I was expecting, and perhaps I looked a bit crestfallen thinking what a daunting task it would be to start my own workshop.

'You will need to apply for a licence from the Bank of England to buy gold and other precious metals from Johnson Matthey. You don't need much room for a workbench; you could work from home, cut down any unnecessary expense and concentrate on design and creation.'

Suddenly what David James was suggesting seemed to make sense. He didn't know that I had no home at the moment, but when I did find somewhere then I would do just as he suggested. 'Thank you so much. I really appreciate your advice and for listening to me,' and got up from the chair to shake his hand, knowing that his time was limited and this appointment with me had been squeezed into his busy schedule.

'It is a pleasure, which is what we at Goldsmiths Hall are here for, to help up-and-coming jewellers. Do not hesitate to get in touch should you need any help or advice,' he said, giving my hand a strong, firm shake.

Leaving Goldsmiths Hall and out into Foster Lane was a very different feeling than I had on entering. A sense of elation now pervaded and the nervousness was gone. Suddenly I had a challenge on my hands, and this I found appealing. The most important thing was to find a place to live, but London rentals being what they were this was not going to be an easy task.

When I recalled the meeting at Goldsmiths Hall to Sarah and Sandy the same evening over dinner at Il Portico restaurant in Notting Hill, they were enthusiastic and agreed wholeheartedly with David James. We would all look out for a suitable flat or a bed-sitter where I could live and have room for a workbench, though I would have to be careful as rented flat landlords would not be prone to having gas bottles and burners on their premises no matter how small these items were. Something special would have to be found.

Buying a bottle of wine one day at the Bacchus wine shop in Kensington Church Street, a contribution to Sandy's supper invitation that evening, I met John Stathers and his girlfriend, Flo; these two people were to become pivotal in my life from that very moment. We chatted like customers do sometimes, with the wine merchant - as camp as coconuts – joining in. Before we all departed and went our separate ways, John and Flo asked me to their flat, in Palace Gardens Terrace, for dinner that coming Saturday. I gladly accepted as I felt a special affinity towards the charming couple and I needed to make new friends.

'But darling, Isabella Spriggs, the writer, is looking for someone to drive her around and cook the odd meal in lieu of accommodation; she owns a mansion of a house in Ladbroke Grove, up on the hill. You should give her a ring.' This suggestion came from Prunella, another guest at John and Flo's dinner.

'Where would I find her number and who should I say made the suggestion? I asked her, thinking that this could be exactly what I was looking for.

'She'll be in the telephone book, just say you met Prunella Fielding and she mentioned that you were looking for someone suitable to live in and do the odd chore. She's a bit formidable but the bark is worse than the bite, you'll get on famously. She also has Cornwall connections so that'll be good for starters.'

'Thanks Prunella, it sounds too good to be true, but I'll give it a bash.'

Four days later I found myself on the steps of

75, Ladbroke Grove, ringing the doorbell then standing there for an interminable time waiting for someone to answer. Eventually a lady opened the door and introduced herself, in the softest voice possible as, Priaulx Rainier, who I instantly loved… and was shocked to find there standing in front of me in Ladbroke Grove. Priaulx Rainier was a well-known composer and lived in St Ives. She was also famous for being a recluse, nobody ever saw her. John knew her a little and had tried hard to get her to accept his dinner invitations but to no avail. So, of course, she was an interesting reclusive myth that fascinated everyone, including me. This had to be her. There couldn't possibly be two people with a name like that, let's face it.

Trying not to look too nonplussed, I introduced myself and told Priaulx that I had an appointment with Isabella Spriggs.

'I know, she's expecting you, please come in. I believe you're from Cornwall?'

'Yes, I lived in St Ives.'

'Isn't that a coincidence, I have a cottage studio in St Ives where I go to get peace and quiet.'

'I believe I've heard your name mentioned in St Ives and read about you in The Cornishman. I lived at Trewyn for quite some time; I believe you know John Milne?'

'Of course I know John, not very well but we have met, I think it was at Barbara Hepworth's. Barbara is a friend of mine, and I might even have been to Trewyn once,' the quiet voice informed me.

Barbara Hepworth was a sculptor whose house was at the end of John's garden on the other side of the adjoining wall. She also had a studio diagonally opposite to her house, a converted cinema, where all her sculptures were made and cast. So this was the illusive Priaulx, who didn't seem in the least bit reclusive.

Priaulx showed me to Isabella Spriggs' door across the hallway and bade me farewell, disappearing up the sweeping staircase. I knocked gently on the frosted glass door and soon it was opened by a small, stern-looking lady with spectacles perched on the end of her nose, unruly hair pulled back into a bun, wearing clothes that I was later to learn were her writing clothes – pyjamas with a cashmere shawl wrapped loosely over her shoulders. An early riser, Isabella Spriggs liked to write in long hand propped up in bed most of the morning, then her secretary would arrive mid-morning and type by dictation.

Isabella was not someone you endeared to easily though I did detect a twinkle in her eyes and the occasional smile once in a while. I was brutally honest with her and said I needed somewhere to live where I could set up a small workshop for making jewellery and then asked what she required and expected.

'I need someone to drive me to various places, not all the time, just occasionally. I presume you can drive? Also I need help with this house and to cook something a couple of evenings a week.'

'Yes I can drive, but where would I live?'

'This house has four floors made into flats or bed-sitters. Priaulx Rainier has the floor above where she has her studio; Nella, her sister, has a bed-sitter on the floor above her, as well as Peter

Lloyd-Jones, an artist; my granddaughter Jane has a flat on the top floor. That leaves the basement, it's pretty huge and completely empty, but you would be welcome to that.'

The excitement rose within me as realisation dawned that we were getting along quite nicely. The house was cavernous and not particularly attractive inside or out but it did have a nice garden which backed onto another private garden for residents of houses in the immediate area that backed onto it – these types of private resident's gardens are quite common in London. I had been surreptitiously glancing out of the French doors of Isabella's' sitting room, looking at the roses growing in abundance right outside.

'Please may I have a look?' I asked, my spirits rising.

'Yes, I think you should, but remember it hasn't been used for many years. Go through my front door and you'll see the door to the basement on the left, please excuse me if I don't come with you.'

A musty dampness hit me as I walked down the stairs into the gloom of the basement. Putting on the light – a naked bulb dangling from a wire in the ceiling – I saw at once that the area was enormous. There were shuttered windows and I opened these to let in a burst of light, revealing a magnificent old flagstone floor throughout the wide hall and passageways. A sitting-room-cum-bedroom, a kitchen larger than the Savoy and a bathroom made up the living space, while the rest of the basement area was as big as all the rooms put together. And best of all, it had its own front door. With windows and doors open and a good swill down, the smell of damp might eventually go. Three quarters of the kitchen would be a perfect place for workbenches.

I returned upstairs and told Isabella the basement flat was fine, trying not to sound too enthusiastic. This was going to be a fifty-fifty deal, my time for that huge space downstairs, but I had to be careful my chores were clear cut and kept to that - otherwise, instinct told me, I could be at this lady's beck and call.

We agreed upon a three month trial period with two weeks first for me to get the flat cleaned, aired and ready to move into. Isabella gave me a key to the basement front door, my very own entrance approached from Ladbroke Grove down a flight of steps, in true London style.

What could be better, I told myself joyfully. I practically skipped all the way back to Elgin Crescent bursting with enthusiasm dying to tell Sarah, and Sandy, if she was there, my good news.

'How fantastic, the place sounds an amazing size, but what on earth will you do for furniture?'

'God alone only knows, I hadn't really thought that far ahead. Beg, borrow and steal I expect, I'll just have to camp there until I can gather some things together, scratch around – you'll see.'

We celebrated with a bottle of wine and one of Sandy's deliciously massive salads which seemed to take her forever to make. To this day I cannot get my head around how it can take someone two hours to make a salad, even if it's the best salad I've ever tasted.

The following Monday morning, I gathered a

bucket, a mop, a broom, some bleach, washing liquid and headed down to my basement for its first scrub and airing. Just opening the doors and windows, letting the air blow through, made a difference. I filled a bucket with warm water added the goodies and literally threw the bucketful over the flagstones and scrubbed like hell. Two hours later it looked like a different floor, the flagstones looked lighter and felt clean. I used the same procedure with each room, then onto the windows. At the end of the day the basement flat looked a completely different place. The following day I would set about painting it. Isabella had offered to pay for the paint if I did the work – fair deal.

By Thursday the flat was looking stunning, even if I say so myself. A large canvas painting was being stored in the basement by Peter Lloyd-Jones so I asked him if I could hang it on the wall of my sitting room, 'Yes,' he said and promptly gave me two more from his studio; these canvases turned the whole flat around making it into an eclectic gallery, a liveable space, and everyone was impressed. Better still, I had accumulated a few pieces of furniture.

'Where did the furniture come from?' Flo asked as I was showing her around the flat, together with Sarah and Sandy.

'I retrieved it all from a builders' skip over three nights.'

They all looked at me in incredulous disbelief. 'I spotted various pieces during the day and in the evening I went back and took them. There are plenty of wealthy people who live around here;

it's frightening to see what they throw away, especially those who are renovating.'

'Blimey!' Sandy commented as she examined each piece in awe.

'You actually took it from the skip?' Flo asked, not quite comprehending that the furniture she was looking at had been thrown away, or that I had plucked it out of a skip.

'Yes I took it all from different skips. I saw the bed in one and got a chap to help me with it. Then I saw a couple of chairs and the chest in another, so on and so on. I felt a bit like a thief in the night but it seemed less obvious to do it that way than in broad daylight with people around who might cotton on to the same idea. Some sanding, gluing and a touch of paint here and there, Bob's your Uncle – some nice usable pieces. I've collected enough planks and scraps of wood to put together a workbench as well.'

'Well all I can say is congratulations, Chris; you've made this place into something very special,' Sarah shouted from admiring the flagstones in the hallway.

Later, we all went off to dinner at Il Portico. For people such as us it was a good, friendly and inexpensive Italian eatery near our homes. We were all quite poor in those days, but boy! Did we enjoy ourselves on next to nothing? Il Portico was a saviour.

John Stathers helped me with fitting together a workbench into one half of the kitchen. This created an excellent working area, and the kitchen, thankfully, had a large sash window that created good light. I bought a couple of sturdy stools to sit on from a cheap pine shop as it was important to have the right height at the bench on steady legs. My hunting around skips had not produced anything remotely near a stool and knocking together a few pieces of wood to make them would have been tantamount to disaster.

The workroom complete, John and I stood back and admired the results. It was better than I could possibly have hoped for. There would be a need for more jewellery tools, but those could be acquired over time. I was as proud as Punch and could not wait to start. All that was required now was to produce some really good pieces of jewellery that would sell.

Chapter Fourteen

Ladbroke Grove

The two weeks were up and it was time to start filling my role as housekeeper-cum-chauffeur. There had been no clear duties set out as such when Isabella and I discussed the position. 'We can play it by ear once you are in situ,' she had suggested. So I reported for duty that first morning, tapping tentatively on the glass door of her apartment.

'Come in, the door's unlocked,' an imperious voice called from inside.

Isabella was propped up in bed by a mass of pillows with writing pad and pen in hand, extra pens and a dictionary sat next to her on the bedside table, the scene looking for all the world like something out of an Ibsen play of literary genius. She must have been perhaps in her seventies, a birdlike figure with the long straggly grey hair now loose and the glasses still perched on her nose giving her a strange haughty look, and the same knitted shawl draped around her narrow shoulders. The French doors were already thrust open, letting in cool fresh air and the pungent smell of roses from the garden.

'Sorry, I unlocked the door early this morning when I first got up. I'll give you a key then you can come in without disturbing me. How about some nice fresh coffee, I presume you know how to use a coffee percolator?' Were the writers opening words without once looking up from the pad she was writing upon?

'Good morning,' I replied, ignoring her remark, 'I'll put the coffee on, how would you like it, black, white, hot or cold milk, sugar?'

'Black and no sugar.'

No please or thank you. I set about making the coffee and waited for a break in the writing so that we could perhaps discuss my expected duties for the week – I would need a proper routine, otherwise it would make life a bit difficult.

'Ah! Nine-thirty, time for my break. Let's discuss what sort of things that I would like you to do, as well as driving me to where I need to go this week. I can drive myself, which I often do, but lately I am finding it more and more difficult to park, or find parking space which takes up a lot of valuable time. You can drop me off and then take the car to do your own thing and then come back to collect me, how does that suit you?'

So far so good, that suited me very well. If I could drop her off and collect her later and use the car to do my own work, what could be better? Other chores would be to occasionally cook a simple meal, wash up, collect the post for the whole house that the postman dropped through the letterbox and set it neatly on the hall table for the tenants. Generally keep the hallway and land-ings looking swept and clean – not too hard a chore for a free flat and the use of a car in central London.

'It sounds good to me, Mrs Spriggs. I'll do my best and thank you.'

'Isabella, call me Isabella - none of this formal stuff, we're all friends here. Priaulx, above me,' – pointing up at the ceiling – 'is one of my oldest friends; she has her studio up there where she does her composing. Enrico Caruso, Italy's most famous opera singer once used the same studio when he was in London. Alas! A bit before my time I'm afraid. It would have been wonderful to hear that resonant, tenor voice singing throughout this house.'

'Yes, I've met Priaulx. She told me she lived on the first floor. What a charming person. I've also met Nella, her sister and Peter Lloyd Jones who has kindly lent me a couple of his canvases to hang on the walls.'

'Jolly good. They will fare a lot better hung on walls than stacked on the landing upstairs. Have you met my granddaughter yet?'

'No I haven't. I think I passed her once in the hallway but we didn't speak. I will introduce myself next time.'

'I don't see her much either, most probably got some young man in tow. How's the flat coming on and the jewellery making, got anything together yet?'

'The flat is looking good and I've been working hard getting that habitable. I intend starting work on my jewellery once we have established my duties here that gives me a long enough stretch at the workbench to create and make some good pieces.'

'Sounds to me as if you have it all worked out. It's a delight to know that you are downstairs and the flat is being utilised in such a good way. I hope you'll be happy, successful and stay.'

'Thank you Isabella, I hope so too.'

Once in a routine, the times I spent at the workbench were productive as I beavered away cutting, hammering and soldering pieces of metal and turning them into necklaces, earrings, bracelets and rings, attempting at times to set semiprecious stones such as lapis lazuli, garnets, moonstones and sapphires, which, to my own surprise, came out very well. I had little knowledge in this department. In classes with Bryan we had only two stone setting lessons which I tried hard to remember. At my own workbench it became trial and error which, in the end, I mastered, albeit not to world class jewellery standard.

Word of mouth at dinner parties and wearing your own jewellery has its benefits, as I was soon to learn. The friend of a friend needed wedding rings made for her and her fiancée. Then a necklace was ordered for the birthday of another friend's sister. Over lunch at the British Broadcasting Corporation (BBC) I sold a pair of earrings and the bracelet I was wearing. All these orders mounted up slowly but surely, and kept me relatively busy.

One late afternoon, hunched over the workbench beating a shape into a silver bracelet, I heard tapping on the upstairs door of the flat. I went to see who is was – Priaulx stood there her head poking through the door she had gently opened, her kind face and straight pudding-basin haircut peered down. 'I am so sorry to disturb you, I wondered if you would care to join me for a glass of red wine this evening,' she asked, in that careful, old-fashioned manner of hers that was so charmingly endearing.

I looked at my watch and then looked at myself wearing a jeweller's apron and feeling hot from soldering links of silver chain together. The thought of a break and a glass of wine was tempting and an invitation from this lady was not something to pass up, as it might never happen again. 'Thank you, I'd love to. What time?'

'Six o'clock would be good. Come exactly as you are, there is no need to change.'

Half an hour later I was knocking on Priaulx's door, which she opened and invited me inside. A grand piano dominated the room which strangely stood by the large window, letting in good light and a lovely view for Priaulx over the garden below and beyond. There were bluff-coloured blinds that could be pulled down to keep off the sun during the day as this would affect the condition of the piano – they were open now, giving a last glow across the room before the sun set. It was difficult not to stare at everything around me as I noticed paintings by Ben Nicholson, a drawing by Barbara Hepworth, an invitation from Yehudi Menuhin and a photograph of Priaulx with Jacqueline du Pre, the cellist. I was drinking red wine and eating the best olives ever, in very illustrious company.

Other than the grand piano the flat was modest

to the extreme, a bit like Priaulx herself really. This was someone who did not spend money on trivia. Her work was her passion and life around that just fitted in. The kitchen from what little I saw looked small and inadequate, and I doubted that Priaulx cooked much. She must have sensed what I was thinking. 'Nella cooks lunch for us both nearly every day, so I eat very little in the evening. I go to bed shortly after eight o'clock, read a little, then wake up bright and early at six o'clock to start on my work.'

What dedication I thought to myself. I could never do that, be like that, so totally at one with your life's passion - in Priaulx's case, playing, writing and composing music.

We talked about my work and the time I spent in Cornwall and what brought me to London. It felt right and very good being in the studio talking to this gentle, precious person who was beginning to open up and tell me about her life, beginning in Howick, South Africa. I was truly captivated. No bed at eight o' clock that evening for the composer, I did not leave the studio until well after that.

'Nella and I are going to the Isabella Plantation in Richmond Park on Friday for a picnic, I wondered if you would like to join us,' Priaulx asked as I was taking my leave.

'Thanks, I'd love to,' I replied, thinking I had no idea at all what the Isabella Plantation was – maybe it was something to do with Isabella downstairs?

My big breakthrough came in the guise of an invitation by the curator of The Design Centre – a prestigious gallery showcasing the country's best designers covering a wide field. Having taken a selection of Jewellery for the curator to look at, he chose eight pieces which would then be presented to a panel of judges for consideration to go on show at their forthcoming exhibition of jewellers two months later. The curator, whose name escapes me, was as dull as dishwater - no friendly smile, thin, mid-thirties and lacking in humour. He hardly spoke a word as he examined each piece of my jewellery as if it was a particularly bad piece of dead fish.

'We'll send you a receipt for the pieces I am keeping, just write down your name and address here,' he asked, pushing forward a small writing pad.

I took the bull by the horns. 'Why did you invite me to come to the Design Centre?'

'A colleague here met someone at a gallery opening who was wearing a necklace made by you, she asked the person who had made the piece and then for your telephone number... and hey presto! Here you are.'

'It all sounds a bit incomprehensible to me, I have to say.'

'Why should it? We are always on the look-out for up-and-coming talent, we have to keep our eyes and ears open, our noses to the ground – word of mouth – nobody exactly walks into here off the street.'

'Well, thank you for seeing me. How long will you be hanging on to my pieces of jewellery?' I asked him trying not to sound desperate. The pieces he was keeping represented weeks of work with nothing left in stock to sell. It could be a lean time.

'The panel meets next week and will make their decisions as to which jewellers will be represented. We will inform you by letter if you are successful or not, soon after that.'

'Are you on the panel?' I blurted out accusingly.

'Yes, I am on the panel of judges.'

Oh dear! I thought to myself as I stepped out into the Haymarket and the bustling traffic. Not much hope there for my precious dead fish.

Isabella Plantation was nothing at all to do with Isabella Spriggs, merely a coincidence of name. It was a lovely enclosed, ornamental woodland garden in Richmond Park, full of exotic plants designed to be interesting all year round with its mysterious nooks and crannies of streams and wild rhododendrons. That Friday joining Priaulx and Nella for a picnic in Isabella Plantation was beautiful and soon became a pleasurable habit. Being with the two sisters was like venturing into never-never land, mystical people from a make belief world, Nella, fine delicate Nella, also a musician and older than Priaulx, would regale me with stories of her life in South Africa, where she belonged to Table Mountain climbing club and would climb that mountain often – sometimes camping on top of it overnight. She told of the magnificent Drakensberg Mountains in the Natal midlands, and I would sit listening to their stories in silence and awe. Neither sister was married. I presumed that both had dedicated their lives to each other and to their mutual passion for music.

Inner instinct told me that Isabella Spriggs was irked by my friendship with Priaulx. If I was invited for drinks with Priaulx I found myself avoiding being spotted by Isabella through her glass door and partition, as I surreptitiously made my way up the stairs to her studio at the allotted time of six o'clock.

Taking a deep breath and an equally deep slug of wine one evening I asked Priaulx, 'could it be possible that Isabella is jealous of me and my friendship with you?'

Popping another olive into her mouth and savouring it thoughtfully before answering, she replied, 'I am afraid she could be. She likes to keep her friends in little pockets and away from anyone else and each other. It's insecurity. Isabella can be unbelievably impossible at times; in fact she can be downright rude, which does not endear her to people.'

These were the harshest words I had heard Priaulx utter thus far in our friendship. 'Yes I can quite understand, I've been at the other end of her brusqueness which makes me keep my distance and do only the necessary that is required. It's a pity really, because there is such a kind side to her.'

Three major events happened in quick succession. The first one being, Sarah had moved out of the flat in Elgin Crescent and went to live on a Thames sailing barge, The Maid of Connaught, in Newhaven on the south coast between Brighton and Eastbourne – what a wonderful boat. We, her friends, would drive down to Newhaven and spend weekends on board living and sleeping in the hold, which even had a wood-burner in it. The boat was large and comfortable. It rose and fell with the tide which determined when we could embark or disembark. The Newhaven yacht club provided hot showers, a bar and the compulsory pool table where we spent hours honing our skills. It would be prudent to say at this stage that my brother Geoff was a snooker champion of much note in the north of England. Unfortunately his masterly skills at the game did not pass through the genes to his sister – alas!

Priaulx excitedly announced to me one day that her new Cello Concerto was going to be premiered by Jacqueline du Pre. 'Would you like to attend the performance,' she asked enthusiastically.

I have to admit here and now that I did not like Priaulx's music. It went beyond my bounds of musical knowledge; Mozart and Handel, Santana and Jose Feliciano scored at the time – Priaulx's compositions were too highbrow and beyond me. 'Of course I would love to hear your Cello Concerto,' I enthused. It would be an occasion itself to see the famous Jacqueline du Pre perform.

Sorting the post out one morning I found two letters addressed to me. One bore the logo of The Design Centre, which I tore open in anticipation and dread. The letter informed me that the selection panel had chosen six pieces of my jewellery for the forthcoming exhibition. I could collect the remaining two pieces at my convenience, and ended with thanking me for my participation.

Over the moon would be an understatement. I was bursting to share this wonderful news. Priaulx could not be disturbed in the mornings and Isabella would not share in my joy, so I called Flo at her office, and she was delighted to hear my news so invited me for supper that evening when we could all celebrate. The second letter bore the crest of The Bank of England – they had granted me the gold licence. I thought I would burst - this was cause celebre indeed.

'You'll be famous now,' Flo said gleefully un-corking a bottle of champagne, 'then there'll be plenty more where this came from.' She said, pointing at the bottle, a wicked grin on her face.

'Sorry to burst your bubble Flo, but I doubt it. Six pieces in an exhibition at The Design Centre is not going to make much of an impact in the life of yours truly.'

All my new friends were gathered together that evening in John and Flo's flat, and boy did we celebrate. Kerry and Carol, Sandy, Sarah, George, Michael and a few others, lifted their glasses and wished me luck with the exhibition and for the future.

'Thanks to all you wonderful friends for giving me such great support and encouragement, also for spreading the word around to your friends and family, because their orders for a ring here, a necklace there, has kept me going these last months,' I told them with true sincerity.

Now with gold licence in hand, I could pur-chase the precious metal in its various carats and colours from Johnson Matthey (metal refiners) in Hatton Garden. This sounds easy and it is, but gold is very expensive and my very first purchase was miniscule and a touch embarrassing when other customers were purchasing the metals in hundreds of grams. Seriously though, I didn't really care. My small gold purchase would not allow for a complete piece of jewellery to be made, so I decided to make the next pieces working the two metals together. My interlocking silver and gold Russian wedding rings became a great success, as did other pieces of jewellery using this attractive marriage of metals.

Exercise was important to me, especially if I had been working over the bench for an afternoon and evening. Walking was not my choice, although I seemed to do a lot of it without calling it exercise. No, I needed a challenge and tennis was something I liked, so when I was invited for a weekend to stay with John's parents, Douglas and Wendy, in Woldingham to play tennis, I jumped at the chance.

'You're quite a nice player,' Wendy said after our first doubles game.

I wasn't sure if she was referring to me as she had the disconcerting habit of not actually looking you in the eye when she spoke, but not wanting to appear rude I said 'Thank you,' anyway.

It was a grass court and a rambling house of no particular period worth mentioning, set in a garden of wild abundance. This was the epitome of middle-class Britain, with the people to match. John's parents and his sister Susan were thoroughly good people. Wendy wore thick Harris Tweed suits and carried slight, over-shot front teeth and a permanent wave. Douglas, the mandatory tweed sports jacket with leather patched elbows man, was a bald, rather nondescript person with a pleasant demeanour. They produced the traditional roast beef lunch on Sunday, after which John's father disappeared. Wendy carried on a conversation without looking at anyone making it hard to follow to whom she was speaking, or referring to. Tweeds, twills, sports jackets and Gin appeared the norm. After a couple of weekends spent with Wendy and Douglas, we all became great friends and spent many halcyon Sundays, if not the whole weekends, being very English in Woldingham.

After watching Patrick play squash at Tregenna Castle, the game fascinated me. Luck would have it that there was a squash court in Holland Park, near the Holland Park Avenue entrance, practically a stone's throw from Ladbroke Grove. I found a willing partner in Rosemary Walters, an assistant producer at the BBC, which was just down the road in Shepherds Bush. We would play a couple of times a week when work permitted and in-between I had the odd game with whoever wanted to play. It was super exercise for me having sat hunched over my jewellers bench a good deal of the day – a colossal release from the concentration and tension in my body and eyes.

So I was taking regular exercise and feeling pretty good about that. Reading was also an important part of my life, the study of philosophy and the classics. I found myself devouring Balzac, Victor Hugo, Dumas and the risqué philosophies of Simone de Beauvoir, Jean Paul Satre and Albert Camus. A few friends would get together around my scrubbed-topped dining table (skip retrieval) for dinner and copious amounts of red wine, where we would discuss each others' philoso-phies, remonstrate about Nelson Mandela being imprisoned and the abhorrence of apartheid, life in general, and what we should do about it.

Out of the blue came a telephone call from Pat Barnes, a friend of Sarah's, she informed me. 'I would like to learn how make jewellery and Sarah suggested I get in touch with you, perhaps come and see your workroom and get your advice?'

'Well, I don't think I am in any position to be giving advice, but you're welcome to come and have a look at what I'm doing.' Was all that I could offer?

'That's fine. When would it be convenient?'

'Any time really, but the afternoons are better. That's when I do most of my work.'

'Could I come round this afternoon? I would like to make you a proposal?'

This was a bit short notice but, what the hell. 'Sure that's fine, four o'clock, do you know where I live?'

'Yes, Sarah told me and I live just off Por-tobello, so it's not far to walk.'

'Press the basement bell when you get here.'

Well, this would be interesting. A proposal from someone I had never met and knew nothing about.

Pat duly arrived as arranged that same after-noon. She was a short, slim person with dark brown hair of which one side swept heavily across one eye. She was about my own age, early twen-ties and sported a strong Lancashire accent – she was from Morecambe.

'So what do you have in mind?' I asked this curious young lady once I'd showed her the work-room and we sat having tea.

'You could show me how to make jewellery, in return; I will do all your dirty work, like filing, polishing and buffing, collecting, delivery, whatever.'

I thought about this for a moment. I was not qualified to teach someone, but It would be company during the long afternoons and the time spent on cleaning up a piece of jewellery once the making of it was complete, would give more time to design and get on with the next piece. 'We could give it a try two afternoons a week, how does that sound?'

'It sounds great to me.'

We arranged a day for Pat to start, and then I escorted her to the front door. 'I'll teach you what I can, but it'll be a case of the blind leading the blind.'

'I quite understand and what you say is true; I'm half blind, I only have one eye.' And with those words ringing in my ear she disappeared up the steps out onto Ladbroke Grove.

Whoops!

Chapter Fifteen

The Ring of Changes

An opportunity of acquiring my own flat in Albany Street, near Regents Park, presented itself in
the form of a friend, Elaine, who was emigrating
to Australia. The exhibition at The Design Centre
had produced new clients: Liberty's Store in Re-
gent Street and Amalgam Gallery in Barnes, south
of the Thames. These two prestigious places ordered between them, many pieces of jewellery, so
I had my work cut out. Isabella was getting more
crotchety by the day. Priaulx was spending longer
periods in Cornwall and France. I had been there
for nigh on two years. It was time to move on.

Albany Street was another basement flat with
my own entrance downstairs leading from the
street. This was an altogether very different place
to the Ladbroke Grove flat, much smaller, more
compact but it did have an extra room to set up a
nice workspace and above all, it had a small,
handkerchief-sized garden which, for central
London, was a big plus. The house belonged to a
grand old lady by the name of Betts, who was a

retired journalist. Her sight was diminishing and she drank whacky amounts of gin, but what a character she was. Tall, angular, with thinning dyed blonde hair. Betts spoke in the poshest of accents as she related stories of yesteryear in Fleet Street journalism, her eyes focusing desperately through triple magnified glasses getting less focussed as the G&T's went down.

Pat liked the new flat though it was further for her to travel. We set up the new workroom together and got down straight away to get the outstanding orders complete. 'It's great here, Chris, I can go outside in the garden now to have a ciggie,' she nonchalantly remarked.

I was secretly pleased with Pat and her ability of making jewellery with only one eye; it could not have been easy. The corner-cutting on her finishing pieces still irritated me, but it gave her jewellery an individual, rustic look.

'Is that the only reason? I've made this big move and you only think about it as being more convenient for your roll-ups,' I told her.

'No it's not. I really like this flat, more warmth and this workroom is more inspiring, and, lets face it, it's so much nicer to have a break and sit in the garden having our coffee – surely you agree?' she said in her blunt Lancashire accent.

'Well it is when the weather is nice, which is not too often. By the way, how are you getting along with your own orders for jewellery?' I remembered to ask her. Pat had been making the odd pieces of jewellery for her friends and I left her to her own devices. She continued to help me in lieu of using my bench and tools, but she was slowly acquiring tools of her own.

'It's going well, but I'm not nearly as good as you.'

'And you know the reason why? You don't finish things off properly; you're too keen to get them sold.' I told her because it was true, and she knew it. Pat would never accomplish great heights, but what she lacked in being a presentable jeweller, she made up in friendship and humour.

Pat's trademark song she constantly sang to me, or if anyone else was around she would change the you with she: anything you can do I can do better, I can do anything better than you. Well I'm not sure that was a good analogy as she turned out some pretty embarrassing pieces of jewellery.

'I wonder how Sarah is getting on in South America?' She continued ignoring my remonstration about her not finishing her work properly.

That touched a nerve, I have to admit. Sarah, together with her beloved black Labrador, Zach, and a restored old Mercedes car had set off by ship to South America a few weeks previously. At the time, it felt like a large chunk of my life had departed. I put this notion to the back of my mind and preferred not to think why. 'I suppose we shall hear sooner or later. Sarah's mum has asked me to go down to Sussex whenever I want, perhaps I'll go this coming weekend, she should have heard from Sarah by now.'

'What a great idea. Why don't we all go, you, me, Sandy and Bella.'

That was not what I had suggested, but, what

the hell! It would be good for us all to get out of London for a weekend and revel in the Sussex countryside. 'Okey dokey, I'll give Nola a ring.'

Bella Mackenzie-Thomas was a close friend of Sarah's who I had met several times during my sojourn in London. Bella was another remnant from the north of England with a slow deliberate drawl of an accent and stunning auburn hair. Bella's humour was Tommy Cooper through and through and she worked in the medical records department at the Middlesex Hospital in the centre of London, a five minute walk from my flat in Albany Street.

I invited Bella to dinner one evening where-upon she told me the rudiments of her job, the shortage of staff and the influx of patients. 'I could volunteer to do some part-time work there,' I suggested rather foolishly. Collecting medical records for incoming patients sounded an easy task and giving a few hours a week of my time to a needy hospital seemed a good idea.

'I'm sure they'd jump at the chance of someone like you volunteering – it's the NHS (National Health Service), they can bloody well pay,' said Bella in her no-frills drawl.

'No, I don't want to get paid. I'm happy to do four to six hours a week on a voluntary basis if you think I could be of any help,' I told her, and left it at that. We enjoyed the rest of our dinner, talked about Sarah and her trip across South America, her reasons for going and a myriad of other things. It was a pleasant evening and I got to know Bella a bit more before she left to catch a bus home to her flat in Kilburn.

At nine o'clock the following morning the telephone rang; it was Marigold Walters, head of the admissions office at the Middlesex Hospital, the voice at the other end told me. 'I believe you would like to do some part-time work at the hospital?' she enquired.

'Yes, I would like to help out if I can; my friend Bella from medical records was telling me about the hospital being under-staffed.'

'Could you come for an interview this morning at ten o'clock?' she asked abruptly, ignoring my under-staffed remark.

My heavens! This was short notice with no time to think. Bella obviously reported my offer the moment she stepped into work that morning, letting no grass grow under her feet, that's for sure. 'Ten o'clock is fine. Where, and to whom should I report?' I heard myself reluctantly say.

'Go to the main entrance of the hospital at the top of Berners Street; ask the hall porter to show you to the admissions office, I will be in there.'

This all seemed very formal for just volunteer work; still, I suppose that everyone under the hospital umbrella had to be vetted.

The mighty Middlesex is one of London's premier teaching hospitals. Its neo-gothic and classical architecture is imposing, and Florence Nightingale herself would not look out of place scurrying through its corridors. I entered the portals into the main hall, which housed a massive inlaid walnut table with an equally massive Constance Spry flower display upon it, and then I found a porter dressed in black tails. The Savoy Hotel would be proud of this entrance I thought to myself as David the porter escorted me around the corner to the admissions office and the formidable Ms Walters.

'So pleased you could make it,' Marigold said, shaking my hand. This was a woman who meant business. Her slightly Hapsburg undershot jaw thrust forward in defiance and I could see the other women in the office were eyes down and silent.

'Come along I want to introduce you to Hilda before she goes off duty at twelve,' she said, shuttling me out of the office I had just entered.

We went back to the front hall again and over to a desk where a pleasant-looking lady sat. 'This is the admissions desk, this is Hilda. Hilda, this is Christine, who is going to be working here in the afternoons,' Marigold informed us both.

'But I can only do a couple of hours here and there down in medical records, that's all I want to do, all I can do. I don't want to be on display here,' I told them both, now that I realised why Marigold had wanted to meet and interview me. Perish the thought; I was not going to be on display. I would work in the bowels of the Middlesex where the medical records are kept but not up top for all to see.

'Rubbish, you'll be wasted in medical records we need someone like you at this desk to admit the in-patients. We have a lot of cancer sufferers who are admitted every month for treatment, radiotherapy, chemotherapy so they need someone bright and cheerful to take their admission details,' Marigold stated in no uncertain terms.

Compliments are not lost on me and the bright

and cheerful image was not something I associated with myself, so that was refreshing to hear but not enough to sway me. But the word Cancer was. 'Okay, I'll go home and think about it,' I told Marigold and Hilda.

'Also bear in mind, if we work this job together we can do alternate weeks of morning and afternoons and Sunday mornings we can take in turns,' Hilda suggested.

Sunday mornings, nobody had mentioned Sunday mornings. This was getting out of hand. Last night I was a free person offering a few hours voluntary work, this morning I'm about to be employed and working hours that I don't actually have. I would kill Bella.

I had only been in the house an hour when the phone rang, it was Marigold. 'Have you decided yet?' she asked without preamble.

'No, I've only just got back.'

'Can you come in on Monday morning then Hilda can show you the ropes, there are a lot of admissions so it will be a good opportunity to see what you have to do?' the persistent lady asked.
There would be no harm in going to see for myself what was required. There would be no obligation to take the job. 'Alright, I'll be there on Monday morning, what time?'

'Nine is fine. Hilda starts at eight but it begins to get busy at nine.'

'I'll be there at eight. Best to learn from the very beginning so I'll know what to do.'

That weekend, Pat, Bella and I had arranged to go to see Sarah's mum Nola, down in Sussex, where the Halls have their country home, Herriots, in the prettiest village of Sutton. Nola, a great lady and the most intelligent person I have ever met, has been a life-long friend ever since those halcyon days that we all spent together in her lovely home. Arriving on Friday evening, we kicked off our London gear and instantly got into Sussex mode, starting with champagne cocktails, and discussed the latest news from Sarah, who was an inveterate letter writer. Nola read the latest ones out to us as we listened, completely enthralled.

Saturday morning we each did our own thing, which in my case was to cycle through the Sussex country lanes, admiring the hedgerows, revelling in the green fields – something I just loved to do. On my return to Herriots, Nola and I decided to have lunch at the local pub, The Pig's Snout – whose Ploughman's platter and massive bowls of pea and ham soup with crusty bread were famous far and wide. 'This is so wonderful, darling,' Nola remarked, as we sat beside the babbling stream in the pub's small but lovely raised garden full of flowers and herbs. 'You have no idea what it means to me to have you girls for the weekend, Sarah's friends.'

Nola and Sarah were very close, as mother and daughter, as intellectuals and best friends. The deep bond between them left a big void in Nola's life when Sarah decided to do her South American journey, especially and unbeknownst to Sarah at the time, that Nola and her husband James, were going through an acrimonious separation due to James's infidelity with his recently deceased best friend's wife. Hence our visits to Herriots became a lifeline for Nola.

'I want a divorce and James won't even consider it. The law Society frown upon extra marital
relationships and divorce. Being a barrister and a
QC at The Inner Temple, this latest affaire of
James's could well get him de-barred, so he stub-
bornly refuses,' she told me in no uncertain
words.

Dearest Nola, my heart went out to her. A
dedicated wife and mother brought to this by
man's infidelity. Beautifully poised and elegant,
Nola was the epitome of the upper-middle-class
lady. Of medium height, with blue twinkling eyes
which were always alert and inquiring, her voice
spoke the Queen's English in perfect diction as she
did in another five languages. Her brown greying
hair always looked smart and the clothes she wore
had a kind of latent elegance with the whisper of
Dior perfume ever present. 'Do you really want to
divorce him?' I asked inquiringly.

'Yes Chris, I've had enough. This isn't the first
time that this has happened. Why should I cook,
clean and give dinner parties for his colleagues
when he is busy philandering. No, I want to be
my own person from now on. I've decided to sell
up and go to South Africa.'

'Well, that is certainly a major decision, why
South Africa?'

'My Goddaughter lives there with her husband
and I quite like the idea. I shall go for a visit first
and see how I like and feel about it.'

'That's very interesting. My sister Brenda and
her husband, along with their three children, have
just moved to South Africa, Cape Town; in fact, I'll

put you in contact with them.'

'Wonderful. Why did they move there?'

'Neville, a civil engineer, was sent on a one year contract, they loved Cape Town, so when the company he was working for offered Neville a permanent Job, they jumped at it and the family have gone lock, stock and barrel.'

'So already I have several contacts. I feel like going already.'

'What will Sarah do if you move so far away?'

'I don't think she will return to England. From South America, she is going across to Majorca to stay with Donald, my brother, and his wife Rosita. It would be impossible for her to return to England because of Zach, she will never put him into quarantine.' Nola said candidly.

South Africa? That seemed a long way away, I thought to myself. A permanent break for Nola, upping sticks at her age would not be easy. How wrong I was. That idyllic weekend at Herriots – the South African seed was sown.

On Monday morning following our lovely weekend I reported for duty at the Middlesex Hospital at 8am. Hilda took me down to the linen room in the basement, whereupon I was given a starched white coat to try on… this, I thought, was going beyond the pale, but I put it on as encouraged and could see the advantage of wearing a white coat… it would look clean and professional to the in-coming patients. So back I went to the front hall feeling like a Doctor and a fraud. Funny how a starched white coat can transform you into a completely different persona.

Admitting the patients was never going to be

easy, I knew that straight away. Emotionally, it was heart-breaking. During my second week a lady came to my desk for admission, I had read through her medical file and was flabbergasted that she could still be alive as she seemed to have cancer of everything. But there sat this lady with a cheerful smile and told me, 'God must have made me the chosen one for doctors to experiment with these cancers of mine. If in the end it saves other peoples lives – then my life and suffering will not have been wasted.' She then got up and went off to her ward for another bout of unpleasant chemo-therapy treatment. I burst into tears and had to leave my desk. 'I can't do this job anymore,' I told the lady in x-ray who was consoling me. I cannot bear to see such suffering, lovely people with bright smiles.

'That's a good reason to carry on. Even with the cancer that dear lady has, she can smile. You can be there for those people who are admitted on a regular basis for treatment – with your familiar face and reassuring smile.'

She was right, of course. If I have to be per-fectly honest I think the smiling lady in question reminded me of my mother – so I carried on for her and all those other sufferers. When Hilda left the Middlesex and went to live at the coast – where she subsequently committed suicide by walking into the sea – Pat took over her job and for many years after we worked the shifts very successfully between us.

My boyfriend at the time, Robin Ellis, lived in a tiny cottage in Esher, fourteen miles outside Lon-don. The cottage was in the family trust and sat on the edge of Sandown Racecourse – stockbroker belt. There were two cottages in fact – both tiny and not particularly attractive, each with a small, postcard-sized garden. I liked Robin a lot. Although he was attractive, energetic with a mop of dark blonde hair, good looking in an Eton schoolboy kind of way, he turned no lights on. He enjoyed good food and wine. As his family were in the wine business, he classed himself as quite a connoisseur. We would visit different restaurants in London and in the countryside when our busy lives allowed. Other than that we really did not do much else. It was a pleasant fling for both of us; we accepted that and just enjoyed ourselves.

'I've got to go to Australia for a couple of years.' Robin announced to me totally out of the blue one evening. 'An opportunity has come up in a wine conglomerate there and they have asked me to consider it.'

'And you've accepted?'

'Yes. It's a golden opening and I would be foolish not to seize it with both hands – this could marry the family company with the fast growing Australian wine merchants.'

This news did not particularly bother me one way or the other. The thought of seeing and being with him were no more exciting than a good game of squash. 'When are you going?' I asked trying to put in a blurb of regret which did not quite come off.

'Well that's it, within the next two weeks. They want me to start in two weeks time. So, I was wondering. How would you like to have the cottage in Esher, Grant's cottage? The trust will let you have it for a peppercorn rent if you keep an eye on the two properties?'

Now that was more of a shock than hearing of Robin's imminent departure. A sweet little cottage in Esher – that would be something to behold. Fourteen miles to work and fourteen miles back, plenty of room for a workshop, a garden and the countryside – with a view over the fence of race days at Sandown. 'Robin, that sounds fantastic,' I told him trying desperately hard to juggle in my head how it could work.

'Good, then the cottage is yours. I will get my brother Richard to send you confirmation of tenure and what the peppercorn rent will be. Does that give you time to sort things out from your end?'

'Yes, it does. I will give Betts a month's notice and gradually move in over that period of time. What's more, I know just the person who would like my flat.'

'And who is that might I ask?'

'Robert Day,' I told a bewildered Robin.

Chapter Sixteen

The first rung of the ladder

I moved into Grant's Cottage over the following three weeks after Robin's announcement that he was leaving for Australia. The Ellis Trust had made me a generous offer in the peppercorn rent, as long as I kept an eye on the two cottages belonging to the trust and maintained their small gardens. As predicted, Robert Day happily took over the flat in Albany Street, and all was hunky dory.

Robert owned a small but impressive florist shop at the Holland Park end of Ladbroke Grove. I had called into the shop one day to buy some flowers and we immediately struck up a rapport with each other; Robert had recently purchased the shop from the previous owner, Fred, who happened to be there another day as I called by. Robert and I were discussing the logistics of my travelling to the hospital from Esher. 'You should get yourself a car,' he suggested.

I thought about it for a few seconds. 'That's all very well, but I don't exactly have the money to go out and buy a car.'

This banter went on for a bit when Fred suddenly announced, 'I've got a car I want to get rid of which I can let you have. You can give me a deposit and pay the rest off over the next six months. Only problem is, it's at my caravan in Brighton.'

Well, I thought. I suppose I could get to Brighton and the offer sounded something I could manage, but the thought of driving into and out of London every day, and where would I park, was a daunting prospect. 'What sort of car is it, Fred?' I asked him, trying hard not to let my eyes keep drifting to the painfully bad wig he was wearing that lay slightly skew with his face.

'It's a little green MG Midget, needs a bit of TLC but engine wise she's fine and goes like a bomb.'

That was a shock - I imagined Fred as a Ford Escort man. I imagined me whizzing up the A3 to London in the MG and every other reason I should not have a car literally flew out of my rationalising mind. 'When can I come to see it?'

A couple of years previously and with great reluctance my beloved frog-eyed Sprite had been sold. John had a friend visiting him at Trewyn who saw it in the garage and fell in love with the frog – the friend made me an offer and I accepted. Heart rending though it was, I did not have to go to Cornwall for the handing over, John dealt with that and saved me the sadness of doing so.

'Whenever you like, I'm there most of the time now; just give me a call to let me know when and I'll have her up and running.'

That sounded a bit dubious, I thought, but refrained from saying as much. I would have to put my faith in Fred; he trusted me enough to let me pay for the car over six months, I would do the honourable thing and trust him. 'I will make a plan to come down next week by train.'

'I'll collect you at the station otherwise you might never find the caravan park,' Fred suggested.

Pat covered my hospital duty for me and the following week I made the train journey to Brighton. Try as I might I found it difficult to imagine the previous owner of a flower shop in upmarket Holland Park, living in a caravan on the outer perimeter of Brighton. I was as intrigued by this scenario as I was about viewing the MG.

Fred was there to collect me as he said he would, the ridiculous wig still in place as skew as ever. His gap toothed grin and mock sheepskin coat, worn and grubby, greeted me and I felt totally out of sync and a tiny bit stupid to be looking at a car belonging to this strange-looking man who was driving me off to a caravan park. We skirted Brighton in the Ford Granada without much driving skill on Fred's part – bumbling and cumbersome both - to arrive at a lowly looking area whereupon stood derelict-looking caravans. My stomach plummeted and all my high hopes fell despondently until Fred turned a corner and there sitting pretty as a picture was the British Racing Green MG Midget... out of place, outside Fred's caravan. It was love at first sight and even if it had no engine I would have driven that car back to London. Fortunately the MG did have an engine, so I gave Fred the down payment, thanked him, and with road map in hand I leapt into the car and drove off.

'Let's work one week on and one week off,' I suggested to Pat. This made sense. It cut down on travelling expenses and gave us both more time to pursue our own work. Pat was delighted. Marigold and the hospital administration office accepted wholeheartedly as long as the shifts were covered. It was just the parking of the MG that was the big stumbling block.

'Albert will never let you park at the hospital, it's strictly reserved for consultants and doctors and even then it's packed to the hilt, and he's such a miserable old sod,' Pat soberly informed me as we sat cogitating where I could park the car each day. In fact there was nowhere.

'I'll work on him. There is no other choice.'

'You are insane.'

I made a point of observing the hospital car park attendant of a thousand years, Albert, during the following days. He was a short, miserable, German man in his late fifties who loved to listen to the football and cricket on the radio. Taking the bull by the horns one day, I drove the MG from Esher to London, leaving at six forty in the morning. This gave me a fairly straight run into work and I stopped in the hospital car park. Albert, alert now and wondering who on earth had the temerity to darken his car park doorstep, ambled over in his black grubby suit, 'Albert I'm so sorry, I had to travel by car as the trains and buses are on strike in Esher and we have important admissions this morning, could I please park here for ten minutes until I can go and find a parking space somewhere?'

'Okay, give me the keys and I'll tuck it in somewhere,' He said in his gruff manner and guttural German brogue.

'Oh thanks. You can use it to listen to the radio if you want,' I said with great relief, handing him the keys.

It worked perfectly. Every other week I left home at six forty in the morning, drove to the hospital, Albert parked the car. I played a game of squash, showered, had a take-away cappuccino from the local Italian café and would be sitting at my desk by eight o'clock. The little MG was always somewhere, moved about during the day, tucked in amongst the Porsches, Mercedes and Jaguars of the Middlesex Hospital's consultants', anaesthetists' and doctors' prestigious collection of vehicles. Not a peep or remark from anyone. Not so insane after all.

The jewellery was going well and I was having regular exhibitions at Amalgam Gallery in Barnes, as well as a permanent display there for people to buy off the street. I was also having trouble with my eyes. Doing such close work and soldering finely with a gas torch, I was finding it more and more difficult to focus my eyes again once I had finished a particular soldering job. I went to see a top eye specialist, Patrick Trevor-Roper, who examined my eyes and told me there was nothing to worry about, it was lazy focussing, and other than that my eyesight was excellent. It felt as if my eyes crossed when I was working and I could not uncross them once I had finished – it was a strange sensation.

I had been at Grant's Cottage a year and no word from Robin. In fact I did not want to hear from him, it suited me to be at the cottage. The second cottage was rented to two friends of mine, Carol and Dean from Cornwall, and we all lived quite happily there in Esher. It was preying on my mind though that one day Robin might appear out of the blue and demand his cottage back. I should offer to buy it, I said to myself one day in the workroom – but what with? I had no steady income other than the hospital salary which would not count in applying for a mortgage; neither would my unsteady income from the jewellery. What to do? First, find out if it would be remotely possible to purchase the cottage. I was sure the Ellis Trust was not short of a bob or two; little Grant's Cottage would be a blot on the landscape of their portfolio. I gathered some Dutch courage and phoned Richard Ellis. We arranged for me to visit him at his house just off Kensington Church Street, the following Tuesday evening at six o'clock.

It was an imposing mansion of a house I arrived at that memorable Tuesday. The architecture was typical Georgian Terrace, popular in the area surrounded by the Art Deco of the famous department stores in Kensington High Street, with one of Christopher Wren's architectural masterpieces, Kensington Palace, a stone's throw away. Everywhere drooled expensive and well to do. I rang the doorbell with great aplomb.

Richard Ellis opened the door. I had never met him before and he looked nothing like Robin. 'Come in,' he said widening the door for me to step inside. 'Let's go into the study.' Richard pointed to a door to the right. 'Can I mix you a gin and tonic?'

'Yes please.' I hated gin and tonic but felt churlish to say so. A glass of white wine would have been more preferable, it was summer and it was warm.

'Tell me,' he started. 'You mentioned on the phone that you wanted to discuss Grant's Cottage.'

'That's right. I would like to buy it.' There - I'd said it. Silence followed.

Richard was still tinkering at the drinks table. 'Have you any idea how much it's worth?'

'No idea at all, I thought perhaps you might?'

'Well I know the cottage is small but it is in Esher's stockbroker belt. Properties change hands for a lot of money, very large or very small, and Grant's is bang on the edge of the racecourse – we'll have to get a valuation.'

'It's not really a matter of what the cottage is worth; it's what I can afford to pay for it.'

There was another silence and still no gin and tonic.

'And what might I ask, can you pay for it?'

I swallowed hard. 'Well, I've done my sums and ten thousand pounds is all that I can afford.'

Crash went the gin and tonic; at least it landed on the tray and not the precious Aubusson carpet. One of life's embarrassing moments indeed. In theory I was a sitting tenant, but far be it from me to mention this. I was being totally honest, in fact I couldn't even afford ten thousand pounds, but I would grovel to the ends of the earth to find it should my ridiculous offer be accepted.

Richard put the refreshed gin and tonic in my hand and I took a mighty gulp, trying hard not to grimace at the taste. 'You can't be serious?' he asked at last.

'I'm deadly serious. I have worked out everything down to my last penny and that is all I can afford and therefore offer. The cottage needs quite a lot of renovating and repair so I'm not even sure I will get a mortgage.'

He pondered and pondered, looking at me in disbelief. Frankly I think I had rendered him speechless. This rather nice healthy looking young man with blonde wavy hair and a touch of Sandhurst, in tailored pin-striped trousers and yellow polo shirt – casual for six o'clock drinks - was bemused and bewildered.

We finished our drinks in polite chit-chat, mostly about my work, and with an update on Robin, who appeared to be doing well in Australia. As he showed me out to the front door his parting words were, 'I will speak to the trustee's and get a valuation on the property – we should have a decision by Friday of this week. I'll phone you and let you know.' With that we said our goodbyes and I made my way back to Esher. Richard had not said no, which I expected him to do outright. The glimmer of hope was still alive.

It was a nail-biting three days to wait - luckily I don't bite my nails so they remained okay apart from the hammering they took making jewellery. My biggest dilemma now was should the trust, for some inexplicable reason say yes to my offer, where on earth would I find the deposit and more importantly, how would I secure a mortgage on my earnings? In the back of my mind I did remember, quite some time ago, Auntie Doris saying that she would give me the money for the deposit on a house should I ever find one to buy 'This could be it, Auntie,' I said to myself in jest rather than truth.

Late on Friday afternoon the telephone rang - it was Richard Ellis, who came straight to the point. 'After a bit of research and price valuation, the trustees have come to a decision. You can have both the cottages for twenty-three-thousand pounds, what you do with the other cottage is entirely up to you, but that is the deal. Purchase both cottages.'

My abacus mind quickly sprang into action as I tried to work out what this meant. A huge jump from ten thousand to twenty three did not take the branch of science concerned with numbers long to work out; thirteen thousand more and I had not even got ten. 'It's a deal,' I told Richard, wondering why on earth those words had popped out of my mouth.

'Good. Congratulations, I think you've just got yourself a fantastic bargain. I admired your spirit and your honesty. I'll get the ball rolling next week, and we can arrange for our respective solicitors to start the conveyance.'

He said goodbye and rung off. Shell-shocked would be a mild description of how I felt at that very moment. Not one but two cottages I was committed to purchase in the twinkling of an eye, and not a penny to my name. What had I done? Panic made me phone my friend Patience to off-load what had happened. No sympathy there. 'Those two cottages must be worth a fortune, buy them and sell one off,' Patience advised matter-of-factly.

'Buy with what and sell to whom?'

'No problem selling. You just have to find the money to purchase, borrow from family, friends, whatever. You have to do it, you cannot miss this opportunity.'

That was the end of that brief conversation.

Saturday morning and I was still in a quandary, having lain awake most of the night willing some sort of magic to happen that would enable me to produce the wherewithal to buy the two cottages. The phone rang and it was Patience. 'I've just been talking to Holly over at Loseley and telling her about the cottages, she might well be very interested in buying the other one. Her family are insisting she has her own home and the family trust will help her – she can't live in tied cottages all her life. I suggested we come over to Esher on Sunday for her to have a look, would that be okay?'

Holly ran the dairy for the Loseley Estate near Godalming where she lived in a delightful bothy belonging to the estate, and from where we often went horse riding. Holly would be an ideal neighbour and my whole being soared at the prospect. 'Sunday would be good, come for lunch or tea whatever suits you and fits in.'

My spirits lifted with that phone call. I popped around to see Carol and Dean and to check with them that it would be alright to show someone the cottage. They informed it was fine and they would leave it neat and tidy and go out for the day. I knew they were in no financial position to purchase the cottage themselves, their relationship was in tatters, and they were both moving on. It was a good time all round for change.

Phoning Auntie Doris was never an easy thing. She treated the phone as an alien and spoke through it likewise; it was nerve wracking to say the least. 'Auntie I need a thousand pounds for the deposit on my cottage which I have the opportunity of buying, remember, you said you would help me when the right time came?'

'Who's that? What did I say? A thousand pounds, what for?'

'Auntie, I need a thousand pounds for the deposit of the cottage that I'm living in. There is the opportunity of buying it for a fraction of what it's worth, can you help me?'

'That's a lot of money. I don't think we have that kind of money lying around.'

Trying to keep the exasperation out of my voice but wanting to hold the momentum, 'It's probably in the bank Auntie, ask Uncle Stanley, you did say you would help me if I found somewhere, well I have. I need to know urgently this weekend or I will lose the property.'

'Eh Christine, a thousand pounds is a lot of money, I'll see what I can do. Your Uncle Stanley is very tight, you know?'

Yes, I did know that Chief Inspector Finney was tight. I'm sure he had a good salary with a thumping pension to boot; they had lived in upmarket police accommodation all of their lives with one memorable holiday, a cruise trip on the

QE11 to America and a flight back. Auntie Doris was going to have to provide a lot of pies and promises to extract a thousand pounds from her husband.

It consumed my mind about applying for a mortgage, which I would certainly have to do. The income from the hospital was not enough to convince a bank manager and my earnings from making jewellery had been haphazard, putting as much as I earned back into gold and silver stock – so no-go there. One lifeline was my friend Sheila, whom I had met when she was the secretary/bookkeeper at Chapman's garage which I used in Blenheim Crescent. Sheila was a whiz at documentation and both our heads together, I was sure, would produce a financial portfolio worthy of a handsome mortgage.

Holly and Patience arrived as duly expected on Sunday and would be staying for a light lunch. To ease the tension I offered them a glass of wine, before letting Holly have free range to explore the minute cottage at her leisure. It wasn't the prettiest of places, but it had great potential.

'I really like it,' Holly enthused, as we sat outside enjoying the clement weather and our lunch at Grant's Cottage.

This was surprising and encouraging as I never imagined her to actually like it. It was a good investment, yes, and perfect for a first-time buyer. Heavens! Who was I to know what people liked or didn't?

'How much do you want for it?' Holly asked.

Without hesitation I told her, 'Thirteen thousand pounds.'

'That's not a lot for this area, in fact it's very little. I'm going to talk to my parents this evening on the telephone and see what they think. I know they will be delighted. They don't like me living in farm-tied cottages connected with my work; they think it makes me too vulnerable to my employers.'

Holly looked exactly like Jane Eyre with her long dark brown hair parted in the middle and held back in a bun. Facially she looked like Jane Eyre as well, and her manner was pretty much that of the literary heroine – old fashioned, genteel, and from another time, despite being practically my own age. The dated use of the word telephone said it all. Holly had started the dairy at Loseley and her speciality was the ice cream which she would try out on us when we visited. I had visions of Holly arriving home with a tub of her latest ice cream experiment for me to sample – life suddenly felt good with the idea of Holly living next door.

Later that evening the phone ringing jolted me out of my reverie - it was Auntie Doris. Telephone calls were cheaper on Sunday. 'Is that you, Christine?' she asked without preamble. 'Yes Auntie, it's me,' I answered as I did every time she phoned, bless her; she sounded animated. 'About that money, your cousin Billy will let you have a thousand pounds, I'll see he gets the money back somehow.'

This was very good news indeed. I felt very emotional and tearful about Auntie Doris having gone to such trouble on my behalf. 'That's wonderful news. How did you broach the subject, was

Uncle Stanley there?'

'No, he knows nothing about it. I was telling Billy and asked him what I should do, he just shrugged and said he would let you have the money; it wasn't worth the long drawn out process and time that your Uncle Stanley would take to even make a decision. No, Billy's got the money spare; his plumbing business is doing very well with all this new central heating they're putting in.'

I felt very humbled. My dear cousin Billy, nearly forty and still living at home mollycoddled and adored by his doting parents. Washed, ironed and fed, why should he live somewhere else? I adored Billy and wondered constantly why some really nice woman had not snapped him up. He was attractive with thick black hair, sporting a wonderful quiff that would make Elvis Presley envious; he had a nice figure and scrubbed up well. He had his own successful plumbing business, and was a mean drummer of some note. Now he was helping me out. 'Tell Billy he's a star, Auntie.'

'He says he'll give you the cash, I'll send it by registered post, do you think it will be safe enough to do that?'

'It will be perfectly safe, you have my address?'

'I do, but you must let me know the moment it arrives, I'll be on tenterhooks until I hear from you.'

We chit chatted for a bit and I made promises to visit as soon as I could. When I put the phone down I realised that Auntie Doris had enjoyed this tryst unbeknownst to Uncle Stanley. I knew my

Aunt so well; just the slightest hint of excitement that I detected in her voice, gave her away.

During the next week a surveyor and various other people came to look over Holly's Cottage. To put a massive dampener on it, all the cottage needed underpinning. After much ado about a lot, the Holt's decided that the price of the cottage was low; therefore the cost of having it underpinned made it more than worthwhile. Sheila helped me to fill in the documents to obtain a mortgage. I falsified letterheads and wrote myself a whacking income together with references and hey presto! I got the home loan. Both sales of the cottages eventually went through and Holly and I became the proud owners of numbers two and three Grant's Cottages, Esher. Number one had been sold some years previously.

Friends and relatives were impressed, friends especially as they also wanted to get onto the property market but found it difficult due to requirement of earnings, an affordable property to purchase, so who did they turn to? Yes, I can quite honestly say that I helped approximately five to six of my friends to purchase their first homes who would otherwise never have been able to do so. And I am quite proud of that.

Chapter Seventeen

The Winds of Change

With the move to Esher and the eventual purchasing of Grant's Cottage, my own personal Winds of Change were gradually happening. I knew deep down that making jewellery was not going to be a career; it had been an extremely successful and exhilarating experience, for which I would always be grateful. The job at the hospital was also reaching its zenith. It was time for a big change.

Neville, my brother-in-law, making a quick business trip to London bringing his daughter Alison, with him, came to supper one evening at Grant's Cottage. Being a civil engineer; Neville looked over the cottage with a critical and observing eye and suggested changes to improve and make the cottage more spacious. I appreciated his advice and moreover it had been truly great to see Neville and my lovely niece. How I would love to visit them in Cape Town.

Apartheid was something I abhorred; it went against my own philosophy that all people are equal. The injustice of incarcerating someone like Nelson Mandela whose fight was so passionate for justice and freedom of his people, the black African, niggled and turned like a corkscrew into my very psyche. I vowed to go to South Africa one day and do something to make the lives of the African people a better one. Nola had already moved there, met my family and loved it.

My deep-rooted fascination of the law, and to keep the grey matter working, I had made a huge decision eighteen months previously to study and take a degree in law, criminology and forensic auditing through the Open University... this would cover the gambit of my past experience and give credibility to the future and whatever it held in store.

We never know at what moment the subtle change that sends our life onto a different path and into a new dimension. I met Dennis Lake through a friend, Ann Bell, whose recruitment agency was underneath an office Dennis used in Kingston-upon-Thames, a mile or two down the river from Esher. Dennis was tall, very attractive with sandy blonde hair and was the spitting image of Charles Dance, the actor who we all so loved in the film of Kenya's colonial past, White Mischief. He was without doubt a policeman and this is what we had in common when I inadvertently bumped into him one fine day having coffee at the River Café.

'This is a great coincidence; I was going to coax your phone number out of Ann today. I wanted to ask if you could help me out with a case,' Dennis asked without much preamble.

When first introduced, albeit briefly, instinct told me that Dennis was a policeman, so I asked him. 'What makes you think so?' he'd replied. 'I was practically brought up in a family of policemen.' And promptly went on to tell him about spending a great deal of my childhood holidays in and around the various houses that usually came attached to the police station that Uncle Stanley was commissioned to at the time. Dennis had appeared interested so I carried on telling him about how much the law fascinated me and with my accounting and financial ability I was seriously thinking of making a career in the Civil Service as a forensic auditor, or better still, an international legal investigator, that was what really attracted me. 'Of course I'll help you out, just tell me what's required and when I'm needed.' I replied trying not to sound too excited, but appear calm and professional.

'It's an interesting case of fraud. The employees of a well-established firm of estate agents have set up on their own, whilst still employed by the company using their database, contacts, telephone, advertising and funds. As far as we know they are unaware that anyone knows about their outfit. We have to get a special court order to enter each of the employee's homes and basically raid it and take any incriminating evidence away. This means there has to be a team outside the home of each suspect, prepared. Each team leader, that's you, will knock on their allotted suspect's door simultaneously at a specified time. This will not allow the suspects time to phone and warn each other. There will be five people to a team, you, two plain clothes, and two uniforms. What do you think; do you still want to help out?'

I was still trying to get my head around all Dennis had said. 'Yes, I want to help, but why so many people for each suspect? Surely you could do it quite easily with just two people - feels like overkill to me?'

'It's the law and a prerequisite of the special court order. There could be one or five people inside each home, they could be armed, anything. The important thing is to find evidence and remove it instantly, which the two plain clothes will do while you unplug the phone and keep an eye on the suspect.'

Realising that this was actually going to happen gave me the jitters, but forensic auditing was tantamount to suspected fraud, so I might as well start somewhere. 'Fine, I'll do it.'

'Good, you'll be in safe hands. We'll have a briefing the day this is going to take place, but I'll let you know a couple of days beforehand so you can make arrangements to be available. Please can I ask you to keep this top secret and tell no-one, absolutely no-one?'

This was TV and movie drama enacted right there on the banks of the river Thames. Of course I wanted to tell everyone. It was like winning the lead role for the latest blockbuster but... I could not tell a soul.

An encrypted message via telephone came through a few days later. The multiple raids were going to take place on the Thursday evening of the following week, where it had been established by surveillance that was the evening when each of the suspects would be at their respective homes. I met with Dennis for a briefing at a nondescript coffee bar in Surbiton where he explained exactly what was required of me and stressing that the timing had to be exact, there was no room for error.

When the Thursday of reckoning arrived, at exactly 8pm I found myself with the backup of four other people ringing the doorbell of a house in Teddington, Surrey. The house was converted into four flats. Our suspect's flat was on the first floor and she answered through the intercom, I told her I was the friend of her cousin Frankie in France who had asked me to deliver a small parcel to her personally... click went the door and we were in and up the stairs faster than flash lightning, meeting the suspect standing in her doorway with a look of surprise and then horror once she was read her rights as realisation dawned upon her what it was all about. It all happened in short, sharp, fast movements by an experienced team as I watched over the suspect who would not have got it together until long after our departure, even if then, to phone and warn her colleagues in crime.

Not a pleasant thing to have to do, but if one believes in law and justice these unpleasant encounters do unfortunately have to take place. It was good that I had first-class experience in the good hands of Dennis Lake; it would stand me in good stead for my planned future. I had been telling Dennis this when we first met, which prompted him to ask for my assistance in the raid. 'Give you a taste of what it's like from grassroots level,' he had said, when I must have shot him a quizzical look.

On Saturday morning after the raid I met Dennis for coffee at the River Café. It was a warm, calm day and boats trundled up and down, commercial and private, their owners enjoying balmy weather and the freedom of the weekend. How pleasant it all looked. 'You did well on Thursday,' Dennis said, conversationally breaking my mood.

'Thank you kind Sir, but it's not something I would like to make a habit of doing.'

'Well that's a pity. We have several jobs coming up and my boss would like to have you on board.'

'Doing what exactly?'

'As part of the team, we would like you as part of the team.'

'What team are you talking about and who is your boss, Dennis; I'm not following you at all?' I asked him rather irritatingly.

'Let's take a walk along the embankment, get some exercise and fresh air. I will explain it all as we go along.'

We ambled leisurely towards Kingston-upon-Thames, taking in the sights and sounds of river life going on around us. Dennis told me who he worked for and why they wanted me on the team. I thought I was beyond being shocked but this revelation of Dennis's sent me orbiting onto another planet which I could not comprehend. MI5, Spooks, Official Secrets Act, Civil Servant, Undercover Government Mumbo Jumbo; I was certainly in the wrong movie, that's for sure.

'Why are you telling me all this, I don't understand, it means nothing to me - and who are you exactly?'

'I am Dennis Lake and I work for Her Majesty's

Government. I'm a Civil Servant.'

'You're not Dennis Lake at all, are you?'

No answer. We reached a break on the towpath and Dennis guided me away from the river and into a road on the perimeter of the town, whereupon we were met by a dark grey, almost black, sinister-looking Jaguar, and I was asked to please get in and go for a ride. I was definitely in the right movie now.

We drove masterly, but not fast, into Central London and on towards the embankment, where we arrived at a large building and stopped. I was escorted out of the car and into the building by Dennis and another gentleman who I had not been introduced to. Having passed through security control we stepped into a lift which did not seem to move, but it must have done, as we entered an office of magnitude several floors above ground level with a spectacular panoramic view of the Thames and London as far as the eye could see.

'Please take a seat,' said the gentleman sitting behind an impressive antique desk.

I did as bid, whist at the same time assuring myself that there was no way these people were going to intimidate me, no matter how important and powerful they appeared.

'My name is Ian Hunter. I am the head of the Special Investigation Service. No doubt you are wondering why we have brought you here today under such a mysterious guise, for which I apologise. Unfortunately, that is the way we work. I have a proposal to put forward to you in the hope that it might humbly apologise for our actions today, but might also interest you enough to take cognisance, be of enormous interest and, if the statute and terms allow it, for you to become one of our agents.'

This couldn't be me sitting here listening to this, was my first thought before realisation kicked in. 'They must have drugged me,' I muttered to myself, but no, I did not feel drugged. I was very compos mentis and in full charge of all my faculties, whilst at the same time trying desperately to think of something intelligent and erudite to say in response to Ian Hunter's opening gambit. The tall, thin cadaverous-looking man before me with a shock of blonde greying hair and quick, intelligent eyes, dressed in a Saville Row suit and Turnbull and Asser shirt, cuffs showing fashionably to the inch, cut a formidable presence, as my mind ran riot wondering if the elegant, Swedish-designed silver cufflinks with a pimple of a diamond in each corner, were in fact, a microphone.

'If I hear you correctly, Mr Hunter, you are suggesting that I might well become a Special Investigation Service Agent should I meet with your terms and conditions. Why on earth would I want to become a SISA, may I ask?' I responded, sounding pompous and patronising even to my own ears.

'For your country would be a good start. We have singled you out over the last few months; your interest in the law, finance, crime and justice makes for good candidature plus you are fit and healthy with a keen mind. Your assistance in the raid this week did not come under our jurisdiction but it was a test of a kind. Sorry for the cloak and dagger, wheels within wheels, but that is the way it is.'

I could have got up and walked away there and then, but I didn't. Curiosity, fascination, got the better of me and I sat rooted to the chair I sat upon, looking Ian Hunter straight in the eye. 'Tell me more, Mr Hunter; tell me what could be interesting enough for me to become one of your agents?'

And a story unfolded. What Ian Hunter had to tell me was as fascinating as reading a James Bond novel. Of course they knew where my strengths and weaknesses lay. The SIS had moved on a notch from what I believed it stood for, espionage, spying and undercover agents. Ian Hunter touched a nerve when he hit my favourite subjects - fraud in international funding and the illegal poaching of wild animals by large, powerful syndicates, when the bells started ringing and he knew he had me hooked. 'Here was the very chance I had been waiting for to do something positive and worthwhile in this life,' I am sure he heard me saying, without uttering a word.

'There will be a trial period of six months where you will undergo intensive training both physical and mental, along with a thorough medical examination and an IQ test.' I heard straightforward talking Ian Hunter describing these conditions before I had even ventured into a protest.

'But,' was all I managed to get out.

'No buts. You'll make a damn good agent if you pass the SIS requirements. Britain needs people like you. I think we're finished here now.

Dennis will take you downstairs to see Mr C, who'll be your immediate boss and see where you go from there. Sorry, no pun meant.' Dismissed I was.

No terms of reference, no schedule of pay, no conditions - in fact, absolutely nothing at all. Meeting Mr C was no better; he gave me the once-over, handing me a brown A5 manila envelope with all the instructions I would require for the next six months. After that I would have to wait and see. Dennis dropped me back at the River Café in relative silence. I don't know if he was embarrassed at hoodwinking me into this situation, but I doubted it. I think he just gave me time to reflect upon it all, to make my own decision on being presented with this unique, but dangerous, opportunity.

I drove back to Grant's Cottage in a daze. Once inside the safety of my home I opened the manila envelope to find a stack of money in crisp flat notes, together with the instructions which I was asked to read and then burn, which I did - the instructions, not the money. It was this very act alone that made me realise I had made my decision, otherwise I would have put it all back in the envelope and returned it to Dennis. The situation was frustrating that I was unable to tell anyone at all; unable to share one tiny morsel... it was part of the deal... a vow of silence.

None of it made sense. The SIS did not cover international fraud or the poaching of wild animals across the world. There was a bigger picture and for the moment I was not allowed into it.

Not long after the meeting with Ian Hunter an

offer was made to me to accompany an elderly lady from Petersfield in Hampshire on a trip to Cape Town, South Africa, all expenses paid. I jumped at the chance. The lady in question was a family friend of Arabian horse stud and farm owners, Richard and Diana Sykes, whose horses I often rode during the weekend whenever I was invited to stay at their farm just outside Petersfield. The lady, Eleanor Douglas, had once been a famous dressage judge but was now in her late eighties, feisty and formidable.

'You only have to accompany her on the journey there and back. Eleanor always stays at the Mount Nelson where she is comfortable and her every whim will be taken care of,' Joanna assured me when the proposition soured somewhat after meeting Eleanor, who was spoilt and unpleasant to say the least. I think it was very clear to her that she would not get her own way with me, free air ticket or not.

Taking the bit firmly in my mouth, Eleanor and I left Heathrow Airport for Cape Town in February 1977, I was thirty-four years old. The excitement of travelling so far away and seeing my sister, brother-in-law, nephews and niece was thrilling, and not only that but Nola was living not too far away from them and was now happily settled in her home there. Excitement abounded as I scrunched into Second Class on the Boeing, whilst Eleanor lounged sulkily in First Class; this only added to the joy that I did not have to sit next to her long, drawn, miserable face that only uttered an abuse of negativity.

During the long haul flight to Cape Town I did

give some thought to my new boyfriend, Mark Stanley. Mark was also a friend and neighbour of the Sykes, who ran his family farm near the village of Hawkley, outside Petersfield, where he lived alone with his mother who made wedding cakes for the rich and famous. I liked Mark a lot with his handsome, bucolic farmer's face topped with a mass of dark blonde curls. Of medium height and rugged, not at all out of place in Last of The Summer Wine, Mark was as adorable as a Labrador puppy. We had started dating in ad-hoc fashion, the distance between Hawkley and Esher being a fair drive away and with farmers needing to be up early and a mother asking constantly where you are, poor Mark always felt torn. We met at the weekends and occasionally we would take the horses and ride out together through the Hampshire woods and lanes exploring the beautiful villages and countryside – he was a true farmer and I kept imagining myself as a farmer's wife, breeding dogs, mucking out horses, making jam, I shuddered at the thought. I saw how Diana Sykes had to work.

'We are about to make our descent into Cape Town, cabin crew please prepare for landing.' The flight Captain announced over the tannoy of the Boeing. I looked out through the window of the plane and saw the awesome sight of Table Mountain below me to the right, then we circled to port and flew over an expanse of white sandy beach with the indigo-blue Atlantic Ocean lapping its white foam upon it that seemed to stretch for miles upon miles, before the plane circled away inland towards D.F. Malan airport.

The heat was the first thing that met us as we left the aircraft, at least 38 degrees Celsius, bliss after leaving London at about 30 degrees less and freezing. Eleanor had completely disappeared, First Class being allowed to disembark before Second Class, and there was no earthly sign of her anywhere to be seen. Everyone was tired after the long-haul and when we did eventually get through the officiousness of the South African customs officers it was a relief to see Brenda's smiling face waiting for me. After greeting each other profusely we set about looking for Eleanor, no sign even inside the airport. I was eventually told that the Mount Nelson Hotel – Cape Town's most famous and luxurious hotel – had its own personal chauffeur service for its visitors, we presumed she had been met and whisked smoothly away in style.

My sister's family home was in the suburb of Tokai on the outskirts of Cape Town. It was a lovely modern house all on one level, open and airy with an inviting swimming pool. After check-ing to see if Eleanor Douglas had arrived at the Mount Nelson, which she had, I threw off all my winter clothes, donned a swimming costume and swam in that cool, cool pool.

What a fabulous country South Africa was. I even managed to put aside my anti-apartheid objections and just enjoy the spectacular scenery. We explored some wonderful beaches surround-ing the Cape Peninsula and the Atlantic Ocean that produced some great surfing areas – I was in seventh heaven. Brenda and I lunched one day on the terrace of The Black Marlin restaurant near

Cape Point. We had beautiful fresh crayfish washed down with crisp white wine – life could not get better than this, I thought, as we sat there companionably on the terrace as the water lapped up against the rocks in front of us.

Nola and I spent a couple of wonderful days and nights at her house in Milnerton where she was now living quite happily, having re-located from Sussex following her divorce from James. Nola's house was also on one level, a traditional Cape Dutch house full of charm and character. Nola took me to the Cape Winelands where we visited the exquisite village of Franschoek (French Corner) set in the mountains beyond Cape Town. Franschoek, famous for its many restaurants as well as its vineyards, sits in a valley surrounded by mountains and vines as far as the eye can see. Le Quartier Francais where we lunched remains one of my favourite restaurants to this very day.

We talked a lot about Sarah, who was now living in Mallorca in Spain. She could not return to England because Zach would have to go into quarantine and Sarah wouldn't tolerate that. Nola's brother Donald and his wife lived in Mallorca, Donald became seriously ill and Sarah went to support him and his wife Rosita, on the island where she eventually stayed and made her home for several years. Bella and I had visited Sarah a couple of times in S'Arraco, a small village inland from St Elmo where she and Nola had bought a spit of land upon which Sarah had built herself a small farmhouse.

South Africa would make a lasting impression. The wide open spaces with pale blue skies, sunshine, warm weather, mountains and the great outdoors. I had even climbed down Table Mountain, which rendered me disabled for almost four days – I loved it all. Even Eleanor Douglas seemed pleasant in South Africa on the couple of occasions she allowed me to visit her at the Mount Nelson.

England in March and in the grip of very cold weather was not a pleasant experience to return to; in fact, it was pretty awful. A kind of malaise hung over me which was difficult to shake off. The permanent grey skies, dark at four pm, always cold and wet, set into me like a heavy slab of cement. Then one day the telephone rang; it was my brother Geoff. 'Thought I should let you know that Lily died a couple of weeks ago, I read it in the newspaper.'

Silence, as I wasn't quite sure why Geoff thought this piece of news about my step-mother might be of interest to me.

'Are you still there?' he shouted down the phone. Geoff had the habit of shouting down the phone if he thought you were a long way away like we were from Nottingham to London.

'Yes, I'm still here. Is that the only reason you've phoned?'

'Not exactly. I decided to go and pay father a visit after I read the obituary.'

'And?'

'All he talked about was you; he wants to see you more than anything in the world. I told him I would phone and talk to you, he asked for your telephone number but I told him I'd have to ask you first.'

I hadn't seen my father in twenty two years. I had no desire to see him now. He had made a half-hearted attempt to make contact with me when I first left the house he and Lily shared, but Brenda had told him in no uncertain terms that unless he was prepared to help me financially there would be no hope of him seeing me. Lily held the purse strings and would allow him nothing. I had never in a million years expected his much younger wife to pre-decease him. 'How, what did she die from?' I asked Geoff.

'Cancer, she was riddled with cancer. He's nursed her through the last two years; apparently it was a very unpleasant death.'

The thought of my father witnessing the death of two wives under the same circumstances where he has had to endure the pain and suffering as well as help with the nursing, tugged somewhere deep within me. 'You can give him my number, Geoff,' I finally told him.

Chapter Eighteen

Love You Dad!

It never occurred to me that my father would outlive his second wife, Lily. Somewhere in the back of my mind I always thought how convenient it was that he had a new, younger wife who would be able to look after him in his old age. How ironic was that? He hadn't really featured much in my thoughts over the years. Given an ultimatum by Lily so many years ago – her or us - he had made his choice then, which ostracised him from the rest of his own family and left him alone with Lily and her three girls.

Taking my brother-in-laws suggestions about renovating Grant's Cottage, I approached a local builder to get quotes. There was no need apparently to get planning permission so when the costs came in I gave the go-ahead to start the work. It became a source of fascination to watch the fireplace being knocked out and replaced by an RSJ (reinforced steel joist) which when bricked and plastered transformed the entire building. With a good clean up and new carpet, Grant's Cottage became an Esher gem. It also became the start of a lifelong interest in buying and renovating Grade Two listed properties in England.

One evening I was sitting in the cottage admiring the changes when the telephone rang; once answered there was silence from the other end. 'Hello, who is that?' I asked.

'Is that Christine?' shouted the voice at the other end.

I went stone cold. It sounded like Geoff bellowing over the distance as if it makes a difference if you shout, but I knew it wasn't Geoff. 'Yes, it's Christine.' I answered.

'It's your father here.'

'Oh yes, Geoff said you might call. How are you? Sorry to hear about Lily.' Was all I could think of saying? It's hard to have a conversation with someone you haven't seen for twenty-odd years and didn't know that well before.

'Where are you?'

'What do you mean, where am I?'

'Where are you speaking from, where do you live, Geoff wouldn't tell me anything?' came another bellow

'I'm at my home just outside London in a place called Esher in Surrey, you probably won't have heard of it.'

'I'd like to come and see you but it sounds a long way away. If I pay your fare will you come and see me?'

That's when the tears started falling down my cheeks. I was so choked up that I found it so very difficult to answer without giving myself away. 'Okay I'll think about it. Give me some time, Geoff

276

or I will get back to you.'

'You can catch a plane if you like, I'll pay for it,' he bellowed again.

'Thanks for the offer but I don't need to fly to Manchester. I can drive if I decide to come up there.'

'Let me know when you're coming then I can have a nice dinner ready for you.'

That really finished me off, tears streaming away while trying to sound offhand and distant. I was a lot more emotional about hearing from my father than I would ever have believed. 'I've got to go now; I'll be in touch, bye.' And put the phone down as years of pent-up tears spilled uncontrollably.

Did I really want to see this man after all these years, I kept asking myself? It was a raw reminder of the past that I had put well behind me. But, he was my father at the end of the day. I felt that I needed someone to talk to about it and in the absence of my sister I decided to call my sister-in-law Margaret; she had been quite close to my father when she stayed with us when Geoff was away doing his National Service stint in the navy.

'I think you should see him. Come and stay here for the night and Geoff can go up with you to Manchester. It will be easier if Geoff is with you, once you've met, Geoff can make himself scarce which will give you time to talk to your father alone,' Margaret advised when I phoned to talk to her.

'That's a good idea. Geoff being with me will break the ice a bit. I can't even imagine what he looks like now,' I told her.

'What you must not do on any account is stay with him. Have a meal, afternoon tea, go for breakfast on Sunday, but don't stay overnight with him.'

'Why do you say that? I'm not going to, but just out of interest.'

'You should both give yourselves time. Your father appears to have lost everything, including his family. He will be feeling very vulnerable and latch onto you. You've made a success of your life thus far, don't let him emotionally destroy any of that.'

I was not sure if those were wise words, but it was sound advice - I know that now. My admiration for Margaret was paramount. After marrying Geoff at just eighteen and promptly having five children one after the other, Margaret then went on to resume her studies and eventually won a scholarship to Manchester University where she graduated with honours in Drama and English literature, whereupon she commenced a lifelong career in education and teaching. She was a very attractive and intelligent woman, and Geoff adored her.

Oxfam came into my life quite unexpectedly. I was offered a job as regional co-ordinator for Surrey... no mean task. It came with a car and an office in Guildford. How this position came upon me I have no idea, and if I did, I would prefer not to think about it. The position gave me free range to travel extensively throughout my designated Surrey area. It also gave me a terrific insight into the work of Oxfam, especially in its long term support of overseas programmes in the poorer countries of Africa, South America and India. Oxford Committee of **Fam**ine Relief, an amazing success story started by a group from Oxford in 1942, during the Second World War, was an organisation I was proud to work for and be associated with.

The SIS training and work carried on as instructed and this seemed to work hand-in-glove with the position at Oxfam. My whole world now centred upon Surrey. The hospital job came to its natural end. I made the odd piece of jewellery which took me occasionally into London, which proved convenient for other work I was required to do, and even had the odd jewellery exhibition thrown in to boot! I continued to see Mark who travelled up from Hawkley once a week. At weekends I sometimes went to stay at the Sykes farm where Mark and I would do some horse riding, go out to dinner or just do whatever took our fancy. I was never invited to his farm and never met his mother, which everyone thought was a bit odd. Tales told that Mrs Stanley was a domineering woman and relied on Mark completely. She did not encourage or tolerate other women in his life. This did not bode well; reminiscences of my father and his domineering wife Lily sprang to mind. I did not find weak men an attractive proposition.

The weekend that Geoff and I had decided upon for visiting our father suddenly arrived. I drove up to Nottingham on the Friday evening where I would stay the night, and then we would travel together up to Manchester. Geoff had forewarned father and the plan was for us to arrive by lunchtime on Saturday for the promised dinner prepared I believe, by my step-sister, Doris.

It was pretty nerve-wracking the thought of seeing my father again after such a long, long time. What would he look like? How would he behave? Having last seen him as a teenager it was hard to fathom, or indeed come to terms with the fact that I did have a father after all.

We arrived at a housing estate of single-storey bungalows which I had never seen or heard of before. This was a new addition to Radcliffe, Geoff informed me. We parked outside fathers' house and walked to the front door. I knocked quite loudly as Geoff stood behind me, my heart fluttering wildly like the Union Jack in a strong breeze. I could hear movement inside and saw the outline of father making his way towards the door through its mottled glass panes. 'This is it,' I said to no one in particular. And the door opened, to reveal a tall, thin, slightly stooped seventy five year old man with tears in the pale blue eyes I so clearly remembered.

'Come in love,' he said opening the door wider to let both Geoff and I inside.

I followed him into the sitting room where he just stood and stared at me, tears still falling but more profusely than at the front door. 'I can't believe it's you, Christine; you look so like your mother, for a moment I thought it was her,' he sobbed hopelessly.

The next moment I was in my father's arms. We just stood there forever with our arms around each other, desperately trying to bridge the twenty two year gap between us, both tearful in our different ways. It was emotional to see this man again telling me how much I looked like my mother. Whatever resentments we both harboured could wait; we would sort it out between us, for now it was the present that counted. Geoff had discreetly disappeared telling me later that he had found the whole scene between father and me quite moving which had even reduced him to tears, hence his hasty retreat leaving us alone to talk and get to know each other.

'That was a lovely dinner, Dad, I'm sure you didn't make it, did you?'

'No love, Doris insisted, she came around earlier to get it all prepared. She's been really good to me since Lily died.'

'Well, I'm sure she has, and why shouldn't she be?'

'She'd like to see you.'

Now this was really the worm coming out of the woodwork. 'Doris would like to see me, I wonder why?'

'She's always been very fond of you. Her mother's jealousy isn't her fault, we had to do as we were told or all hell was let loose.'

'Threatened you, more like it. Lily had a chip on her shoulder the size of Mount Everest.'

'She got her just desserts in the end.'

'What do you mean by that, Dad?'

'The cancer, she was so riddled with jealousies and meanness I think it caused the cancer which literally ate away at her.'

'Oh dad, I don't think that's really true,' I said while thinking exactly that very thing.

'You don't know the half of it.'

281

'I think I should brew us a nice pot of tea and go back and sit in the sitting room, then you can tell me all about it.'

We cleared away and washed up the dinner plates together and I brewed up a pot of tea and took it through. 'So dad, what's the problem, you looked very peeved when you said I didn't know the half of it?'

'She took all my money.'

Deathly silence as I took this statement in. Father was not a rich man but he'd had a house to sell, he'd worked all his life even beyond retirement age, and now he was telling me his wife had taken all his money.

'How exactly did she manage to do that?'

'We made up a joint will stating that should anything happen to me you would get half of my estate and Lily the other half.'

'And what happened, since she has predeceased you?'

'She made another will after that by herself without my knowledge, leaving everything to her three daughters.'

'So, she was at liberty to leave whatever she had to whomever she wanted to.'

'Lily also opened a separate bank account in her own name and transferred everything from our joint account into it, leaving me with absolutely nothing.'

'Please don't tell me, Dad, that you knew nothing about all this?'

'I knew nothing at all. I handed over my salary, got spending money and left the rest to her for shopping and running the house.'

It was unbelievable what I was hearing, though funnily enough it did not surprise me. It was so ironic I wanted to burst out laughing. Even words escaped me; there was nothing really much to say.

'I want to contest her will,' Father suddenly blurted out, taking me completely by surprise.

'What on earth for?'

'Because I want my money back so that you can have your fair share.'

'Oh Dad, no, I don't want anything at all and to contest a will you would have to go through the courts which would be a long and drawn-out process. Whatever amount you might or might not get would only go on lawyers fees. No, Dad, don't even think about it.'

'But she's deceived me and basically stolen my money.'

'You just have to put it down to experience and a hard lesson learned,' I told him, having actually wanted to say "down to stupidity" but thought better of it. 'She was your wife and you gave her the money. You would find it difficult to prove otherwise in a court of law. It's a waste of time, Dad, lets just move on.'

He wasn't convinced and from what I could ascertain, the amount was insignificant. It was justice he wanted but I think poor old Lily had already given him that. He would at least have the chance to be reunited with his family she had been so against, and perhaps, given time, he could also have his daughter back.

Overall the weekend went well. I stayed with Margaret's mother, Marion, overnight on the Saturday, and Geoff stayed with one of his children. On Sunday morning I went to spend some more time with my father and really enjoyed talking to him and telling him about my life since we had last seen each other. I told him all about Brenda and her family now living in South Africa and their wonderful lifestyle there. More importantly he needed to know about Brenda's three gorgeous children, his grandchildren he had never seen; that brought much sadness to him I could see. In all probability father would never see those grandchildren that he would have been so proud of.

Geoff I knew would be seeing our father more often now that the ice had been broken. He would see to it that his five children got to see their grandfather and visa versa. Thank goodness something had been salvaged out of the long, miserable interlude that was my fathers' second marriage, but an eternal sadness that his ties with Brenda would remain severed forever.

Being back in Esher on Sunday evening after dropping Geoff off in Nottingham was a startling relief. I'd promised to phone dad as soon as I returned safely, though the minute I entered the cottage the phone started to ring and it was dad, worried about me driving down the M1 and getting home safe and sound. Once again, a lump stuck in my throat; after all these years of living, working and managing on my own, suddenly there was someone, a father, my father, who really cared.

Margaret was so right in her advice. It was easy to see now, the vulnerability of both my father and myself. For whatever reasons we needed each other, I had to be strong and not succumb to feeling sorry for him, whilst on the other hand it seemed natural to want to spend time together. Fortunately the distance between North Manchester and Esher made the choice for me; it was logistically prohibitive.

Training and studying at the Cobham academy was going particularly well. Intensive work on law and finance were gruelling and the pace of it all, death-defying. 'What on earth was I doing in all this?' I had to ask myself a thousand times over. The six month period had come and gone and I was still undergoing intensive studying in the same fields over and over again, intelligence, psychology, criminology. My constant consolation being that most people would have to study for years at university to acquire such knowledge. Oh yes! You had to reach degree level, no question about that, something of which Ian Hunter had failed to inform me.

Mark suffered the most, or at least I think he did from the constant complaints uttered forth from him when yet again I cancelled an evening, a weekend, a lifetime really in the scheme of things. What minute time I did manage to scrape together I whizzed off up to Manchester to visit father, often travelling dangerously through the night as there seemed to be less traffic then.

Out of the blue came a phone call from Robert Day to tell me he had to move from his shop in Ladbroke Grove. The lease had expired and he needed larger premises. The shop next door but one to where he already was had come on the market and it was ideal, also there was a lovely double-storey flat above which would make a fabulous space for his flower décor business . He wanted to know if I would like to go in with him and have the shop as a jewellery outlet. My first instinct was no. 'I don't think it would work, where would I live, there would be no point in travelling all the way from Esher once again?' I told him.

'Sell the cottage and buy here; it has a fourteen year lease.'

'Yes, that's all very well, but it would never belong to me.'

'Does that matter very much? You'll get a fortune for that cottage being in Esher's stockbroker belt, you'll see.'

'And where would I live?'

'On the top floor of the flat, I only need the first floor - there's plenty of space. You will be next to Holland Park, the squash courts, Portobello and Priaulx up the road.'

'Let me give it some thought, I will get an idea what this property is worth first and we can go from there.'

'Okay, but the shop will be snapped up very quickly being in such a prime position, I've got first refusal but he won't wait forever.'

We ended the conversation but a seed had been sown. I missed London in a funny sort of way; the theatre, Covent Garden, Kensington Gardens. John and Flo had moved to Devon, Sarah was in Mallorca, Nola in South Africa, Pat, who was continuously doing her jewellery still, would be delighted to have the outlet of a shop. I could masquerade as a manufacturing jeweller, a workbench in the shop where people could see us working. My mind was agog at the possibilities as a plan began to form.

This period of my life reminded me of John Mortimer's book "Voyage Round My Father" set in the town of "Bugger All". It really was a voyage round my father, and Radcliffe the town of Bugger All. I worked endlessly to squeeze father into my busy schedule when I would race off up the tedious MI and spend time, whenever I could with him. It felt as if a strange premonition was driving me on and when the inevitable phone call came it was all too clear that in the back of my mind, time was not on father's side.

'He collapsed in the house and Doris found him sprawled on the floor. They'd phoned him and got no reply so she and David went round and found him, thank goodness. He's in Rossendale General, here's Doris's number if you want more information.' Geoff explained as sympathetically as he could. Men were never good at these things.

'Any idea what's the matter, heart attack? Tripped up? Has anybody said anything?'

'Not yet, Chris, he's only been in hospital a few hours, they'll need time to assess him and find out what's wrong.'

'I'm coming up straight away, I'll drive through the night, and the hospital should know something by the time I get there.'

'That's up to you, but I think you're daft. Wait until you get news from Doris. The weather is horrendous and it's dangerous on the roads.'

Panic stations struck in. I didn't want Doris to

tell me about my own father, I wanted the diagnosis from the doctor himself even if I had to drive two hundred odd miles for him to tell me. 'I'll take care Geoff, promise.'

'Where will you stay?'

'In Dad's house.'

'Good, well let me know how you get on and what news of father.' And with that Geoff rang off.

Several phone calls later and a small packed bag I set off for Manchester once more, but this time with a heavy heart. It was very cold and the road conditions were bad, really bad. It had been a foolhardy decision to leave straight away, but I never would have rested staying cooped up in the cottage. One of my phone calls had been to Doris to say I would like to collect my father's house keys the following morning. We were cordial with each other and she kindly invited me for supper the following evening, which I accepted.

The service stations along the M1 were my life savers. Atrocious as the motorway might be at times the services function well, and I was even able to get some sleep in the car at one or two, while fresh coffee and a snack kept the car and me on the straight and narrow. I arrived at Rossendale General Hospital early the following morning, not exactly refreshed, but compos mentis. The ward sister frowned upon my arrival on the ward until I told her I had travelled through the night from London and insisted on seeing my father no matter how early it was. It did the trick and she showed me to his bed. There he lay half propped up with pillows, fast asleep and looking like a much older version of Geoff.

He started to wake up once I had plonked myself down on the bed, throwing off my sheepskin coat as the heat of the hospital suddenly became overwhelming. 'Dad it's me, Christine, I'm here with you,' I assured him as his eyes tried to focus in confusion.

'What's this?' he asked as his hands fumbled around on the bed. 'Have you brought the dog with you?'

I looked and saw he was stroking my coat. 'No dad it's not a dog it's a coat. It's very cold and icy outside; it's a fur coat to keep me warm.'

'What've ye done with the baby?'

'What baby, Dad?'

'Our Christine, what've ye done with her?'

Oh dear! It suddenly dawned on me; he thought I was my mother. This was not good news. I decided to go and speak with the imperious ward sister and ask to see the doctor in charge of my father. It was patently obvious from her lemon-lipped expression that a mere lowly visitor should never request to speak to a holier-than-thou, doctor. I think ward sister Merrion had just met her Waterloo.

'He's on his rounds and won't be on this ward until late morning,' she told me in her pinched, clipped expression.

The urge to tell ward sister Merrion that she should perhaps get herself between some of the starched white bed sheets that surrounded her and get a life was oozing out of me, then I thought better of it. 'I shall wait here in this office until the doctor deigns to make an appearance,' I informed her with as much aplomb as I could muster.

'He won't like it one little bit,' she said shaking her head in exasperation.

'No, and I don't like waiting here one little bit just to see a doctor and get a diagnosis of what is the matter with my father.' With that she bustled off, ramrod straight and indignant.

Dr Barton, who was as pleasant as could be, informed me that my father was suffering from kidney failure. The fall at home had shaken him up a lot and senile dementia had started to kick in. All they could really do was to make him as comfortable as possible in the hospital, time would take its own course but it was doubtful he would recover enough to be allowed home.

So there you have it. I told Doris and David that same evening over dinner, having repeated to them what Dr Barton had clearly explained.

During the next couple of days I spent nearly every moment at the hospital that was possible, and the nurses were very helpful and sympathetic. Sister Merrion ignored me as best she could. Dad was hell-bent that the nurses or visitors were stealing money from his wallet on the bedside table, and kept saying so in no uncertain terms in a loud voice. He'd forgotten having paid for a newspaper and other bits and pieces every day and it took all that I had to try to keep him quiet. This was all part of the illness, the doctors and nurses assured me.

Once dad became stable and settled I decided to return to Esher. The hospital or Geoff would keep me informed of any change for the worse. He seemed at peace and vulnerable in his hospital bed and my whole heart went out to him lying there with tears in his eyes. 'Love you, Dad,' I whispered, kissing him goodbye.

A few days later I received the dreaded phone call from Geoff that our father had taken a turn for the worse and was inevitably on his way out. I raced once again up the M1 and reached Rossendale General to find him still alive, but only just. He had been transferred to a room of his own; Geoff and Doris were already there at his bedside. When I took his hand he opened his eyes and looked directly at me as I held, talked and comforted my father until the sad, heartbreaking end.

On a cold winters day in March 1980 my father, Robert Barrington, was buried in Radcliffe Cemetery next to his second wife Lily. Ironically, a stone's throw away from where his first wife, my mother, lay buried. We spent six months together after a separation of twenty-two years. A wonderful six months I would not have missed for the world.

'Love you, Dad.'

Chapter Nineteen

Life goes on, yeah!

Life did need to go on having spent six months in a voyage round my father. There were decisions to be made about the cottage and taking on the shop in Ladbroke Grove. In the end I decided to put Grant's cottage on the market and take it from there, if the shop was still available should the cottage be sold then it was all meant to be. Robert would just have to keep his friend, the present leaseholder, happy and at bay.

A summons arrived via telephone from Dennis Lake that Ian Hunter had requested to see me. We arranged to meet at the River Café near Kingston-upon-Thames and from there we would drive into London as we had done before, a great long while ago, or so it seemed.

'You've excelled yourself,' were Ian Hunter's opening words as I sat in front of the very same desk, with Ian Hunter dressed and looking exactly as I had left him the last time I was in his office, the same file in front of him though looking a lot thicker in volume than it was before.

'Good,' I offered when he didn't seem to want

to elaborate further.

'Pretty impressive, you've passed with flying colours,' he went on.

'I'm pleased to hear that because it was very hard work, tough going both physically and mentally. In fact I would go so far as to say it was tantamount to cruelty.'

A smile came at last from Mr Hunter. 'Oh come now, we're not as bad as that, are we?'

He was quite attractive when he smiled and I suddenly warmed to the man sitting before me. 'Well, it felt like it at the time,' I told him with a hint of humour.

'Please read this through very carefully and sign it if you agree to the terms and conditions. Take your time; it's a fairly comprehensive and important document,' Ian Hunter said, passing over what turned out to be a government-crested tome.

Reading the twelve page document was mind-boggling and totally incomprehensible. I asked Ian Hunter a few questions for which he gave eloquent answers; he asked me some questions in response. An hour later I was being whisked back to the River Cafe having signed the document making me a Civil Servant, bound to a vow of secrecy. I also acquired a coveted number… not quite 007, but not far off.

I had absolutely no idea really why I had been singled out. Deep down I knew that trying to find the answers would be like banging my head against a brick wall. I just hoped in my heart of hearts it would lead me to Africa. Ian Hunter had mentioned that in our first meeting, which ignited my interest as he knew it would. Only time would tell.

Grant's cottage sold for four times the amount that I had paid and spent on it. This was a colossal amount for me and I decided to go ahead and purchase the lease of the Ladbroke Grove shop from Robert's friend. Together Robert and I looked over the shop premises, which were delightful, and the flat above was convenient and ideal. We arranged to meet at my solicitor's to sign the lease agreement, but Robert never turned up. In fact no one could get hold of him by phone, letter or dropping round to his flat in Albany Street; he just appeared to have fallen off the face of the earth. Obviously I was furious as the cottage was sold and I had nowhere else to go, and there was no option but to purchase the lease on my own, which I did.

'It'll be fabulous,' said Pat enthusiastically when I showed her around the shop and flat. There were a few alterations being made in the shop itself; a workbench was being installed, and a few showcases. Window shoppers would be able to watch us working through the window and customers could see their designer pieces being crafted, should they so wish. The shop was at the prestigious end of Ladbroke Grove, almost on Holland Park Avenue surrounded by some of London's most stunning homes owned by film stars, pop stars, TV personalities, politicians and the aristocracy. All we needed to do was ply our trade.

The Christine Barrington, Goldsmith shop opened with a fabulous bang, amid a host of guests including friends, family, clients and the media with food and champagne in abundance – it was fantastic. Both Pat and I were delighted with the accolades and positive response from everyone there.

'It's such a wonderful place to work from, much better than being cooped up in a workroom with nothing to look out on, here we have the best of it all,' Pat enthused after a few weeks of working in the shop.

'Better still; we only have to go two strides for our after work drink at the Ladbroke Arms.'

'That is definitely a plus to this new setup. I really like the Ladbroke Arms, where you can sit outside and the food is good.'

'It's so much better than that dreadful place in Albany Street,' Pat added pulling her face at the thought. We both laughed. 'Talking of a drink, I need to ask you a big favour and I invite you to the Ladbroke Arms in order to wine and dine you in preparation.'

'Okay, let's shut up shop and repair to the Laddie.'

It was a cold day so we plumped for inside where it was cosy and warm; we ordered drinks and food and sat next to the warm open fire burning fiercely in the grate.

'I want to buy my flat in Maida Vale,' Pat started without much preamble. 'I'm basically a sitting tenant and this is a golden opportunity for me to buy the flat as the owner of the mansion block wants to sell, but I don't have the necessary requirements like a full-time job for me to get a mortgage, any suggestions?'

Pat had lived for some years in quite a massive flat in Maida Vale where she let out the occasional room to a tenant. It would be a colossal investment if she could secure it. I knew where Pat was coming from and why she was seeking my help. 'What do you want me to do?' I asked her.

'Tell me or advise me how to go about it as you did with getting a mortgage for Grant's cottage. How on earth do I start?'

'It's not at all easy, Pat. It takes a lot of skill, skulduggery and a touch of forgery to beat the system. You've got to be prepared to do all of that.'

'Will you help me?'

The pregnant pause spoke mountains. I wanted to help Pat because the owner of her mansion block was a crook of the highest order, and it would give great pleasure to outwit him and for Pat to acquire the property at a much lower price being a sitting tenant. My Robin Hood alter ego clicked into the fore.

'Okay, I'll help you.' I told a relieved Pat as we chinked our glasses together in celebration.

Three months later a delighted Pat became the owner of her first property for a fraction of the market value. She was over the moon and we wined and dined again, though this time in her very own home with family and friends. The girl from Morecambe had done well.

Mark appeared to have flown out of the window; logistically our relationship died its own death. There hadn't really been time to nurture it from my end, and if the truth be known it irked me that I was never invited to his home. We always met at Grant's cottage or at the Sykes farm; this was not a natural basis for a relationship in my estimation.

No sign of Robert Day as the shop swept gently into success. It was of no interest to me to find out what might have happened to him though the natural course of the human being with its penchant for gossip brought tales of a serious drink problem, financial mismanagement of his shop, et cetera. It was no surprise about the drink problem but I would have no idea about the financial side, though I suppose it made sense his not coming to the table with his half of the finance for the lease. In hindsight the shop was probably a better place without him.

Early in the year of 1981, Pat arrived one morning to work and to look after the shop. We usually took it in turns to do this, thus giving ourselves time to do other necessary chores like going to Hatton Garden for metals, seeing clients, supplying Liberty's or Amalgam Gallery with new stock. Other times we worked together enjoying the camaraderie, great company and a lot of fun. 'There's a strange buzz going on outside,' Pat said taking her coat off and rubbing her cold hands together to get warm.

'What sort of buzz?'

'I don't really know. Something in the air, not buzz as in the noise, but in the atmosphere.'

'Well I did go and play squash this morning and nothing in the atmosphere penetrated through to me,' I teased her mockingly.

'Holland Park squash court is approximately five hundred yards away from this shop, I would hardly think you would pick up a buzz in that short space,' Pat quipped back in Morecambe twang.

'Ha ha, you have no idea what I can pick up between here and Holland Park.'

'Perish the thought I should want to know about that.' Pat laughed.

'It's Charles and Diana, that's what the entire buzz is about. Excitement in the air, a royal engagement, Britain thrives on nothing better than a royal celebration. It uplifts the spirits. Good for the country.'

'Do you think it's going to happen?'

'Oh! I most definitely do.'

'You always seem to have some insider information.'

'Think what you will, but I can assure you it's purely gut feeling.'

Pat thought about this for a minute. 'It could bring us a lot of business you know; a royal wedding always attracts millions of visitors.'

'How do you know? When did you last witness a royal wedding?'

'I must have seen one on the telly.'

'I think you're dreaming, our Pat. The sort of people coming to witness Charles and Diana's wedding are not the kind of people to be roaming at random down Holland Park Avenue. They will come just for the occasion and nothing more... trust me on this one.'

A few days after our conversation someone came into the shop where I was working in deep concentration on a piece of jewellery at the workbench, I looked up, and there stood before me was

Diana Spencer. 'I wondered if you had a pen or a pencil I could borrow?' she asked looking just like one of the millions of photographs plastered across every media newspaper in the country. Several evenings after that I was invited to a dinner in The Bolton's, an exclusive area of London, by a client of my friend Patience, whose home she had interior designed with a little help from me, and they invited us to dine with them by way of a thank you.

Fabulous food and the finest of wines were served by seriously wealthy people without one hint of snobbishness about them, in fact so ordinary were they that I would have felt perfectly comfortable inviting them to my humble flat in Ladbroke Grove serving up a pizza and a bottle of red from Oddbins – that's how they made us feel. Having said our goodnights we got into my car parked in the road between two other cars. As I turned on the ignition I said to Patience, 'There's someone crouched in the back of the car in front of us, what do you think they're doing?'

Patience tried to focus but it was dark, eleven-thirty or thereabouts with only street lights overhead. 'There look, more than one person, two or three all crouched down - and what have they got in their hands?'

I tentatively looked in the rear view mirror at the car parked behind me. There were people in that car as well – what on earth was going on? Then it dawned, realisation clicked in. 'Those are people with massive zoom lens cameras and they are lying in wait for someone,' I told Patience.

'It must be some pop-star. It's the most fashionable place in London at the moment to own a home in The Bolton's.'

'These amounts of cars with hidden cameramen, look see over there,' as I pointed over to more cars parked on the other side of the road, 'are not gathered here for some pop star. They are all lying in wait for Diana Spencer; I believe she lives around here.'

'Good grief. I can't believe so many cars with those massive zooms are spending the night out here just to get a picture of that poor girl,' Patience remarked.

'Lets get out of here,' and I steered the car out of the almost bumper to bumper parking space. In hindsight I most probably could have charged a high price to move on from the awaiting vehicle ready to slot into my spot.

Prince Charles and Diana Spencer got engaged in February 1981. It was later announced that their wedding would take place on 29th July 1981. England became gripped in wedding fever and little else was spoken of for months.

An invitation arrived for me to attend the wedding festivities from a vantage point on the procession route to St Paul's Cathedral. This was something I really did not want to do, and after many telephone calls later it was accepted that a member of my family could attend in my absence so I asked Margaret, my sister-in-law to go in my place. She was delighted. Due to the very high security, every person invited up to a certain area around the royal procession route had to have credentials scrutinised, and be on the official list for up to two months before the wedding took place. No one after a certain date would be allowed to attend. We had to work hard to get all Margaret's information and credibility through in time, but we did.

The area of Holland Park would also be cordoned off to traffic the night before the royal wedding. Pat suggested that we all meet at the shop as Geoff and Margaret were travelling down from Nottingham, Pat's family were coming from Morecambe and a host of friends decided the shop was the nearest place for getting to the firework display in Hyde Park that same evening.

Amid great excitement, the 28th July dawned. Geoff and Margaret would be staying at the flat with me, along with a couple of friends. Pat's family were staying with her in Maida Vale. We all congregated together at the flat at six o'clock for drinks; all twenty of us, from there we made our way by foot up Holland Park Avenue and on to Bayswater Road and into Hyde Park carrying picnic baskets full of food and drink. It was the most amazing experience I have had in London. The walk to Hyde Park, along with thousands of other people was peaceful, calm and happy with everyone in festive mood and all chatting to each other. This was the English public en masse at its best.

What a firework display, what a fantastic evening Prince Charles put on for the eve of his wedding that night in Hyde Park. It was a superb moment to cherish in most peoples' lives. Certainly my guests and family were pretty bowled over at the entire event.

The following morning I was awakened by the

sound of the doorbell ringing, and I felt it was not yet light outside. 'Who on earth could that be?' I thought to myself. I put my head outside the bedroom door and found Geoff just coming up the stairs. 'Don't worry it's the chap come to escort Margaret into London.'

'I'd no idea he was coming so early, it's only five-thirty; why on earth are they going at this time?'

'Apparently all invited guests have to be through the cordon by seven o'clock, and Phillip suggested going at this time in case of any hitches. They have to catch the tube to get there, no cars allowed. If they are not checked through by seven, that's it, too late.'

'No point in me going back to bed now, I'll curl up on the sofa and watch the start of the proceedings, which I'm sure will have started even at this unearthly hour.'

My decision for not wanting to go and see the wedding procession up close and personal was quite simply that I wanted to watch it from the comfort of my own home. Travelling on the tube and being security-checked was not my style, also once you were in you couldn't get out.

The sitting room of my lovely flat became the viewing sanctuary for the entire day from six o'clock in the morning until twelve o'clock in the evening. Geoff made coffee and toast for breakfast, before leaving to try and get as far as Buckingham Palace to watch from there. 'I think you're bonkers.' I told him. 'Stay and enjoy it with us in the peace and tranquillity of this flat.'

'Rubbish, what's the point in being in London

302

for such an occasion if I'm going to watch it on the TV. Might as well have stayed in Nottingham - no, I'm off to where it's all happening.' And with that he took his leave and left us to our viewing devices.

He was right, of course, but if you live in London it doesn't have quite the same appeal when you have it on your doorstep and travel around the capital sometimes on a daily basis - a declared national holiday meant resting and doing things other than traipsing around London. With windows thrown open and the whisper of a gentle summer breeze drifting into the flat, it was perfect for those of us who opted to watch the wedding on the television. There was a supply of smoked salmon, colourful salads, strawberries and cream, chilled white wine and champagne - really, who could ask for more? We hardly took our eyes off the screen for almost eighteen hours of unadulterated British bliss, only interrupted at times by the odd person drifting in or out.

Geoff arrived back from an exhausting day at Buckingham Palace where he viewed everything through a periscope above the heads of the massed crowds. 'It was really worth it,' he assured us lazy lounge spectators.

Our reverie was broken in the late afternoon by someone hanging onto the doorbell and making a ridiculous noise. Geoff went to investigate and returned with his somewhat inebriated wife. Margaret had, she repeatedly assured us, had the best time of her life. 'The carriages going past our balconies to St Paul's were so close that I could have touched them,' she explained. And from the photographs she showed us later I could well believe her. Describing the moment from her arrival at the invited function, Margaret went on to tell us about the banquet that was laid out for the two hundred guests. Champagne had flowed from the moment she walked through the door and her glass was never empty for the whole duration. Caviar, fresh salmon, smoked salmon, canapés, roast beef, every cheese known to France and the world were in abundance together with puddings, fruit, gateaux and gallons of fresh cream.

Three hours later after Margaret had finally exhausted herself and us regaling the wedding from her spectacular vantage point, we came to the conclusion that her day had been pure magic. She excused herself and went off to bed where she slept the sleep of the dead.

Life after such an event was difficult to resume. The build up and excitement of it all deflated like a lead balloon. Geoff and Margaret went back to Nottingham, Pat's family to Morecambe, and we were left to open and run the shop as if nothing had happened. It was hard to pick up any enthusiasm but I knew it would blow over and come right in the end. All I could say to Pat in mitigation was, 'Thank goodness we don't have such celebrations more frequently, otherwise I think Great Britain would come to a standstill.'

Chapter Twenty

The Gold Rolls Royce

During their stay of the royal wedding, Geoff pointed out a large vertical crack in the brickwork at the front of the shop building, which gave rise to some serious alarms. The building is made up of a row of five shops with double storey premises above each shop. I reported this immediately to the owner of the property who lived round the corner in Holland Park Avenue. The crack was bang in the centre of the property, exactly in line with the shop and my flat above. Municipal building inspectors arrived along with the owner's construction engineer to assess the extent of the damage. Bells started ringing.

The once hairline crack was opening up into a large abyss, declared unsafe and a public liability. A large chunk of the front of the building would have to be pinned back which in lay terms meant extensive construction repair and evacuation of my part of the property. What to do? No shop and nowhere to live for perhaps months – it was a disastrous situation. But not one to be deterred, with the proceeds of the sale of Grant's cottage, I bought a small terraced house in the village of Sheet, in Hampshire, a Grade Two listed building which I would make some improvements to during the reconstruction of the shop building.

Another wedding was in the offing. This would not be the lavish affair like the fairytale wedding of Charles and Diana, but it would be extravagant in its way by having a famous pop star as a guest. My niece and godchild Virginia, Geoff's second eldest daughter, was getting married and my sister Brenda was coming over to England for the special occasion.

Brenda and her family had been living over in Teheran for two or three years as Neville's company in South Africa had sent him there on contract. Their children, now teenagers, kept travelling back and forth from South Africa to Teheran with the usual stopovers in London. During that period I felt I knew Heathrow airport like the back of my hand as I went to meet or collect them from there on a frequent basis.

It was really great to see my sister again. She stayed at the flat with me for a few days as the builders had not yet appeared, let alone started on pinning the front of the building, and we enjoyed a rare and special time together, chatting, shopping and eating out at good restaurants. We were able to discuss our father and I would tell Brenda of the last six months of his life father and I had spent together. It was a great sadness to her that he never met her children, his three grandchildren. How dearly he would have loved them.

We left for Nottingham on the 28th April 1982, together with a friend of mine, Rosan Jones –

whose great desire in life was to see back-to-back houses in the north of England – Rosan, coming from the leafy bourgeois suburb of Guildford found the thought of people living in back-to-backs incomprehensible. What a shock she was in for. The three of us would stay at Geoff and Margaret's for the night then travel on from there the following day to Radcliffe for Virginia and Gary's wedding on Saturday 1st May at St Thomas's Church, Radcliffe. Brenda was to stay with her good friends in Whitefield and Rosan and I were staying with Auntie Doris.

'The first thing I do when I land in Radcliffe is to go and put flowers on my mother's grave and give it a bit of a tidy up,' I told Rosan, 'hope you don't mind. Radcliffe cemetery isn't a morbid place, in fact it's rather pleasant up there.'

'That's fine by me. It will be interesting to see where your mother is laid to rest, she sounds such an interesting person and you obviously loved her very much.'

Laid to rest? I thought that sounded an interesting euphemism to use for a twenty-four-year-old. 'Yes I did love her very much. Also my father's burial place is very near and I want to see if Doris, my step-sister, has managed to get his engraved tombstone erected yet.'

'After that can we go and see the back-to-back houses?' Rosan asked as if she was going to miss out on something really important like discovering the Holy Grail.

'Just you try keeping me from showing you such a northern heritage, my heritage,' I teased her.

It was the last day of April and bitterly cold for the time of year. Radcliffe cemetery was slightly elevated above the town in a large acreage open to the elements. It was always a peaceful and comfortable place to me. Often I would go there and sit on an old bench under the trees, reading or writing poetry. It felt like being in the countryside after the grim, dark mill town of Radcliffe… a saviour, in a way.

The morning of the wedding arrived to a cold but sunny day. At least it was not raining and we were thankful for that. I had shown Rosan some of Radcliffe's historic sights the previous day, such as the Pioneer cotton mill that dominated the town and where my father worked for a great deal of his life, the Bealey maternity hospital where I was born, and the world famous Bury Market, the home of black pudding. This morning we were off to visit the back-to-backs. The wedding ceremony wasn't until 3pm so we had plenty of time to explore.

Lancashire at its best; the abandoned cotton mills, the canals, the river Irwell meandering grimly through Radcliffe's industrial area, warehouses stand empty, hauntingly sad with their smashed windows the destruction of teenage boredom and drug abuse, the indoor market with its few smattering of stalls, once a packed market and the hub of the towns busy and prosperous existence so many years ago.

'It has an amazing charm, what a terrible pity it's gone to the dogs like this,' Rosan said as she looked incredulously at the now defunct Odeon Cinema, boarded up and derelict.

'That Odeon has a lot to answer to. It was the pinnacle of Radcliffe entertainment for both young and old for many good years before it became a bingo hall and before the advent of television,' I told Rosan.

'Now look at these,' I said, stopping the car down a side road, giving a long view of the oldest back-to-back houses in Radcliffe.

'Wow! Do people actually live in these houses?' Rosan asked, mouth aghast.

The long row of terraced houses I was showing her had front doors straight onto the street and a small back yard with a door opening onto a narrow alley so that in two steps you were at the back door of the house that backed onto the alley from the other side – hence 'back-to-backs'. 'Of course people live in them. They used to be referred to as mill workers houses and they never had time to think about gardens.'

'Let's have a look; I presume it's okay to walk down the alley?'

'Sure it is. We can take a walk right around both streets, which will give you the complete picture. Two different streets with houses backing onto each other separated by a narrow alley, interesting eh!'

'You wouldn't want to fall out with your neighbours living in such close proximity, would you?' Rosan commented gazing around in disbelief.

'I think they all lived in each other's pockets in those days. Born and brought up in Radcliffe, sometimes people never left the town or went as far as Manchester in their lifetime. My paternal grandfather never saw Manchester, which is merely a fifteen minute train ride from here.'

'It's hard to believe that in this day and age.'

'Best get going, get ourselves togged up for the wedding and meet the entire family – that in itself will be an experience.'

We arrived at the imposing St Thomas's Church at 2.15pm. As we turned into New Church Street to park near the entrance, there, parked outside the main church gates stood a very impressive gold Rolls Royce and parked directly behind that was my cousin Sheila's canary yellow Reliant Robin three wheeler car, together with tied-back curtains in the rear window. There was a crowd of onlookers surrounding the Rolls as if it were a UFO just landed from Mars. If Rosan thought back-to-backs were weird, this amusing sight was weirder still. The gold Rolls Royce belonged to the pop singer, David Essex, whose girlfriend was Gary's sister Donna.

St Thomas's Church - the mainstay of the Barrington family, where my parents got married, where I was christened and confirmed - was packed. The organ belted out The Wedding March. The bride looked stunning. Tears fell and voices sang loud and sonorous. Cousin Sheila could not stop crying for love or money. You could honestly say it was a truly successful wedding ceremony. The church bells peeled in triumph as we all filed out of the church ready to throw confetti and congratulate the newly married couple, only to be met with the shock of a white wonderland, a world covered in snow and freezing.

We'd be lucky to get to the reception being held some miles away at Smith Hills Coaching House near Bolton. I could not believe it had snowed like that whilst we were in the church and on the 1st May, in fact, nobody could. It should have been spring in all its glory, new leaves, flowers in the hedgerows, a hint of warmth in the air, newly mown grass – alas! This was England.

Following Cousin Billy who, together with his new wife Audrey, was transporting Auntie Doris and Brenda in his car, we did – taking it very carefully – make it to the reception. It was a great occasion and memorable in that Brenda had not seen Cousin Billy, Auntie Doris and Cousin Sheila for many a long year so there was plenty to celebrate and talk about. Speeches were given, jokes were told, merriment got under way, but, alas, David Essex, keeping a low profile, did not thrill us all with one of his songs. No limelight taken from the bride and groom, for which I admired him.

Mark had disappeared off the scene and out of my life, only to be replaced by the beautiful Oliver. Oliver came into my life via the front door of the shop and it was love at first sight. An eight-week-old bundle of beauty wrapped up as a Doberman given by a friend who thought it would be safer for me to have a dog on the premises being a jewellery shop in London. Whether I objected or not, the deed was done and it was too late anyway, Oliver had conquered my heart, there was nothing more to say.

Living in such close proximity to Holland Park was a godsend. I would take Oliver for a long

311

walk through the park every morning and every evening, fantastic exercise for both of us. At weekends we ventured further to Richmond Park where we would spend a whole afternoon. Oliver grew into a sleek and extremely handsome Doberman with top-notch breeding. He was a complete joy to have and take anywhere, and somehow it did feel safer being in the shop knowing he was there. He would sit on the first bend of the spiral staircase leading up to the flat – on guard from every aspect.

At last the workmen arrived; scaffolding was erected in front of the shop and went high above the top window of the flat. At first I believed the shop could stay open while the work was being done but there was no chance of that and even less of living in the flat as all the brickwork at the front of the building had to be removed to fit in an RSJ. Apart from the dust and debris it was too dangerous to stay there, so I shut up shop, lock, stock and dust-wielding barrel and moved Oliver and myself to our new acquisition in Village Street, Sheet, not having any idea how long the construction work was going to take.

We loved being at the old terraced house. I renovated and upgraded the kitchen first, putting in a new red, oil fired AGA which was to prove a massive bonus as it heated the whole cottage throughout during the cold spells and the winter months. The back garden went from a courtyard up two terraces of flower beds onto a small lawn at the top, where the garden gate led onto an open piece of municipal land, absolutely ideal for exercising a boisterous and much loved dog. The front of the house was set directly onto the street; fortunately there were no houses opposite, only an ancient stone wall covered in moss and wild flowers surrounding the lovely old church within it.

One evening it occurred to me whilst looking at the 1950s tiled fireplace in the sitting room of the house that it most probably had, in its day, a huge hearth with an open fire and bread oven off to the side. So intrigued was I with this idea that I got up and started to knock in various areas of the chimney breast. It most certainly had a very large beam somewhere hidden behind the plaster, so there must have been something there. Taking the bull by the horn the following day I decided I was going to knock through the wall and find out. Stuff of madness said friends, idiotic to try, warned the neighbours. 'The house might fall down,' shouted the negatives, 'I bet you it won't,' insisted the positive... that was me.

With sledgehammer, pick axe, heavy hammer, chisels and a surfeit of dust sheets, I wielded the first blow praying that my instincts were correct and that the wall I was about to demolish would reveal its true identity and expose a walk-in fireplace together with a bread-making oven – God help me if I was wrong.

Three days later I knew that God had given a helping hand in the matter. Covered from head to toe in dust with aching arms, aching back, jewellers fine hands reduced to sandpaper and hair matted with plaster bits and pieces, there before me was a magnificent oak beam and the original fireplace taking up the whole length of the wall and big enough for me to stand up in at 1.7 metres tall. As predicted, recessed in the right-hand side of the fireplace was the old baking oven. Standing in the fireplace you could look up the chimney and see metal rungs set into the brickwork for the chimney sweep to climb up. It was a wonderful find and a few days later when I had cleared everything up, swept, vacuumed, dusted and polished I invited friends and neighbours to come and inspect – suffice to say that everyone was mightily impressed. The Heritage Trust's Grade Two listed building inspectors came to have a look and give their expert opinion – splendid, came the unanimous verdict.

There was still no sign of the construction workers finishing at the shop, and on my weekly visits to inspect the progress I found myself disheartened and disillusioned. Basically the place was a mess. I still had to keep paying rent for the premises which to me was money down the drain, with no respite from the landlady. When eventually the builders did finish I went to inspect the flat and found they had been using it to sleep, bath and cook in. I was furious. The shop itself was dirty and dusty, which would take weeks to transform to its former glory. In the end I did not have the heart to carry on with the shop and decided to put it on the market – it sold within two months. That was the final nail in the coffin of my jewellery career.

Special assignments were taking precedence. A long spell working at the Middle Temple with some eminent barristers and at The High Courts of Justice compounded my fascination and intense interest in the law. For a brief time I was invited to use the top floor flat in Dr Johnson's building next door to the ancient Temple Church (built for and by The Knights Templar), belonging to a barrister friend. Late in the evening I would look out over the Temple buildings to see barristers working away over briefs and cases in preparation for their High Court trials.

I loved the atmosphere of the Middle Temple and its surroundings from Fleet Street to Victoria Embankment. It reminded me a bit of Oxford. The buildings steeped in history, barristers walking to and fro from their chambers always a hub of activity, and the Temple Church where you could sit peacefully, and if you were very lucky, you could listen to the outstanding choir practicing... such lifting of spirits and food for the soul. The surrounding trees and lawns leading down to the embankment were a haven and one found it hard to believe you were in the heart of The City of London? Oliver would have loved it too, had he been allowed to enter through the Middle Temple's holy portals.

It was high time for a holiday and I decided, together with Oliver, that we would go to Cornwall. The thought of those long sandy beaches, wild surf and moors to explore were beckoning, and anyway I had hardly been back there since I left to find my fortune, like Dick Whittington, in the streets of London, paved with gold.

The all-too-familiar drive to the West Country along the A303 onto the A30 then the scenic route across hauntingly beautiful Dartmoor, onto Bodmin Moor and down into Cornwall, was like going home. I never realised until then how attached to the county I had become. Years of homesickness fell away as I drove further south towards St Ives until there she sat, the loveliest picture imaginable, with fishing boats bobbing on the water in the little harbour, Smeaton's Pier protecting them, with the Island standing behind like a pretty sentinel surrounded by the Atlantic Ocean, as blue as could be. I was back there in a thrice, thrust into the heady days of the Copper Kettle and the romantic, roguish smell of Gauloises cigarettes.

Of course a lot of my friends and contemporaries had left when I did, or shortly after. We were young and not the drop-outs we liked to think we were. So it was natural we would all find our own particular paths in life. There were some friends remaining, mostly artists, potters and one songwriter, Betty Thatcher Newsinger, who had been the 'bête noire' in my life during the early, heady St Ives days. Betty had, what I can only describe now, as a mad, mad crush on me which seemed to go on forever. She was a talented and interesting person, slightly of the beatnik type, small, thin and emaciated with long blonde hair and a pale, pale complexion. Betty's claim to fame was the song she wrote called Northern Lights, it became well known and put Betty firmly on the songwriter road. Unfortunately her obsession and fatal attraction to me was unrequited, so much so that one day I paid her to leave St Ives and return to where she came from, London. Thinking that had done the trick I relaxed with relief and was able to venture around St Ives freely without having to duck and dive round back streets and shop doors trying to avoid Betty.

It was not to last. A month later she was back. 'I thought I gave you money to go to London,' I said when she nonchalantly strolled into the Blue Haven coffee bar where I was helping out.

'I did go to London, but I've come back.' Betty quipped back.

'You were supposed to go forever,' I said, getting cross.

'Nothing is forever. I didn't like it back in London.'

'That's where you come from, that's where your home is, Newcross. If, as you say, nothing is forever, then please leave me alone and keep well out of my life.'

'Why? I'm not doing any harm.'

'You're doing me a lot of harm following me around, turning up wherever I happen to be, pretending it's coincidental.'

'You're my inspiration. I wrote Northern Lights for you.'

'What a load of cobblers.'

And so it went. I can't actually remember an exact time when Betty's obsession eventually, started to wane. I do believe however that she did write Northern Lights for me no matter how much I pooh-pooh'd it at the time.

Now I was back in St Ives, some catch up time with friends and long, long walks with Oliver. What could be better?'

I rented a ground floor flat at Piazza Studios which led straight out onto Porthmeor beach and the Island to the right. Extremely handy for our early morning and evening walk with a fantastic view of the Atlantic waves lapping onto the beach in front of us. Porthmeor was a big surfing beach and you could sit for hours just watching gorgeous young men, and some women, riding the waves. Brandon, he of the frog-eyed Sprite, my first sports car, met for lunch a couple of times at The Sloop Inn, having a ploughman's or a pasty and a half pint of bitter shandy sitting on the wall of the harbour slipway. Brandon no longer lived in St Ives; he now owned his own successful pub and restaurant in Helford, Near Falmouth.

The Penwith Art Gallery was a favourite place to visit and so was the Marjorie Parr Gallery. I was becoming quite an art collector which meant that I was always on the lookout for a new picture or two to add to my growing collection. Modern, contemporary art appealed to me more than anything else. I loved the St Ives artists in particular, Alfred Wallis, Willie Barns-Graham (Wilhelmina), Ben Nicholson, and Patrick Heron. Alfred Wallis's primitive art depicting St Ives and its surroundings always reminded me of Lowry's paintings of the northern industrial areas. To me, both were stunning painters. The vibrant colours of the St Ives modern artists appealed enormously with their cobalt blues, cadmium reds and oranges, others subtle and subdued like Ben Nicholson. The sunshine and a particular bright light made St Ives very special. The little town became an inspiration to all artists who gravitated towards it.

The Tinner's Arms at Zennor was a must place to visit. They really did make the best Ploughman's lunch served with warm, freshly baked bread. The Tinner's, as it was fondly known, was a real blast from the past and hugely sentimental. Glynn, a very good looking ex-boyfriend and fabulous surfer, and I met up one evening where we discussed going for lunch to Zennor. I told Glynn that I wanted to walk the cliff path from Clodgy Point to Zennor Head, it would give Oliver a fantastic run, then have lunch at The Tinner's after.

'You must be out of your head,' Glynn replied with a look of horror on his face.

'What's wrong with that? Plenty of people walk it,' I said, rather indignantly.

'Yes they do but usually experienced walkers. You'll be exhausted by the time you get to Zennor Head and then it's another hike inland to the village.'

'Good, I'll surely walk up an appetite then, won't I?'

'If you insist on getting to Zennor in this idiotic way, I think I should come with you. I'll get Mary to drive to the village and meet us there. We can all have lunch together then give you a lift back to St Ives.'

'That sounds mighty fine to me,' I told Glynn jovially.

On the morning of the planned trip to Zennor I woke up to find a thick heavy mist lying over the Atlantic and halfway up the beach, obliterating anyone and everything. My heart sank. Clodgy Point was at the end of Porthmeor beach to the extreme left facing the sea; it was out of sight hidden under the bank of mist. Oliver was champing at the bit to be let out, he was all too acutely aware that we were going somewhere... walking shoes, anoraks and back-packs are a dead give-away to my highly intelligent companion.

The buzzing of a doorbell jerked me out of my reverie. It was our doorbell I went to answer and it was Glynn all togged up and ready to walk.

'Is it safe to go in this mist?' I asked him before even saying hello.

'Mist'll be gone in half an hour. If we start off now we can avoid some heat. It's eight-thirty, so we can get a head start before the sun comes out to bake us.'

'It's like pea soup out there, is it safe to start? What if the mist doesn't lift and we're on that precarious coastal path and we can't see where Oliver goes.'

'Oh! Have faith my friend, I keep telling you the mist will lift, now let's get going,' Glynn retorted impatiently.

The scenic coastal path from St Ives to Zennor was quite a hike up and down the cliff coves with astonishing sheer drops straight into the Atlantic to the right. Oliver bounded on up ahead, frolicking in the gorse and fields to the left of the path. For some wonderful reason he seemed uninterested in the cliff-face on the right, obviously sensing the danger. Good Dog!

It was a wonderful, if not an exhausting walk, when three hours later we reached Zennor Head. Glynn, Oliver and I spread ourselves out on a grassy bank and had a well-earned rest. Looking out across the vast blue ocean before us, I found myself dreaming of sailing far away into the distance and beyond, thinking about South Africa and wondered how long it would take to sail there, and did the legendary Mermaid of Zennor ever swim that far.

'A penny for your thoughts,' Glynn asked.

'Strangely enough I was thinking about the Mermaid of Zennor. And then, I was wondering how long it would take to sail to South Africa from here.'

'About two to three months depending on what size of boat you were sailing in. Do you have any burning aspirations to sail?'

'Always, whenever I see a yacht I long to be on it sailing away. My goodness, three months to sail to South Africa, that's a hell of a long time.'

'It's a hell of a long way. Come on, I think we should make the last hurdle to the Tinner's or Mary will think we've got lost or fallen off the cliffs.'

Eating lunch sitting outside the Tinner's Arms was as special as I remembered. Mary had bagged a good table and was relieved to see us when we staggered towards her for the last few yards. Never has a half pint of bitter and a ploughman's lunch been more welcome. We even had hot apple and blackberry crumble with Cornish clotted cream to follow. What pigs we were, and who cares?

Mary was Glynn's girlfriend and the relationship was still fairly new, so after lunch I told them I was going for a little walk around the village in order to give them some space before we headed off back to St Ives.

Meandering off to the right of the Tinner's, up past the lovely Norman Church of St Senara –

where a six hundred year old carved mermaids chair firmly sits – I spotted a row of the quaintest terraced cottages which I had never seen before. Not exactly pretty, Cornish cottages tend not to be, but they were old, very old, and obviously steeped in history. Each cottage – there were five – bore the name of a person. The first end cottage in the row was called, Winifred's Cottage, and was the prettiest out of the five. A young gentleman stepped out from the doorway of the second cottage and asked if I was interested in Winifred's; he was the owner and it was for sale.

Richard Penryn showed me around Winifred's Cottage with its thick granite walls, a front door you had to bend down to enter, beamed ceilings so attractively low, windows set deep into the two foot thick walls, nothing to look over you from the front with its small, attractive garden, and only fields between the back garden and the wild Atlantic beyond. I was captivated.

'I've just bought a cottage,' I told Glynn and Mary when I rejoined them at the Tinner's.

Silence is golden, and from the look on Glynn's face I truly believe he thought I had caught a touch of the sun. Mary's mouth stood open in disbelief.

'You have only been gone twenty minutes, how could you have bought a cottage in such short a time?' Glynn asked

'Quite easily, as a matter of fact. I was admiring the cottage when the owner, a young man was leaving his house next door to go back to work. He saw me looking at the cottage and asked if I was a prospective buyer as it was for sale with agents in Penzance. I told him no, but asked if I could have a quick look anyway. He duly obliged, told me the asking price, I made him an offer which, after five minutes of negotiation and compromise, he accepted. The rest is history.'

'You are truly mad my friend, truly mad.' Glynn said shaking his head.

No one was more delighted than Oliver and I. We were about to become the proud owners of Winifred's Cottage in the ancient settlement of Zennor, Cornwall.

Chapter Twenty One

Back to Cornwall

As luck would have it, Rosan Jones's mother, Lindy, wanted to buy the house in Village Street, so there was no need to even think about putting it on the market. When Lindy heard that I wanted to sell she phoned me immediately. We negotiated a purchase price, and Bob's your uncle, the deed was done. I could not wait to get back to Cornwall.

Quite a few friends were living in and around the Petersfield area and it would be hard to leave them. Although Mark lived near we never bumped into each other. He was still single and hanging onto his mother's apron-strings, people were too ready to inform me. Riding at the Sykes farm and spending time with the horses would also be a wrench but, it was time to move on... or was I moving back?

A meeting with Ian Hunter was arranged as it was imperative at all times that he knew my whereabouts. I made the trip to London and was collected by Dennis in our usual place, The River Café on the embankment at Kingston-upon-

Thames. This all sounds a bit cloak and dagger but it was the easiest and quickest way to head-quarters without being noticeably seen. As I suspected, Ian Hunter was not in the least bit enthusiastic about my move to Cornwall, although it did have its advantages, he seemed to think. He suggested, or should I say insisted, that I have one of the flats in the Barbican as a temporary London base. This was rather appealing as I could then visit the art galleries, go to the theatre and concerts whenever assignments required me to be in London and work permitting. I simply had no idea to whom the flat belonged. As Ian Hunter explained, it was safe, fairly luxurious, and very contiguous to all that one required in the City.

'You are going to be given a new car as well. You need something reliable and fast. It's not exactly a new car but an ex squad car, a BMW 5 series, it's being re-vamped as we speak. With your penchant for sports cars I think you'll find this has plenty of poke in it,' Ian Hunter informed me without the blink of an eye.

'But I have a perfectly good car, what shall I do with it?'

'Get rid of it. Sell it. Put it in storage if you're sentimental about a car, but I want you in this BMW with plenty of space and comfort to carry passengers, like your colleagues, when necessary,' he answered in no uncertain and final terms.

This was Ian Hunter at his most imperious. It was difficult to work him out, much as I tried. He could be polite and charming one minute, dicta-torial and commanding in the next. For some reason he was hell bent on me using the BMW, so

I must just get rid of my car - no explanation, no discussion, just do it. Somehow I did not and would not let this man intimidate me. It all came with the turf for which I had signed a code of conduct. It would be best to remember that. 'A 5 series BMW sounds great. At least it will get me from Cornwall to London in supersonic time,' I said to no-one in particular with jocular enthusiasm.

A faint smile quivered on Ian Hunter's lips. 'Mind you don't kill yourself. We don't want to lose you at this stage; you're one of our teams' best assets. Oh! And by the way, you will have a week's driving instruction at our school attached to the academy outside Cobham. You'll be an expert driver by the time they've finished with you.'

'Will I have to travel in every day from London?'

'No. You will be accommodated. There's a small house attached to the compound which will be at your disposal for the week.'

'Thank you, Mr Hunter. Is that all?'

'You asked for this appointment. Is that all from your side, Miss Barrington? It most certainly is from mine until further notice. Mr C would now like to see you.'

Dennis and I made our way through the corridors of SIS Intelligence as I liked to think of our headquarters as being. Large glass action rooms spurting out papers and ticker tape from hi-tech machines, phones continuously ringing, mobiles buzzing, banks of computers flashing, messages, times, zones, pictures. This was the heartbeat of life on the edge. Dennis could sense my excitement as I looked down through the glass panels at the action, reminding me of the trading floor at the stock exchange. 'You look as if you would like to be in on the action down there,' Dennis suggested.

'It just looks so fascinating, exciting with a myriad of things all going on at once, such a cacophony of electronic sounds pumping information, finding people, finding places,'

'They are the people behind us, tracking, filming, listening, checking, bugging, protecting. You would not like to be on that floor for more than a day, believe me, it's scary.'

I tapped on the door of Mr C's un-glassed office. In complete contrast to Ian Hunters more traditional office, this represented more state-of-the-art of a modern day professor.

'Come in, Christine,' Mr C said in his gentle but firm and very English voice. 'Ian tells me you are moving your home base to Cornwall, is that correct?' he asked without preamble.

'Yes, I'm afraid it is.' Then I went on to tell Mr C the extraordinary story of acquiring the Cornwall cottage. 'Perhaps I should have thought it through before making such a dramatic change?'

Mr C looked very thoughtful; his face softened and his intelligent eyes always inquiring and clear looked into mine with almost fatherly intensity. 'Whatever we do in this life, Christine, we do for a reason. It's not ours to question or reason why. Follow the path chosen, be honest, clear and concise at all times – you will never go wrong.'

'So you don't think my hasty decision to move

to Cornwall is a retrograde step and being distanced away from the SIS is going to be a problem?'

'Indeed not. Come and take a look at this map, the SIS covers the whole of England including Cornwall as you can see and we affiliate with these countries overseas.' Mr C's hand swept across the massive map of England and onto other large maps covering the rest of the world spread across one wall of his office. 'I think your decision is remarkable. It will come with its own significance in due course, just you wait and see.'

If this last remark of Mr C's had not been made with a certain sparkle in his eye and the clean whisper of a smile on his lips it would have sounded ominous, instead it made me feel better. He was a wise and lovely man who, I felt, shared a similar kind of philosophy to my own.

'Would it be permissible to take Oliver, my dog, with me to Cobham?'

'I don't see why not. A woman on her own in the house should have a four-legged companion for company,' Mr C agreed.

A week at the Cobham driving school proved very productive. I always thought myself to be a fairly competent driver, but being put through intensive paces under the guidance of scrutinising trainers and inspectors was an eye-opener. There were four other agents on the course, three men and one woman called Bea. We were advised not to speak to each other about our respective work and positions in the organisation, putting an immediate damper on a week we could have spent having a bucket-load more fun and camaraderie than we unfortunately did. Oliver, of course, had a ball. He enjoyed being on office duty when I was otherwise engaged. He was cosseted by big bosomy Brenda, the secretary and given the occasional run by one of the off-duty instructors. In my time off Oliver and I would drive to Wisley Gardens and have a long walk through the woods. Bea occasionally joined us and she would have me in stitches of laughter mimicking the guys on the course and taking the mickey out of the seriousness. Bea was an interesting looking woman with shoulder-length blonde hair, slightly skewed teeth, which gave her a comical but endearing look. She was a five foot six inches strongly built, feminine lady, a comedienne of note with a wicked sense of humour who could turn her voice into any accent. She was a breath of fresh air.

The conveyance of the house and cottage was going ahead according to plan, without any irritating hitches. During this time I was able to get life in order, sell the car and put various things into place ready for the move, my biggest problem being people to have or dog-sit Oliver when I couldn't take him with me. In the end this became the least of my problems as everyone wanted to look after him, which enabled me to set up a healthy network of dog-minders for my beloved Ollie.

Owning a cottage in Zennor, or indeed Cornwall, had been a dream since arriving there in the sixties. So it would be prudent to say that owning Winifred's Cottage was realising that dream. Historically the row of cottages were tied and lived in by local farm workers. When the owner of the farm passed away, he had bequeathed each and every cottage to the resident farm worker who had worked unstintingly for him. The cottages were each named after their owner, Winifred, Gerald and Doris etcetera. A wonderful story and I loved Winifred's Cottage all the more for it.

It rains in Cornwall. I never remembered it raining twenty years ago, but of course, those were the halcyon days of sunshine, surfing, flower power and love. Now I was seeing Cornwall in quite a different light, where it always appeared to be raining, wet, windy, very cold and eternally damp. In sheer determination I bought an outdoor wooden table and benches to put in the delightful front garden in the hope that one day the sun might shine – it persisted in raining throughout my first summer and autumn but I persisted in barbecuing, serving drinks in the garden and sitting out until bedtime, even if we all shivered through it.

Taking Oliver for walks to Zennor head and along the coastal path was a daily bonus. Having friends to stay and showing off Cornwall, lunching at the Tinner's or Gurnard's Head became a pleasant pastime. I loved the moors above Zennor which stretched along the peninsular towards Land's End, so much so that when the opportunity to buy a horse arose out of the mist I grabbed it with both hands. Bonny Lass, a retired sixteen hands, dapple grey hunter, joined the family and we rode those moors together with Oliver for all we were worth, fair weather or foul. Sure-footed Bonny Lass, used to the Cornish terrain, guided us superbly and we spent many happy hours together exploring and enjoying those moors.

The five series BMW was now in my possession. It was an ex-police squad car; now revamped, it moved like nothing else on earth. Being white in colour it tended to stick out in Zennor where most vehicles were farm trucks or small cars more suited to the narrow winding roads. I always felt somewhat of a yuppie using the BMW and tried not to whenever possible.

Demands from London were coming hard and fast. I felt I was using Cornwall as a refuge instead of a home. The Barbican flat served its purpose well, though the idea of visiting art galleries and theatres became a joke - work took precedence and there was absolutely no time for anything else. When I was away, Oliver was well looked after by Tom, a retired neighbour who lived in a detached cottage down the lane from Winifred's. I remunerated Tom for this service, for which he was grateful; though he loved Ollie passionately the money helped eke out his old age pension to provide that extra pouch of Golden Virginia and a pint of bitter.

In 1986, England seemed to be going through a depressive time. I had to go on an assignment to Leeds and to my great shock and horror saw that there were streets of houses for sale, not one or two houses, but streets with For Sale signs outside each house, all the way along. It was depressing to say the least. Penzance fared no better. Everyone appeared to be on the dole; social security was rising, no jobs, and very little tourism permeated through the town like a contagious disease. I found myself longing to be away from it all, to see sunshine, blue skies, smiling faces and healthy-looking people instead of miserable faces dragging themselves up past the Humphrey Davey monument in Penzance high street. The closure of the tin-mining industry in Cornwall had a lot to answer to.

One day, out of the blue, an urgent summons came through from Ian Hunter. Unusual in that he had never contacted me personally before, but this particular day he did and I was requested to travel to London as soon as I possibly could. It was intriguing and I made the usual arrangements quickly for Oliver and drove like the wind up the M5 and the M4, trying hard not to kill myself before I reached headquarters.

'We have a most unusual situation,' Ian Hunter started to tell me without preamble, almost the moment I stepped through the door into his hallowed office. We greeted briefly before taking my usual seat on the opposite side of his desk. 'I believe you are acquainted with South Africa?' he asked quizzically.

'My sister and her family live in Cape Town and I have visited them there, but I would not go as far as to say that I'm acquainted with the country.'

'How would you feel about going to South Africa for a few months?'

My heart started to race. Ian Hunter looked deadly serious and the excitement of perhaps working on another continent for a few months was a thrilling prospect. 'It would depend on what it would entail. I love the country, it's spectacular but what would I be going there to do?'

'You would be taking on a somewhat danger-ous mission actually.' Ian Hunter pondered before going on. 'The poaching of wild animals in Africa at the moment is at its zenith – especially the horned species and in particular the elephant and rhino – rhino horn and elephant tusk bring mil-lions on the black market. This is massive business and of course is run by a professional syndicate headed by prominent and wealthy people across the continents. It will be your job to find out who these people are – we need the names of the head or heads of the syndicate. That is what's required.'

'Is this at government level, Sir?' I asked, knowing full well that I would not get the re-quired answer.

'Unfortunately I cannot say. You will have a contact in South Africa and various help there at your disposal which Mr C. will brief you on. I think you should take someone with you, how did you get on with Bea Donovan in Cobham?'

'We got on well together; she has a rare sense of humour but is pretty professional underneath it all.'

'Good, then I shall arrange for her to accom-pany you.'

That seemed to be a fait accompli as far as Ian Hunter was concerned. I felt a bit shell-shocked that this was something I was ordered and not asked to do, but hey! The job description came with enormous responsibility and being told at the drop of a hat, where I was required to work was all part of the territory. Having Bea along would be light relief as she did have a superb sense of the ridiculous and something told me, after hearing Ian Hunter's brief on the poaching syndicate, that a sense of humour might well be needed. 'Thank you, I think we'll make a good team,' I assured him.

'It could be a dangerous operation so you will have to draw upon all your resources and take particular care. These people are ruthless, from the lowly poacher through to the head of the syndicate – where such vast sums of money are involved; these people will stop at nothing to protect themselves, and I am deadly serious when I say, stop at nothing.'

'I completely understand what you are saying Sir and I'll ensure that Bea and I will be as proficient as we can be without ringing bells. Bea is brilliant with changing her voice from one dialect to another. We are going to have to use our intelligence and acting abilities par excellence on this one as we cannot go about brandishing firearms ad nausea, otherwise we shall soon cause alarm.'

'That is the way it will have to be, I'm afraid. I'm putting you in charge, your disguise to be tourists, researchers or voluntary workers can be your camouflage; whichever you choose will be entirely up to you and Bea. The special investigation service team has complete faith in you. But be warned, for the greater part of this assignment you will be on your own.'

'The brief is understood, Sir.'

'Good, Christine, very good indeed, Mr C is waiting in his office to give you all the information we have at hand and to provide you with documentation, money and contacts in South

Africa that you will undoubtedly require. You will need to get your house in order, as you might be out of the country for quite some time.'

I bade my goodbye to Ian Hunter and made my way to the other world of Mr C., feeling excited about the daunting prospect ahead. My strong beliefs in animal rights and wildlife conservation spurred me on, and after what Ian Hunter had told about the horrors used in the poaching of Africa's rhino and elephant, I was determined to use my own full resources to hunt out the perpetrators of such dastardly deeds.

My briefings with Mr C were always a pleasure. I found this man gentle, but powerfully strong, with an acute intelligence. He made me feel special and protected as a member of his elite team. Today he explained in detail what was required of me in South Africa, the boundaries, the limits and back-up contacts plus a myriad of documentation which would be necessary to move around freely and without suspicion. This was butterfly excitement at its best.

It was going to be a spell-binding change spending time in Africa. We would be based in the Transvaal and Natal where the larger national and private game parks featured in abundance, and not in Cape Town, which was the only place I knew. It would be difficult to leave Winifred's Cottage and Zennor but a well-rooted sense of déjà vu was sending out a signal that this was the right thing to do. Deep down and three years later I knew that it had been a mistake to return and live in Cornwall. With the halcyon days long gone, it felt as if I was drowning into the past instead of forging ahead into the future.

In a weak moment I decided to sell Winifred's Cottage. That was also the right thing to do. It was soon purchased by a local farmer friend (the son of a well-known writer with strong ties to the Zennor area), who's family already owned another cottage in the same row. He would eventually live in Winifred's Cottage with his new wife. In an even weaker moment I bought myself a brand new town-house in Surbiton the size of a postage stamp. It was somewhere to call home until I decided what next to do with my life.

Oliver was my largest problem. Not Oliver himself, but a problem for me. I loved the dog passionately but it was unfair to move him away from Cornwall where he was happy. Tom loved him and wanted to keep him, but I could not make the decision to let go. He was now six years old and in fantastic form but Dobermans only live to approximately nine or ten years old. It would be cruel of me to leave him with Tom and then take him back after, what could be months away; the choices were all heartbreaking but it had to be done. Eventually Tom and I agreed on a six month period of shared ownership where I would pay for all his food and any vet's bills that might occur. Tom would provide free lodging, endless walks and companionship. I cried buckets of tears on the long drive up to Surbiton, for Winifred's Cottage, Zennor, Cornwall and my beloved Ollie.

There was a bigger world out there and rather than be an armchair critic of apartheid in South Africa, I had for many years longed to put my abhorrence of the regime into practice – this assignment, I secretly hoped, would lead me to further this ambition.

'Well this is a turn-up for the books,' Bea said in greeting when we met for coffee at the River Café. 'You're one moment in Cornwall, the next in Surbiton, and now off to South Africa.'

'Makes life pretty exciting, doesn't it? I can't believe nearly three years have gone by since we met in Cobham and now we're off to work on another continent together. How do you feel about that?' I asked her.

'It's a golden opportunity as far as I'm concerned. My sister Amour lives in Pretoria where she co-hosts a morning talk show for Radio Five. She's quite a comedienne and has made somewhat of a name for herself in South Africa; it will be good to see her again after so many years. She has offered us the use of her apartment.'

'That's brilliant, Bea. What an amazing coincidence that we both have a sister living in South Africa. Amour's apartment could prove pretty useful sometime as we shall need to be based in the Transvaal near the Kruger National Park. I've already been doing some logistic research in the areas that high concentrations of poaching have been carried out. The KNP and its surrounds are high on the list due to easy access from Mozambique which borders on the east side of the KNP. I also heard yesterday that we have a house at our disposal, a remote house in an area called Nooitgedacht outside Johannesburg. It's also near a small airport in Lanseria that caters mostly for small private planes.'

'That sounds pretty amazing. I just hope they

supply a suitable vehicle if we're to be that remote. Lanseria could prove mighty useful as well.'

'I think that's why we're being based in the
Nooitgedacht house, apparently all the surrounding areas are farmland and this is a house on one
of the farms.'

'Oh well, I'm sure all will be revealed once we
land in SA?'

'Is everything going okay with you, Bea?'

'All is very fine, got mother sorted out and
she'll keep an eye on my flat whilst we're away.
She's busy working at the car showroom in Kings-
ton so that will keep her out of mischief. She's
seriously envious about me going to SA and seeing Amour.'

'Yes, I'm sure she feels that you going to SA
and not her, is somewhat unfair?'

'I think she does, actually. She even mentioned
about emigrating to South Africa to be near her
famous daughter whom she adores.'

'Maybe you'll both move there one day. What's
to keep you in England?'

'Sweet nothing really, the weather's crap, the
cost of living is rising by the minute and there's a
serious recession. I've never been to South Africa
but I know the sun shines, it's warm and you can
swim in the sea and sunbathe on clean white sand
– sounds like my sort of place.'

'It is pretty spectacular, I wouldn't mind living
there myself,' I told Bea not knowing for a moment how true those words might become.

The last weeks before leaving for South Africa
were pretty hectic. Briefings galore, inoculations,
planning and clothes for the African bush took up

an inordinate amount of energy that proved a good thing as it gave no time to reflect or think about Oliver and any regrets I might have about leaving him. It was all for the better good of wild-life conservation, I had to keep reminding myself, and if we were on a mission to save and protect the decimation of Africa's beautiful wildlife it would be a significant mission accomplished and something to be proud of.

On the evening of 12th April 1987, Bea and I left Heathrow airport for South Africa with hope in our hearts and revenge on out minds.

Chapter Twenty Two

Assignment in Africa

The plane touched down at Jan Smuts airport on the morning of 13ᵗʰ April 1987, to beautiful sunshine and warm balmy weather. We were met by Bea's sister Amour. If I thought Bea had a sense of humour, Amour out-humoured her by miles and had me in stitches from the word go. A popular radio personality and comedienne with attitude, Amour was an extremely attractive thirty-four-year old, with long blonde hair and a five foot four figure of sexy dynamite, whose volatile moods were the bane of her life and everyone else's that happened to be around her. At first it was easy to see why Bea's mother, Joanne, adored her baby-doll daughter Amour over Bea who was exactly the opposite to look at and in personality. Bea was by far the more intelligent, but on a good day Amour's superb sense of humour outshone everything. On a bad day she was like something from hell!

Amour drove us to her apartment overlooking the attractive jacaranda city of Pretoria, from

where you could see the impressive Union Buildings, the seat of the South African Parliament. It
was quite resplendent and I found the city attractive. During our brief stay at the small apartment,
Amour introduced us to some of her Afrikaans
friends who in turn, invited us to their homes for
lunch or dinner on a few occasions. I came to like
and appreciate these friends who insisted, when
we were present, that everyone must speak in
English instead of their native Afrikaans. We met
such warm and interesting people from Boer
vortrekker stock, who produce good food and
braai (barbecue) delicious steaks the size of Africa
like no other race can do.

After a week of acclimatising ourselves with
the people, the climate and the country, we were
contacted by JV – our man in Africa. We were
collected in Pretoria and taken to his Johannesburg office. JV was a young, handsome, rugged
game ranger with a deep rooted penchant for
murdering each and every poacher that touched a
whisker of his beloved wildlife. He would string
up the heads of the syndicate from the highest of
trees to suffer a very slow and agonising death.
Passionate would be a good description of JV,
together with his unruly sun bleached hair and
dark weathered tan, he cut a fine specimen of man
that most girls would die for. Bea and I immediately liked him.

We discussed in length a proposed strategy
with JV; we would need all the help that we could
get. It's very difficult to explain to anyone in detail
the extent of an investigative strategy without
giving away our particular and successful recipe

of modus operandi. I made JV aware of this, which he quite understood. More importantly he needed to know that we would need all the help that we could get. Already there was a small team at our disposal that we could call on night and day. JV would introduce us once we had our temporary home in order and familiarised ourselves with the Land Rover provided.

Belcharto, in a rural area called Nooitgedacht, turned out to be a very pleasant surprise. The single storey house was set in twenty-one hectares of land surrounded by trees and woodland, remote and set far off a dirt road by a half kilometre drive. A German family owned the house and lived on the plot next door, so there were no neighbours within easy walking distance. The house itself was well-appointed with two bedrooms, lounge, kitchen and bathroom. A wide veranda surrounded the house for sitting and entertaining outside. This was African terrain without a doubt and being far removed from everything felt vulnerable at first, but we soon got used to it and grew to love being there, which was just as well as our assignment in Africa took almost two and half years to conclude.

It was such a fascinating, gruelling and horrendous experience tracking down poachers, middlemen, buyers and suppliers until finally I discovered Mr Big, the instigator who, surprise, surprise turned out to be British. The man behind it all – landed gentry with a pad the size of Blenheim Palace - was supplying rhino and elephant horn to China, Taiwan and South Korea as a potent aphrodisiac, its use in traditional medicines, and to to the Yemen and Oman for ceremonial daggers. All this was masterminded electronically from the comfort of Mr Big's beautiful study overlooking the Capability Brown designed and landscaped gardens of his splendid home.

What a coup it turned out to be, brilliant and successful. A lot of very hard and dangerous work was put into the assignment; risking lives when some poachers were caught, questioned and thrown into jail, others that got away became vengeful that their source of income was being threatened and their lives were in jeopardy. The Big Man himself was arrested, together with his Asian colleagues. I received a commendation from the Special Investigation Service and Bea scored a zillion brownie points. We were on a roller with nowhere to go. The story was big, very big and I decided to record it by writing a book – Cry for the Wild was born, and I resigned from the SIS.

In a nutshell our time in South Africa was exciting and I personally grew to love the country. Its people, the warm weather gave me a sense of freedom that I never felt in England. Much to our huge surprise, Bea and I became celebrities in Johannesburg. We were hailed as the new Charlie's Angels – where this originated from I have no idea – but the Sunday Times Magazine did a full page feature on us, and so did a couple of glossy magazines. The SABC made a short film about our undercover assignment and we were interviewed on talk shows. All this culminated in being inundated with offers of work; some we accepted, a lot we turned down. Without actually orchestrating it, we started our own successful SIS International in conjunction with the SIS in England. One thing became very certain to me after our Assignment in Africa experience; I wanted to dedicate my future to writing and give a great amount of time and energy to the Conservation of all Wildlife in Africa and around the world. If there was a chance that I could save one rhino, one elephant or one lion then I would have achieved something worthwhile.

The glitz and the glamour prevailed in Johannesburg but it was not something that we revelled in. Basically I had retired from the civil service for good reasons, and I did not want to carry on, regardless of the fame Bea and I found ourselves having. My dream was to make a life and a future in beautiful Cape Town, surrounded by mountains and the Atlantic Ocean. My sister and family were there and so were Sarah and Nola, it was familiar and friendly; that is where I dreamt of being.

Mere chance, guided by an invitation to play tennis with the neighbourhood tennis group in Nooitgedacht, introduced us to Sue, who, together with her husband Graham, owned a holiday flat in Simon's Town, a thirty kilometre drive from central Cape Town.

'You must go and stay in our flat,' Sue insisted when I told her of my plans to live in Cape Town, 'it's gorgeous and looks over the yacht basin. What's more, you can walk everywhere, to the shops, the beach and it even has a train station. The railway line hugs the coast halfway through to Cape Town.'

Sue certainly made Simon's Town sound very

attractive, and why not stay there? It would give a base from where to take a good look around before deciding which area might be a nice place to settle down and start my new life in South Africa together with Toby, a beautiful six-month-old African wild cat that I had adopted.

1990 – Uprooting from Belcharto was a lot more emotional than I would have believed. It had played a passionate role in our assignment as a home and a place of refuge. On the rare occasions when we sat out on the veranda in the evening, sipping chilled white wine and watching the African sky - at times thunderously magnificent like a massive canvas of modern art with wide brush strokes of black, red and cadmium orange blazed across it, at other times a deep indigo blue amassed with a zillion stars - Bea and I would remark in wonder at how lucky we were to be sitting there enjoying such beauty.

Simon's Town from the first moment became the place for me. Bea decided to move to Cape Town at the same time as we were still doing work together – she would look for a flat once we were there, in the meantime she could stay with me. Sue and Grahams' flat was superb, it was one of thirteen flats converted from the old St George's Hotel in the main street overlooking the yacht basin exactly as Sue had explained, but seeing it for real was overwhelming. Two days into my stay there I was chatting away to the manager-cum-caretaker who enthusiastically told me that there was a flat in the same building a few doors away from Sue's and the owners wanted to rent it out. I took no time at all in setting the ball rolling, and a few days later the flat was mine – lucky lady.

Jubilee Square, the statue of Just Nuisance with a myriad of yacht masts standing proudly behind him and the ocean spread out beyond, were my immediate views from the flat's spacious balcony - it was pure heaven. Bea was also temporarily renting a flat on the ground floor at the rear of the building, it was a small but perfectly adequate flat leading out onto the garden where there were barbecue facilities, a handkerchief of lawn, and pretty flower beds.

Joanne, Bea's mother, made a spontaneous decision to re-locate from England to South Africa, surprising us all. Her reasons being that both her daughters were living there now, the climate was perfect and the quality of life was much better. Bea was pleased on the one hand but dreading it on the other. When Joanne informed her that she was going to make her home in Johannesburg, Bea was thrilled, 'I've had mother for the last ten years, Amour can have her for the next ten,' she mused trying to make a joke of it, but underneath I knew Bea harboured undercurrent resentment about her mother.

For months South Africa and the rest of the world were sitting on eggshells. F.W. de Klerk, the President of South Africa, and Nelson Mandela were deep in talks, causing world speculation that Mandela's much awaited release from twenty-seven years incarcerated in prison might be imminent. The talks were not unfounded and on 11th February 1990 Nelson Mandela was released from Victor Verster Prison in the Western Cape. This

346

was cause for mass celebration across the universe and we in Cape Town celebrated Madiba's release in ecstatic style.

'Nola and Sarah have been constant followers and admirers of Mr Mandela for years. Don't you think it would be appropriate to invite them for lunch to celebrate?' I suggested to Bea shortly after the release.

'A damned good idea,' retorted Bea, 'we can have a roast lamb Sunday lunch in the garden.'

'That's fabulous; I think you enjoyed meeting them when we first visited Cape Town?'

'I certainly did. Nola must be the brightest button in the box when it comes to intelligence, and her daughter doesn't come far behind.'

'You're dead right on that one. Sarah bravely started her Montessori school some years ago in the apartheid era with children of mixed race. This was a first in Cape Town if not in the whole of South Africa. I think it was very courageous of her.'

'How does she manage, I mean how can anyone run a school with mixed race pupils when you are not allowed to eat in the same restaurants or use the same carriage on a train because it's against the law of the country?'

'The school isn't registered with the Department of Education, but it is registered with the local authorities. Sarah just ploughs on regardless, it's a private school and as long as parents keep sending their children to her, the door remains open.'

'What about the parents - if the school is not registered won't it affect the child's future once it reaches senior school, which might well be a government school?'

'As far I know it has not caused a problem yet and the school is going from strength to strength. Perhaps you should ask Sarah, she's the one who can answer your questions.'

Our invitation was happily accepted. Nola and Sarah came for lunch the following Sunday. It was a glorious day weather wise and we were able to dine outside on the balcony of the flat while Bea barbecued the lamb in the garden next to hers. It was a great catch-up time and we chatted endlessly, drank champagne and put the world to rights, including the future of South Africa now that Nelson Mandela was at last a free man. Sarah explained to Bea about the school and answered the questions that concerned her. The lunch felt homely and familiar with my close English friends, and I was singularly pleased the three of us were now living in South Africa.

Bea was temporarily helping out at the local estate agents which also covered as a sub-branch of the Allied bank. These sub-branches were quite important in Simons' Town as this was the home of the SA Navy. On navy pay day it was easy to see why. One afternoon I was busy finishing off a report when Bea knocked on my door and walked in. 'I'm not feeling too good so I've taken the rest of the day off,' she announced, looking pretty grim.

This was unusual as Bea always seemed to be in fairly good health apart from an irritating cough. 'What's the matter - headache, stomach, chest? Is there anything I can do, like make you a cup of tea or coffee?'

'No thanks. Mrs T in the office thinks I might have TB she's really worried about my coughing and thinks I should go and see a doctor.'

'Is the cough bothering you?'

'It's quite exhausting and the fact that it's not clearing up is worrying.'

'Then you had better make an appointment to see a doctor, if you don't then I will.'

Bea started to feel about with something on her neck. 'There's a strange lump on my neck here,' she said bending down to show me. It was a small hard lump resembling a tiny cyst. 'To the doctor we go. Let's get this sorted out,' I told Bea in no uncertain terms.

We went off together to a surgery in Fish Hoek where, during a break between patients, the doctor saw Bea. I sat in the waiting room and when she emerged Bea looked crestfallen. 'The doctor has made me an appointment to see a specialist at Constantiaberg hospital to have a look at the lump.'

Agonising days followed after a biopsy was taken on Bea's neck. The cough was not improving and generally her morale was low, but Bea, being the eternal joker that she was, tried to make light of the situation. It was a week before we went to see the doctor in Fish Hoek for the results. It was not good news. Bea once again emerged from the doctor's room and hurried out of the building before she told me it was cancer, a rare form of cancer, and the lump in her neck was a secondary. Horror and devastation would be a mild expletive to describe her feelings on hearing this news, and mine were no better.

Six months of action followed, which seemed to be spent in a complete haze. The prime importance being that Bea needed to go into hospital for tests to locate the primary cancer. After long deliberations with her mother it was decided by Bea herself that she would go to Johannesburg General Hospital to have the tests, there she would be near her mother and sister who could visit and look after her. I drove her to Cape Town airport and saw her off on the plane. It was a terribly sad moment; we had worked and got on so well together, but as she disappeared through the departure gate, a sad kind of premonition told me I would never see Bea again.

They were still short-staffed at the Allied, even more so now that Bea had gone. When I offered to step in and help, they welcomed me with open arms. My work was on the reception desk which gave me an insight into the people and characters of Simon's Town and how the small town worked.

Sarah phoned me one day enquiring after Bea. I gave her an update which was not good news. 'I wondered if you would like to join me on a walk this coming Sunday,' she asked.

Not being a walker gave for some apprehension - ah, what the hell, I thought. 'Great, why not, give me a time and place. I never knew you'd taken up walking?' I commented.

'I haven't really; it's just that my doctor suggests that I should take up walking as there are signs of osteoporosis in my spine.'

'Okay, that's a good enough reason to join you, just bear in mind that I don't much like walking, any amount of tennis or swimming, yes, but walking, no. Have you any ideas where you might want to walk?'

'Why not Redhill and across the Simonsberg mountain behind your flat, there should be stunning views from up there?'

'That sounds good to me. Let's do what you suggest and then stay for a late lunch at the flat when we're finished.'

Sunday dawned; the weather was good, not too warm with a light breeze whispering off the Atlantic Ocean surrounding the Cape Peninsular. In fact, perfect conditions for a brisk, hearty walk. Sarah arrived and with back packs a-ready we set off following the contours of the hills around False Bay and Cape Point – how breathtaking it all looked. Sarah and I chatted away companionably, and she regaled me with stories about her life since leaving London those many years ago and how she made the conscious decision to move to Cape Town. 'I felt that I was frittering my life away holed up in Mallorca, Don and Rosita were dead, Mum was in Cape Town and the future looked bleak,' she explained.

'So you went to Mallorca because of Don and Rosita?'

'I went to help Rosita when Don died, he was an alcoholic and only thirty-nine, and Rosita she was distraught. I just stayed on and made a scrappy life there. Mum came over for a visit and together we bought a piece of land in S'Arraco whereupon I built a small farmhouse, Es Pujol. When Rosita eventually died, most probably from a broken heart, there seemed little point in staying in Mallorca, no money, no future.'

'You obviously made the right decision. You've created a successful school from nothing; look at you today with Ambery House.'

'The school is not doing as well as it should be, or as it looks on the surface, we're in financial difficulties. Some of the parents don't pay the school fees, the teachers have to be paid, maintenance has to be done on a regular basis, my salary is a pittance. We desperately need a financial genius, an administrator to take it all in hand, free me up to do what I do best, teach and be a good school principal.'

Bells not only rang but clanged in my head; why did I have a distinct feeling that Sarah was trying to ask me something. I don't flatter myself at me being the financial genius, more like good at finance, was this a call for help? 'Is there anything you'd like me to do, have a squizz at the books perhaps?' I asked tentatively.

'Well, as a matter of fact I wanted to ask if there was any chance that you could, I just wasn't quite sure how to approach it.'

'I would be happy to, Sarah, just tell me when would be convenient.'

'The sooner the better as far as I'm concerned.'

'Very well, I'll come next week for two days and see how it goes.'

We ended our walk and collapsed back to the flat, tired but exhilarated. Some good food and a few glasses of wine later all was pleasantly back to normal; for once I was pleased that making the effort had been worthwhile.

Ambery House finances were in a mess, and it

didn't take a rocket scientist to work that out rather quickly. Being a person who enjoys a challenge, there was no doubt from the onset that I would take this particular challenge on. Having worked my way through the debits and credits it became plainly obvious where things were going wrong. I believed with the tightening of ropes and a firm hand, Ambery House School could be saved.

What a wonderful school it was to be part of. The large Victorian house was in Kenilworth, an affluent, suburb of Cape Town. Considering there were over a hundred children ranging from the ages of 3 to 12 years old at the school, it always remained peaceful, which in my observation meant the children were happy and content. I just loved it.

Having been at the school for a couple of months I began to make inroads into the finances, paid all outstanding accounts, and managed to get the unpaid fee parents to cough up which did not make me Miss Popular - but did I care? No I did not. My mandate was to try and get the school into a healthy financial position, which would take time; each month was showing a marked improvement. Six months later when Ambery House had its annual AGM the Chairman of the school board, Professor Maurice Keeble, announced that the other board members were delighted with my results thus far. He then asked if I would take up a permanent position at the school. Delighted and humbled, I accepted.

It was agreed that I would work on a part-time basis, allowing time for me to concentrate on writing and other work that kept coming in from overseas. Kenilworth was a thirty minute drive from Simon's Town so it made sense to start with four full days to begin with, and then take it from there. This would allow me time to interact with the parents, get fees paid on a regular basis for those who could not pay the full amount at the beginning of each term. It worked well.

Not too long into my work at the school, Sarah introduced me to an ex-teacher called Cait Andrews, an ethnomusicologist from Cape Town University. Cait had taught pupils at Ambery House some years previously, now she was working with the Bushmen of the Kalahari, studying their music. Cait was having a meeting with Sarah at the school when I met her; she was there to seek Sarah's advice at the request of the Bushman leader Dawid Kruiper, who had explained to Cait that he wanted some kind of education for the Bushmen, especially the Bushmen women and children. Cait immediately thought of Sarah, whom she admired, and thought the Montessori teaching method would be ideal for them. Sarah had asked me to join her and Cait at the end of the meeting to see how best the school could incorporate an education programme for the Bushmen. Logistically they were a long, long way from Kenilworth; we would have to work out a plan to take the education required to them.

Cait was known as The White Bushmen. Her knowledge of the fast diminishing group of Bushmen in the Southern Kalahari was amazing. She had lived with them for weeks upon end over several years studying their haunting trance dance, the songs and guitar playing as well as the Bushmen hunting skills, their habits, moods and survival. Apart from being a school, Ambery House was also an Educational Trust, therefore we were in a position to raise funds and take the Bushmen under our wing to provide them with appropriate education that they themselves were requesting.

Sarah suggested that I spear-headed this particular mandate, financially and logistically. Once we were in a position to move forward, the educational part would fall into place. Nobody could have been more thrilled. This was an exciting and challenging project which I could not wait to start.

Chapter Twenty Three

Bushmen of the Kalahari

It was difficult and exciting to imagine what it would be like to meet and become involved with the Bushmen. What little I knew about this fascinating race was through having read the many interesting books written and immortalised about the Bushmen by Laurens van der Post. Over many years I had been an avid reader of the celebrated writer and his stories of Africa. Tales of the vast Kalahari Desert and the gentle hunter gatherers were still as prevalent in my mind as they had been over twenty five years of reading them, inspiring an enormous longing to visit the Kalahari.

Now, here I was about to embark upon an incredible journey. A group of Bushmen were living in the mountainous region of the Cape Cederberg. Kagga Kamma farm, belonging to a Cape wine farmer named De Waal, is an expensive game and nature reserve set high up atop of the mountains. When the Bushmen were kicked out of the Kalahari Gemsbok Park by the National Parks Board and had nowhere to go, the media got wind of this and became headline news in South Africa. Enter Mr De Waal. Seizing a prime opportunity, De Waal offered the Bushmen a place to set up camp on Kagga Kamma in return for letting tourists see how the Bushmen live, hunt and ply their crafts. This partnership would give the Bushmen the opportunity of making money by receiving a percentage of the tourist takings and selling their crafted jewellery, bows, arrows and ostrich eggs, etcetera. On the surface it seemed a practical solution for the Bushmen, but like all good intentions large potholes soon surfaced. The Bushmen were not receiving the agreed percentage of takings from performing for the tourists, and whatever crafts they sold to them at the Bushman camp, they had to share with Kagga Kamma.

The Bushmen, having created a typical environment to the kind of life that they led as hunter gatherers in the Kalahari - both male and female appear totally naked apart from wearing a scant, animal-skin loincloth to cover their genitalia - the Bushman are a massive draw card for local and international tourists to visit. Mr De Waal was making a killing.

Education was what the leader of the Bushmen requested and education was what Ambery House Educational Trust would do our very best to supply. It was not going to be easy but logistically Kagga Kamma was the best place to start from, being a mere two hour drive from Cape Town whilst the Kalahari was a nine to ten hour drive. Some of the Bushmen group had chosen to stay up in the Kalahari region setting up a small camp on the perimeter of the Kalahari Gemsbok Park. The rest were lured by promises of earning money and chose to live in the Cederberg.

At an Ambery House Trust meeting Jennifer Moore, one of the school's senior teachers, was identified as being the right person to co-ordinate the education programme in liaison with Sarah. I would oversee the programme from the financial side.

One Friday morning very early, the three of us set off in the school microbus making the first of many, three day trips to meet up with Cait Andrews at Kagga Kamma to be officially introduced to the Bushmen group who were settled there, this included the leader, Dawid Kruiper and his wife Sanna. I felt the excitement brewing as we entered the reserve. Surrounded by amazing sculptured rock formations and dried-up salt pans, it held a sense of timelessness from another world.

We arrived at the Kagga Kamma office, who were expecting us and to make ourselves known. The Manager, Michel Draper, and his girlfriend, Belle, greeted us enthusiastically; they were both Afrikaners who appeared charming and helpful. Taking us immediately to one of the spacious self-catering houses we had booked, they were eager to explain that the accommodation was free gratis for the three days we were booked in at Kagga Kamma.

'That's a good start,' remarked Jenny when Michel and Belle finally left us to unpack.

'They could be currying favour. Cait mentioned at some point during our discussions that

Belle was a teacher and might perhaps be incorporated into the teaching programme – it would make sense as she's here on the spot,' Sarah remarked.

'It would certainly make sense. We'll see what kind of mettle she has in her first,' I piped in.

We showered, changed and treated ourselves to a steaming hot cup of fresh coffee before embarking into the microbus for our short trip to the Bushmen camp and the large impressive thatched barn that De Waal had specially built – a place for the Bushmen to entertain and impress his clients and the tourists.

First and foremost, Cait explained, the Bushmen do not like to be called or referred to as the Khoi San, despite the popular belief of some Europeans, Americans and anthropologists who insist on doing so. Dawid Kruiper comes from a long lineage of Bushmen and he says his people are Bushmen of the Khomani San and must not be referred to as the Khoi San. We understood this completely. In other words it would be like calling a Scotsman an Englishman! Perish the thought.

We drive about half a kilometre away from the game reserve into what could pass as the African Bush, until we reached the imposing thatched barn, long low and well built to blend in with the surroundings. We emerged from the microbus to find nobody there; we searched the impressive barn – empty. A strange quietness pervaded the still hot air around us, when quite soundlessly, one by one, the Bushmen appeared out of nowhere, children, men and women, followed lastly by Cait.

Seeing those first Bushmen children was captivating. Meeting the men and the womenfolk was an added bonus. Although small in stature, the Bushmen are perfectly proportioned with lithe sinewy bodies, tiny high cheek-boned faces and hair resembling black peppercorns spread over their head. How lovely they were and how humbled I felt in their company.

Cait stepped forward with an elder man who I presumed to be the leader of the group, Dawid Kruiper. 'Dawid, these are the people who are going to start an education programme for your women and children, this is Sarah, Jenny and Christine.' And to us, 'This is Dawid Kruiper, the eldest son of Regopstaan Kruiper, the leader of the group who is ninety-six years old and very ill at home in the Kalahari, so Dawid is the acting leader.'

The broadest smile and the dirtiest teeth I have every seen beamed back at us, a dentist's dream to die for. Dawid spoke in the tongue-clicking language of the Bushmen, indecipherable to me and my colleagues, but somehow we caught the gist with all the hand gestures and Cait's response. Dawid seemed very delighted we were there and as far as he was concerned we were very important and there to help his people – the last remaining Bushmen of the Kalahari.

Without even knowing it I fell hook, line and sinker. The Bushmen made such an impression upon me that I made a pledge to put my energies and resources in the very best way that I could to these first people of Africa. Having seen the afternoon group of tourists arrive at the Bushmen camp, it was blatantly obvious that a show was being performed. The Bushmen group had met us in Western clothes, t-shirts, shorts, skirts and blouses; now they appeared naked except for the traditional loincloth and brandishing spears, bows and arrows. Instinctively we as a group did not like the set-up at Kagga Kamma, but it was the Bushmen's choice to live and work there, so we had to devise an educational plan around that.

'I think a Montessori mobile classroom is the answer,' Sarah suggested when we gathered together later in the barn after the tourists had left.

'What is a mobile classroom?' I asked.

'Look, I'll draw you a picture in the sand so you can all get an idea.' Whereupon she looked for a long stick and began to map out her plan. 'Basically it is two wooden book cases approximately one metre square with deep shelves to put the Montessori teaching equipment on. These two cases would be hinged together to open out like a book, which could be locked up and safe when not in use.'

'Bloody brilliant idea,' enthused Jenny, temporarily forgetting the company we were in using such expletives. 'But wouldn't it be very heavy to move about, one wooden book case of that size is heavy enough.'

'It would have about four to six heavy duty castors on each case, thus enabling it to be wheeled about wherever the Bushmen have a classroom setup. The educational trust has some funding in hand for such a project, I think this would be perfect. We can then apply to donor organisations for sustainability funding to keep the project going on a long-term basis.'

'If the Bushmen decided to return to the outskirts of the Kalahari area then the mobile classrooms could be taken there - is that the idea, Sarah?' Jenny asked

'That's the basic idea. Wherever the Bushmen choose to eventually settle, or even if they remain nomadic, these mobile classrooms can always be utilised as long as it's logistically possible. For instance, if they decide to travel into the interior of the Kalahari then it would be impossible.'

'Just as a matter of interest, the Bushmen are applying to the South African Government to get land re-appropriated to them after being removed out of the Kalahari. A human rights lawyer together with the Minister of Land Affairs is working together with them,' Cait matter-of-factly informed us.

This was something I could get my teeth into. Re-appropriating land for the Bushmen to at least have a permanent place to settle would be something worthwhile. With their nomadic days numbered as the onslaught of western civilisation dug deep into the African interior, it became all too clear that time for the Bushmen had irrevocably changed. I had contacts, a certain amount of clout which I could bring to the table. On our return to Cape Town I would set upon putting the wheels in motion.

Enormous enthusiasm and a fair whack of money later, the Southern Kalahari Bushmen Trust was formed with the sole purpose of re-appropriating a sizeable chunk of land that could be given over to them in lieu of the vast tracts of desert that had been their nomadic home for centuries, long before the black African arrived on the continent.

During my time at Ambery House the school's involvement with the Bushmen became an integral part of the educational process; and from my part, and on a personal level, it delved deep into my conscience what we, as human beings, do to each other in the name of progress and humanitarianism, beggars' belief. The Bushmen themselves had requested some kind of education and when approached by myself with regard to their land claim, Dawid Kruiper and the rest of the group had been more than enthusiastic that they gave me a written mandate to act on their behalf together with the human rights lawyer, Mark Reynolds. In 1994 South Africa was abuzz with the upcoming fair and free elections and the advent of the African National Congress party winning the elections making Nelson Mandela the first black African to become President of the country. Such an exciting time, and the way forward was becoming a reality – I would fight for the injustices of the previously disadvantaged with courage and passion, starting with the Bushmen.

We were surging forward in the new Rainbow Nation. Ambery House School was able to apply for registration with the Department of Education, and I was there to bear witness when the dour-looking inspectors arrived to carry out a thorough and intensive inspection. 'They're a pretty foreboding couple,' I remarked to Sarah when she popped into my office to collect something.

'They are quite dour, but pleasant. Just getting on with the job at hand, and quite frankly I would prefer them to be like they are than flippant and talkative.'

'What do you think our chances are of getting registered?'

'It's an unusual situation, to say the least. The inspectors seemed pleasantly surprised when we met in my office. I gave them a brief tour around the school to show them where everything is. They will observe and do their inspection over a couple of days, that is all I can do; the rest is up to them. Let's just keep our fingers crossed that the school conforms to the expected curriculum, size, health and safety.'

'Nobody runs a school better than you do, Sarah. It's completely transparent for everyone to see how happy the children are and when they move on to senior school our children seem to excel. You can't get better than that.'

'That's the way we see it and you're right, but the education authority see things in a completely different light. Let's just see what they come up with. How are things going with the Bushmen land claim?'

It's a long process. We're having a big indaba in Welkom the weekend after next with the entire Bushmen group, including old Regopstaan who is still holding on to life by a thread, the human rights lawyer, Mark Reynolds, the minister of land affairs, Derek Hanekom and Andrew Martin, the elephant expert from the Kalahari Gemsbok Park. The meeting should be very interesting.'

'I wish I was coming with you. It will be a piece

of history in the making to have these important people together on the red sand dunes of Welkom where the Bushmen have temporarily made their home.'

'Please come along, it would be great to have you there; some input from you would be much appreciated. We will travel there in the microbus and stay for the weekend, the meeting is on Sunday morning in Welkom.' I told Sarah because I knew that the Bushmen would be delighted to see her there. To have more on the Bushmen side – the better.

'Well, I have to say it would be fantastic to be there. Let me look at my diary and see if I have anything else on over that weekend.'

'There's sure to be a philosophy school function.' I heard myself say rather churlishly.

'If there is then maybe I can excuse myself.'

'Please try. Your presence there would mean a lot to the Bushmen.'

It felt as if I was pleading a bit, but Sarah has a wise head on her and it would mean a lot to both the Bushmen and to me if she could make the meeting, Andrew Martin and David Hanekom together would be a force to be reckoned with, so the more batting on our team, the better.

There is nothing at all like waking up in the early morning around 3.30am to begin a journey. Still dark and silent with an empty eeriness, I started the already packed-up microbus and we were off. Much to my delight, both Sarah and Jenny were accompanying me. We would meet up with Cait and her friend Andre in the Kalahari. A couple of hours out of Cape Town we were driving over mountain passes with dawn breaking and the sun rising, creating such a spectacular sky it took our breath away – this is what makes Africa so very special. We stopped for an early breakfast which would set us up for the rest of the seven-hour-long journey up into the Northern Cape and the Kalahari.

The indaba turned out to be a great success. Set amongst the red Kalahari sand dunes, we gathered together and thrashed out the pros and cons of re-appropriating land for the Bushmen. The great leader of the Khomani San and Dawid's father, Regopstaan - at ninety six years old and seriously ill... attended. For him it would be a lifetime's dream to see justice for the Bushmen. Andrew Martin was against the Bushmen returning to any part of the Gemsbok Park as it was protected by the South African National Parks Board, and the Bushmen were still hunter-gatherers. However this point brought home the necessity for the Bushmen to have somewhere of their own where they could put down some roots in an area as close as possible to their natural habitat.

We left the Kalahari feeling elated. Dawid Kruiper had been summoned to an appointment with Nelson Mandela and asked us for a lift to Cape Town. So off we set with Dawid perched in the back seat of the microbus, dressed in a beautiful, brightly-coloured cashmere sweater which Sarah's mother had donated to the Bushmen women - Dawid had claimed it instead, because he could. He presented a comical figure sitting back where he could spread out his recently broken leg, and was not impressed when told he couldn't smoke in the bus. At our first petrol stop he was out of the bus and away for a smoke, it took us half an hour to find him again – surrounded by a group of local people who had seen him on television – Dawid sat puffing away on his roll-up relaying old Bushmen stories with not a care in the world. Unfortunately this happened at every stop that was needed to get petrol, making the nine hour journey a good deal longer than it should have been.

We dropped Sarah off first. 'Thanks a million, Sarah. I'm sure your presence there was paramount to the negotiations. It was really great to have you along,' I shouted after her as she disappeared into her welcoming front door.

'What a fantastic weekend it was. I would not have missed it for anything – it will go down in the annals of history. The Bushmen deserve recognition and securing an area where they can call their own would be something very special,' Jen said passionately as we at last neared my home and the end of an eventful journey.

Falling into a much-welcome bed that evening, my mind kept drifting back to the wondrous look on the faces of the Bushmen, women and children, all there in support of their leader on such a historical occasion. I admired the high-cheeked, slightly Mongolian-looking Bushmen with their caramel-coloured skin, kind hearts and welcoming hospitality. I fell asleep and dreamt of wide expanses of savannah with a river running through it and trees abundant on its banks – how perfect a place that would be for my Bushmen.

One morning soon after our trip to the Ka-lahari, Sarah called me into her office and handed me a letter. 'Read this,' she said, with little enthusiasm. I saw it was from the Department of Education and a cold chill went up my spine as I started to read it. Glossing over the paragraphs that meant nothing to me, at the very end it read: We are pleased to inform you that Ambery House School has been recommended for full registration with the Department of Education. 'That's bloody fantastic!' I almost shouted before realising I was in the school.

'I though you'd be pleased,' Sarah said with a smile as wide as the cat that got the cream.

'So those dour-looking inspectors have come up trumps. Would you ever have thought it?'

'When they left the school they did come in and thank me and both said what a pleasure it had been – it was the nicest school they had been to.'

'Congratulations Sarah, you deserve it. After all you've put into making the school what it is to-day; this is a superb compliment to you.'

'Rubbish, it's not just me; it's everyone in-volved, the staff, the children, even you. Had you not put the school back onto a financial track it might well have folded by now.'

'That's not the point and it's not up for discus-sion. After these long years and against all odds you have made a very successful school. I think we should celebrate in style – champagne on Friday after school with all the staff.'

'You took the same idea out of my head.'

'Good, at least we know that great minds think

alike.' I finished with a big smile and a hug for Sarah.

Some months later, after lengthy amounts of form filling and a zillion questions answered and one or two small changes, Ambery House School was, after fourteen years in existence, legally registered with The Department of Education.

The Bushmen land claim went through a quiet period as far as the trust and I was concerned. We had done everything that we could, and it was now up to the lawyer, Mark Reynolds and the Minister of Land Affairs, Derek Hanekom to present it to parliament and await the outcome. There were many people making land claims during the mid-nineties, so the Bushmen land claim was no exception – patience was a virtue and we would have to await our turn like everybody else. In the meantime the Bushmen school was going well, Belle was teaching the little ones in the big barn, and Jenny or another teacher would travel to Kagga Kamma once a month for a few days to check Belle's progress and take over some teaching themselves as the Bushmen women were also part of the learning and teaching programme. On some occasions I went with one of the teachers, merely as co-driver and company, but mostly I liked spending time with the Bushmen who never ceased to enthral and amaze me with their hunting techniques, their running abilities, their extraordinary acute hearing and the mesmerising trance dance. I hadn't quite taken to the Bushmen's favourite speciality of cooked donkey, but they did bake mean dough bread over the coals, which I loved.

We were now deep in post elections. Nelson Mandela became the first black President of South Africa and the rainbow nation was born. It was a fantastic time to be in the country, to experience all the changes and to bear witness to the transition of equality between the blacks and the whites, where everybody was equal. Although things cannot be expected to change overnight, it was encouraging to see low-cost housing being built, African tellers in the banks, African entrepreneurial businesses taking shape and Black Economic Empowerment put into force. They were exciting times.

In 1999 the South African Government expropriated farms and state land on the outskirts of the Kalahari Gemsbok Park, in total amassing to some 25,000 hectares. This land, together with the farm houses and outbuildings, was awarded to the Khomani San in respect of their land claim. The South African National Parks made available 55,000 hectares of land in the Kalahari Gemsbok Park to the San and Mier (a coloured community also making a land claim) communities to be used as a contract park. This was a fantastic offer and one that would appease the Bushmen to a great extent. Although not in the Gemsbok Park itself, these farms were very near and had the same type of terrain, bushveld, sand dunes and vast open spaces. They were allowed, under strict regulations, to hunt small buck up to a certain size for food. With one of the farms, Erin, it was thought that they might turn it into a Bushmen Guest Lodge as the farmhouse itself was in pretty good order and could be transformed for overseas tourists to experience Bushmen life at first hand. Together with their hand-crafted artefacts, ostrich shell jewellery, bow and arrows, spears etcetera, which sold like hot cakes – this could prove a perfect opportunity for the Bushmen to create an environment with which to maintain sustainability for the future.

Deep in my heart I knew this was never going to happen. Steeped in hunter gatherer tradition and a love of freedom and their nomadic instincts in wide open spaces, the Bushmen would never conform to being anything other than who they were. The newly acquired land brought bouts of heavy drinking, home grown dagga was smoked from morn till night, and fighting amongst them became prevalent. In hindsight, had one done them a favour? I had to keep reminding myself that the land claim had been their request, as was the request for education. Every human being has a constitutional right, and who are we to say otherwise. The Bushmen, like everybody else enjoys wearing jeans, drinking a bottle of Coke, listening to the radio, much as the purists would like to keep them exactly as they are, an original Bushmen group unspoilt by human and Westernised interference. Unfortunately, my friends, they are too late. The human being did what he does best and ruined the Bushmen by plying his Westernised ideas in the first place.

The world was agog, and South Africa was no exception, as the new millennium was upon us. It was to be a monumental party of all proportions and I decided to celebrate it in my beloved Simon's Town. The centre of the town was closed to traffic and the street parties were in abundance and every shop open celebrating in bottles of glorious champagne. With the fantastic participation of the South African navy – who really know how to put on a show – the New Year 2000 rocketed in amid firework displays between ships to shore in a dazzling display.

Chapter Twenty Four

A Beautiful Marriage

During the second year of our relationship, when our life together in Cape Town was beginning to settle down, Alex suddenly announced over dinner one evening that she would like us to get married.

'Pardon?' I asked, thinking I had misheard her.

'I love you and I'd like to be married to you,' she repeated in no uncertain terms, which I now clearly understood.

This was not in the larger plan in the scheme of things. I was at a loss what to say. It had never been mentioned in our affair so it came as somewhat of a surprise when this suggestion suddenly appeared on my plate. 'I don't think it's legal for two women to get married in South Africa, in fact I'm sure it's not.'

'We can get married in Germany, it is legal there now,' Alex responded with determination.

'It might well be legal in Germany but to get married I am perfectly sure that the two persons concerned have to be in the country for some time before a marriage can take place,' was my only reply, in fact I hadn't a clue what I was talking about. I knew nothing about marriages taking place anywhere, really - just vague glimpses from the past in England about having banns read etcetera and living in the parish for a certain length of time.

The whole idea seemed preposterous and un-necessary. We were happy as we were – marriage wouldn't change anything. 'What suddenly brought this on?' I asked out of interest.

'Nothing brought it on. It's the most natural thing that if two people love and want to be with each other then they usually want to get married.'

In my eyes you only got married if you wanted to have children but I refrained from making such a crass remark, I felt it was too sensitive a subject and was getting out of my depth. Security was another thing; maybe Alex would feel more secure with me if we were married? The only thing that ever marred any decision about anything for me was the tremendous age difference. When we first broached into our relationship it was from my part to take every day as it came. I lived under no false illusions that it might last, I was just grateful for every day that I spent with Alex; every day was a bonus.

'How would you propose going about it. I ha-ven't the faintest idea where one would even start?' I replied unromantically, as this had really caught me on the hop.

'We could go and see a lawyer and ask his opinion. In the meantime I could ask my mother to get in touch with the authorities in Bad Oeyn-hausen and find out what is legally required for us to get married.'

It was obvious that Alex had been thinking about this for some time before mentioning it to me. She had all the answers ready and a plan of action in place; this wasn't something she had thought about on the spur of the moment. It felt scary. What to do?

'Have you any idea what kind of lawyer would be tolerant to such a case as two women wanting to get married?'

'You know plenty of lawyers; I thought perhaps one of them might be suitable.'

'Yes Alex, I do know quite a few lawyers but that's on a professional level. I wouldn't use any of them for such a personal matter as this.'

'Why not?'

Why not indeed, I thought to myself. What was I afraid of? It had startled me to hear Alex mention involving her mother in this process. Alex had no qualms or hidden agendas and was proud of who she was and who she loved. It never came into her equation that people might be shocked. If she had the courage of conviction then so should I, and anyway I was beginning to warm to the idea; it would be a first for me and no doubt the last.

We made an appointment with a nice young lawyer, in Cape Town, Christian van Zyl, who had recently done some work with me on a professional case. His work was excellent, and I also liked his name. Chris had expressed his delight in being able to help us if he could, when I phoned to make the appointment, and appeared totally unphased when I briefly explained what it was about.

It could not have been easier. Christian van Zyl listened to Alex who did most of the talking as she appeared to be more clued up about same-sex marriages and partnership agreements than I certainly was. Chris, after our phone call, had done some research into the legality of same-sex marriages. It was not yet legal in South Africa; therefore Alex had been correct in suggesting that we should get married in Germany where it was legal. Chris suggested an affidavit partnership agreement be drawn up between Alex and I that could then be submitted to the German authorities as proof of our binding contract to each other. It was impressive listening to Chris and Alex's exchange in all this; they appeared to know what they were talking about. It seemed to flit over my head… just had to trust them on this one.

'Michaela will be here in a couple of weeks' time, she will be perfect to witness the affidavit of our partnership contract,' Alex said as we chatted amiably on the journey back from Christian van Zyl's office.

Michaela is Alex's best friend, happily married with two children; she lives in Germany in the same town, Bad Oeynhausen, where Alex was born and where her family still live. Michaela was leaving behind her husband Torsten and their two children for a long awaited visit to South Africa to see Alex and to meet me. 'Frankly, I can think of no better person to do so,' I responded sincerely.

I was very involved with the Yacht Club during this time. I had become a committee member that meant taking responsibility and this was something I felt strongly about. The members vote you onto the committee and if you accept the position then you take all that goes with it. I took my duties seriously, which meant putting in time and effort. None of this ever infringed upon our sailing and racing schedule. Twilight racing on Wednesday was my real love and at the weekends we raced in whatever races were scheduled, depending upon crew availability and weather conditions.

Michaela arrived for her holiday amid enormous excitement. Tall, blonde and willowy, with a kind homely face, she was at once very likeable. This was the first time she had really been so far away from home alone, without Torsten, Nikolas and Phillip. She loved her children and was on the phone to them immediately she arrived at the flat, but after that she settled down and was going to make the most of every moment that she had with us and seeing South Africa. Of course, Michaela got her first priorities right, she wanted to go for a sail on my yacht, Tradewind. Never needing to be asked twice, I was delighted.

A few days later when the weather and sea conditions were perfect, Alex, Michaela and I set sail from the marina and out into False Bay. For me, nothing can be more perfect than hoisting up the main sail, sheeting out the foresail, cutting the engine, the yacht heels into the groove and you are away, at one with the elements, sailing silently, beautifully across the water. 'Look Michaela, that's Cape Point,' I said, pointing to a massive rock form looming on the horizon. We had sailed south from Simon's Town following the peninsular all the way along until we reached a safe distance from dauntingly spectacular Cape Point rising from the sea, massive and impressive as spuming white waves smashed and crashed against her.

'Wow! That really is something, wow! I never thought I'd see Cape Point from this position, it will never look the same when we go there later in the week by road,' Michaela exclaimed looking pretty impressed.

'It's awesome, really awesome, I've rounded Cape Point several times now, once as the sun set behind it which was breathtaking. Every time I sail to it or round it, Cape Point never ceases to captivate me.'

'One good thing, Michaela, when we take a trip to the Cape Point Nature Reserve you will be able to walk to the view up there and look out across the ocean towards the South Atlantic - how fantastic is that?' Alex told her friend cheerfully.

It was good to see Michaela and Alex enjoying each other, such wonderful camaraderie and chatter. They were really close growing up and remained good friends. They were both members of the same tennis club, and played league together – until Alex left Germany to work in India and then Malawi. Such a nice bond between them and they never, at any time, made me feel like the odd one out.

The sail back to Simon's Town was glorious as we ventured further out into the bay instead of following the coastline back. It felt perfect and suddenly seemed the right time to ask Michaela about being a witness to the affidavit for our partnership contract. Alex and I had spoken about it; she had told Michaela about our intended wedding, and she was delighted. We agreed that I should be the one to ask her about witnessing it.

We did a quick tack, setting us back on the course to home. Once Tradewind was heading up steadily for a straight run, I broached the subject. 'Michaela, Alex and I would like you to witness the affidavit for our partnership contract. How would you feel about doing that?'

Silly of me, of course she didn't quite understand what I was saying as her English was smattering, so to be quite clear of what I was asking, Alex repeated it in German.

Michaela's face lit up as she took in the question. 'I no want anyone else to witness my friend wedding, I will be proud to be part of this ceremony,' she replied with determination.

'Thank you, Michaela. It will have to be done while you're here at our lawyers' office. Unfortunately there will not be a ceremony; we will hopefully have that in Germany at the end of the year,' I explained to her slowly so that she could understand.

Over in Germany Alex's mother, Karin, was being a busy bee and dealing with the Rathaus authorities in Bad Oeynhausen who were a bit flummoxed, as a same-sex marriage had never taken place before in the town – however they were apparently being helpful and supportive, so no negative vibes coming from that quarter. Karin informed us what documentation would be required, birth certificates, the sworn affidavit of the partnership contract and other personal information. Karin had also contacted a civil servant appointed by the Rathaus with special dispensation to conduct civil marriages in the registry office who would be happy to conduct our marriage ceremony.

An exciting day was about to happen. Christian van Zyl informed us that he had the partnership contract drawn up ready to sign. The three of us, Alex, Michaela and I, went to the appointment at his office during the late morning; so that once the signing was over we could then celebrate by having a slap-up lunch at Cape Town's fabulous V&A Waterfront.

I'm feeling quite nervous,' Alex said as we went up in the lift to Christian's office.

'So am I, and there's nothing for me to be nervous about,' responded Michaela, half-laughing.

Funnily enough we were all got togged up a bit more than usual, especially for me. Jeep shorts and t-shirts were my norm of attire; today saw a white blouse and long clean shorts, earrings and perfume. Alex wore a smart blouse and slacks, Michaela a pretty dress. Christian greeted us with a nice smile and welcomed us into his inner sanctum; I could see he felt pleasantly amused by the moment, especially when we introduced the witness, coming all the way from Germany – not worth bursting the balloon to say she was coming for a visit anyway, coincidental that this was perfect timing.

Although Christian had sent us draft copies of the partnership contract to peruse over until we were both satisfied with the final draft, at Christian's insistence, we now sat and read through it again before signing. When we both agreed that the terms and conditions set down were correct he showed each of us where to sign. From the elaborate way in which we produced our own black ink pens you would think that we were signing the Magna Carta - who cares, I always use my own pen. Alex used the lovely Cross pen I gave her when she started the MBA and Michaela flourished something of an unknown quantity but it wrote her signature bold and true... all finished amid sighs of relief. The secretary made copies of the contract for Michaela to take back to Karin in Germany, Christian's office kept a copy, Alex and I kept the original. We bid our farewells and thanked Christian profusely for all that he had done and for paving the way to this moment so smoothly.

As planned we lunched at a rather snazzy restaurant on the Waterfront. Sitting outside, surrounded by the busy tourist harbour abuzz with boats of every shape and size offering fishing trips, pleasure sails, ferries taking people for tours to Robben Island – Nelson Mandela's prison island for many years and now a museum – it was a superb cacophony of people enjoying life, just the right atmosphere for the three of us to be celebrating in. It was also nearing the end of Michaela's visit so a double reason for spending such a special time together in a place like no other, eating succulent prawns and crayfish washed down with chilled white wine.

With sad hearts we saw Michaela off back to Germany. Her visit had been all too brief but, should our plans turn out as we expected, we would all be together again in late December, so the parting was not as difficult as it might have been, especially for Alex. We had given Michaela a wonderful time, showing her as much as possible of the Cape, spending time in Stanford, and generally enjoying each others company – a successful visit, and I looked so much forward to meeting her husband Torsten and their two children.

Alex and her colleague on the MBA course, Rachel, had made up their minds to do their dissertation together on the Bushmen. This was a first for The Graduate School of Business, unusual in that most graduates stuck to more conventional business based dissertations, but why not the Bushmen situation? There was no hard and fast rule to say otherwise. Indeed the lecturers were pleasantly delighted. I was delighted and proud that these two women had gone off the conventional track and decided upon such an assignment. In view of the Land Claim and the sustainable future of the Bushmen, this would provide an important reference paper. Also it would mean spending time with the Bushmen in the Kalahari – this was to be a real bonus.

The year was moving on fast and furious; Alex was now deeply into the MBA course which was intensive and demanding. I was working at the school and spending any spare time at the Yacht Club either yacht racing, or doing committee duties. The weekends were spent playing tennis at Springfield or visiting Wisteria Lodge in Stanford when Alex was not otherwise occupied on her course.

'Rachel and I have to go to the Kalahari, we

need to interview the Bushmen, especially Dawid, would you like to come with us? Rachel and Kevin are going, we thought it would be great to all go up there together; they have their old Land Rover and Rachel said they would travel on from there further into the Gemsbok Park for a few days break, apparently Kevin is exhausted, this is his final year at medical school.'

I did not need asking twice, being drawn inexplicably to the Kalahari Desert; it was always an exciting pleasure knowing I would be visiting there soon. 'Yes I'd love to go; wild horses wouldn't keep me away, especially as this visit will be based on something quite different.'

'That's wunderbar! Kevin speaks fluent Afrikaans so that will make it easier for us,' Alex exclaimed with joy.

'Unfortunately we'll have to go in the BMW otherwise we could have made it further into the park. I would love to visit Mata Mata – still, I don't think we have the time to do that.'

It turned out to be a superb trip. We booked into Twee Rivieren camp at the southern end of the Gemsbok Park and shared a large chalet. Kevin and Rachel were in their element. Arrangements were made to visit Dawid and the rest of the Bushmen group where they had set up camp deep into the dunes on the Erin Farm land. It was a hike to get to and only the discerning would try – but the four of us made the trek in 40 degrees of unrelenting heat. We were richly rewarded by the girls having Dawid, Sana and a good turnout of the rest of the group's undivided attention. Sometimes you might have to wait hours or even days for Dawid to appear – the girls and Kevin got the lion's share of input and information, recorded, written and photographed.

Our last evening we spent around a roaring camp fire braaing supper and drinking red wine with jackals hovering on the sidelines, their eyes glinting in reflection as flames danced and the distant roar of a lion sounded hauntingly in the dark starry night. The following morning Kevin and Rachel left for a deeper trek into the Gemsbok Park, while Alex and I returned to Cape Town.

News came from Germany that a date was set for our wedding ceremony to take place in Bad Oeynhausen at the Civic Offices on 21st December. The enormity of this did not sink in and as usual I simply went along with the flow. This meant that we would be spending Christmas in Germany with Alex's family; it was difficult enough trying to get my head around the marriage, now it would be meeting the family and surviving the cold, cold European winter.

Alex's MBA course finally came to a close. There were several end-of-course parties put on by The Graduate School of Business which I attended and enjoyed, set in the spacious outdoor courtyard of the superb building that was once a prison. Graduates and friends gathered together to pay tribute to the GSB Principal, lecturers and tutors who had become their mainstay during an intensive year, through sadness, happiness, ego, frustration, tears and failure, but there was a general feeling of great camaraderie between everyone involved – a GSB family affair. I was intensely proud of Alex's achievements; there had been moments for her of despair and frustration, but she had worked her way through each situation that produced difficulties and at times, a brick wall. But being the person that she is, Alex bounced out of it with a smiling face to become a very deserving Master of Business Administration Graduate.

Alex and I arrived in Germany five days before the wedding, not a lot of time in the scheme of things. We were staying in her parents', Karin and Kalle's one bed-roomed flat with not a great deal of room for manoeuvre. But, like all weddings, there was a general buzz and atmosphere as flowers, champagne, wedding cake talk dominated the short time before the occasion. All this took me by complete surprise, I had imagined just the two of us in a registrar's office with Michaela and Alex's mother as witnesses – no such thing – this wedding was going to be the whole bang shoot.

Nervousness did not elude me on the morning of the 21st December 2004. At sixty years old I was about to get married for the very first time. It made no matter that the marriage was to a woman; most important it was to someone who I loved very much and who loved me. I was excited, scared, happy, all the things that no doubt go through every person's mind who is about to commit themselves to the one that they love for the rest of their lives.

After much bustle and a light breakfast we got ourselves ready for this special occasion. I basically had the clothes that I had brought from South Africa, which was totally inadequate but passable - a little black jacket atop a smart white blouse always works wonders and together with a buttonhole spray of ivory white roses, I almost looked the part. Alex wore a smart skirt, blouse and jacket and as always looked gorgeous. We were both completely underdressed for the dangerously cold weather, but who cared?

In Bad Oeynhausen Karin and Kalle dropped us outside the registry office, situated in a pretty area of the town, and we went inside. Hallelujah! Half the world seemed to be crushed inside and they were all waiting for us. If I was nervous before, I was horrified now. There stood brothers, cousins, nieces, nephews, all there to witness our marriage. Duck and run was my first thought – but of course you don't do that, so I composed myself and tried to look as if I was taking it all in my stride and politely greeted each person as they were introduced.

We were all asked to assemble in the special registry room. There was even a music player provided, we chose a special favourite, the wonderful Nigel Kennedy playing Vivaldi's Four Seasons for the ceremony. A large highly-polished table sat in a prominent position in the room with our guests seated all around. We were told to sit at the table along with our witnesses, Karin and Michaela, the officiator who would conduct the ceremony and a Rathaus official presided on the other side. The officiator looked very formidable, but having talked to him beforehand he was a charming and very likeable man who instantly put me at ease.

The ceremony itself took all of ten minutes, documents were signed and witnessed. We were then pronounced officially married. The gentleman in charge from the Rathaus then presented us with a lovely folder for our documents and then to me a special gift from Bad Oeynhausen of a beautifully bound sailing Log Book – I was very moved by this kind gesture, which really brought tears to my eyes. Then it was all over, and amongst hugs, kisses and congratulations we made our exit from the building only to be met outside by Alex's league tennis team waiting for us with tennis racquets arched over the steps leading down from the Rathaus – what a fantastic surprise. We all gathered together outside, family, relatives, friends amid flowers and glasses of champagne we chatted and took photographs.

We then repaired to the pub of Michaela's uncle for a celebratory lunch. Michaela had made a fantastic wedding cake and we all had a superb time. Alex and I were presented with a very, very large card in the shape of a red heart, signed from all of Alex's immediate family – it was a wedding gift of a two night stay in one of Berlin's snazziest and modern hotels. We were to leave later that day. What a fantastic gift.

'That was the best day of my life,' I told Alex when we were eventually alone in the sumptuous hotel room together. 'Thank you for everything, I feel like the luckiest person on earth. I love you very much.'

'I love you too, my darling. What a fabulous wedding and all those people? Great of the tennis girls to show up like that, they really have been supportive, I was pleasantly surprised and pleased that so many people turned up at Uncle's pub for the reception.'

'And now we're in this fabulous hotel with the tallest, most elegant Christmas tree I have ever seen, standing in the reception area surrounded by modern works of art on the walls that made the Tate Modern look dull.'

'So you approve?'

'Of course I approve, it's pretty amazing. Swimming pool, saunas, gym, waiters who serve you breakfast in bed and the whole of Berlin to explore - this is the stuff of luxury personified, and I'm revelling in it.'

'Good, then we'll go to the Christmas market later this evening, it's only a short stroll down the road, I noticed it as we were arriving, Christmas markets are a must in Germany.'

'That's perfectly fine by me. Then tomorrow and the next day I want you to show me Berlin, stroll through the park, see the broken wall, lunch at Einstein's and in the evening, visit a pub with singsong and laughter.'

And we did do all of those things. Alex showed me Berlin through her eyes, her thoughts, and her perspective. I loved it, I loved it all. We were happy and we were in Love. I wrote for her:

Oh how I love you as I do
You entered my life like a shining star
Your bright eyes, your lovely smile
Captivated and lost me forever
Oh how I love you as I do.

Chapter Twenty Five

Waterford

What a wonderful Christmas-time we had in Germany, followed by New Year in Devon, taking us into 2005. Arriving at Flo's house we were welcomed by a festoon of silver balloons bearing congratulations strung up everywhere, and champagne waiting in the bucket. This dear family had made it so special for us, and I was once again overwhelmed. Geoff, my brother, arrived the day before New Year's eve and I told him about my marriage to Alex; he seemed pretty taken aback but said very little.

Alex had been upstairs changing when I told Geoff this news, when she eventually appeared in the sitting room to greet Geoff; he got up from his chair and gave her a hug. 'Welcome to the family, I believe I'm your new brother-in-law?' he said with a sense of amusement.

'Indeed you are, and I am your new sister-in-law,' she said hugging Geoff affectionately.

'I don't mean to be rude or ignorant here, but how exactly does it work, the name situation, whose name becomes who's?'

A very fair question not asked by anyone thus far. 'Chris's surname stays the same and I take on the Barrington, making my surname Barrington-Stromberg, pretty impressive don't you think?' Alex told him proudly.

'It's a bloody long-winded name if you ask me.'

'Yes its twenty eight letters and twenty nine if you add the hyphen.' I butted in, 'but Alex likes it and she's the one who has to say and write it.'

'Fair enough, but it's still a mouthful.'

'Alex for short, Geoff, you'll most probably never need to use or remember her surname.'

We all spent the funniest New Year that I can remember in lovely Kingsbridge, at The King's Arms. I have no idea how we decided to go to this pub but it was hilarious. Although dressed as a woman, the pub singer was of unidentifiable gender. Then we were joined by friend Julia, our very own pub singer who took over and belted out some of her sassy songs. We drank, we were merry, it was a fitting end to be with close friends, Alex and my brother, to what had been a memorable and fabulous year.

Life and work had to go on after the MBA for Alex. It concerned me quite a lot when she had given up her post in Malawi, and now I could tell that she was not interested at the moment to resume work in her African field.

We were driving across Dartmoor National Park one day shortly after New Year and before our imminent return to South Africa. 'What do you intend doing work-wise when we get back home, have you given it any thought?' I asked her conversationally.

'No not really. Being so engrossed finishing the MBA followed by the wedding; I have to admit I haven't given it much thought. But I'm going to have to do something soon as my savings are fast running out.'

'You obviously don't want to go and continue doing NGO work in other African countries. Black Economic Empowerment in South Africa is making it difficult for white people to secure good employment. Perhaps you should work for yourself on a consultancy basis?'

'That would be first prize and something I would like to do eventually, but it takes time and quite a lot of money to set up. No, I think I need to look for immediate employment, anything will do for a start.'

We stopped for lunch at The Warren House Inn, high on top of Dartmoor, giving views across the cold, bleak, hauntingly beautiful moors. Huddled in front of the Inn's famous grate where the fire has been burning continuously for over a hundred years, it was snug and warm. Feasting on Scotch broth soup, crusty bread and Cornish pasties, I regaled Alex of my frequent journeys, many a long year ago, to and from Cornwall using this road in all weathers, deep snow and ice in winter, the moors carpeted in wild flowers and lambs in spring, warm sunshine, picnics and hikers in summer and the burnished gold of leaves and gorse in autumn. Throughout the seasons Dartmoor ponies roamed wild and free.

Lunch over, we faced the cold outdoors; donning beanies and Barbour's we walked over the moor directly in front of the Inn until our noses were frozen as a biting bitter wind howled into our faces. 'Was this the Dartmoor I loved?' I muttered to myself. But it was and it is and always will be.

Once the heater got going the warmth of the car was welcoming as we trundled along the deserted moors looking out for the few wild ponies astray, and wondering how they survived the harsh desolate winters. Of course not all did survive, as I witnessed many years ago whilst staying with a friend, Stephen Church, who lived in Belstone on the edge of Dartmoor. We would walk the moors often in those days venturing into places not many people would roam. There during the winter months we would see sad remains of horses and ponies that had not survived – heartbreaking to see nature having taken its course in this way.

Finally making our way back to Kingsbridge, a good idea sprang to mind. 'Why don't we buy a property for you to renovate, something in Cape Town or thereabouts. There are plenty of old cottages in need of total refurbishment or a face-lift, especially in an up-and-coming area?' was my enthusiastic suggestion

'Goodness, I'd love to do something like that but I would much rather it was in Stanford than Cape Town. It would be much nicer to work there.'

'Well I'm not so sure there are many bargain properties in Stanford but we can have a look-see when we get back. It can be a joint venture, I will purchase the property and you can renovate it –

how does that sound?'

'Fantastic,' Alex enthused, her bright smile radiating the car.

'Good, then that's settled.'

A few days later, having bid tearful farewells to such special friends in Kingsbridge, our plane landed at Cape Town International airport to blue skies and warm sunshine of 30 degrees – such a welcome contrast to the weather we had left behind in London. Dear Lynn was there to meet us for the lift home to Simon's Town.

Not wishing to let the grass grow under our feet, we unpacked, washed clothes, aired the flat, and had a lovely dinner with Lynn who imparted all the latest gossip and generally we settled back to being in South Africa. With our immediate future plans still hot in our minds, we then headed off to Stanford to stay at Wisteria Lodge and check out if there was any prospective property for us to invest in.

On a whim I called into my friend Jill Smith's house from where she runs her office. Jill is one of the best estate agents that I know and the company she works for are the top property agents in South Africa. As estate agents go I trusted Jill – alas, she was not in her office so I left a note stuck on top of the telephone saying we were looking for an old property to renovate, and mentioned a maximum purchase price.

Later that same afternoon Jill popped up to Wisteria Lodge, apologised for not being in her office when I called, but, 'you'll never guess what Chrissie, I read your note as I checked the answering machine and – can you believe – there was a message from Clive Pearce saying that he wants me to sell the little thatched house down in Sillery Estate. He bought it years ago, nobody has ever lived in it and it's on a 1000 square metre plot, and it's within your maximum price range. It might be just what you're looking for,' Jill sounded out enthusiastically.

'That's amazing coincidence. Any idea what it's like inside, Jill?' I asked her.

'No idea at all. I've never seen inside or looked at the property yet, I came straight round to tell you so why don't we all go and have a look tomorrow? I'll have to find out from Clive who has the keys.'

'That would be great,' I said, nodding at Alex who was giving the thumbs-up sign.

As soon as Jill left we hopped into the car and took a turn down to Sillery Estate to look where the house was situated and get a feel that it might be what we were looking for. It was not difficult to find this sweetest, pretty thatched dolls' house sitting in a rather large field – enchanting was my first impression – small but irresistibly enchanting, it felt right and Alex thought so to, we would unfortunately have to wait until the morrow to see inside.

Renovation went out of the window. The Doll's House was too small to do much with it, so my imagination took riot like a swirling dervish and I came up with the bright idea of building a barn type of house onto it. It was quite a huge step from renovating to actually building a house, but we both loved the location, the size of land… so why not? Clive accepted my offer and a short time later we were off and away. An architect friend, together with our input, drew up a design for a long barn which would be built on one side of The Doll's House - affectionately called the pondokkie, theoretically making a tee shape. Planning permission was granted and the joint venture began.

We hired a one-man-band builder called Ray, who lived across the road from Wisteria Lodge and he in turn hired local artisans. Once the foundations were down, Waterford was born. Alex and Ray worked like Trojans to get the place built; they worked well together and had a great local team of builders, plasterers, carpenters and painters.

Having given my input design wise, I stayed away from the building site and got on with my own work, writing. There was plenty of other work besides with yacht club responsibilities, meetings, yacht racing, staff problems etcetera, and I found this to be unbelievably time-consuming, having to make the journey to Simon's Town and back with more frequency than I cared to admit.

Things were going well on the building site and a couple of months down the line Alex phoned while I was working in my study at Wisteria Lodge. 'It's a beautiful evening, why not come down to the building site - I've got a chilled bottle of white wine, we can have sundowners' on the pondokkie veranda while looking out at the mountains?' she suggested.

'That sounds a nice idea. Give me half an hour and I'll pop down.' I told her.

Of course, I should have smelt a rat. Alex does

not normally drink alcohol apart from the odd glass of wine every blue moon. She had obviously gone out of her way to buy a bottle, a chilled one at that, so the warning signs were there ringing bells.

It was a gorgeous Overberg evening as we sat together sipping our delicious wine, admiring the Klein River mountains sitting to the right of us with the sunset illuminating the sky to our left. 'Quite a spectacular view from here, don't you think?' Alex commented.

'Yes, I have to say it's very special with these uninterrupted views of the mountains and those cows in the fields beyond the river – I had no idea it was so lovely.'

Wisteria Lodge had no views to speak of, it wasn't something glaringly important when buying the place – it was really an investment which had turned out to be a very useful and practical retreat. Stanford was becoming an important place for Alex and I to be; we enjoyed living in the village and spending time with our many new friends and neighbours.

'So, darling, what do you think?' Alex suddenly said making me jump out of my dreamy reverie.

'Think about what?'

'Don't you think the views from this house are fantastic?'

'Yes, I've just said the views are very special. I can see, darling, they are very special and thanks for asking me to share this lovely evening with you.'

Before we went back home to Wisteria Lodge,

Alex showed me around the building which was coming on a pace, and it looked huge. The design was based upon something I had always dreamed of, a French split-level farmhouse with solid wood floors and open-beam trusses. At this point it was hard to imagine it turning out as planned and I tried hard not to think about it. This house was to be built and sold on, then perhaps another house or a renovation after that… who knows?

For the next couple of weeks I ignored several remarks Alex made about the building of the new house. Every evening she would amuse me with stories about one artisan or another doing this or not doing that. Windows having to be ordered as the builders were now up to window height in the bricklaying. She had a budget to work within and the sash windows were going to have to be imitation and not the real thing, she kept stressing, 'real sash windows cost four times as much as the imitation ones, but they look so much better. Darling, you always keep telling me you would never have imitation sash windows in your own house.'

'You're quite right, Alex, I wouldn't have imitation sash windows in my own house, but it's not my own house. You're going to build it and we're going to sell it – that's all there is to say.'

'Well, I think it's a terrible shame. Such a beautiful house with such fabulous views is going to have imitation windows.'

This had been building up for some time now and I was doing my very best to ignore Alex at every turn. Without actually coming out with it, I knew she wanted us to keep the new house. 'So what exactly do you have in mind?'

'We're at the level of building now where we have to decide whether to put in real and beautiful sash windows or imitation ones - they have to be ordered tomorrow at the latest or it will hold up the builders.'

'We cannot afford to keep this house, Alex, if that's what you're barking at.'

'If you sold Wisteria Lodge, we could keep this house.'

'You would rather live here than up in the village?'

'There is no comparison in my eyes. I like Wisteria Lodge but as a permanent home I think this is far better for us, and don't forget I've got two other building jobs lined up after I finish this. It's your decision, my darling, but I have to order the windows tomorrow at the latest.'

So the decision was made to sell Wisteria Lodge and keep the new house with its now-attached pondokkie. Beautifully made sash windows were ordered and the building forged ahead at the rate of knots.

It was time for me to give up my position at Ambery House. I had been there for twelve happy years and felt that I had become stale without enough energy to take the school a step further. It needed new blood and input which I could not resurrect within myself. Heartbreaking it would be, but most definitely time for me to hand over. Ambery House was my pride and joy. It was hugely successful, having reached a much higher level than when I first set foot on the premises; it now boasted another property backing onto

Ambery House property. I had negotiated the purchase of this house and surrounding garden with the owner, against a property developer – not an easy task when a developer is dangling carrots in millions and a new house – but, persuasion and the owner's moral conscience won the day. Ambery House became the new owner, making the two properties together a more sizeable area for the children's outdoor recreation. With this addition it made Ambery House School an extremely valuable property.

Much against my wishes, Sarah arranged a leaving party. It was to be held at the school one late afternoon. Everybody attended, children, parents, staff and friends. A splendid cake was produced, speeches were made, cards were given and a wonderful book made by the children with a drawing and kind wishes from each and every one of them – it was unbelievably moving. Sarah made a tear-jerking speech which brought tears to my eyes and then presented me with a gift from Ambery House – not a gold clock but a set of fabulous Celtic design Waterford crystal wine glasses – very heavy and extremely precious. Another Chapter closed; I bid a joyous but sad farewell to Ambery House. After this emotional occasion and presentation of the beautiful glasses, Alex and I decided that the new house in Stanford would be called Waterford.

On Valentine's Day 2005, Alex gave me a dazzling surprise – a trip to see a performance by the famous Lipizzaner horses at the Spanish Riding School in Vienna. This was one of my lifetime ambitions to see these magnificent horses perform, and there presented beautifully in a hand made Valentine card were the tickets to go later in the year. I felt completely spoilt and very, very lucky.

Alex's parents, Kalle and Karin were visiting from Germany for Alex's MBA graduation ceremony at the University of Cape Town, it was June and very cold. The four of us were staying at Wisteria Lodge together so that Alex could show her parents, with a lot of pride, the project management work she had done on what was to become our new home. The folks were delighted and amazed - not only at the size and beauty of the new building, but the work Alex had put into the project to produce such a fine and interesting house.

My sister Brenda and I, together with Kalle and Karin, attended the graduation ceremony. It was really moving to watch these two humble parents seeing their daughter, together with her fellow graduates, dressed in gown and mortar receiving her graduation certificate from the Dean of the University. Both Kalle and Karin were dressed for the occasion, he in a smart navy blue suit and starched white shirt, his short thick grey hair immaculately cut and Karin, always so smart, wore a floral two-piece dress and jacket. Both faces beamed with proud smiles throughout the ceremony.

Afterwards we all joined the graduation reception being held in one of the faculty halls of the impressive Cape Town University building campus. Set at the bottom slopes of Table Mountain National Park and overlooking Table Bay and the

Atlantic beyond. In my opinion, Cape Town University is the most beautifully-placed university in the world.

We took Kalle and Karin on a trip to the Addo Elephant Park in the Eastern Cape which was not the greatest success. On arriving there after a seven hour journey from Cape Town, we were promptly told that there were very few elephants in the park as the elephants had been rounded up and relocated to the far end of Addo, for some mysterious reason we were never to discover. It was a bitter disappointment, and we felt that the Addo Park should have let clients know there would be no elephants about. After all, what's the point in travelling all that way to see elephants only to be informed there are none to be seen? It's called hoodwinking the tourists. We were booked into the park for one night where a couple of elephants did in fact gather at the water-hole in front of our chalets. Early the following morning we went on a rather pathetic game drive, there was no game to be seen and it was freezing cold. Arriving back at the camp we had breakfast, hot coffee and thankfully left the Addo Elephant Park vowing never to make the return trip.

On the return journey back along the garden route to Cape Town we stopped for a night at a friends house in Wilderness, where they breed champion Welsh ponies. Andrea and Rhoda welcomed us wholeheartedly and our stay with them more than compensated for the disappointment of Addo. Andrea, a tall, thin blonde lady of mature years, was a professor of Law, a writer and intellect once married to a General in the Zimbabwean army. Her companion Rhoda was a theatre sister, now retired. These two women from completely different backgrounds were a delight and entertained us royally in their splendid home perched high on top of the wilderness hills, commanding a view across to the blue Atlantic. Kalle and Karin were in seventh heaven.

Life at the yacht club was hotting up as we were nearing the annual AGM to be held in August. There was always a general buzz around the club during this time; positions would be coming up for the General Committee, club members whispered or banded about names, proxies flew around hither and thither. Bottom line... a lot of people wanted me to stand as Vice Commodore at the forthcoming AGM. This was flattering indeed and would be a first for a woman to have this role in the history of the club. Apparently and, according to rumour – I got things done. So it was, in August 2005 I proudly became the Vice Commodore of False Bay Yacht Club.

At FBYC the yacht racing season starts with the annual spring regatta held towards the end of September, I was dead keen to enter Tradewind with our usual crew, Roger, Alex, Hannelie and I - they were all enthusiastic so we entered accordingly. My friend Margaret, who worked six months of the year in London and stayed the other six months in Simon's Town, liked to sail. Margaret was on her London stint at the time, so I e-mailed and suggested she should come over for the regatta. Marge jumped at the chance.

This particular spring regatta turned out to be a test of endurance and sailing skills, to say the least. The weather was pretty foul with gusting winds and huge sea swells causing damage to many of the participating yachts in its wake – but like mad salty sea dogs we soldiered on, hoping with each hour that passed the conditions would change. The regatta is spread over two long weekends so during the middle you can take a break.

'Let's go out to Stanford for a couple of days,' I suggested as we sat in the Crow's Nest bar after the last race of the first weekend, discussing our race statistics and being finally out of our foul weather gear.

'That's the best idea I've heard, please, please let's go,' pleaded Margaret who happened to be sitting with us, she was crewing on a hectic racing yacht called Pure Magic, and the strain was obviously getting to her.

'Okay, we'll go on Tuesday morning and return on Thursday evening - what do you think, Alex?'

'I have to go anyway to check with Ray how the building is coming along, and give him some money for the builder's wages on Friday, see if they need anything urgently,' Alex remarked, raising her eyebrows.

Off to Stanford we went, the three of us. It would only be a mini-break but that would suffice as a brief respite before the next weekend bout of yacht racing. Margaret I knew loved spending time at Wisteria Lodge. She would get up early in the morning and go for a swim in the nearby river, this, she seemed to enjoy more than anything. Alex and I would attend to matters of work and home then just chill out.

Early the first morning there we were disturbed by a telephone call from Jill, the estate agent. 'Sorry to bother you Chrissie, but I have a client who wants to have look around your house, he's from the UK, would it be convenient if I brought him round this morning… soon?' Jill asked with tongue in cheek.

We were a bit flummoxed to say the least; of all times to come and show a prospective client around the house, three women in a state of undress with foul weather gear drying out around the place… oh what the hell. 'Sorry Jill, we've just arrived here on a quick break from the spring regatta, clothes are all over drying out and we're half-dressed, if he's okay with that then do bring him round.'

Half an hour later Jill arrived with her client, Mr. Tomlinson. He apologised for the intrusion then said nothing more. Jill asked if he could take some pictures of the house to take back to show his wife - I agreed, while wishing they would hurry up and leave. Jill showed him around with the usual estate agent patter – Mr. Tomlinson showed no sign of either liking or disliking the house when they eventually finished. But I was curious; Mr. T had on a sailing jacket and sailing shoes the same make as my own. None sailing people did wear them sometimes as fashion statements, but this man was not into fashion statements, of that I was sure. 'I see you're wearing a Musto sailing jacket, are you by any chance a sailor?' I asked him just as they were about to leave.

'Yes, as a matter of fact I am. My job at the

404

moment is managing the Global Challenges Round the World Yacht Racing Team.'

This was the stuff of serious yacht racing. 'Wow! That's amazing, so you'll know Ellen MacArthur and Dee Caffiri?' I asked sounding like a fan club groupie.

'Yes I've certainly met them. We managed Dee Caffiri's, single handed, round the world the wrong way yacht race, so I know her quite well, not so well Ellen MacArthur though.'

'What an amazing coincidence,' I remarked to the other two when Jill and her client disappeared down the road. 'Here's us in the middle of a spring regatta and this Global yacht racing manager turns up as a prospective buyer for Wisteria Lodge.'

'Well let's hope it's a good sign. Wouldn't it be wonderful if he bought it?' Alex enthused.

'Absolutely nothing about him gave any indication he was even interested. Why would the Global Challenges Manager based in England want to buy somewhere in Stanford?' I wondered aloud.

Without giving Mr. Tomlinson another thought we enjoyed our brief sojourn in Stanford then returned to finish the last weekend of the regatta. In a nutshell, Tradewind did not win her division in the spring regatta, the weather conditions were not on our side. As crew we did our very best - Tradewind is, after all, a cruising, not a racing yacht. But we had plenty of fun, honed up on sailing skills and enjoyed the camaraderie of our fellow sailors – all great guys and good sports.

Jill phoned to tell me that Mr. Tomlinson and

his wife wanted to put in an offer for Wisteria Lodge; it was not the asking price, so we negotiated back and forth a couple of times before reaching an agreeable compromise. I was secretly delighted when Jill told me she was sure the fact that I was the Vice Commodore of FBYC clinched the deal as he had once sailed there in his younger days. Apparently he had seen the yacht club letterhead on my desk and Jill imparted this information to him. I am with certainty sure that being Vice Commodore of the club had nothing to do with the Tomlinson's choice but if Jill wanted to believe so – why burst her balloon?

It now became urgent to get the new house finished and ready to move into no later than November when transfer of Wisteria Lodge was due to take place. We would have to move out as the Tomlinson's were spending Christmas in South Africa and obviously wanted to be in their new home. So the pressure was on Alex to get ours completed.

Our trip to Germany and then on to Vienna to see the much awaited Lipizzaner horses perform at the famous Spanish Riding School was upon us.

We flew off to stay with Kalle and Karin and visit the rest of Alex's family for a few days, then from there took the short flight to Vienna. What a historical, architectural and cultural shock Vienna was, after Africa or even England the richness and opulence of the many churches and cathedrals was spellbinding. Horse-driven carriages trotting through the street, cafés overflowing on pavements filled with beautiful people, strong Viennese coffee permeating the senses as we passed by in wonder. We were like two people in wonderland, unable to take it all in.

The Spanish Riding School in Vienna is the only institution in the world where the classic equestrian skills has been preserved and is still practiced in its original form from the Renaissance to the present day. Here we were at the Imperial Palace in the most beautiful baroque riding hall in the world watching the Lipizzaner horses in what I can only describe as an unforgettable perform-ance in precision of movement and perfect har-mony with the music. Watching these white stal-lions perform brought tears to my eyes. The occa-sion, the beauty, and sharing this with my beloved Alex was nothing short of perfect.

On leaving the riding hall we were drawn to the courtyard of the Imperial Palace where a small ensemble of musicians were playing the most incredible and heart-stirring music. We stood captivated listening to Beethoven's Appassionata, Bruch's violin concerto, and a superb renditioning of On My Own from Les Miserables rounded off a stunning evening. We walked arm in arm through the intoxicating streets of nightlife Vienna back to our hotel. The Lipizzaner performance followed by such hauntingly beautiful music had left us both breathless.

Chapter Twenty Six

Proudly Commodore

At the end of November 2005 we moved into Waterford. It was not exactly finished, but we couldn't wait any longer we needed to remove ourselves out of Wisteria Lodge. Part of the purchase deal with the Tomlinson's was to leave practically all my furniture which they liked very much. I had simply negotiated a fair price and went promptly out and bought the same, only new.

Moving in and with me up their backsides, finishing the house commenced at a greater pace. The carpenter fitting in the kitchen was laboriously slow. Johan, a tall, blonde Afrikaans man of dubious background – whose claim to fame was having been in the South African police force – tested my patience ad nauseam, working one day, off for three, feigning every excuse known to man why the kitchen cupboards he was making were not materialising. It was getting nearer and nearer to Christmas. 'No more payment until you finish,' I told Johan in no uncertain terms. Innocence, his wife, also of dubious means and birth to add to it, shook in her shoes at my vehemence to get the job completed. Always by her husband's side with baby Johan in tow, this couple were scraping the financial barrel of life... I stuck to my guns. By hook and by crook the kitchen was finished an hour before the Christmas Turkey got popped into the spanking new, eye-level oven.

Waterford was complete. It was a tremendous accolade to both Alex and to Ray; they had worked their butts off building the house and renovating the pondokkie to spectacular proportions. Ray was a rough, hard little worker who when not supervised cut corners, scrimped here, saved there. His building cock-ups in Stanford preceded him, but we liked Ray a lot; he was fun, and under Alex's wing he excelled.

I invited Ray and his wife Steph over for a drink to celebrate the completion of Waterford. I'd known Ray for some time; he was an amiable, funny kind of chap, an ageing hippie I think he liked to call himself. When he and Steph stepped into the house all I can tell you is that Ray was totally gobsmacked. His building work had been completed some weeks previously so he had not seen it since the interior was finished.

I cracked open a bottle of champagne and filled our glasses, 'I wish to make a toast to Alex and Ray for building the loveliest house in Stanford.' Then I handed Ray an envelope - he opened it and cried. I'd been so delighted with the house, the work and effort put in by Ray I decided to give him a bonus and together with a card of thanks, that's what was in the envelope.

'Nobody has ever given me anything like this

before,' Ray blubbed into his handkerchief, handing the card over to show Steph.

'Well, you deserve it, my friend. I know it's not been easy but you got the job well done and this example should restore faith into your building capabilities to the Stanfordians.'

'Hear, hear, thanks Ray for everything. We've worked well together and it's been a pleasure most of the time, the other times I won't mention – but thanks a lot. May I also thank Chris for having faith in us taking on this project, a truly resounding success?' Alex announced emotionally.

So there we were, the mutual admiration society gathered together in the lovely Waterford drinking champagne at the first success of Alexandra's venture into project management.

'What made you call the house Waterford?' Steph asked matter-of-factly.

'Sir Robert Stanford, who our village is named after, came from Balina in Southern Ireland. I was looking at the map of Ireland and saw Balina was not too far from the area of Waterford, famous for it's crystal glassware. When I was presented with a set of Waterford crystal wine glasses from Ambery House School, I felt Waterford was the perfect name and Alex agreed with me.'

'That's so romantic,' Steph said, looking wistful.

Romantic wasn't how I would have described it, more sentimental if you like, but delightful, frowsy Steph, an ardent Eastenders disciple, perhaps looked upon it in a different light. Romantic, historical or sentimental, Waterford was born.

During the building taking place Alex had been

approached by several people to either renovate their newly-purchased house or build a new one on a vacant plot, so the work was coming in fast and furious. Alex has such a fantastic and pleasant demeanour about her that people immediately liked and trusted her. Waterford was a testament to her abilities for all to see, praise or criticise as village people are wont to do, facts alone, speak for themselves.

Happily, Alex transferred promptly onto the next job, building a house from scratch for a young couple living in Cape Town. Having bought the plot some years previously, this couple, Willa and Glenn had seen Alex at work on the building site and approached her – they got on extremely well and the new project of building their dream home in Stanford became a reality.

Alex and I settled nicely into our new, rather large home together with Hettie, Harry, Josh and Toby. The dogs of course loved it; you could walk out of the gate and around Stanford quite freely with fields and the river path at our fingertips. Stanford boasts many dogs per capita with Sillery Estate being the favoured dog-walking promenade. Every evening between 4pm and 7pm the entire dog-walking populace of the village walked past our house. People would stop and talk, others ignored. Friends often popped in, dogs-and-all to enjoy a sun downer on our terrace – once I counted twelve people around the table and ten dogs sitting in the kitchen – well! That's Stanford village life.

We were staying at the flat in Simon's Town for our weekly Twilight Racing on Wednesday evening. Alex called me outside. 'Josh is finding it difficult getting up the steps,' she said pointing out Josh's rather strange stance. Josh, our more than beloved Dachshund who, for the best part of his life, flies like the wind. Going up the few steps to the car park was a doddle; he just flew up them, but now he looked pathetic. I had never seen this bright intelligent fellow look anything like he did now. 'I'm taking him straight to the vet in Glencairn,' and picked Josh up as gently as I could trying not to show any panic.

'I'll come with you, you hold him and I'll drive. I think there's something wrong with his back.'

'Please God, I hope not.' My heart was clutching with fear as I said it.

The big kindly vet, Seamus, gave Josh a thorough examination, 'I think it's his spine, unfortunately it's very common in these dogs. We'll give him an injection now and you can take some anti-inflammatory tablets with you, if he improves all well and good, but you must keep a strict eye on him and don't let him leap about or jump onto anything without support.'

Josh did improve, and our spirits with him. Then a couple of weeks later at a park in Rondebosch he stood shivering and looked awful. A well-known veterinary clinic was a couple of minutes away and we took him there. The vet who saw Josh decided to keep him in for a few days over the weekend. We phoned every day and were told there was marked improvement. On Monday morning the vet phoned to say Josh had deteriorated overnight and that we must take him to see the specialist at the Flora animal hospital on the other side of Cape Town. We collected a very sad Josh from Rondebosch, drove like the clappers across town, and hit the veterinary hospital at pell-mell. The rather sombre vet, Dr David's, a specialist in animal back problems, examined Josh with a fine-toothed comb. 'There is a fusion in his spine which is causing him a great deal of pain, we'll have to take a scan to be absolutely sure but I'm afraid we're most probably going to have to operate, which can be successful, but not always; otherwise the kindest thing would be to have him put down.'

That was the bottom line straight in our faces. Ten years of happy-go-lucky Josh looked pleadingly at me, as I tried so very hard not to cry. 'Operate, Doctor; if it's only a faint chance, I want him to have it.'

Dr David's verdict was as he suspected from the scan and Josh was operated on early the following morning, the operation was deemed successful. Huge relief for Alex, and I was beside myself with joy. Josh would remain at Flora hospital for a couple of days for observation, then we could go and collect him. Dr David's phoned me quite late on Tuesday evening and said he was not altogether happy with Josh's response; he didn't look as perky as he should, but the veterinary nurse on duty would keep a close eye on him.

Alex phoned the hospital the following day to be told that Josh was pretty much the same; they informed her that Dr David's was in the operating theatre most of the day but would give us a ring on Josh's condition later, after his rounds.

We did our usual twilight yacht racing on

Wednesday evening in Simon's Town, getting home around 10pm. At 11pm my mobile phone rang, and it was Dr Davids; at that time of night my heart sank. 'Bad news, I'm afraid. I found Josh dead in his kennel when I went to do my late evening check on the animals. I'm sorry. The operation was successful and everything else was fine so I have no idea at this point what has caused his death like this. We can carry out a post-mortem if you would like?'

'No, no thank you. Leave him in peace. Thank you for informing us, I'm a bit dumbfounded at the moment. We'll call the hospital tomorrow and make arrangements for whatever needs to be done.'

Alex had heard the conversation, everything. We were both gutted. Josh had been with me since he was twelve weeks old, from the local hardware store. I went in for some weed-eater twine and came out with Josh, or should I say, Josh followed me out and jumped into the microbus I was using at the time. Returning to the shop I gave them one hundred rand, which was all I had in my pocket, and said 'The dog is mine, take it or leave it?' They took it, so we both drove happily home. Ten years of pure joy, what a fabulous legacy for Josh to have left.

Being very involved with the yacht club took my mind off Josh quite a lot, though whenever I thought of him I got a big lump in my throat and often just cried. One thing I did learn from Josh's death was how emotionally it had affected me that this one little character had burrowed itself so deeply into my heart and broken it.

Ob-La-Di, Ob-La-Da; life goes on and it did. Alex was now knee-deep into her new house building. I was being lined-up and encouraged to become the new Commodore of a premier yacht club in South Africa in the forthcoming 2006 yacht club AGM. This was greatly supported by a majority of Past Commodores and plenty of the yacht club members. Bar flies had their say, yea and nay as bar flies do – but in the main the general consensus was Christine for Commodore.

Personally I did not go into this lightly, having served on the General Committee for quite some time before becoming Vice Commodore. I felt I should be doing it for the right reasons and not for the accolade and historical ones. Of course I discussed it with Alex who was as proud as punch and insisted I go for it. I also discussed it with a friend and neighbour in Stanford, Dave McCarthy, whose opinion I valued highly. Dave put everything into perspective. 'If the members have chosen you Chris then in my opinion, there's nothing further to discuss,' Dave finalised in a nutshell.

Due diligence followed as I allowed my nomination for Commodore to be put forward. One of the most important things to me taking on such a position was to have a very good supporting Vice Commodore and members on the General Committee made up of people who were like minded and not there for self-aggrandisement, something I had experienced in a few Committee members over the years. Fortunately I already had my man, Lionel Dyke, chosen and battened down. Together with Lionel, we discussed our modus operandi for the AGM; I would stand for Commodore, Lionel for Vice Commodore. We would have in place, nominations for the General Committee made up of members of our choosing.

When the great day arrived there appeared to be no other nominations put forward for the position of Commodore, though the club's constitution does allow for nominations from the floor at the AGM; in all likelihood this would probably not happen, and at such short notice be unlikely to attract the majority of members present. So Lionel and I went into the meeting backed up and prepared to the hilt. As Annual General Meetings go it was non-contentious, fairly straightforward without verbal event. I was elected as the new FBYC Commodore amid great applaud and Lionel became the new Vice Commodore, eight club members – most of which were the ones we wanted – were voted in to make up the General Committee. The meeting was declared closed, the bar was opened, congratulations and celebrations went on for the next couple of hours in a very packed Crow's Nest. What an evening!

The inauguration of the new Commodore takes place on a Saturday at the start of the yacht racing season in September, about three weeks after the AGM. My particular Saturday was here as we sat in the Simon's Town flat overlooking False Bay – my whole domain set out before me, exciting and daunting.

The Commodore's reception party held in the Crow's Nest was packed. Local dignitaries, Rear Admiral of the navy, other naval dignitaries, Commodore's past and present, friends, relatives and club members made up a very, very packed room while others spread out on the lawns below. What a proud moment this was. Dressed in a lovely white blouse and three-quarter pants, silver yacht-drop earrings and for once, a smart pair of shoes - even I thought the effort I had taken looked quite good.

Speeches were made by the out-going Commodore, Andrew Mackenzie, and Lionel as Vice Commodore followed by an address from the Rear Admiral of the navy. My speech as the new Commodore was mainly addressing the fact of being so proud of at last breaking through the tradition of male domination and becoming the first female Commodore of FBYC, which ended the formal proceedings – we then repaired out onto the lawns of the clubhouse to fire the cannon in salute. It was my duty as Commodore, under the guidance of a professional cannon firer, to put fuse to the cannon, which set off a God Almighty ear-splitting blast across the Bay.

Next came the really exciting and fun part of the inaugural ceremony – The Commodore's sail past out in the bay, our theme being Pirates of the Caribbean. To take this traditional salute I chose to be on board a lovely yacht called Swimlion, where there was plenty of space for Alex, the Rear Admiral and invited guests who would be accompanying me. Swimlion sailed out into the bay and anchored in position. The flotilla of yachts taking part in the sail past were gathered a nautical mile further out to sea and made a breathtaking sight with a myriad of brightly coloured sails and spinnakers flying at full mast. Fifty to sixty yachts we counted sailing beautifully towards Swimlion, making my heart burst with pride. As each yacht rounded our bow it dipped or flurried a sail in salute - the crew on board every boat dressed up hilariously as pirates or some other such thing, one young man dived naked off the back of his yacht, Brightwater Fox. All the yachts in the sail past were decorated, dressed up in pirate style, and the entire bay became a big fanfare of celebration.

That evening the Crow's Nest turned into a disco complete with a live band, plenty of food and a good supply of drink. Alex and I danced the night away and had a ball. Being the new Commodore and setting an example, I felt it best to leave at a reasonable hour and we did, leaving the young ones and some of the elders to party until the wee small hours. The day had been a wonderful success, with a fabulous and encouraging turnout of yachts, no newly elected Commodore could have asked for more.

Newspaper articles followed soon after, both local and in The Cape Times. It obviously made good, interesting news having a female Commodore in a previously dominated male position.

False Bay Yacht Club, for the past few years has been the host club for The Governor's Cup Yacht Race from Cape Town to the island of St Helena in the south Atlantic, a race of 1702 nautical miles. The GCYR occurs every two years; it was to take place later that same year of my Commodore-ship. I yearned to participate, but didn't have a yacht big enough. One day Stuart, a friend and fellow sailor, approached me and said,

'How do you fancy joining me for the race to St Helena?'

'You're not serious are you?' I asked, feeling a small flutter of excitement.

'I'm dead serious, I want to do the race and then sail Allegro on up to the Caribbean, you can return to Cape Town on the RMS St Helena with the rest of the race participants.'

'Wow, you are serious, aren't you? How would you feel about Alex joining us, is there room for two more?'

'Eh Chris, I wouldn't ask you without Alex - of course I want you both along.'

Stuart is a fellow Lancastrian with a strong northern accent. I liked his no nonsense matter-of-fact approach. Mid-fifties, tall, with a good lean body, I knew we'd feel safe with Stuart at the helm. I excitedly discussed the prospect of the race with Alex who was not nearly as enthusiastic as myself but was not letting me go alone without her. Stuart duly entered us for the race as part of Allegro's crew.

Entering a yacht race of this magnitude is no easy feat. Apart from costing an arm and a leg to enter, the boat has to be weighed, pass a hefty safety inspection and be in tip top condition. Allegro, a 41ft Lavranos yacht was strong and superbly maintained both inside and out. She was Stuart's pride and joy and he had spent a good deal of time and money over the years making her into the lovely boat that she was. Apart from being a qualified electrician, Stuart was also a musician and a superb, well known saxophone player par excellence, hence the yacht's name

Allegro.

From my point of view competing in this particular Governor's cup was perfect timing, being the present Commodore of the host yacht club. It would also be good public relations for St Helena, who had just appointed their first female Commodore. Us two Commodores were now corresponding, and longing to meet each other in the hope of exchanging ideas, thoughts and experiences.

In the scheme of things there was little time to prepare before the race was due to start from Cape Town's V&A Waterfront harbour on the 28th December 2006. Stuart together with his wife Evelyn would prepare the victualling for Allegro. Two other race crew were to join us - Jacqui, a FBYC member and a keen sailor whose boyfriend was crewing on another yacht taking part in the race, and Martin Fine, a competent sailing friend who I had persuaded to join us. We were now five crew up which was perfect.

Alex and I chose to spend a low-key Christmas that year. It was my birthday on Christmas Eve when family and friends dropped in to Waterford for a drink and a Happy Birthday toast, also to wish us well for the race – most people think you're mad just stepping onto a yacht, let alone set sail across the South Atlantic on one. But if it's your sport and your passion, that's what you do. Other people climb mountains, walk across the ice cap to the North and South poles. People get into tin cans every day where the accident and death rate is too phenomenal to mention, and think nothing of it?

The 28th December dawned into a beautiful, warm sunny day. All the yachts entered in the race were moored in a strategic position at Cape Town's V&A Waterfront where family, friends and visitors could see and join in the hustle and bustle going on aboard the yachts before they set off. The navy band was there playing some har-rumphing music, jollying the proceedings along. In the hospitality tents food and drinks were served, dignitaries and sponsors chatted to, race officers and press trying to grab yacht crew for last-minute information – it was a complete ca-cophony of sound, laughter and at last, a prayer conducted by the Reverend John Storey, bringing a few tears and seriousness to the occasion.

As each yacht left its mooring, eighteen in all, stereo sound played a piece of music chosen by the yachts skipper – Stuart had chosen Dave Bru-beck's famous jazz recording - Take Five – to send us on our emotional way. At twelve noon sharp, decked out in our navy blue Allegro t-shirts, we proudly motored down the V&A shipping chan-nel and out into Table Bay with a fanfare of crowds, waving and cheering from the busy quay-sides and bridges along the way.

In Table Bay all the participating yachts assem-bled together with a flotilla of other boats of every description that were patiently waiting to give us a good send off. The Royal Mail Ship St Helena sat anchored in the bay with The Governor of St Helena, sponsors, invited family and friends on board having a slap-up lunch after which, they could view the start of the race. This charming mail ship – one of the last in existence – would be the starting bridge for the 2006 Governor's Cup Race.

Once in the bay we had to literally float around until lunch was finished on board the RMS. Psychologically this was not the best laid plans of mice and men. With the fanfare over and a twelve to fourteen day long journey ahead of us, the yachts wanted to be off, not bobbing around in Table Bay – also the weather was changing, it looked a bit ominous, dark clouds loomed in the far distance, and we were all champing at the bit.

By the time the race committee and the RMS St Helena were ready to officially start the race all yacht participants were pretty fed up, to say the least; also the support boats had to wait making us all feel uncomfortable. We had long range weather forecasts and were aware that the weather conditions would be changing, so the sooner we got a move on the better. Finally we saw the RMS St Helena pull up anchor and move further out into the bay - this was it, folks. VHF radio instructions were given for the starting point, all yacht motors were cut, full sails hoisted, and at 15.00 hours a mighty blast from the bridge declared the start of the 2006 Governor's Cup Yacht Race. We were off.

Race buoys had to be rounded in the correct order before setting out to sea proper – the yacht in front of us we could see already having a contretemps with another yacht rounding the first buoy, if this happens the yacht at fault is supposed to do a three hundred and sixty degree turn and start again; neither of the yachts concerned turned back.

An hour into the race we were all starting to get chilly, the weather was changing rapidly. On the horizon we could see a very dark mass of cloud and presumed this to be a bank of rain coming towards us. Fortunately Stuart decided in time to reef in the main sail and hoist in some of the fore sail. We sailed past Dassen Island, following the coast in a northerly direction. The dark bank hit us and before we all realised we were in the full blast of a horrendous storm which lasted for twelve hours non-stop. Shell-shocked would be an apt description for all of us on board Allegro that night. We wore foul-weather gear and safety harnesses at all times – this was very frightening stuff. Martin and Stuart were brilliant in helming the yacht and keeping her upright, though at times I had my doubts that we would make it. Alex and Jacqui handled the conditions admirably - the art of survival does that.

At 09.00 hours the following morning, we took stock of all the damage the storm had caused. Part of the sail rigging had catapulted off which had been similar to bullets flying around us, Stuart and Martin had temporarily repaired the storm damage. Collectively and seriously we had to make a decision whether to carry on with the race or abandon it. The weather conditions had calmed down a little from the previous twelve hours but it was still pretty bad. We were lying just off the west coast of South Africa and could easily get to Saldanha and to safety. It was clearly obvious that nobody wanted to abandon the race but the last hours had given us all a great fright, including Stuart, as waves taller than Table Mountain crashed down upon Allegro. Both Alex and Jacqui had been brilliant and quick-thinking during the storm, assisting Stuart and Martin whenever necessary, I felt unutterably guilty having put Alex through such an experience but it would have to be her decision I told her, if we were to carry on or not.

Obviously there were no defeatists on our ship; mad or not, the unanimous decision was to carry on. We had heard by radio contact that three or four yachts had abandoned the race, including Lionel on his beloved Marty Alessa due to a very seasick teenager on board. The weather conditions remained sensationally bad for the next three to four days, so much so that on New Year's Eve we did not celebrate with the bottle of bubbly Stuart had on board ready to toast it in – instead we sat huddled in Allegro's cockpit cold, wet and miserable wondering if we had made the right decision to carry on with the race. We were all pretty baffled as this yacht race is a downwind race subject to fair winds and fine weather and a pleasant sail – what had we done to deserve this? We kept asking ourselves.

Night watch was the scariest due to very high sea swells, huge waves and no moonlight. Looking out for hazards such as submerged containers floating on the surface of the water was a nightmare. Spotting lights from ships on the horizon became hallucinations.

Eventually the wind did abate and it even became calm enough to throw off our foul weather gear and safety harnesses. We had hot showers, baked bread, cooked some good food, and generally settled into life on board Allegro. One evening Stuart produced the champagne and we toasted to the New Year and the fact that we were alive and well. But we apparently were one of the luckier ones. The only tri-maran in the race passed us late one evening, promptly sank, and the solo skipper, in a dangerous attempt, was luckily rescued and hauled onto a massive container ship. Another boat lost its rudder and a brave mission to get into that cold South Atlantic Ocean by one of the crew to secure it for the rest of the race was a brilliant job well done.

If a dangerous situation pulls people together, then the St Helena race this year did just that. All five of us got along fantastically well. We shared the cooking, cleaning, took it in turns doing night watch – always two up. There was great camaraderie amongst us and a bond of team spirit pervaded. My twice daily task was communicating with Cape Radio and doing chart work. Studying the sea charts one day I saw that we had approximately five kilometres depth of ocean and an entire mountain range beneath Allegro... that was scary.

Days dragged on endlessly with nothing in sight. The sighting of superb Albatross we had left far behind. An odd container ship might be seen in the far distance if binoculars allowed. The sun never shone and the promise of moon only briefly peeped out of its cloud cover. No bikinis, kikois or suntan lotion for us. Sailing jackets, jumpers and warm woolly beanies were our constant attire. Had all those people I kept asking myself, been joking when they told us of the wonderful downwind conditions, the warm sunshine and moonlit nights that the Governor's Cup Race devotee's promised?

Day fourteen loomed, and still no sighting of land, ship, bird or fish. Stuart kept popping up from the chart table to tell us that St Helena should be coming into sight very soon, according to his reading. We three girls kept an anticipated lookout while Martin calmly steered the yacht, hopefully towards the island. Four hours after Stuart first announced St Helena should soon be in our sights, there through the mists of time was the outline of a massive mound – the Island of St Helena. No wonder the British exiled Napoleon Bonaparte there out of harms way. Some two hours later as we neared the island, members of the race committee plus a couple of Saints, as the locals are affectionately known, as well as Steve, Jacqui's boyfriend, came out to welcome us and escort Allegro into Jamestown harbour.

My! How good it was to be on land and to meet up with our fellow competitors, whom we had been worried about due to one mishap or another having heard about via Cape Radio. Odette, the Commodore, greeted me with enthusiasm, and we made arrangements to meet up soon. Alex and I rented a car, a beat-up old thing, but it worked. Jamestown is the capital and administrative head-quarters. It's carved like a fissure into the volcanic rock face, when reaching the end of the town you turned either right or left which takes you pre-cariously up, up and up with a breathtaking drop on one side of the narrow road all the way to the top. Another way of ascending this is to climb the

699 steps of Jacob's ladder from Jamestown, one of the Island's most notable features.

We were booked to stay in charming historical Prince's Lodge, the home of Robin Castell, St Helena's very own historian and poet. Robin, a FBYC colleague, was not resident on the Island at the time and had kindly offered Prince's Lodge to us. When we arrived at the house it was a shock to find the race committee had based themselves there – we were disheartened as this information had not been passed on to us. However the house was large enough to keep out of their way. This was our special time, and we intended keeping it like that. As Commodore I could have been at their beck and call, so I made it quite clear from the outset we were not to be disturbed - our part of the house was strictly taboo.

There were several functions to attend in my capacity as Commodore - one of them being at Plantation House, the home of the Governor of St Helena as well as that of Jonathan, the Seychelles tortoise, said to be one of the world's oldest known vertebrate who, with his fellow tortoise dominate the extensive grounds. A grand reception was held by the Governor for all the race participants where the actual Governor's Cup itself would be handed to the race winner. We were all superbly entertained, fed and watered by the Governor and the Plantation House staff, who did us all proud. Speeches were made, prizes handed out, a toast to this, a toast to that; an excellent time was had by all.

Annie's Place Restaurant and bar in central Jamestown became the gravitating point where all the race participants seemed to gather. It was fun, friendly with a laid-back atmosphere. One evening Stuart, having safely weathered such an amazing storm together with his precious Allegro and even more precious saxophone, played his heart out – giving one of the most superb, sensual and emotional performances I have ever had the privilege to hear. Annie's Place exploded with applause and cheers. Stuart, at one with his saxophone, had touched everyone.

Along with Martin we did a tour of the subtropical Island, visiting, of course, the famous Longwood House where Napoleon lived in exile and where he died. We visited his chosen burial place in a beautiful wooded glen. His body was later exhumed and taken back to France so that Napoleon could be buried on French soil.

The Island holds no redeeming features to speak of that we could find. There are coffee plantations, lovely walks, but the shoreline around is completely devoid of a beach anywhere and what little spit we did discover was dark brown and gritty. The Island was a sheer and dangerous drop into the Atlantic – no escape routes here for poor old Napoleon. How longingly he would have looked out of those Longwood House windows.

We enjoyed our week-long stay on St Helena; it was interesting and quite an education to see and experience how the Saints lived and existed on such a small mound of volcanic rock a zillion miles from anywhere. Once a flourishing sisal industry long since forgotten, St Helena now seemed to produce nothing other than a few coffee beans and tea leaves sold to locals or visitors to the Island. There was a Victorian charm about Jamestown we liked a lot. The Saints were a strange mixture of nationalities, English with a touch of Creole and African thrown in, speaking in a twisted tongue language of English that was difficult to decipher. Odette and I got on well together, she was worth her weight in gold help-wise, and rest assured this was a large young lady. We bade our goodbyes to St Helena knowing that in all probability we would never return.

Stuart waited for us to leave on the RMS St Helena before pointing Allegro northward to continue his journey to the Caribbean with one young man as crew on board. Jacqui, Martin, Alex and I were returning to Cape Town. The five day journey turned out to be great fun. Although Alex and I were squashed into a small cabin in the bowels of the ship due to our late booking, we were however, seated at the Captain's table every evening for dinner. Captain Smith told us that a Commodore ranked higher than Captain, so etiquette prevailed.

Plenty of games, shows, films and a concert were enjoyed by everyone on board. A game of cricket is mandatory on RMS St Helena between passengers and crew. FBYC got a team together and, in the first time for many a blue moon, whacked the RMS crew clear off the ship. Alex, who had never held a cricket bat before, hit more runs than anyone else and bowled out the ship's doctor in the first over – were we jubilant, or were we jubilant? Thrilled and chuffed to pieces is the answer. A shocked crew left the deck with their tails between their legs.

The spectacular sight of Table Mountain was soon upon us. We entered Table Bay from where we had left three weeks previously, pleased now to be returning home and alive. Our race with its fair share of casualties would be talked about for weeks to come. In the history of the race they were the worst weather conditions recorded.

I'm very proud of Stuart, Alex, Jacqui and Martin for having the courage to carry on with the race under such appalling conditions. A special bond was created between us on board brave, courageous Allegro. We had fun, we had laughter, we gained enormous experience, and we learned to survive.

Chapter Twenty Seven

Back into Africa

Work for Alex in the building and renovation trade continued. We were happy enjoying life at Waterford, playing tennis and sailing for relaxation and pleasure. Life was good. For Hettie, our thirteen year old Staffie, life was not so good; she developed cancer which spread to her liver and the end was in sight. We nursed her and made her as comfortable as possible. The moment she stopped eating I called Olga our cherished vet who came and euthanased Hettie in Alex's arms. Tears for Africa followed as Alex dug a deep grave in our lovely Waterford garden where we laid Hettie to rest.

'Two gone, two to go,' I remarked sadly as we planted a rose bush on top of Hettie's grave.

'Yes, and they've all had a pretty good life. Harry's nearly twelve and Toby is an unbelievable twenty-year-old cat living long past his sell by date.'

'I suppose once they're gone we'll be loose and fancy free to do and go where we like without having to worry about the animals?'

'We don't have to worry about them anyway whilst Raymonde is around.'

We were very fortunate in having a Florence Nightingale of a dog-sitter in the guise of Raymonde, who not only dog-sat but house-sat as well. This truly blessed retired lady had enabled Alex and me to do the yacht race, travel overseas and have weekends away without having the slightest worry or concern. The dogs and cat worshipped the ground Raymonde walked on, we just happened to be their owners who did not warrant the same adoration.

'That won't be forever. Raymonde is getting on and she might go and join her daughter in Australia – then where would we be?'

'You're quite right. We'll have to play it by ear and see what transpires. Oh and by the way, that piece of land I mentioned the other day is for sale, what do you think we should do?' Alex asked, changing the sensitive subject of our animals.

I pondered over this for a moment having forgotten the conversation about this particular venture we had discussed. 'It's a very small plot but a nice position. Do you seriously want to build a cottage on it from scratch?'

'Sure, why not - as we discussed, it could be a good spec house to build and sell on.'

'Okay, if you think you and Ray can do it then I'll give Sarah a ring and ask her if she wants to come in with us. She did ask me last time we had dinner together that if something worthwhile came up for her to invest in I was to let her know.'

That evening I phoned Sarah and put our proposal to her. She was delighted, and then stipulated an amount which she was prepared to put in. The cash Sarah mentioned was perfect in enabling me to purchase the land and use Sarah's cash to build a pretty nice cottage.

And that's exactly what we did. Rose Cottage was a miniature version of Waterford. Alex scaled down the plans of our house, got the architect's signature of approval, presented them for planning permission which was granted, and away we went. When Rose Cottage was complete and a garden established, we decided to try and sell it privately. Alex had the bright idea and temerity to email Rose Cottage details to friends around the world. Lo and behold a friend, Marika, who Alex knew from working in Malawi, took the bite and bought it. Marika, a tall, thin attractive mid-thirties blonde, came from Finland and works for the European Union. Marika did not see Rose Cottage before the purchase; she believed in and trusted Alex completely.

We three investors were delighted with the sale of Rose Cottage and more so that it was sold to a friend. It was a charming little cottage and emotionally we had become attached to the place. When transfer went through, we split the profit three ways as agreed, Sarah was as pleased as punch and Alex now had some money of her own with which to speculate, if she so wished.

By this time Alex had project managed the building of four houses and renovated the same amount. It was time, she informed me, to build her own house together with the builders and artisans of her team. A plot around the corner from Waterford was for sale with lovely views of the mountains and vineyards, so Alex bought it. She decided to base the house design upon Wisteria Lodge, adding a spiral staircase leading up to a large, spacious studio. Outside a swimming pool was built into the terrace leading off from the main bedroom – an indigenous garden surrounded the perimeter of the land with a small herb garden to the rear. It was a truly delightful house.

'I've had enough of building and project managing,' Alex suddenly announced one day shortly after completing her house. 'I feel I need to get back into my work in Africa, be properly employed by an organisation, that's what I'm used to.'

It would be foolish to pretend I hadn't seen this coming. Although Alex had done extremely well in the building and project-managing world, in the long scheme of things it was not her life's ambition. Alex's personality and integrity made her popular, so much so that she was in great demand and the project-managing contracts kept rolling in. After four years of putting her life and soul into this work, which after all had started as a temporary measure, I began to see the signs of wear and tear. It was clearly time for a big change.

'What is it you would really like to do?' I asked her.

'I enjoy working with the local people. I know I can make a change, look at this last house where each worker on the project had a stake – it gives them pride and uplifts them.'

Indeed, Alex did have a very special rapport

with the local people, meaning, in her case, the non-Caucasians. It was wonderful to see how she interacted with them and how they responded to her. It was truly a mutual admiration society between them.

'How do you propose to work in this field, any bright ideas? I know you've tried the Overstrand Municipality in connection with training and come up against a brick wall, so where to from here?'

'Well, it's totally impossible trying to start anything here in Stanford with the local community. Brick walls are nothing compared to the heads in the municipality in Hermanus, they are a complete waste of time. I've sent off my CV to a few organisations in Germany who specialise in development programmes throughout Africa, so let's see what happens.'

A few months previously my term as Commodore came to its natural end and Lionel Dyke was voted in as the new FBYC Commodore at the 2007 AGM. My time as a General Committee member, Vice Commodore and then ultimately the top position, and one that I am extremely proud of, The Commodore, was enough. New blood was needed, fresh ideas and a clean sweep I felt could take the club, which was rapidly growing in membership, into a different sphere. A bit like the school situation; I felt that I hadn't quite got enough humph left to take the club forward.

Following that I made the decision, reluctantly, to sell Tradewind. This was a most-beloved treasured possession that had given great pleasure not only to me but to the many people who had sailed on her. With Tradewind we had reached euphoric heights by winning races, spent many happy and fun filled hours just sailing in the bay, sleeping on board over New Year and at Gordon's Bay – she was a brave tub and I loved her. A complete break from the club was needed by me, and keeping Tradewind there would always be a pull. The long term plan or pipe dream was to purchase a larger yacht and sail round the world. So it ended, a decade of good sailing and dedication to the yacht club.

Alex was mightily relieved that I would be spending more time in Stanford. The travelling back and forth, a round trip of 300 kilometres from Simon's Town to Stanford, was hectic and nerve-wracking for us both. I sometimes stayed overnight at the flat but more often than not I returned home to Stanford and my darling Alex.

Stanford village life became another world. Walking the dog, eating out at friends or one of the many pubs and restaurants, sundowners with neighbours, the odd art exhibition thrown in or shopping at the farmers market - we embraced it all. As well as writing I started to make use of our fabulous upstairs studio that lent itself to something large other than my desk, so I started painting small canvases at first, before graduating to very large ones. Being a lover for many years, most probably since my days in St Ives, of modern art, I now found myself experimenting, sploshing and Pollocking to my heart's content. Alex became fascinated and would drop into Waterford at odd times during the day to see what masterpiece I would be working on – the large canvases I usually did on the floor might be one picture at lunch-time, then changed into another one by the end of the day.

It was such a relaxing time just to be able to read, study philosophy and listen to beautiful classical music every day without having to rush off and be somewhere else, have meetings, sort out staff problems at the yacht club. I luxuriated in this new role and made the most of it, who knew how long it would last?

There was no response thus far to Alex's applications she had sent to the development agencies in Germany. She was reluctant to take on any more jobs or get into any contractual agreements. The desire to scale down the project-management and move back into development aid work was becoming paramount. Age wise, it was important that Alex secured a job in her chosen field, the older she became the more difficult it would become to get long term employment in one of the development agencies. She persevered and kept applying, and sending her CV for jobs advertised on the internet.

On the 23rd December, 2008 Alex was up in her study talking in German to someone on the phone for what seemed an interminably long time. I was immediately thinking there might be a problem at home with one of her parents – but even then it was a long call and somehow the difference in tempo of Alex's voice told me it was someone she did not know.

'Well, that was an interesting phone call from Germany. You're never going to believe this one.' Alex said bounding with enthusiasm into my studio.

'I'm all ears; you were on the phone for ages, so it must be something interesting, please tell me,' I pleaded, as the suspense was killing me.

'That was an employment agency for one of the development aid organisations in Germany, who received and read my CV. The organisation is looking for someone with my profile to fill a position in Kenya. Anyone who is accepted will mean that person's husband or wife are also accepted. They are looking for someone to start a pilot project for Fair Trade in Africa.'

'Wow! How brilliant is that. Is it something you would like to become involved in? Is this the sort of position you're looking for?'

'It would be exactly the right kind of organisation to work for, well-established and highly thought of in development aid around the world.'

'So what happens next?'

'The employment agency will put my CV and application forward as a recommendation to the development organisation. They will then scrutinise it for consideration and get back to the agency.'

'How long could all that take?'

'They say the position needs filling urgently, but these things can take months. If I did become a prospective candidate then we would have to travel to Germany for an exploratory interview - how would you feel about that and the prospect of a three-year contract in Kenya?'

'Daunted and excited, I expect. But as that was the first phone-call I don't think you or I should get our hopes up too high at the moment'.

Christmas and New Year flashed by, and before you could blink we were into the second month of 2009. Alex's fortieth birthday on the 6th February was heralded by a big party in celebration of this wonderful girl's special day. Ninety guests of family, friends and neighbours were invited to Waterford. The garden was spread out with beautifully decorated tables and flower displays. Fabulous aromas of food drifted from the dining room where French doors opened out onto the terrace, music played and a superb time was being had by all. At 8pm, as if on cue, a mighty streak of lightning lit up the backdrop of the Klein Riviersberg Mountains, giving a resplendent display worthy of the royal fireworks – an awesome sight. There followed a thunderstorm and welcome rain after the days blistering heat of 40 degrees Celsius. Everyone piled inside Waterford and onto the terrace for shelter; the barnlike sitting room was cleared and there began an evening of fantastic disco-dancing that lasted well into the early hours of the morning.

Alex eventually did receive communication from the German development agency that the donor organisation was extremely interested in her job application. We were both invited to Cologne for a thorough assessment of our suitability for living and working in East Africa. There followed a long period of no word or communication – then out of the blue and with very little warning, Alex alone was invited to Germany for an interview with the donor organisation itself. She was told confidentially at this interview that she had got the job.

Our cat, Toby Twenty-Two, as he was called because he was twenty-two, had become seriously arthritic, and one day his rear end collapsed. Alex shouted up to me in the studio that Toby was on the lawn and couldn't get up. A hand clutched at my heart because I knew it was time. In all honesty we should have had Toby put out of his misery at least a year earlier but Alex insisted he was not in pain, and I always relented. Together we took Toby, wrapped snugly in his blanket, to Olga, where he was put gently to sleep in our arms as tears for Africa flowed once again. In memory to Toby's twenty-two years of companionship, love, and being the most-photographed African wild cat, I had a metal archway made for the garden where he was buried and planted a Blossom Magic climbing rose to ramble over it.

We were both required to undergo extensive, compulsory medical tests and examinations. The organisation allowed us to have these carried out in South Africa. The thought of having these tests put the wind up me, being the age that I was – but, I bit the bullet and went ahead. Fourteen pages of blood test results later, a gynaecological examination, blood pressure and an ECG test all came out with glowing colours and a clean bill of health.

In September Alex and I went to Cologne again for our preparation period at the development agency campus where we stayed in-house for a week. Here we learned about the life and dangers that we might be faced with in the East African countries, for us one of the most dangerous being homosexuality. Same-sex marriages were strictly illegal and therefore banned, especially in Kenya. This was something we would have to be discreet about and be one hundred percent aware of. Alex did a course in Swahili; I had a few brief lessons. During this time and as the job entailed linking East African craft producers into the Fair Trade European market, Alex travelled throughout Europe to meet and get acquainted with Fair Trade buyers. After the preparation time was finished we returned to South Africa.

Time was moving on a pace. It was difficult to imagine that life in Stanford, as it had been for the last few years, was slowly coming to an end. Harry was still alive and kicking at almost fifteen, though a tumour had recently been removed from his side. Our plan was for Raymonde to look after him and house-sit for a couple of months at a time and see how things went. I or both of us would return from Kenya frequently to check on Harry and the houses. Alex's house Kinsale was on the market, but not yet sold.

In October Alex attended a course on Strategic Export being held at her old stomping ground, the Graduate School of Business in Cape Town. This was sponsored by the Development Agency in Germany as part of her employment package. As a partner I was welcome to accompany her at the adjoining, Ports Wood Hotel, where we were booked into. For a few days we acted like tourists in Cape Town, enjoying our time based at the Waterfront.

In early November Alex left for Kenya ahead of me to start her three year contract with Producers of Fair Trade in Africa on the 15th November 2009.

She would have to look for a vehicle, accommodation for us, furniture et cetera. It felt like a daunting task and I had to admire her spirit. I would follow in six weeks' time just before Christmas where, hopefully, there would be a home within which to spend it.

Shortly after Alex's departure, the tumour on Harry's side started to weep and look unpleasant. A couple of days later he refused to eat for the very first time in nearly fifteen years, and he looked unhappy. I phoned Olga for advice whilst knowing the inevitable, but still I had to be told. It would be cruel to put Harry through another day. Raymonde was house-sitting for a neighbour around the corner and I stopped to tell her on the way to the vet. Raymonde came with me as Harry lay on the rear seat of the Land Rover. Olga, already forewarned, came out to meet us and performed the dastardly deed as Raymonde, and I held him in our arms until all life left him. No words can describe what I felt, or indeed how Raymonde felt. Harry had always been my favourite dog and everybody loved him. I mourned for this character of an animal that had given so much pleasure and joy throughout his life. Another grave was dug at Waterford, and three rose bushes given by friends of Harry were planted on top in memory.

During the last few months I had been a sleeping but very active partner in a small, successful antique shop in Stanford aptly named The Red Bicycle. My partner, Janine went into this business knowing that I would be leaving for Kenya at the end of the year. Janine had a choice whether to carry on alone, take another partner or sell the shop, she chose to carry on and I passed the business over to her in its entirety leaving her with a large amount of my personal stock to sell on sale or return. My part in The Red Bicycle was wound up and no longer my concern.

With the demise of Harry, Raymonde was no longer needed to house and dog-sit as we had first planned. She had other eager customers requiring her services, especially as it was Christmas time. After much thought and deliberation I decided to hand Waterford over to Stanford River Cottages for holiday letting; they had approached me and already had clients prepared to pay a handsome rental for Christmas and New Year. There was nothing more to do other than make sure all valuables were safely stored away, the house cleaned from top to bottom, windows glistening and the garden glowing.

There were rounds of dinner parties and fond farewells to our wonderful neighbours in Stanford, followed by plenty of tearful goodbyes and au revoirs to my dearest friends and family in Cape Town. It really was time to be off, and in my heart I knew it was the right thing to do. I stepped onto the aeroplane, whisking me away to be with my beloved, to start a new period of our life together in Kenya knowing that Alex's future from now on was of paramount importance. My own future would fall into place beside her.

Epilogue

The Philosophy

In the months before my mother's death she would speak to me gently about life, enthralling me with her dreams and wishes which, sadly, would never be realised. Her soft encouragement in explaining to me what was happening to her and how I must be brave and get on with life in the best possible way. 'Travel,' she said, 'see some of the world; don't get trapped into another life before you do so. Be good, kind, honest and considerate to other people at all times and use your integrity. Above all, fulfil your dreams and follow your heart.'

This was sound advice indeed to an eleven-year-old girl explained with such love and intelligence to a daughter from a dying mother that instilled into me and built over the years, my own philosophy towards people, animals, the world situation, and mankind in general. It has stood me in good stead and guided me throughout my life.

When I realised that my relationship with Alexandra was serious I agonised for hours, days and weeks over the situation, feeling powerless to do anything about it. I was extremely attracted to this girl who had me in hers sights long before our meeting. Her attraction to me was open, honest and without bounds. Regardless of our twenty-six-year age gap… Alexandra never wavered.

I did not have such openness and honesty. Alarm, fear and incredulity of becoming involved with a woman stood in the way of letting the relationship move forward and develop in its own way… the barriers were in place. In my sport I sailed a lot in rough, shark-infested waters, but this situation felt seriously more dangerous. We were in love and the power of that love conquered all. Alexandra's relentless pursuit and my futile attempts at rebuffing her were powerless. I remembered what my mother had told me those many, many years ago. 'Follow your heart.' And that's what I did.

The last ten years of our life together have been the happiest for both of us. We live in a completely "normal" world; family and friend's neighbours and colleagues accept us for exactly who we are, Christine and Alexandra.

Being contracted for three years into Kenya, a country where same-sex partnerships are illegal, was never going to be easy, we thought. After two years being resident in Kenya, with a little caution and subtlety we have found that the Kenyan community accept us and we lead exactly the same life as we do in South Africa, Germany, England and everywhere else.

What the future holds for us we cannot know or even predict. Alexandra's work is with the Fair

Trade craft producers of Africa, introducing them into the European market. She is an inspiration to these people with her bright friendly smile, her warm sparkling eyes and her constant, encouraging presence… they will succeed.

My dream is to sail around the World in a charity race for the fight against cancer. I would like to save all the wild animals from extinction before it's too late. It would be nice to think that I shall spend the rest of my life with Alexandra, and who knows; if I fulfil my dreams and follow my heart, perhaps I will.

www.ingramcontent.com/pod-product-compliance
Lightning Source LLC
Chambersburg PA
CBHW021841010726
47493CB00005B/1503